REFLEXIVE

FIRE

JACK MURPHY

Reflexive Fire is a work of fiction. Names, places, and incidents either are products of the author's imagination or are used ficti- tiously.

© 2011 Jack Murphy

Printed in the United States of America

http://reflexivefire.com

First Edition

Cover Art by Marc Lee

Also by Jack Murphy:

PROMIS: Vietnam

PROMIS: Rhodesia

Non-Fiction:

Special Forces Weapons Report Card

For Caterina

PROLOGUE

Sergeant Major Bill Keely turned to face to the front of the aircraft, looking towards the cockpit, holding one hand spread open in front of him under the dull red glow of the MC-130's interior lights.

With oxygen masks over their faces to counter the effects of the thin air at altitude, they relied on hand and arm signals alone. Not that it mattered. His men would never hear him over the roar of four Allison turboprop engines in addition to the wind rushing in through the open ramp. The free-fall jumpers held out five fingers, mimicking his movements to acknowledge their understanding.

Four operators plus himself made for a relatively simple jump. Four of them had mustard stains on their HALO wings, indicating multiple combat jumps, but of course that was only on citations locked away in a file cabinet somewhere.

Delta operators were known for keeping a low profile, and none of them wore their combat badges in garrison.

Keely faced back around, easily hefting the hundred plus pound rucksack snapped onto his harness. Looking out into the black void below, it was impossible to judge altitude, wind speed, or where they were in relation to the ground. They'd be dropping from 30,000 feet, locating their drop zone under night vision after they pulled their ripcords at 4,000 feet.

The Delta troops lined up like ducks in a row for an equipment check. Behind him was Pat, the other old timer on the team with twenty three years in the Army, ten with Delta, leaving him with an open disdain for the entire Army command structure. Pat flipped open the top flap on Keely's reserve chute.

The Fucking New Guy, Alex, was behind Pat checking his MC-5 parachute, and so on all the way down the line. The first thing Pat looked at was the CYPRES display. The small console under the reserve flap displayed a four digit number, barely visible in the poor lighting. That number was programmed into the unit on the ground by each jumper at the direction of the jump master, based on the barometric pressure. If a jumper was knocked unconscious in mid air the CYPRES would detonate a small charge releasing the reserve parachute at 2,000 feet.

If your CYPRES fired and you ended up riding in on your reserve you were having a bad fucking day, to say the least.

Next Pat moved on to the cotter pins holding the reserve parachute in place, making sure they were properly stowed through the nylon loops. Slapping the reserve flap down on its Velcro fasteners, he unsnapped the main chute below it and conducted same check on the single cotter pin holding the spring loaded pilot chute in place under the green flaps.

Finally he checked the small oxygen tank strapped on the Sergeant Major's left side. At this altitude you would get a serious case of hypoxia from lack of oxygen, requiring them all to strap bottles of O2 and breathe off a mask for the trip down. All good, he snapped the flap down then pounded his Sergeant Major on the shoulder.

Keely pivoted around, the side of his helmet emblazoned with the words, Shut Up and Squat. A few months prior, Pat had wrote it with a Sharpie marker during a training jump. The boys joked that it was the Team Leader's motto in the gym because he had legs thick enough to resemble the pine trees surrounding Ft. Bragg.

Pat gave him a thumbs up to let him know his chute was good to go.

Behind Pat the new guy, Alex, was holding his rucksack with one hand while conducting his checks with the other; the weight of the ruck was clearly a little too much for him. Finally he gave Pat a thumbs up.

Keely lowered his free fall goggles over his eyes and checked the dual tube night vision goggles mounted on his helmet a final time before moving to the edge of the ramp. Feeling the wind whip at his legs and knowing there was 30,000 feet of nothing below him, the Sergeant Major motioned for the rest of the team to follow him to the lip of the ramp.

Two minutes ticked away in what seemed like seconds, the team taking shallow breaths and waiting for the light mounted on the fuselage to turn from red to green, letting the jumpmaster know that they were over their drop zone.

Pat looked over his shoulder at the New Guy. Alex had just completed selection last year and the Operators Training Course a few months ago. He'd only had a few jumps with the team, which led to a heated argument between Pat and Keely about Alex and whether he had any business being on this mission.

Keely told him that the guy completed HALO school and had the required jumps with the team; he was a career Special Forces soldier; what more did he expect? Eventually Pat had to accept Keely's decision or go look for another job.

Alex, strained by the weight of the rucksack, finally let it hang by the harness to shake out his tired arm. Behind him he heard something pop. Looking down, his stomach suddenly flip-flopped. In a rush, he had attached the rucksack's metal fastener to his rip cord grip rather than the metal ring on his parachute harness where it belonged. The weight of his rucksack had pulled his ripcord once he let it hang. The metal cable that ran from the ripcord to the cotter pin holding the pilot chute in had been released.

Glancing over his shoulder, he saw his pilot chute whipping around the metal floor of the aircraft.

The two operators behind him, Mark and J-Rod, lunged towards the pilot chute a moment too late as it was sucked out of the ramp of the aircraft.

Before the rest of the team knew what was going on, the pilot chute did its job. Catching in the wind outside the aircraft, it yanked Alex's main parachute out of its deployment bag. As he was sucked out of the back of the high performance aircraft, he toppled over Pat and Keely, sending them end over end flying off the ramp and into the darkness.

Suddenly alone in the back of the aircraft over enemy territory, Mark and J-Rod looked at each other as the green light flashed.

Turning toward the ramp, they followed their team out into the night.

One

The garrote wire slid silently under the sentry's chin.

With an aggressive yank on the piano wire, the Colombian was snapped backwards into the jungle underbrush, his rifle falling from limp fingers onto the manicured lawn.

The large palm leaves reaching over the yard shook for the briefest of moments before going still, and the birds began to chirp again, blissfully unaware of the killing below. The assassin reached out from his concealed position, reaching for the M4 carbine the cartel henchman had dropped.

The killer shrugged into the sentry's black combat vest adorned with extra magazines and then pulled the dead man's ball cap over his head. The Colombian belonged to the *asesino*, as they called themselves. The personal bodyguard of Colombia's most wanted man.

From his vantage point he could see two sides of the villa, an expansive fortress built into the almost impenetrable jungle mountains. The compound could only be accessed by winding roads lined with villages and ranches, bought and paid for with cartel money and guarded by cartel check points.

A careful scan of the fortress revealed several teenage girls splashing each other in one of the three in ground pools on the property but no other guards in the immediate area. Emerging from the jungle, the interloper turned his newly acquired M4 rifle over in his hands, drawing the bolt back to ensure that a round was seated in the chamber.

It looked as if money talked and bullshit walked.

The Ramirez cartel apparently had enough cash on hand to arm its paramilitary force with better weapons and equipment then many soldiers in the US Army were issued, the M4 being a short barrel version of the carbine and outfitted with a holographic reflex optic for close quarter shooting.

Looking down at his watch, he could see the numbers ticking down.

For now he would hide in plain sight while attempting to locate his objective. As he moved alongside the sculpted hedges, he knew that his disguise would not stand under scrutiny for long due to his being nearly a head taller than most Colombians.

He had to work fast.

Approaching the villa, the assassin heard voices coming down the wide stairs that led up to the second floor. Leaning against the wall he held the M4 at the ready, listening to two voices converse back and forth. His Spanish was rusty but he could pick out that they were talking about having someone shot. Maybe this was Mr. Murder himself, Ramirez. The extra footsteps the assassin heard must belong to his bodyguards.

Whatever the case, the drug lord wasn't his concern at the moment. Waiting for the party to arrive pool side, he disappeared into an alcove that contained a short flight of stone stairs heading into the basement.

Stepping carefully across the tile floor, he arrived in a kind of underground grotto complete with fake stone walls and hanging vines over a indoor pool. Stalactites made of artificial rock hung from the ceiling over the pool and an adjoining hot tub that bubbled with a low hum, waiting for another Colombian beauty from Ramirez's harem.

He hoped his target was down here somewhere because there was no way he was going to search the entire villa uncontested. It was just a question of when.

Pat sat with his back against the wall listening to the buzzing of several flies circling overhead. Every now and again one of them dropped down to make a dive bombing run on his head, causing him to flinch away.

Across from him J-Rod wasn't looking so hot.

As far as he could tell, none of them made it to the drop zone. He had managed to link up with J-Rod and Mark after stumbling through the jungle for several hours. With the Narco traffickers on their trail, they had been unable to put distance between themselves and the enemy, not with J-Rod's fractured ankle.

He and Mark had taken turns carrying him, but it was only a matter of time before they made contact. Mark was dead; he knew that much for sure. He could only imagine what had become of the rest of the team; then on second thought he would rather not.

Now they sat in a concrete cell belonging to the Ramirez Cartel.

Waiting.

The Delta Operator looked through the iron bars at the two guards lounged back in their chairs listening to the radio, rifles propped carelessly against the wall. It could be a while until his government negotiated terms of release with the cartel. As a soldier captured in the course of what was to be a covert operation he had become the best political bargaining chip a criminal, terrorist, or dictator could ask for.

He had become Khrushchev's Gary Powers, and there would almost certainly be a reckoning.

Constantly drilled to objectively critique the performance of himself and his fellow soldiers from the beginning of his military career, Pat kept rehashing the events in his mind over and over again. What could he have done differently? No. He forced himself to concentrate on his current situation. They had to focus on escape.

He turned his back to the guards as both of them looked up, eyes towards the corridor leading deeper into the Villa's basement. Someone down the hall was saying something in muffled Spanish.

"A worker is asking for help with the pool," J-Rod whispered. "Something is wrong with one of the pumps," he said, finishing the translation.

Once again Pat damned the Army for deciding he should learn Thai when he spent all his time in the Middle East and South America.

One of the guards got to his feet, grumbling something that needed no translation and headed down the corridor.

Pat leaned back against the wall. It was more than just a little disconcerting that the drug lord had a small private prison under his villa. There were several other cells. The floor and walls stank with the blood and feces left behind by former inmates. This wasn't his first rodeo. If it came to that and he couldn't find a way to escape, he'd be damned if he let a similar fate happen to himself or J-Rod.

With his head down, a new guard came walking out of the corridor, his blue ball cap obscuring his face. Even though Pat had his watch confiscated by the cartel gunmen during his capture, he knew that the guards rotated in two hour shifts, this guy being about an hour early.

The guard listening to the radio looked up at the newcomer and must have sensed that something was wrong. He attempted to get to his feet but never made it. The stranger struck first.

With his hand creating a knife cutting edge, he jabbed his fingers into the indentation under the guard's larynx depriving the Colombian gunman of oxygen, Pat recognizing a basic *atemi*. With the guard already gasping for air, the stranger easily put him into a choke hold until he passed out. The newcomer locked the hold in place as the man's face turned blue. He didn't seem worried about the second guard coming back any time soon.

Easing the corpse back down onto the chair the stranger turned towards the prisoners.

"Deckard?" Pat said, squinting his eyes. "Is that you?"

"Hey, Patrick," he replied, approaching the cell.

"Who the hell are you?" J-Rod demanded. "Where is the rest of the rescue team?"

"They called up the best and the brightest for you guys," Deckard replied. "But their risk mitigation worksheet had an improper heading on it, so they are still grounded on the tarmac at

Ft. Bragg. You got me instead."

"Who is this guy?" J-Rod demanded.

"The guy who was available," Pat answered. The younger Delta operator had been expecting an entire squadron of fellow Delta operators, backed up by a battalion of Army Rangers, not some guy wearing a Televida ball cap.

"We need to hurry. The Agency is jumping the gun and sending the Colombian military to crash the party. We only have a few minutes to clear the area."

"The guy with the cell keys is upstairs," Pat said, not wasting any time. "He opens the cell when they bring us food. Saw him down here an hour ago when the guard shift changed."

"What does he look like?"

"Curly hair, mustache; today he's wearing jeans and Michael Jackson T-shirt."

Deckard looked at him sideways.

Pat shrugged as a halfhearted response.

"The rest of the team?"

Pat shook his head. "One dead, don't know about the rest."

Nodding his understanding, Deckard turned towards the stairwell leading upstairs. There wasn't anything else to say. Leaving the dead behind was a tough pill to swallow, but intellectually Pat knew it was the only option. The Colombian military could recover the bodies later even if he couldn't bring himself to say it out loud.

Picking up a small shaving mirror that lay on the stool next to the radio, Deckard used it to peer up the stairs from behind cover, looking for signs of the enemy. Satisfied with what he saw, he moved up the stairs, M4 rifle leading the way.

"You know that guy?" J-Rod asked, while they waited helplessly in their cell.

"Yeah, we were in the same unit for a while."

"Who does he work for now?"

"Fuck should I know," Pat grunted, "and if he gets us out of here, I don't care."

Hearing a series of bumps, they turned to see Deckard

dragging their jail keeper down the stairs, his heavy cowboy boots clunking down every step as Deckard held him under each arm. All three of them winced at the noise even though no one else could hear it over the radio, still blasting salsa music. Finally he set the guard down next to the other corpse, the dead man's faded Michael Jackson shirt pulled up over his hairy belly.

The asesino member's throat bore a ragged wound that looked to have sliced completely through his windpipe and carotid arteries, dark crimson stains now obscuring Michael Jackson's visage.

"Right front pocket," Pat informed him.

Deckard dug around and came up with a key ring, the cell key being an old fashioned type for warded locks. Turning the key, Deckard swung open the barred door, wincing for a second time at the sound the rusty hinges made. J-Rod limped out with Pat supporting him with one arm.

"How bad are you?" Deckard asked, giving him a once over.

J-Rod was white in the face. His ankle was blown up like a soft ball.

"I can manage."

"It's a fracture," Pat clarified. "We aren't going anywhere fast."

"I might have a way cleared out for us."

Deckard disappeared back into the corridor, stepping over the body of the first prison guard he eliminated. Reaching for the door, he could hear the laughs and shouts of the two girls who he had seen in the outdoor pool, now joined by several male voices.

Hurrying back to the prison, he looked back up the stairs.

"What's up?" Pat asked.

"That way is no good, too many people in the grotto."

"The grotto?"

"I don't think you're invited."

Deckard crept back up the steps.

J-Rod propped himself up against the wall while Pat handed him one of the unattended rifles and picked up the other for himself. No extra magazines, but the situation was already looking better than it had a few minutes ago.

Coming up the steps, Deckard was crouched at the top motioning for them to stop. Quickly looking under the bannister and into the room, Pat could see that the cartel don had spared no expense. It was a formal sitting room lined with mahogany walls, Italian leather furniture, and a large plasma screen television on which another guard was now watching a muted AC Milan game.

Rolling up his left sleeve, Pat saw that Deckard was using an interesting but somewhat anachronistic weapon, a garrote wire. On his left wrist Deckard wore a leather bracelet around which was wrapped some medium gauge piano wire that led to a small wooden dowel on the other end. At the moment the dowel was held in place by a rubber band on the bracelet.

Releasing the rubber band, the dowel fell away as Deckard unrolled the piano wire wrapped around the bracelet. It was a technique the Delta operator had never seen before, most garrote wires, as commonly thought of were two wooden handholds attached by a few feet of wire. Deckard's was one handhold, the other secured around the leather bracelet which would protect the wrist.

Remaining in a crouch Deckard moved heel to toe, gaining ground over an immaculate Persian carpet while keeping his target in sight. Only a highly skilled operator could stalk within striking distance to make a nearly silent kill with such a weapon. Pat considered the garrote obsolete; these days' weapons manufacturers had entire secret divisions of their production facilities dedicated to developing proprietary weapons for Delta, DevGroup, and the CIA, such as subsonic ammunition and guns with integrated sound suppressors.

In the pit of his stomach Pat knew Deckard didn't have access to such hardware because he was simply making all this up on the fly.

Successfully reaching striking range without alerting the guard, Deckard came to a high crouch, his left hand hovering just behind the guard's neck. The Colombian cartel heavy grunted at something on the television as the American flipped the garrote wire over the man's head with his right hand.

Deckard immediately pressed his left hand with the wire attached to his wrist against the back of the guard's neck while simultaneously powering straight back with his right hand, grasping the garrote's handhold in an iron grip. It was a virtually instantaneous and silent kill.

While he lowered the body to the ground, the Delta men climbed the rest of the way up the stairs. Deckard rewound the garrote wire around his wrist. Taking the rifle off his shoulder by the sling, Deckard eased open one of the sitting room's two doors, knowing he had to backtrack through the mansion to find a suitable exit.

Deckard shook his head at the further signs of tasteless extravagance. The next room appeared to be a large open air entertainment area with more television screens mounted everywhere and an artificial waterfall trickling down one wall. More asesino members were sitting and standing around the screens watching the soccer game, a few shouting at something happening in the match.

Blinking a few times to make sure he wasn't seeing things, Deckard watched another cartel member walk into the room from outside, guiding a large black jaguar on a chain leash. Ramirez was known to maintain a private zoo, yet another sign of wealth and status, but this was starting to look like a movie set.

On reconsideration, maybe that was the point.

There was no backing down now. They had to get out and didn't have time for anything slick before the assault began.

Ignoring the squad of men standing around the plasma screens for a moment, Deckard sighted in on the Jaguar handler. The Columbian was telling the others in Spanish that the boss wanted the animal around during the party. With the red dot in the M4's holographic reflex sight hovering on the animal handler's chest, the former soldier gently squeezed the trigger.

The handler spun around with the strike of the 5.56 bullet impacting his chest, the chain leash falling to the ground before the handler dropped. The other guards turned from their game, their minds still processing the unexpected. Exploiting their hesitation, Deckard swept the muzzle of his rifle across the room from left to right, firing into the center mass of each gunman he could index, a few missed shots shattering the wide screens behind them.

The jaguar let out a blood curdling roar that instantly filled the room as one of the guards struggled to his feet, tearing a Beretta pistol from his holster. Now agitated and masterless, the jaguar did what large predators do best. Moving like liquid across the floor, he gained momentum before jumping onto the back of the asesino gunman, large paws straddling his shoulders, claws sinking deep into the flesh.

The Colombian let out a scream of his own as the ebony jungle cat easily wrestled him to the ground. The last the gunmen shouldered his own rifle and took aim at the jungle cat.

Deckard blasted the guy twice in the chest for targeting an endangered species.

The trio tiptoed around the bodies and the jaguar to the next room, emerging in a wide foyer with a row of marble columns on each side. The Ramirez villa was like some kind of bizarre fun house someone with a bad sense of humor had dropped in the middle of the rain forest.

By now the small army was alerted to the prison break, and armed men began pouring through the doorway on the other side of the foyer.

Deckard sprinted towards cover, Pat taking longer as he helped J-Rod hop behind one of the pillars. Pivoting at the hips to expose as little of himself as possible, Deckard indexed one of the enemy shooters coming through the door on the opposite side of the room. He fired, several rounds punching through the man's face and dropping him, his head bouncing off the ground like a basketball.

Ducking back behind cover, he took a knee, changing his elevation as he engaged an enemy behind the opposite row of columns. A burst from the Colombian's MP5 sub-machine gun broke apart large pieces of the pillar Deckard was behind as he returned fire, walking several rounds across the shooter's neck and head in an aerosol spray of blood.

The sustained bursts from one of the Delta operator's weapon ceased just as he heard Pat call out to him.

"I'm black!"

Reaching down Deckard tore a magazine from his combat vest and slid it across the floor to Pat's position. Snatching up the full magazine Pat expertly reloaded his weapon and continued to fire, this time at a gunman above them on the balcony.

Sensing movement, the former soldier realigned his sights towards the open doorway just as another gunman came rushing through, oblivious to the situation he had stumbled into. Pat, J-Rod, and Deckard simultaneously triggered bursts that riddled the man with holes before depositing him on the marble floor, a pool of blood quickly growing under him.

With the bolt of his M4 locked back on an empty chamber, Deckard quickly recharged his weapon while nodding towards the french doors that led out towards the pool where he had made his infiltration from. Helping J-Rod to his feet, they moved towards their exit as shouts could be heard deeper in the villa.

Clearing the French doors, the three men began down the wide stairs to the lawn. The humidity hit them like a brick wall; the smell of the adjacent jungle was strong outside.

Halfway down the steps, Deckard cringed at the sound of gunfire, anticipating enemy bullets that never came. Spinning around he saw both of the Delta men leaning over the railing, raining down a hail storm of lead. Below, several of the Don's bodyguards were exchanging gunfire with them from the entrance to the grotto.

Two bodies were already piled on top of each other in the doorway, a third man vying to join them as he wildly fired his Uzi one handed. Stepping beside them Deckard flipped the selector switch on his rifle to automatic and laid on a brief salvo of fire, causing the gunman to duck back down into the passage.

Marble chips tore across his booted foot as an enemy gunshot narrowly missed. Looking over his shoulder, Deckard focused on the cartel gunmen scurrying around the drug lord's helicopter like ants around an ant hill on the far side of the gardens, several of them taking pot shots with pistols and sub-machine guns.

Fast work. The pilot must have been under orders to kick the rotors the moment any shooting began, to prepare for the Don's escape. Kneeling, Deckard carefully aimed at one of the two hundred and fifty meter targets. Squeezing the trigger, he watched as one of the gunmen went down, his hands flailing in the air.

The rotors on the helicopter were beginning to gain momentum, but the pilot couldn't leave until they had Ramirez safely aboard, and that wasn't happening with the Delta men pinning him down with suppressive fire, effectively trapping him in the grotto.

With another bullet zipping over his head, Deckard shot the second gunmen in front of the helicopter, the single rifle round coring through his neck before bouncing off one of his vertebrae and creating a fist sized exit wound on its way out the back.

Turning his attention on the helicopter, he began spraying fire across the pilot's windshield. It would have made for the perfect escape in slightly different circumstances. Deckard could fly a small single engine plane, but attempting to fly the helicopter would be nothing short of a death wish. With the windshield beginning to spider web from the pounding of 5.56 rounds he resigned himself to the fact that if they weren't leaving, neither was Ramirez.

Suddenly the aircraft exploded in a plume of orange and red flame that rose into the air, the entire fuselage lifting off the ground under a tower of fire. The helicopter crashed down on the concrete helipad, the blast washing over them as a larger Black Hawk attack helicopter peeled off from its gun run with another coming in right behind it.

Above them they could hear more gunfire, followed by shattering glass as Ramirez's private army began firing on the Colombian military helicopters from the villa's second floor.

The second Black Hawk nosed up into the air at a vicious

angle before seeming to crest an invisible ridge like a roller coaster. Now the pilot brought the helicopter screaming down towards the villa, opening fire with 2.75 inch Hydra rockets, and strafing the entire side of the building.

The concussion shook the ground beneath the Americans' feet sending them ducking for cover as glass and cement showered down from above, the rockets pounded into the mansion. The settable fuses on the rockets allowed them to detonate somewhere deeper in the mansion, flames erupting from the windows above them. Gunfire could still be heard sporadically, but it was clear that the gunship had significantly reduced the enemy's numbers.

Groaning as he got back to his feet, Deckard brushed concrete dust and glass shards off his shoulders.

"Aw, fuck," J-Rod groaned.

Like a giant dragonfly, they could hear the rotor blades buzzing through the air. Someone had cleared the twin gunships for immediate re-attack. However, across the lawn Deckard could see the silhouette of someone up on top of what had been the maintenance shed for Ramirez's helicopter. The large caliber anti-material rifle the man lugged onto the roof was unmistakable even at a distance.

As the AH-60L helicopter lined up for another gun run, the cartel sniper opened fire; .50 caliber Raufoss rounds echoed across the compound with each shot. The exploding anti-armor incendiary rounds flashed with each strike against the helicopter's metal fuselage.

Seeing the splash off the skin of the helicopter, the sniper continued the lay the fire on, each shot rocking the barrel to the rear on its internal recoil absorbing springs until the ten round magazine had been exhausted. Getting closer to its objective, the Blackhawk amazingly seemed to withstand the barrage of gunfire, if only for a moment.

Deckard and the two Delta operators turned and stumbled back into the villa as smoke began to billow from the rear rotor, the gunship literally going into a tail spin. The pilot desperately auto-rotated the aircraft the entire way down to the ground before it smashed into the ground and spun onto its side.

Rolling over, the rotors chewed into the grass lawn before they broke off into pieces, flying as red hot shrapnel, a few landing in one of the above ground pools with a hiss of steam.

With the wreckage of the first AH-60L still smoking, the second bird continued its assault, walking a line of .30 caliber fire from its M230 chain gun across the top of the maintenance shed in a single stunted burst. Sustained fire from the heavy machine gun created a yawing effect when long bursts were fired, the recoil pushing the aircraft off target, making shorter burst necessary.

The blast caught the sniper completely exposed, tearing him to pieces and leaving nothing but cauterized flesh and a red vapor mist as evidence of his presence just a second before.

J-Rod limped along with agony spread across his face until Deckard ran up behind and threw the operator over his shoulders into a fireman's carry before he had the chance to protest.

"Take point," he said to Pat, as they dashed through the foyer.

Pat nodded, stripping another fresh magazine from Deckard's combat vest.

The foyer took up the entire center of the villa, the now pockmarked marble columns standing in front of a half dozen shelves containing what Deckard hoped were just forgeries of Inca artifacts. The stone faces glared at them through shattered display cases as they ran past. More buzzing, more muffled gunfire could be heard outside.

The three men shouldered their way through the front door to find another two Black Hawks hovering outside. These were transport helicopters, buzzing like giant bumble bees over the front lawn and driveway. Behind the pilots in the cargo area, rope masters were giving the order to drop ropes.

The thick, green nylon fast ropes were dropped from the helicopters, the excess coiling below on the ground under the spinning rotors. With the rope hanging from a boom attached to the side of the helicopter, camouflage clad counter terrorist soldiers from Colombia's Agrupacion De Fuerzas Especiales Urbanas began sliding down, like they were on a fire pole.

The Americans didn't waste any time watching the commandos descending on the drug lord's villa. They ran directly for the oblong warehouse made out of corrugated metal, the garage doors giving away its purpose.

Running down the steps, Pat quickly led them into the hedges, careful to keep them out of the commando team's line of sight. From the initial gun runs on the villa, it was clear that the AFEU were weapons hot for this operation. Deckard followed with J-Rod over his shoulders, manipulating his M4 with one hand as best he could while holding the Delta operator's legs with the other.

Pat approached the side entrance to the parking garage, finding the large metal door already partly ajar. Stepping inside they found themselves in total darkness, stumbling around as intermittent gunfire blasted somewhere deeper in the compound.

Setting J-Rod down on his good foot, Deckard and Pat began sweeping around in the darkness for a light switch. Suddenly the overhead lights blasted on, causing them squint as their eyes attempted to readjust.

The automatic gunfire was deafening as the sound reverberated off the walls. Hitting the cement floor, a fusillade of rifle rounds punched through the thin metal wall behind Deckard as he rolled behind the wheel well of a 1966 Shelby Mustang.

Pat followed Deckard's lead, taking cover next to him, J-Rod crawling behind a Camaro.

"Lights!" Deckard yelled.

The three Americans aimed towards the ceiling, systematically shooting out the florescent bulbs above and around them, creating shadows deep enough to hide in. Hearing a gruff voice barking orders from the other side of the garage, it was clear enough what had happened.

After heading off Ramirez and his lackeys at the grotto, and the Colombian military depriving him of his escape plan, Ramirez had the same idea they did, doubling back and finding another means to make a getaway.

18

Deckard pulled free his final 5.56 magazine and slid it across the ground to J-Rod.

"Keep them occupied. We'll envelope."

The Delta men nodded, J-Rod taking a knee and putting a few suppressive shots down range to give the enemy something to think about. Breaking off, Pat went left and Deckard went right, staying behind cover whenever possible and sticking to the shadows when it wasn't.

Sliding up alongside a Ferrari, Deckard could hear J-Rod sending volleys of fire towards the drug lord and his bodyguards. All he had to do was keep their heads down long enough for his teammates to get into position. Moving in a crouch, he continued to make his way to the other end of the garage, weaving his way through Ramirez's car collection.

Breaking a corner around another Ferrari, he spotted one of the gunmen taking refuge behind a BMW convertible, fixed in position by J-Rod snapping rounds over his head. Taking aim, Deckard was ready to make a head shot from less than ten feet away when the Ferrari rocked up and down on its suspension, glass showering both him and the gunman.

Dozens of holes suddenly appeared in the roof, spilling laser-like beams of daylight into the darkness of the garage. Somewhere above them the Black Hawk gunship must have been made aware of shots fired inside the garage and took action to protect the Colombian assault team outside.

Hundred thousand dollar sports cars were stitched from fiberglass hood to trunk by 30mm autofire, crumpling frames and shattering windows, the massive holes seeming to appear from nowhere. Utilizing the opportunity, Deckard fired. Acting on muscle memory, he put the round right through the bridge of the bodyguard's nose, effectively dropping his target to the ground.

Edging deeper into the warehouse, he picked up the pace as the large bore automatic cannon above tore through the roof as if it wasn't even there. From the sound of J-Rod lowering his rate of fire to just a shot every few seconds, he knew he had to act quickly. J-Rod was almost black on rounds.

At the last row of classic cars he lay down on his side, looking under the frame of the vehicles for any bad guys, finding one foolishly kneeling down on the cement and occasionally firing a shot or two, attempting to seek out J-Rod's position. Still on his side, Deckard swung the M4 up horizontally to his shoulder and lined up the red dot sight on the man's ankle. Triggering a single shot, the Colombian fell to the ground howling, allowing Deckard to easily deliver a fatal shot to the back of his head, spraying a wash of gore across the floor.

Another crack sounded as Pat fired on someone, just as another salvo came bursting through the rooftop from above.

Swinging out around the vehicle on one knee, Deckard gained target acquisition on the nearest asesino standing a few meters behind the corpse he has just made. His finger was tightening around the trigger when a crash thundered down in front of him, throwing him on his backside. With his finger on the trigger he accidentally discharged a round into the air.

The man had been split end from end, a 30mm round tearing down through the ceiling had sliced through flesh and bone, cracking him open like a lobster. Two arms and a leg could be made out amid the intestines strewn out across the floor, but that was about all that was recognizable. Deckard swallowed. His nose filled with the sickly smell of blood, he realized he had been hosed with bits of bone and gore.

Wearing khakis and a collared shirt left open to reveal a large gold cross, Ramirez sat at the edge of the pool of blood. His pistol lay at his side while he had both hands on his forehead, trying to comprehend what had just happened.

Snarling at the turn of events, Deckard got to his feet as Ramirez's face suddenly bulged outwards, the back of his head disappearing as it was taken off by a gunshot. At this point Deckard was so deaf he didn't even register the shot. The drug lord collapsed backwards, his blood mixing with that of his late comrade.

"Mission complete," a voice said from the darkness.

Deckard spun toward the sound.

"Let's get the hell out of here," Pat said stepping out of the shadows.

Two

Depressing the magazine release on his M4, Deckard acknowledged two rounds in the mag, plus one in the chamber.

"Grab what you can. We need to go," Deckard said.

Pat ran back to retrieve J-Rod while Deckard consolidated the enemy's weapons. The battlefield recovery netted a gold plated AK-47, one FN P90 sub-machine gun, a jewel encrusted 1911 pistol that had belonged to the former drug lord, and a CZ75 pistol with a spare magazine that Deckard shoved in his waistband.

A little cliché for a drug baron, but that was the kind of stuff they'd go in for, Deckard figured. The way things were heading, he just hoped they all went 'bang' when he pulled the trigger.

Pat made it back with J-Rod over his shoulder, just as he spotted the key box and flipped it open.

"The Ferrari looks like it's about done," J-Rod said, pointing to the Italian car riddled with 30mm craters. "Maybe we can take the Lamborghini out for a spin?"

"Not with your bum ankle," Deckard said, grabbing a key. "How about something a little more practical?"

"A little more boring you mean," he groaned back, following Deckard to a white Range Rover.

J-Rod sat in the back, handling his M4 and whatever ammunition they had left for it in addition to the AK. Pat racked the charging handle on the P90, watching a 5.7 round drop out from the bottom to ensure that it was loaded. He shoved the 1911 between the seat and the center console just in case.

Turning the ignition and starting the truck, Deckard hit the garage door opener mounted on the sun visor.

"Hold on," he said, stomping down on the gas.

The Range Rover hurtled out of the garage as Deckard spun

the wheel hand over hand taking them in a ninety degree turn toward the villa's front gate.

Ornamental plants and jungle flew by as more gunfire sounded, the rear window imploding and sending shards of glass everywhere. The Colombian counter-terrorist team had no idea they were there and assumed they were with Ramirez's crew.

"Thank the Agency for me," Deckard grunted, as they drove out the front gate. "I'm sure they sent the AFEU in as soon as an inside source reported your capture. They wanted Ramirez dead and didn't care how it got done."

"Nice," Pat muttered, as Deckard sped onto the winding mountain road.

"No worries," Deckard assured, cutting around a fork in the road. "All we have to do is fight our way through a half dozen or so cartel checkpoints and we'll be home free."

"Shit," J-Rod said. "How did you get up here to begin with?"

"Took a taxi."

Shooting down the crumbling asphalt road, Deckard blasted through the first checkpoint, the cartel men manning it screaming and waving their guns in the air for them to stop. On their right side was nothing but a blur of green leading to a sheer cliff face. It was what the conquistadors had called the *infierno verde*. On the other side, the road immediately dropped off the edge of the mountain, at certain points the mountain actually overtaking the road as huge washouts were created by erosion.

Nowhere to go but down.

Downshifting, Deckard eased them around another bend, not knowing what was around the corner. Straightening out the wheel on the other side, they were greeted by another checkpoint, one of the Colombians manning it speaking into a hand held radio.

While the gunman was still receiving the message about a runaway Range Rover over his walkie talkie, Pat leaned out the passenger side window, easily maneuvering the stubby sub-machine gun. Holding down the trigger, he sent a full auto stream of 5.7 armor piercing rounds into the guard's chest, sending him tumbling backwards into a runoff ditch on the side of the road.

As they flashed by, the dead man's partner reacted, firing on the truck as it passed. J-Rod returned fire, getting several shots off with his M4 through the already shattered rear window before running out of ammo and transitioning to the AK-47. He was fairly sure he missed his mark. Firing from a moving vehicle wasn't easy to begin with, especially on the mountain road, and especially with Deckard driving.

"Everyone good?"

"We're kosher," Pat replied.

For a moment the truck was engulfed in a tunnel of green, vegetation spilling into and over the road before they came out on the other side.

The third checkpoint had gotten the word and was on alert. As soon as the truck pulled within line of sight of the gunmen, the Columbians opened fire, muzzle flashes giving them away just an instant before bullets peppered the front of the truck. One shot managed to blast off Deckard's side mirror in a miniature explosion.

Resisting the urge to return fire, he ducked down and kept both hands on the wheel and his foot on the gas, knowing that he needed to focus solely on driving. Pat leaned out the window again and began squeezing off rounds as they rushed up to the checkpoint, his bullets kicking up little puffs of debris around the feet of his target.

Both continued firing on each other as Deckard watched the speedometer climb to nearly seventy kilometers an hour. J-Rod was leaning out the rear window on Deckard's side with the AK and firing at the second checkpoint guard. He held his breath and pointed the Range Rover straight ahead, knowing that the seventy kilometer an hour jousting match would continue until some people starting dying.

Just a few meters away, Deckard exhaled. The two gunmen now lay still on the side of the road, victims of the Delta operator's handy work.

Cutting around the next bend, the Range Rover went right

through the next checkpoint. He hadn't expected another one so close, and the guards looked just as surprised as they bolted by them. Clearly they hadn't expected them to make it this far.

Looking for his side view mirror, he remembered that it wasn't there anymore and turned to the rear view mirror in time to see the cartel thugs pile into a beige colored Dodge pickup truck. Cranking the engine, they powered up behind the Americans.

"Heads up."

"I see 'em," J-Rod answered.

The pickup was quickly gaining on them as they entered a straightaway. Deckard let them, he didn't want them on his tail by the time they hit the next checkpoint. Letting up off the gas pedal, he let them shoot ahead, leaving the cartel shooters leaning out the windows, fingers on the triggers with a confused look on their faces.

Stomping back down on the gas, he matched their speed, coming up on their right side, allowing J-Rod to rake the Dodge with AK fire. Reaching into his waistband, Deckard pulled free the CZ75 pistol. Craning his neck, he flicked off the safety and began pumping rounds into the gunman sitting in the passenger seat of the pickup while steering with his left hand.

The gunman shouted as crimson blossomed on his shirt around the shoulder and forearm, causing him to drop his MP5 sub gun out the window. Pulling the trigger a third time, Deckard skipped a beat, the expected bang never happening.

A quick look showed him the pistol had stove-piped. An expended casing failing to fully eject from the pistol, it got jammed between the barrel and the slide. Turning the Czech handgun upside down, Deckard wedged the rear sight up against the Range Rover's steering wheel and pushed the pistol forward.

The spent shell fell between his legs, and letting the pistol up off the wheel, he heard the slide slam home with a satisfying metallic smack as it chambered a fresh round. Crossing his right arm back over his left, he watched as J-Rod beat him to the punch. The 7.62x39 bullets shook the passenger back and forth in his seat as if he were having convulsions.

Deckard was about to try to fire on the driver, but the pickup truck simply wasn't there anymore.

"Holy shit," J-Rod yelled, looking back over his seat. "The erosion ate up the entire side of the road right there. They just drove right off the edge."

"Long way down," Pat laughed.

The humor didn't last long as they spotted two black Sports Utility Vehicles parked nose to nose across the road. Three camouflage clad cartel shooters stood in front of the blockade, confident in their plan.

"Lay on everything you got left," Deckard ordered. "I have to slow down if we're going to make it through in one piece."

Ducking down, Deckard aimed the Range Rover directly between the two SUVs. Speeding up, the Delta men opened fire as they closed within a hundred meters. Bullets thudded into the truck, sounding like massive raindrops pounding into and through the vehicle's metal frame. Over the dashboard he saw one of the AK-47 wielding shooters go down, the other two still blazing away.

A bullet tore through the headrest, splaying it open in a burst of yellow foam. It would have drilled Deckard in the face had he not ducked down, eyes still looking over the dash.

At twenty five meters Deckard eased down on the brakes. The battered truck squealed in protest as the frame twisted back and forth. Meanwhile, Pat drilled a second AK gunner with a two round burst. Deckard almost brought them to a complete halt. If he attempted a break out at high speed, he would destroy the Range Rover, ending their chances of escape, if not killing all of them in the process.

The truck was stitched back and forth, shattering the few remaining windows, a round burning across Deckard's forearm, causing him to flinch off the wheel for a split second. Pushing the muzzle of his gold plated AK out the window, J-Rod finally put an end to the gunman's erratic fire.

Just a meter away from the roadblock, Deckard grasped the wheel and hit the gas, powering through. The Range Rover made contact, jarring their molars and pushing the SUVs outwards to clear a path out of the kill zone.

Speeding back down the road, Deckard shook out his arm. The bullet had only grazed him but burned like hell.

"You okay?" Pat asked.

"Yeah, we got lucky."

"What do you got for ammo, J-Rod?"

"Ten rounds maybe."

"Shit," Pat said, inspecting the translucent magazine the laid horizontal across the top of his sub-machine gun. He had about the same left in what had been a fifty round magazine. "Me, too."

"Maybe fifteen rounds for the CZ," Deckard added. "Only fire if it's a sure thing."

The road continued to weave its way downhill. Deckard could see his objective in the distance, just passed the two cartel triggermen pulling a Nissan across the road. The ridge line on the opposite side of the checkpoint opened up into a saddle, a thin reprieve from the green hell, and their only chance at escape.

No way were they making it through another half dozen checkpoints lining the road down to the valley floor.

Deckard got them as close as he dared. Hearing the staccato rip of gunfire, he slowed the truck before pulling the emergency break and power sliding to the side of the road. With the Range Rover still rocking on its suspension, Pat and J-Rod threw open the doors and escaped onto the clean side of the vehicle to take cover behind the wheel wells.

Climbing across the center console to avoid coming out on the contact side, Deckard could hear the enemy's AK-47 rounds bouncing off the asphalt and slamming into the side of the truck with one thump after another.

Getting to his feet alongside the Delta soldiers, he saw one of the enemy collapse under his own weight, one of J-Rod's shots coming in a little low and knee capping him.

Lining up his front sight post over the next shooter's face, Deckard knew he had to aim high. A fifty meter shot with a pistol wasn't easy even on a good day. Holding the CZ75 in a modified weaver grip, he rested his hands on the hood of the truck to steady his aim.

Firing, he let the recoil ride up his arms. The gunman doubled over for a moment, touching his stomach in disbelief until Pat fired a shot that took a chunk out of his neck. Falling to his knees, the wounded man did a face plant in the middle of the road.

The third shooter was a little smarter but not by much. He had taken cover behind the Nissan but not behind the protection offered by the metal and rubber around the wheel well. The two Delta operators triangulated in on the man, bouncing their final rounds off the asphalt under the truck. The ricochets shot out as shrapnel into his feet and shins, causing excruciating pain that sent the cartel shooter wailing to the pavement.

Deckard loaded his only spare magazine before breaking cover and heading towards the dead and dying. The Delta men dropped their now empty weapons, and Pat yanked the 1911 out from between the seat before lifting J-Rod over his shoulder to carry him.

Standing in front of the would be killer, now laid out with a neck wound and gut shot, Deckard watched him gasping for breath, knowing from hard experience that it wouldn't be long. Leveling the CZ, he delivered a mercy shot between the Colombian's eyes. Approaching the third gunman behind the Nissan, he found him in a similar state and efficiently repeated the process.

There was no satisfaction; it just was.

Grabbing up two of the dead shooter's AKs, he slung one and carried the other, tucking the pistol back into his pants.

"We're almost there," he informed the others.

Picking it up to a steady trot but not fast enough to lose Pat as he carried his partner, Deckard moved the rest of the way downhill to the saddle. Between the break in the cliff face was a small, barely recognizable foot path. Turning as the Delta men arrived, Deckard spotted two more black SUVs racing up the road towards them from below, alerted to their presence by radio or gunfire, it didn't really matter.

"Follow the path," Deckard said, handing one of the AK's to Pat. Sticking the 1911 in his pants, Pat accepted the rifle. "You'll come out on a spur, just a single finger jutting off the side of the mountain. Take this." Reaching into his pocket, he handed J-Rod a pen flare gun.

"Fire it when you get there."

"And you?"

"The pilot should already be overhead somewhere. I'm going to slow them down, but if I'm more than a minute or two, then get out of here."

"You sure?"

"Yeah."

Having been gunslingers their entire adult lives, neither of the men were much for goodbyes.

Shifting J-Rod's weight on his shoulders, Pat began stomping through the muddy trail, quickly disappearing into the foliage. With the sound of his passage fading, Deckard took a knee behind the largest tree he could find. At this altitude the forest didn't grow into the massive triple canopy normally found in the region, but it would have to do.

The black SUVs continued to speed up the road towards the wasted checkpoint, unaware of Deckard's position in the underbrush. Flipping the AK's selector down one notch, the former soldier shouldered the rifle with sweat running down his face and stinging his eyes.

Initiating his ambush on the first truck, Deckard fired, the tinted driver's window exploded revealing a bloody corpse behind it. Effectively driverless the truck sped out of control, careening off the road and smashing into the cliff.

The stinging in his eyes forgotten, the burn across his forearm no longer registering, he shifted his grip on the rifle and took aim at the second vehicle as armed cartel members unpacked themselves from each door.

Panting with exhaustion, Pat set his teammate down, trading him the AK for the pen flare gun. He could hear the faint buzz of a helicopter and hoped it wasn't the Colombian gunship searching for them.

They easily found the finger of dirt and rock that stretched out off the side the mountain. There was just enough open ground for a small helicopter to hover in for a high angle pick up. Screwing a flare into place, he pushed back the spring loaded firing mechanism and released it, firing the red flare up into the sky.

Behind them the sounds of a full on gun battle raged alongside blast after blast of what sounded like grenades detonating in the distance. J-Rod sat in the mud, angling himself back the way they had came from, silently pulling security until their ride arrived. Another burst of gunfire echoed through the jungle. Pat scanned the sky as he screwed another cartridge into place on the flare gun.

Pat fired the second flare as the gunfire grew closer.

J-Rod trained his sights on the path.

The trees and brush swayed as a green colored civilian helicopter buzzed right by, the pilot giving them the once over with a curious frown and a lit cigarette in his mouth, before disappearing from sight once again.

"What. The. Fuck."

The Jet Ranger III completed an orbit out over the valley before swinging back toward them. The pilot cautiously eased his way closer to the clearing, careful of the distance between the trees and his rotor blades. As the bird came in closer, he could make out the words 'Amazon Tours' on the side of the aircraft.

"Let's go," he said, picking up J-Rod.

"What about Deckard," he screamed back, over the sound of the rotor blades beating at the jungle around him.

"If he's going to make it then he'll make it."

The truth was that the younger Delta operator had to come

first for him. He hadn't seen Deckard in years but still hoped to hell he'd hurry up and join them.

The pilot grimaced as he set one skid down on the ground, the other hovering precariously over the edge of the mountain. Pat tugged open the side door and dropped J-Rod inside.

The younger man's eyes went wide as he spotted something over Pat's shoulder.

Glancing back he saw Deckard running down the path into the opening. He turned and returned fire with an MP-5 he had gotten from somewhere, or taken off of someone. Bullets swarmed around him like angry hornets, chopping through the wide palm leaves and turning the small tree trunks into splinters.

Suddenly Deckard kicked backwards as if struck in the chest with a sledge hammer and disappeared into the tall grass.

Pat cursed. Grabbing the AK, he thrust the drug lord's 1911 toward J-Rod.

"If the pilot makes a move, I want you to splatter him."

Taking the pistol, J-Rod nodded his understanding.

Charging forward, Pat cut loose, sending several bursts down the jungle path as he made his way toward where he had seen Deckard fall. Through the dense vegetation he could see the silhouettes of several sets of gun-toting cartel gunmen.

Aiming at the closest asesino taking cover behind a sapling tree, he fired several rounds through it, dropping the man into a sprawl across the trail. It had to be enough to buy him a few more seconds.

Coming alongside Deckard, he glanced down, seeing the side of his face covered in blood, the MP5 laying absently alongside him.

There was nothing he could do for him now.

Firing another burst to keep the enemy's head down, he prepared to run back to the helicopter when he noticed the receiver of Deckard's MP5 was bent, the steel core of a bullet tunneled into the metal frame.

"Deckard," he said thumping him in the eye with a finger.

Deckard squirmed as if he had just smelled something bad.

Down range, a cartel shooter attempted to bound forward, Pat catching him in mid stride with several well placed shots.

"Deckard! We are leaving right goddamned now!"

Coughing he rolled over on his stomach and saw the helicopter.

"Go!"

Stumbling to his feet, Deckard limped towards the Jet Ranger.

Bullets snapped over Pat's shoulder, causing him to fire back at a muzzle flash deeper in the jungle brush.

Realizing it was now or never, the Delta operator emptied what remained of his magazine, crisscrossing the jungle with automatic fire, the AK heating up in his hands until it went dry.

Throwing the rifle to the ground he turned and ran full speed, catching Deckard halfway to the helicopter and tossing him over his shoulder. His legs burned like they were full of battery acid, but he refused to slow down, not now, not so close.

Bending at the knees, he vaulted through the helicopter's open door, him and Deckard landing inside in a confused mess.

The pilot didn't wait for permission and peeled off under a barrage of gunfire.

J-Rod struggled, still holding the 1911 to the pilot's head as the exterior world swirled, mountains turning into valley and then into sky as he banked away and took them into a dive. The three Americans were weightless in the aircraft for one strange moment before slamming back into the floor.

"What the hell is going on?" Pat asked, sliding the door shut.

They were dumping altitude fast, the valley floor quickly rising up to meet them.

"I don't fucking know," J-Rod yelled back. "The pilot speaks fucking Arabic!"

"What?"

"No," Deckard sputtered. "He speaks Kurdish."

Pat blinked, confused, physically and mentally exhausted.

Deckard wiped some of the blood from the side of his face,

32

looking surprised at the sight of it. The bullet had struck his submachine gun, the splash catching him in the face and causing some shrapnel wounds.

Trying to untangle himself from the arms and legs of the two other men, he snatched a headset off a fastener from above and slid it over his ears. Readjusting the microphone, Deckard said something to the pilot.

"Fuck," he muttered, as they continued their decent down into the valley.

"What?"

"Johnnie says we're coming in hard. He's got some weird feedback in his pedals. Thinks we ate a few rounds on the way out."

Pat and J-Rod looked at each other.

"Hold on," Deckard said, listening over the head set. "He sees a soccer field he thinks he can get us to before we drop out of the sky."

J-Rod's eyes were like saucers.

Sitting up, he began fastening his seat belt, his companions following suit.

"Hold on," Deckard repeated, looking out the window for the field. "Yeah, there it is."

The helicopter was dropping fast, the skids passing just meters above some electrical lines.

"Where is that coming from?" J-Rod blurted.

"Where is what coming from-" Pat said turning from the window.

The entire cabin was filling with black smoke.

"What the-" Deckard coughed.

The pilot pulled on the collective pitch control, making a final push toward the soccer field as the helicopter went into free fall.

THREE

Twenty four hours later:

"I can't hear you," Deckard screamed with a finger stuck in one ear, the other pressed up against his cell phone. "I can't hear shit!"

The firefight in the mountains had left him hard of hearing for the time being, and the whining jet engines on the airfield weren't helping.

"I said, I need you in California tomorrow."

"What the hell for?"

"A recent job opening," the voice on the other end of the line said. "We were tracking the guy who was to take the job, but he had a nasty run-in with some Chechen separatists in Ardahan yesterday. It was over a woman, from what I understand. I want to dangle you out there to see if you can't get hired to do the job in his place."

"Hired by who?"

"I already created your cover and managed to get you a meeting with Chad Morrison through one of my contacts. You ever hear of him?"

"No," Deckard said, looking back at the C130 transport aircraft. The pilots were waiting on him.

"He runs a black bag PMC," he said referring to a Private Military Company. "At the moment he is looking to recruit some fresh meat."

"Recruiting for what?"

"People to protect certain industrial interests. People like you. Oil fields in Nigeria, alluvial diamond deposits in the Sierra

Leone, Coltan Mining in the Congo, that sort of thing."

"Wet work. He wants trigger pullers who don't mind getting their hands dirty."

"You got it. The resume I put together is fail-safe. You have backstops for backstops, solid covers, references with people I know personally waiting on the other end of the line if they get called. Besides, I know he won't be able to resist your charms once he meets you in person."

"Fuck me," Deckard yelled into the phone. "You already put my name in the hat, didn't you?"

"No, I put O'Brien's name in the hat, which is who I want you to be when you meet Morrison."

Deckard looked back at the aircraft.

After Johnnie nearly killed them by dropping into the soccer field, they had improvised their way to the nearest CIA safe house in the province. Using the communications set installed in the apartment, they had set up their extraction out of country.

Pat stood on the C-130's ramp, motioning for him to hurry up.

"Double my normal rate," Deckard told the man over the phone. "I also want you to personally supervise the recovery operation."

"Recovery?"

"Of Sergeant Major Keely and the rest of his team."

There was a pause, and for a moment Deckard wondered if he lost the connection.

"No problem," came the reply. "So, can you be in California tomorrow?"

"I'll be there," Deckard said, terminating the call.

Slipping the phone into his pocket, Deckard strode towards the open ramp of the aircraft, wondering what was waiting for him in the United States.

A wrinkled hand slapped a cellular phone shut as Deckard terminated the call on the other end.

Somehow, the son of a bitch had pulled it off again.

Colombia made for a hat trick having followed up assignments in Zimbabwe and Iran.

The older man ran a hand across his chin. He didn't get as much sun these days as he would have liked. The exterior of the building he worked in looked like a furniture warehouse while the inside looked like a military command center despite its small staff.

He had plucked Deckard out of the ether. After a falling out with the US government he had gone freelance a number of years ago. The older man was a veteran of the same world, the same battlegrounds in decades prior. Some members of the group thought that someone as reckless as Deckard would be a liability.

Then they had gotten word through the grapevine about the freelancer's job in North Korea. There were whispers about a derailed train outside Pyongyang and the bodies of dead Syrian nuclear scientists. That had been enough to put Deckard over the top as a candidate and given the Vietnam veteran the ammunition he had needed to ensure that he was accepted into the group.

As a member, Deckard still operated independently but he now had access to the group's stockpiles, safe houses, and sophisticated surveillance equipment to make use of.

The old man spun in his seat, looking at the picture frame hanging on his wall. It was the only personal memento that resided in his office, the only reminder of his past life. It was a tattered American flag that had flown over his fire base the day they had been nearly overrun at Command and Control North, or CCN, on the coast of the South China Sea.

His organization had worked for decades to place an infiltrator in the midst of the global elite, the cartographers and king makers of world history.

A grin tugged at the corners of his mouth as he realized that he never really had any doubt that that man would be Deckard.

Tens of millions of dollars had been spent creating the fictional O'Brien cover. Ghost writers had penned documents in his name, lines of credit had been opened and closed under the alias by support staff, retired spooks sat on telephones waiting to pick up and pretend to be former employers. Everything had been set in motion years prior.

For Deckard's sake, if nothing else, he could only hope that Lady Luck was watching over both of their shoulders.

"Mr. O'Brien?"

"Yeah," the man replied, stepping forward to reveal sutures running down the side of his face.

"Please follow me," the attendant said. "They are ready to receive you."

"They? I'm supposed to talk to a Mr. Chad Morrison."

"You were meant to think so," the attendant huffed. "Now please follow me."

Deckard's jaw tightened.

He wasn't in the mood for cryptic nonsense.

Turning, he followed the attendant down the dirt path, allowing him to lead the way, heading somewhere deeper into the estate that sprawled across a good portion of Southern California. The invite-only event was held once a year for America's powerful, wealthy, and- maybe most importantly- the influential.

Morrison was supposed to be a headhunter for several major defense contractors, but now that someone had pulled a bait and switch on him, Deckard had no idea what to expect. In this crowd, he shuddered to think what it could be. Certainly nothing good. If any minutia of his cover was blown, he may well be a walking dead man in a place like this.

Following the forest trail, they passed by a former US President along with his son, the CEO of a major international corporate conglomeration, and the owner of three major news networks and a good portion of downtown Manhattan, all within a few seconds of each other. Different people living in a different world, Deckard thought.

Leaving the forest behind, they approached one of the lodges reserved for the event's biggest power players. Deckard looked up at the mantle over the door. It bore a skull and crossbones with Latin text on each side. Deckard shook his head. What the hell had he gotten himself into?

The call he had received in Colombia, that had initially sent Deckard to the gathering, was from an old hand, someone deeply embedded in the intelligence apparatus that was the Department Of Defense. Deckard trusted him, to a point, but still wondered how the DOD operative managed to secure him, if under the guise of Jake O'Brien, an invitation to what these old men called Bohemian Grove.

Walking up creaky wooden steps, the attendant held open the door for him, closing it as he crossed the threshold. Deckard felt like he was being taken to the woodshed, and maybe he was. Looking around the inside of the lodge house, his chest tightened.

The only good news was that if his cover had been blown, he never would have been ushered to such a high level meeting.

Three men rose to their feet in unison to greet him.

"Thank you for coming on such short notice," the first of the three said, shaking his hand.

"O'Brien. Not a problem," Deckard said. The man opposite him didn't bother introducing himself. It was just assumed that Deckard already knew who he was.

He did. Jarogniew had been a staple of the defense intelligence community since before Deckard had been born. Belonging to *szlachta* Polish nobility, his family was hit hard during the Second World War. Immigrating to America, he had attended the finest universities before being picked up by various foundations and think tanks.

Jarogniew had gone to the top, acting as a national security adviser to one President and serving as secretary of defense for another. Since that time he had somewhat retired from public life but continued to serve on councils and non-governmental organizations, even appearing as a commentator on television from time to time.

Looking past the deep lines in Jarogniew's face, Deckard saw a look in his eyes that bewildered and chilled him all at the same time.

"Thank you for coming," the second man said, shaking a little too hard with one hand while squeezing a half smoked Cuban cigar between the fingers of the other.

His name was Kammler, and at about fifty pounds overweight he was another national security adviser and also owned an international consultancy firm with clients stretching from Saudi Arabia to Argentina. It was also a well-known fact that his phone number had been on the White House's speed dial for decades going back to the Vietnam War.

"We've heard good things," the third man said. "Very good things."

Since Deckard's fake resume under O'Brien consisted mostly of cold blooded murder and ethnic cleansing, he could only imagine what he meant by that. Hieronymus was another heavy hitter, maybe the heaviest. His family was old oil and old money, owning everything from real estate to insurance companies to banks. His foundation fielded self-appointed experts to all sectors of government and business. Together with Jarogniew, he had founded the Trilateral Commission.

All three were high level members of the Council on Foreign Relations and the Bilderberg Group as well.

"Happy to be here," Deckard said with a forced smile.

"We have it on good authority that you are of just the pedigree we have been searching for these last few days," Jarogniew said, motioning for everyone to take a seat.

"What pedigree would that be?" Deckard asked.

The former national security adviser shifted in his chair.

"The kind of man who can get things done. A professional."

"Kind words."

"Yes," Kammler said, pointing to the side of Deckard's face where his sutures were. "We can see you are the kind of man who takes a hands on approach."

"I have my moments," Deckard replied, ignoring the urge to scratch at the stitches he had just been reminded of.

"While our man, Chad Morrison, does not know you personally he says he knows of you. Apparently, you have all the right credentials," Kammler said, his jowls shaking with a chuckle as his two friends joined in at the inside joke.

"It's a job. It pays the bills."

"True, and we have a job that will pay the bills for the rest of your life."

Deckard leaned forward in his chair.

"I'm listening."

"We had, should I say," Hieronymus cleared his throat, "a falling out with a former employee. We think that you would be well suited to take his place."

"We have a private army standing by," Jarogniew stated bluntly.

Even Deckard was surprised by such an unguarded statement.

"In a central Asian nation," he continued. "We would like you to begin training and equipping them immediately. When the time comes, you will be charged with leading them into combat."

"Interesting," Deckard replied, his curiosity genuinely piqued.

"You would have full access to several accounts; this will be a well budgeted operation."

"The mission?"

"When the time comes," Hieronymus interjected. "When the time comes, there will be a culling."

"Yes, the useless eaters," Kammler muttered.

Jarogniew looked at his partners as if they had said something wrong.

"The bottom line is, we need someone who can get the job

done, once that time arrives. You will have full operational authority on the ground; we don't care how you conduct your business. Only results matter," Hieronymus finished.

"When do I start?"

The old men smiled crooked smiles.

It was dark by the time they exited the lodge and the old men began to lead Deckard down towards the pond. Deckard followed them down the winding path from the lodge, soon merging with a larger road where the Grove's patrons shuffled along.

At the pond, Deckard stood among Hieronymus, Kammler, and Jarogniew, waiting for the Grove's final ceremony to begin. The pond, along with the altar on the other side, was illuminated with torchlight. Around the altar stood robed men wearing hoods, some in white, others in red. Behind the altar was a massive statue made to look like a stone sculpture in the shape of an owl.

Deckard's guts churned at thoughts of what might be coming next.

He had heard rumors about the ridiculousness that the so-called global elites engaged in, but this was surreal. A scan of the crowd revealed many that he didn't recognize, but some were unmistakable from television and movie appearances. Within his own clique Jarogniew seemed slightly amused if nothing else. Hieronymus and Kammler leered.

The owl represented the ancient Canaanite and Babylonian god Moloch, to whom those civilizations offered human sacrifices thousands of years ago, or so he had read in history class years ago. Personally, he found the scene comical but was disturbed by how seriously it was being taken by the Grove members. They were the elite of politics, Hollywood, banking, business, and here they were like a bunch of mouth breathers at a peep show.

There were hundreds of spectators now, clamoring around the shore of the pond, watching, waiting. As bagpipes began to play somewhere off in the darkness, more robed men began to stroll towards the altar, carrying what looked like a bound body between them. The crowd cheered.

The robed men disappeared behind a black canvas, shielding them from view. What was happening behind the black curtains was unknown and no explanation was given. The old men simply continued to breathe hard.

Without warning, one of the black-robed men in front of the visible altar began to speak,

"The owl is in his leafy temple," his voice boomed. "Let all within the grove be reverent to him. Lift up your heads, oh, ye trees and be ye lifted up, ye everlasting spires...for behold! For here is Bohemia's shrine, and holy are the pillars of this house."

A gong being struck rang above the sound of chirping frogs.

"Weaving spiders, come not here!"

The gong sounded a second time before the speaker walked from the altar and a new procession moved forward.

"Hail, Bohemians! With the ripple of waters, the song of birds, such music as such inspires the sinking soul, do we invite you into midsummer's joy. The sky above is blue and sown with stars," the new speaker continued. "The forest floor is heaped with fragrant grit. The evening's cool kiss is yours. The campfire's glow. The birth of rosy fingered dawn. Shake off your sorrows with the city's dust and cast to the winds the cares of life. But memories bring back the well loved names of gallant friends who knew and loved the grove."

As the torch light illuminated the faces of the crowd and the surrounding trees, Deckard wasn't sure whether to laugh or to cry. The only thing he was sure of was that most of the attendees took the ceremony deadly seriously.

"Dear boon companions long ago. Aye! Let them join us in this ritual and not a place be empty in our midst. All of his battles to hold in this gray autumn of the world or in the springtime of your heart!"

As the speaker carried on, Deckard was struck not so much by the sinister implications of the Bronze Age ritual, but that it was in fact a simulacrum of older rites. A dulled fabrication. The trio of old men, his new employers, seemed nonplussed. Perhaps the Grove was simply another steering committee for the three puppet masters. A place for them to fill the lives of their high level minions with purpose.

The narrator wrapped up his speech about Mother Nature as old horror movie music blasted over a sound system mounted in the surrounding trees.

"Bohemians and Priests!" A new speaker called out. "The desperate call of heavy hearts is answered. By the power of your fellowship, dull care is slain!"

The crowd cheered once more. Deckard was left confused. What had happened behind the curtain? Had he been party to a real human sacrifice or a simulation of one? Maybe not knowing was part of the ritual in order to intrigue and stimulate new Grove members. To Deckard it still reeked of parlor tricks better suited for a dime store novel.

"His body had been brought yonder to our funeral pyre, to the joyous pipings of a funeral march. Our funeral pyre awaits the corpse of care!"

More creepy music played while a robed man paddled a dugout canoe across the pond, a reference to the river Styx, to be sure. On the boat was what looked like yet another bound body. Reaching the other side of the pond, the robed men placed the body on the altar.

"Oh thou, thus ferried across the shadowy tide in all the ancient majesty of death. Dull care, ardent enemy of beauty. Not for thee the forgiveness or restful grave. Fire shall have the will of thee and all the wind make merry with thy dust! Bring fire!"

The crowd shouted with glee. Maniacal laughs came over the speakers as pyrotechnics were set off around the pond.

"Fools!" the speakers sounded. "When will thy learn that me ye cannot slay? Year after year you burn me in this grove.

Lifting your puny shouts of triumph to the stars when again ye turn your faces to the marketplace...do ye not find me waiting, as of old? Fools! Do you dream you can conquer care?"

"Say, thou mocking spirit," the narrator fired back from the altar at the imaginary deity. "It is not all a dream. We know thou waiteth for us when this our sylvan holiday has ended. We shall meet thee and fight thee as of old, and some of us will prevail against thee and some thou shalt destroy."

The mock battle between the Grove's narrator and the crowd's apparently burdensome responsibilities back in their real lives continued. Finally the effigy on the altar was set ablaze, flames flickering in the night as the deity of the crowd's burden walloped over the loud speakers.

At last the Grove members applauded.

As music continued to play and fireworks were fired off alongside the pond, Deckard finally placed the sickening feeling in his gut. It wasn't the childish and immature display, a charade of a pagan ritual. It was the three men who stood beside him who had crafted this elaborate hoax to corrupt, entice, and compromise the leading minds in America.

It was the look Jarogniew had given him the lodge as he shook his hand. The tugging at the corner of his lips, the warm look in his eyes, the well honed mimicking of real emotions he had never felt. The phrase that had been digging at him all night finally came to the forefront of his thoughts, and with the red glow of fireworks on his face, he remembered.

They traffic in the souls of men.

Four

The steppes reached out to the horizon in every direction, the landscape unchanged since time immemorial. It looked barren, inhospitable, and even alien. Something was to be said for the men and women who called this place home.

Shadows shifting throughout the cabin, the passenger aircraft banked, internal pressure changing as the plane lined up on heading for approach to Astana International Airport.

Deckard closed his laptop computer. He had read nearly unblinking for the entire trip. Decades ago, Jarogniew had published a book about global geopolitics and the shifting paradigms that influenced long established cultural motifs. In that last thirty years, nearly every prediction he made in his massive fifteen hundred page tome had come to pass, by design or by coincidence, Deckard didn't know.

The only sure thing at this point was that the man was as brilliant as he was ruthless.

The human terrain was what was really shifting. Ignoring borders, transnational groups floated above national sovereignty, power drawn from new centers of gravity. The Balkanization of the entire world occurred under the guise of modernization. Mini-states and micro-states competed with super powers on an increasingly level playing field.

Deckard closed his eyes and sat back in his chair, wondering who or what would meet him on the ground.

The Gulfstream 500 slowly rolled to the secluded industrial sector of the already nearly empty airport to meet with Deckard's liaison. Descending down the folding stairs, the wind blew across the open plains, biting at his face. Standing in front of the commercial hanger were two men wearing black trench coats, with an airport baggage handler close by with a dolly.

Stepping towards them, Deckard shook hands with the nearest man.

"Jake O'Brien," Deckard said, introducing himself under his cover name.

"Stevan Djokovic, Executive Officer."

Mind turning, Deckard suspected the older Serbian man was responding with a cover to a cover. He knew this man, but from where?

"Fomenko Korganbaev. Sergeant Major." Six foot three or so and carrying himself with obvious military bearing, Deckard had no other background on the Kazakh.

Having loaded Deckard's two black tough boxes off the private jet, the bag handler rolled the dolly into the warehouse. Korganbaev led the way, and the three began walking through the industrial pavilion and out to the street where a driver was waiting for them in a nondescript black van.

Climbing into the van, the driver and the bag handler finished loading Deckard's equipment before getting back into the truck and taking off towards the Kazakh capital.

"Your first time in Astana?" Korganbaev asked.

"It is," Deckard answered truthfully. He had been to most of the 'stans', but this was a first even for him.

Djokovic lit a cigarette, neglecting to roll the window down.

"Did you retire from Sunkar or Arystan?" Deckard asked the Sergeant Major.

The tall Kazakh chuckled. "Sunkar, but we have recruits from both units, as well as the 37th Air Mobile Brigade."

"Strong troops."

"I know you will be satisfied."

"What kind of access will our unit have to the facilities here at the airport?"

"A hanger will be set aside for us prior to deployment. We have no dedicated aircraft at the moment."

"How many men do we have assigned to us?"

"Four hundred and fifty-one. Full strength on combat troops but still lacking support elements. Mechanics, intel, supply, and such."

"They've been in training for two months now?"

"Nearly," the Serb interjected. "We will get you settled in your personal quarters and give you a tour of the compound when we arrive--"

"No need for that now. Take me to whichever platoons are currently training."

Samruk International had its compound set up forty kilometers outside Astana proper, and as expected the conditions were spartan. A Soviet era warehouse, with the roof half collapsed, and a dozen surplus army tents served as the headquarters and barracks. Fans of fire had been established out into the empty steppes where training, when ammunition was available, could be conducted at any time. Open air toilets rounded out the facilities.

Directing the driver to the range, the Serb pointed towards where one of the platoons was using the shooting range. There wasn't much to it, but you don't need much to train. The troops were on line in the prone position with AK-47's, taking careful, deliberate shots that punched through paper targets posted fifty meters down range.

"Which platoon is this?" Deckard asked, as they exited the vehicle.

"Third platoon, Bravo Company," Korgan responded. "Led by Sergeant Serik."

"No officers?"

"None."

Deckard's appearance stood in stark contrast to the rugged descendents of nomads and warlords now training for combat. He wore western clothes and trail running shoes while these men wore ragged boots and tattered fatigues, firing nearly ancient but still serviceable AK-47 rifles. A few of the Kazakhs looked in his direction, barely acknowledging him before returning to their task.

While Deckard passively observed the training, Sergeant Serik shouted orders and the men ceased fire. Clearing their rifles as one, they carried them down range for a target inspection and critique by the platoon's senior NCO. Deckard followed behind, examining the paper bulls eyes himself. The shot groups were decent but not great, except for one talented young soldier. Deckard committed the kid's face to memory. The battalion would need several sniper teams.

It wasn't so much the marksmanship that he had come to see but the method of training and discipline of the troops. Having worked with indigenous soldiers all over the world, Deckard had seen much, much worse. These guys had potential.

Following the mercenaries back to the firing line, the gears were turning in Deckard's head. Ideas and improvements would be discussed later once he had more than just a snap shot impression of the battalion's operations.

Nodding towards the XO and Sergeant Major, they got back in the van, the two seeing the look on his face and wondering what was in store for them in the near future.

Looking more like the Kazakhs under his command, Deckard walked into the interior of the warehouse, covered in sweat and dust. The morning light streaked through the huge gap in the ceiling, reminding him of the amount of work that needed to be done at Samruk International.

The warehouse had already been partitioned off by the former Kazakh military and police veterans with plywood, sheet metal, and whatever else they could scrounge into makeshift offices for the battalion's leadership and a war room consisting of a table and a ten-year-old computer. The rest of the warehouse was left open, one corner having been converted into a gym.

With his body warmed up from the five mile run in fatigues and boots, Deckard walked over to the weights, what Russian Spetsnaz units called the courage corner, a tradition that had obviously bled over to the Kazakhs, among many other influences from the former USSR.

Hitting the ground, he knocked out fifty pushups, alongside the Kazakh NCOs conducting their own physical training, and then followed up by sticking his boots under some dumbbells and executing a hundred sit ups. Next came a hundred flutter kicks, fifty dips on the dip bar, and a hundred squats. That was one set. Four more came after.

Taking a few deep breaths and stretching for a moment, he picked up one of the twenty-five-pound kettle bells. The AK-47 of fitness equipment. He began by doing five kettlebell swings before moving up to a thirty-five-pound kettlebell, then a forty-four, and finally a fifty-three. This made for one set. Two more followed.

Finally it was time for pull ups.

Legs feeling as if they were about to give out under him, he refused to show it in front of the mercenaries. It was his new found responsibility to provide an image of absolute confidence and strength in front of them. However, sitting down in his so-called office he knew he would be hurting for it by the time tomorrow morning rolled around.

Last night had been fairly productive. After observing training, Deckard had called a team pow wow to meet the battalion's leadership, which was basically platoon sergeants, along with the XO and Sergeant Major. After the troops went back to the tents to get some sleep, Deckard placed some calls on the satellite phone. As promised by his new benefactors from the Grove, several open lines of credit had been made available to him in New York, London, and Hong Kong.

While changing uniforms, he thought of what needed to be done. The former soldier wanted a full day to evaluate the organizational and equipment needs of the unit before placing any large orders. A few weeks was what was needed, but he didn't have that long. Based on the conditions he had seen so far, he had already contacted contractors in Astana to deliver pallets of water, portable lavatories, and some metal workers to fix the collapsed roof. Next would be electricians to make sure the place didn't burn to the ground, once the generators began showing up.

Looking at the situation as small manageable tasking blocks, the job in front of him looked fairly straightforward.

However, the truth was that Deckard had deep reservations.

The truth was that he was no George Patton.

The Kazakh mercenaries fanned out across the steppe in a linear L-shaped formation around a building mockup, isolating the objective while reducing the chances of friendly fire. The Kazakhs lay down in the prone with AK's facing inwards while the assault team moved in a line towards the objective.

Deckard had shown up unannounced to watch the maneuvers, the Sergeant Major close at his heels.

The reality of the situation was that Deckard had never commanded anything even approaching this level. While a part of several Army Special Operations units, he had worked as a part of small teams of highly trained soldiers. Afterwards, he had mostly conducted singleton operations in rather austere parts of the world. Given the opportunity, it was an environment he had thrived in.

The assault team halted at the gaping hole left in the sheets of wood representing a doorway. The second man in the stack threw a rock through the door, simulating a grenade. Waiting a few moments, the assault team rushed through the door, each member making gunfire noises as they cleared the single room to let their sergeant know they were engaging invisible targets.

Commanding a battalion of hundreds of soldiers was something else entirely. It meant tracking operations, training, and personnel on a very detailed basis. It meant training meetings, intelligence meetings, and meetings for meetings. Paperwork and teleconferences. Death by Power Point. All the things he had avoided like the plague.

With the objective secured, the assault team moved out of the mockup, and the team leader counted them back into the platoon to have accountability for everyone. At this point the sergeant ended the drill and instructed them to do it again. The men looked bored, and Deckard couldn't blame them. Some of these guys had been doing much more advanced training and even combat operations in Kazakhstan's Special Forces.

Watching them continue to drill on the objective, Deckard was already forming ideas for future training objectives.

"What is the purpose of this type of training?"

"Cordon and search operations. Weapon confiscation," Korgan said shrugging his shoulders.

"Why focus on this specifically?"

"Not for us to know," the Sergeant Major grumbled in his thick accent. "Instructions from the Samruk offices in Astana."

Interesting.

FIVE

"Here is what I need to happen," Deckard ordered. After a pause the Sergeant Major translated to the platoon sergeants. "Two five-man assault teams will constitute a squad. Three assault squads per platoon plus one weapons squad."

One of the Kazakhs spoke up, a confused look on his face.

"He wants to know what you mean by weapons squad. All squads have weapons," Korgan translated.

"Weapons squad will consist of three, three-man machine gun teams. Three PKMs per weapons squad."

As the Sergeant Major translated, the younger NCO frowned, the two speaking rapid fire Russian for several seconds.

"But we have no machine guns..."

"Give me a week."

Korgan again spoke to the platoon sergeant, and now his frown was replaced with approval.

"I want four radio operators, two snipers, and five medics per company, in addition to the first sergeant and company commander. These positions will be filled by those who show the most ability as we continue to train. Monetary bonuses will be put into place, based on duty positions and performance.

"At the battalion level I want one mortar section and one anti-tank section, manned and ready to begin training once the necessary equipment arrives. Until then have these men continue to train as assaulters."

The meeting went on deep into the night with Deckard outlining what would be the battalion's new Table of Organization and Equipment before launching into weapons and equipment procurement and requests, living facility upgrades, training schedules, and attracting and recruiting more Kazakh veterans to the unit, until he realized it was nearly four in the morning.

Everyone was grateful when the sun finally began to crest the horizon and break the oppressive cold that lingered in their bones. Even with their bodies warmed up from running several miles, the cold stung at their faces. Somehow, Deckard couldn't help but feel that he was the only one who wasn't used to it.

The dusty road seemed to go on across the steppe forever until finally the firing range could be seen in the distance. Alibek, the Alpha Company Second Platoon Sergeant, took the lead by picking up one of his privates and slinging him over his shoulder in a fireman's carry.

Deckard followed suit, picking up the nearest Kazakh mercenary, a private named Oraz. He was one of the younger troops in the platoon, but like the others he had the Asiatic features typical of many Kazakhs. Once the entire platoon had paired up, Alibek took off running towards the range. Again, the American was impressed with the level of leadership shown by the young military veterans he had under his command.

Maybe it was the culture. Maybe it was a meal ticket.

Whatever they may have lacked in hard skills, they made up for in enthusiasm. It was no fault of their own that their military wasn't as developed as in the West, but then again, maybe it was an asset. The technology and bureaucracy of modern armies often led to a loss of focus on combat proficiency.

Quadriceps burning, he was relieved when Sergeant Alibek finally set his partner down halfway to the range and switched positions. Oraz hefted Deckard's weight with a grunt and began charging down the road. Finally they arrived at the shooting complex, little more than flat ground with some stakes stuck in the dirt to indicate range fans and meter distances, every member of the platoon with a cloud of hot steam coming off their bodies.

Alibek began shouting commands in Kazakh and pointing

to the targets posted down range. Deckard needed no translation and simply followed along as the mercenaries began loading magazines and racking the charging handles of their AK-47s.

The next twenty minutes were spent sprinting across the range in buddy teams, bounding while the other remained in over watch, laying down a suppressive fire on targets. Next, they repeated the same maneuver in four-man fire teams, Deckard joining in with an odd group of three. The drills continued until each soldier had expended sixty rounds on the targets down range, not much but for now it was their allotment.

Alibek and his peers made an impressive display of making the best with what little they had, but Deckard knew it was going to take a lot more for them to pull off what he had in mind.

"No, dammit, that's not what I want!"

Rapid fire Russian was spat back and forth on the other end of the line.

"Hold on," Deckard sighed, picking up the other phone.

"Samruk International?"

"Yes, this is O'Brien."

"This is Raul Fernandez. My supplier is inquiring about end user certificates for the merchandise, and we are already at the loading bay with three pallets. I-"

"Is this about the surplus GME-FMK2-MO grenades that Argentina dumped in your country and you've been trying to sell at marked up prices to the Iraqis for the last three years?"

"Um, well-"

"Yeah, I know about that. Listen, you tell those fuckers that the Ministry of Defense provides the EUCs, not myself or Samruk. They have already been forwarded to your people, and I have a signature of delivery, so you need to start communicating with them."

"I will call them immediately after I hang up, but we still have the issue of-"

Fernandez rattled on about the HAZMAT reportable quantity of Research Developed Explosives and the proper markings and packing materials for the pallets while Deckard stared at his email's inbox. It was filling up at an alarming rate, with messages from manufacturers and dealers all over the world.

These days Deckard's credit card had a triple A rating that went straight to the top. Some items would be procured in a more clandestine manner through front companies, but for some of the major end items, there just wasn't time for any kind of elaborate subterfuge.

The voice on the second cell phone switched from Russian back to English.

"Give me a second here, Fernandez," Deckard ordered, grabbing the line with the Russians on the other end.

"What's the deal Niko?"

"We have agreed to your proposal for the AK-103 rifles, Mr. O'Brien; however we request that you also buy the corresponding M43 ammunition, using us as your broker."

"Which plant do you go through?"

"The old factory 21."

"Copper washed steel?"

"Green lacquer."

"I also need T-45 green tracer."

Niko paused. "How about type Z red tracer?"

"Good enough."

"Sounds like a deal, and listen, tell your brother I need someone to source some M-23 vests."

"How many?"

"About a battalion's worth."

"Fuck."

"You can't do it?"

"Uh, give me two days."

"Alright, Niko, don't fuck me on that ammunition. I want you to test fire each lot number before you ship."

"Yes, Kommisar."

"No one likes a smart ass," Deckard said before hanging up and going back to Fernandez.

"Fernandez, you track down those EUCs yet?"

"My secretary is faxing them to our export control office right now."

"Good, let me know if you find those Portuguese commando mortars I asked about, okay?"

"No problem, Mr. O'Brien."

Deckard hung up and turned back to his laptop. He was making international arms dealers shit themselves with delight these days.

Beginning with the first emails, Deckard began to work his way through his inbox. There were emails from a guy who ran a small business in North Carolina sewing together custom nylon gear for Special Forces teams at Ft. Bragg. Samruk needed some chest rigs made for their sniper and recon troops that couldn't be sourced elsewhere.

There were a few more messages from the manufacturer of holographic reflex gun sights. Deckard had put in a mass order several days ago. They wanted the business, but now his order was competing for space on the factory floor with several government contracts. With Deckard sweetening the deal, the owner agreed to run his workers on twenty-four hour shifts until his order was fulfilled.

Next came emails from a representative of Glock in Austria. After attempting to go through an Italian arms dealer, Deckard ran into a wall when he discovered the guy had actually been jailed by Interpol for a dirty deal he acted as the agent for between the Chinese owned Liho Inc. and the Libyan Government. Not willing to waste more time, he was now going directly to the source, and they were not fucking around with the letter of credit transaction or insurance costs for shipping.

There were more messages from South Africa about 40mm grenades and an American based company building PKM machine guns with titanium frames, but it was the misspelled email from a textile plant in Wujiang City that really gave Deckard a headache.

Most First World military forces now outsourced production of their uniforms to China, and through several contacts, Deckard had managed to find one textile plant that was printing off rolls of fabric for Canadian desert uniforms as well as Italian 'vegetato' woodland camouflage fabric. Mr. Yao had understood that once the freight forwarder sent the bill of lading to the textile company's bank, the documents would then be forwarded to Deckard's accountant and the monetary transaction would then occur.

Now he was asking for a down payment. Deckard was already paying a huge overhead for Yao to source and supervise the cutting and sewing of the fabric by a third source. He had contemplated having the fabric shipped to Tamil Nadu where the old ladies could take some time off from sewing lingerie and deliberately trashing pairs of jeans to make them look more trendy for American kids and construct the uniforms. Once again it was an issue of time.

He just didn't know how much or how little he had.

"Why have you fucking done this!" Djokovic hissed. "*I* already had an arrangement."

Deckard's Executive Officer had cornered him coming out of his office.

"Regarding?" Deckard said, refusing to allow himself to be baited out.

"You know what," the Serb practically spat. "The AK-47s I ordered."

"That was a bad call," Deckard shot back. "The Century Arms AK-103 rifles are superior to those Bulgarian made ones you had your eye on."

Djokovic's resistance proved to Deckard what he had

already suspected.

"I had made deal!"

"And I canceled it."

"You are still new here, O'Brien. It is not good idea for you to make trouble."

"Tough titties. I run this outfit and I'll be damned if I have my boys running around half-cocked carrying rifles made with frames that are not properly riveted and will fall apart in a year."

The truth was that Deckard had made some phone calls regarding his second in command. His real name was Dejan Serbedzija, wanted by the International Criminal Courts for war crimes in the Balkans. He knew he recognized him from somewhere but couldn't quite place him until now. Deckard had been part of a task force charged with apprehending several war criminals in the region years ago.

Of course after the UN brokered cease fire, all that went away. The under-the-table deal for peace was amnesty for many of those responsible for the ethnic cleansing that had taken place. Since then Serbedzija had bounced around, a no-job to dirty gun for hire.

The Serb sneered at Deckard. Clearly the conversation was not going as Serbedzija had expected.

Now he also understood his irrational argument for the Bulgaria deal. He could only be this passionate about such a non-issue if he was getting kickbacks from the manufacturer.

"You had better watch yourself," Serbedzija said, turning on his heel and skulking off.

Deckard smirked.

He knew the corporate offices would never let him fire the Serb. He was clearly a plant put inside Samruk by the old men at the Grove to keep tabs on Deckard and what he was up to.

No, he couldn't fire him, but he could sure as hell arrange a friendly fire incident.

As the Serbian war criminal must know from personal experience, the best place to hide a murder is on the battlefield.

Six

The long drive into Astana had given Deckard plenty of time to think, and the more he thought about it the more he was convinced it was time to take a closer look at Samruk International. Driving his company-issued BMW all the way into the capital on *Sofeivskoe* Highway, he passed by the bazaar and the train yard, noticing that signs of industry and construction were everywhere. The expected Soviet-era apartment blocks or *microroyans* were nowhere to be seen. Instead it reminded Deckard of a developing city like Dohuk at first glance, but with its own Central Asian twist.

Crossing a newly built overpass, he could see a large steel arch, smaller but similar to the one in St. Louis, Missouri. Beyond that, far on the other side of the city was some kind of giant structure with a spike sticking out of the top. On the flight into Kazakhstan two weeks prior, he had read that Astana was the first capital city built in the twenty first century, and built for the twenty first century, according to the tourism brochures the government promoted.

The Samruk corporate offices were somewhere on *Ryskulov* Street, but with some time to kill before nightfall, he decided to spend some time reconnoitering the city before making his unexpected visit.

Making a left towards the large spike-topped building in the distance, Deckard did a double take as he drove past a monument that looked like a burial mound surrounded by rune stones. Everyone from the Etruscans to the American Indians made use of burial mounds, some dating back thousands of years, but he had never seen a mock-up like this used as a modern memorial.

Even more interesting was the giant flying saucer shaped building across the street. Judging from the statues of unicyclists

59

and seals balancing inflatable balls on their noses it was probably a circus.

Pulling over alongside a construction site, he stepped out of his car and buttoned up his jacket against the cold. In front of him was the enormous steel structure he had first seen from the other side of town. Grasping his cell phone in one hand, he began searching the web for any information regarding construction projects in Astana.

It was called the Khan Shatyr Entertainment Center, designed to be the world's largest tent which would eventually be the home of an entire self contained community. Underneath the glass and steel frame would be a shopping and entertainment center, an indoor beach resort, golf course, and more, with enough floor space for ten football fields. Obviously Astana's city planners had some strange concept of crossing the tribal yurt with post modern design and convenience.

Weird.

Turning to the immediate west was an open park filled with sculptures and a fountain. Flanking it were a series of circular apartment buildings and a gold domed mosque with four spires surrounding it. Getting back in the BMW, Deckard pulled into the street and followed it past the park to an open mall encircling another water fountain.

A few minutes later he was standing in the center of the fountain, which had been turned off for the winter. In front of him was the tallest building yet. Like a large golden column it rose high enough that Deckard had to strain his neck to see the top of it. A placard outside declared it as the Ministry of Transport and Communication.

In the cold breeze that blew in off the barren steppes, the city center felt empty and barren. It was as if someone had just decided to one day build a city in the middle of nowhere and that was exactly what had happened by presidential decree.

Farther down the boulevard was some kind of tower or needle like the one in Seattle. Walking through another park, he could see the tower capped with a massive golden sphere. The trees around him creaked in the wind, the only noise in the mall seeming to echo across the buildings on both sides. On the right was the cube-looking Kazakh World Trade Center and some buildings whose architecture mimicked the wavy northern lights. Walking stiffly he passed the circular shaped railway headquarters building and a triangular housing complex.

What is this place?

The tower with the golden sphere was called *Bayterek* according the web page displayed on his cell phone. It looked like a giant torch to Deckard, but apparently it was representative of the Tree of Life. Deckard did know that the tree of life was part of an ancient mono-myth, an archetype found in all cultures from ancient Babylon to the Jewish Kabbalah. In Kazakh mythology the Tree of Life featured prominently in a folk tale involving a magic bird.

A bird called Samruk.

Farther down the park boulevard sat two massive golden pillars, representing what, and to whom, he did not know, but between them at the end Astana's gallery of ancient modern architecture sat the presidential palace. At first glance it looked like a czarist castle of some sort with a large blue dome and spiked pinnacle.

Walking back to his vehicle, Deckard felt overwhelmed. He never expected to find all of this out here in the center of the windswept Kazakh waste. What was the meaning behind all the mysterious and clearly occult designs? He felt like the only one in the world who even knew all of these things existed.

Turning over the engine, he turned up the heat, trying to warm up, at least until he could no longer see his breath in the air. Getting back on the road, he decided to circle back around and begin looking for *Ryskulov* Street, when something caught his eye silhouetted against the twilight sky.

Driving around the presidential palace, he saw a pyramid reflecting the red glow of the setting sun. With glass and steel sides, the pyramid reached high into the sky, four entrances located in each cardinal direction. Pulling alongside, he left the car behind and rushed down the stone walkway, almost unable to believe his eyes. The sun had finally sunk below the horizon as Deckard pushed through the door and was confronted by one of the uniformed greeters.

"Welcome," the young Kazakh woman said, "to the Palace of Peace and Reconciliation."

"What is this place?"

"The Palace of Peace and Reconciliation was built to unite the world's religions and to denounce all forms of violence," she recited pleasantly.

"Uh, is it okay for me to be here?"

"The Palace is open to the public for another hour, sir." the greeter warmly stated.

"Thanks."

The entire bottom of the pyramid was an open-air lobby, painfully white and sterile. Thousands of panes of glass lined the inside walls, effectively making a second inner pyramid minus the capstone, which was a separate room far above the atrium he stood in. Looking for a way up, Deckard first found the way down, a set of stairs leading into the basement.

Shuffling down the steps, Deckard found himself in the darkness of a vast opera hall. The stage was empty but lit up, a few workers moving around, preparing the lighting for a later performance. Like many others, this opera house was multi-terraced, but unlike other venues this one had a giant sun symbol painted on the roof above it.

Turning, he dashed back up the stairs. In the atrium, Deckard found the spot directly above the sun pictogram below. Raised above the floor was another giant sun symbol, with rays of light reaching out in all directions.

"Ma'am," Deckard said, finding the greeter again. "What is this room used for?"

"Sometimes meetings of state, or traditional music, but this space was constructed by the British architect Lord Norman Foster as a meeting place for the world's religions. All of the leaders of the world's religions met at a three-day forum for a roundtable discussion several years ago."

"I see."

"Please enjoy the rest of your visit, sir."

Finally he found the stairway that wound around the inside of the pyramid up to the apex. While making his way upward, Deckard considered what he was seeing. The public was entertained in the darkness of the opera while the world's religious leaders met for some kind of reconciliation around a sun pictogram.

Being a student of war also meant being a student of history, and as Deckard recalled, a scholar had once said that the pyramid was the perfect symbol of the secret doctrine, as well as the mystery schools that taught it.

Taking a small elevator the rest of the way to the top, he stepped out into the capstone level of the pyramid. The center of the room was left open with a circular table constructed around an oculus. The walls that reached up to form the point of the pyramid were all glass, now allowing him to see Astana lit up in the darkness. The city glowed, golden in the night.

Looking up he could see that the panels of glass at the very tip of the pyramid had been stained yellow and streaked downwards as rays of light.

It hit him like a sucker punch.

That was what the pyramid and really the capital itself was built to honor.

Not the peace and reconciliation of the world's religions but worship of its single oldest religion.

Sun worship.

It was a good thing he had brought his bag of tricks with him because it took the better part of twenty minutes to pick the door lock and then the dead bolt, and then another ten minutes for him to find the switch contact on the magnetic alarm and bridge them at the splice point. Finished, Deckard eased open the door, hoping that there wasn't a tertiary system like motion detectors in place.

Seeing no sign of motion sensors or pressure plates under the area rug in the room, he stepped inside the lobby and closed the door. Behind the secretary's desk in large raised letters was the company name, Samruk International along with its logo, the bird of Kazakh mythology.

Getting into the offices required a numerical code for the keypad at the door. Blowing a small portion of talcum powder on the keypad, the former soldier could see which buttons had fingerprints on them. Four digits, three, seven, six, and nine. With the design of this particular keypad lock it actually didn't matter which order the user entered the digits in. Pressing each of the digits with fingerprints on them Deckard twisted the knob and opened the door.

Making sure to wipe the talcum powder off the keypad with his sleeve, he closed the door and proceeded into the offices. While the three old men at the Grove had placed Deckard in charge of Samruk's private army, he was not made privy to what was going on at the corporate level. That was going to change tonight.

Samruk had been established not long after Kazakhstan declared independence and although it was a private enterprise on paper, it was well known that Samruk was owned by powerful men in Kazakhstan's government, not to mention some of its larger financial institutions. Past dealings had been legit for the most part, mostly executive protection work for the politicians and bankers who had started the company.

This recent rapid expansion into a full-blown private military company at the behest of the old men back in the US showed who the real puppet masters in Astana were. The remaining question was, to what end?

A row of file cabinets lined one wall, packed full of corporate documents. Sticking a switchblade above one drawer, he unlatched the gang lock easily enough. Turning on a red LED flashlight, Deckard browsed through the documents. Although they were mostly in Cyrillic, he was able to tell from the numbers involved and what English nomenclature there was that he was looking at tracking forms for the equipment he had been ordering over the last few weeks.

Putting the files back in their correct place, he sat down behind one of the computer terminals. Moving the mouse, he watched the screen light up, taking him directly to the corporate website's log in screen. Deckard noted that since they were using the web rather than a local area network that meant that their data was being stored off-site.

A SQL injection attack was enough to get him into the system, but now he had to queue up individual files, one command at a time. Reaching into the backpack he brought along, Deckard pulled out a USB drive and stuck it into the computer. After a few hiccups he got the keylogger installed on the corporate server.

Retrieving the USB drive and closing out of the system, he began installing eavesdropping devices around the offices. Wireless cameras went into the light fixtures, which would draw electricity from the existing power lines. The fiber optic cameras were simple but effective. Letting himself into the executive offices, he planted several wireless listening devices in desks and briefcases left laying around.

Heading back into the main offices, Deckard used his Leatherman multitool to unscrew one of the electrical outlets to install another fiber optic camera, which would look out through the socket panel. He wanted audio and video of everyone who worked at or visited the offices. The camera went in easy enough, but Deckard found himself cursing under his breath as a piece of sheet rock fell away when he tried to screw the panel back on.

Finding the nearest bathroom, he began looking underneath the sink for something to repair the damage he had done to the wall. Behind a bottle of bleach was someone's half-used tube of toothpaste. Grabbing it and a handful of toilet paper, he mixed the two together, mashing it up into a paste.

Using a wad of the paste, he was able to stick the piece of sheet rock back into place. Checking over his work with the red light he was convinced the damage would go unnoticed to the casual observer.

The outlet panel was almost completely screwed back on, when Deckard heard the office door abruptly open and the lobby fill with laughter. Cursing a second time, he gave the multitool a final twist and crouched behind a desk as the door to the offices was opened and the lights flipped on.

Now he could hear both a man and a woman's voice.

Great.

The two continued to giggle to themselves as they stomped around the office on heavy feet, obviously drunk. The Samruk executive had probably picked the girl up at a bar somewhere and brought her to the office because he was married.

Peering from behind the desk, Deckard saw the drunken couple engulfed in each other. A moment later the rhythmic slapping of skin on skin began that had the former soldier rolling his eyes.

Why did this sort of shit always happen to him?

He waited to make sure they were fully distracted before making his move. It had to be now or never because it didn't sound like the executive was going to last much longer. On the balls of his feet, Deckard crept to the office door and slipped out before his ears began to bleed.

SEVEN

Camouflage clad soldiers had been scurrying all over the compound since well before dawn. A detail of men had been woken up and sent down to the airfield in Astana in the early morning before the aircraft arrived and were now beginning to trickle back in on several deuce and a half trucks acquired on the local market.

Deckard observed the scene for a moment before moving on. His second in command, Djokovic, was supervising the equipment breakdown and the issue to the troops. After signing for the pallets and moving them into the warehouse, the platoon that had been detailed began breaking down the shipping containers.

Cracking open the metal frame door, he watched another platoon literally running back from the range. A massive front was moving in from the west. A Central Asian sandstorm that would literally turn broad daylight into a bizarre kind of twilight. In their hands were the brand new AK-103 rifles that they had been out zeroing and grouping with until the sandstorm moved in.

The AK-103 was chambered for the same 7.62x39 round as its predecessor but included a folding stock, flash suppressor, and had the wooden furniture replaced with a composite plastic. The fore grip heat guard was also replaced with a rail system, and rifles would soon be fitted with the holographic reflex sights that had arrived.

Deckard made a mental note to get a field report on the new rifles from the platoon sergeants in order to ensure that the rifles and ammunition were functioning properly. Turning back inside, he was glad the contractors had finished repairing the roof because in a few minutes a wall of sand would be washing over the entire compound.

As the pallets were broken down, the troops sorted the

67

equipment out item by item and stowed them in green kit bags. Once everything was broken down and accounted for, each soldier would be issued one of the kit bags, which would contain his four uniforms, two woodland and two desert, spare AK and Glock magazines, M-23 chest rig, jungle and mountain boots, compass, boonie caps, t-shirts, socks, poncho, poncho liner, rifle sling, pistol holster, camelbak water bladder, Ka-Bar fighting knife, rucksack, and a few other odds and ends, all of which they would sign for from the new quartermaster.

Dastan had been in Alpha Company until last week when he broke his ankle during morning physical training, a Sambo match that got a little too heated, from what he had heard. Deckard had the injured Kazakh mercenary driven into the capital for medical treatment, even while his platoon sergeant argued that it was his own fault that he got hurt. But Deckard knew there was a perfect job opening for a broke dick soldier and kept him around.

Dastan had just been voluntold to be the new supply sergeant.

With this shipment also came most of the mortar systems, some of the sniper systems, and many of the grenades he had ordered. The PKM machine guns were due in next week, and hopefully the rest of it wouldn't be far behind.

Most of the instructors and translators he had hired were already in London signing contracts and non-disclosure agreements with a Samruk legal representative and would start filtering in within a few days. Everything was coming along nicely.

Just in time to have the rug pulled out from under your feet, Deckard thought.

"Where is Adam?" Deckard asked.
"Fucking dead hookers, for all I know."

68

"Good to see you too, Frank."

"What do you go by these days? Brown? Roberts?"

"O'Brien," Adam said, walking up behind the two. "Head of operations for Samruk International."

The ground crew was surrounding the 737 out of London, preparing for refueling while the passengers walked down the movable stairs pushed up to the side of the aircraft. Dozens of instructors had been brought in to conduct more advanced training with the Samruk troopers and a few had been hired full time to fill specialized positions. Two of those were the black bag operatives, Adam and Frank.

"I don't actually maintain any official title that I'm aware of."

"So what kind of operation are you running here?" Frank asked. The ex-Ranger was almost as wide as he was tall.

"Your favorite kind; I'm making it up as I go along."

"Nice."

"I've got a couple guys I want you to train as technical surveillance specialists."

"That all?" Adam seemed skeptical.

"No, I'll brief you on extracurricular activities later."

"I thought so."

The two intel and recon boys threw their gear bags on the back of one of the deuce and half trucks before climbing up the tailgate. Both were highly talented operators, and Deckard happened to know that both needed the money, which was substantial, with him offering eight hundred to twelve hundred dollars a day of Samruk's money, depending on the experience level of the operator. Bonuses would be based on tangible improvements in the mercenaries they would be training.

Deckard squinted, looking across the tarmac at two other trainers heading towards one of the other trucks. One of them looked like the largest Rastafarian in the world, standing at about six foot four with dreadlocks and a beard. He had one load out bag rolling on wheels in one hand and a cooler also on wheels in the other. Had to be a full of beer, Deckard thought, shaking his head.

Only in the SEAL teams do you find people like Charles Rochenoire.

The shorter man next to him was Kurt Jager, a former German GSG-9 counter terrorist operative. Both men were on loan to Deckard from GUARD, an American based private military corporation.

A few dozen other trainers carried their bags to the awaiting trucks, some of them seconded to Samruk via subcontract from other PMCs, while some were strictly freelancers that he had crossed paths with in the past or knew by reputation. A few months with these guys, and Samruk International would be up to par with other elite light infantry units, such as US Army Rangers, Princess Patricia's Canadian Light Infantry, and British Royal Marines. If Deckard had his way, Samruk would even surpass those units in a few key areas.

Now that the trainers were here, Deckard could focus on other priorities.

The keyloggers he had installed in the Samruk Corporate offices had begun dumping data into his email account on regular intervals, and what they had revealed was interesting to say the least.

The translator looked terrified as he literally watched a black man get red in the face.

"Do it the way I taught you!" Charles Rochenoire screamed, while grabbing the Kazakh soldier by his collar and lifting him off the ground.

The Kazakh translator was barely out of his teens when Deckard had found him on monsterjobs.com and contracted him to translate for his military trainers. For the first time in his life the young man was thankful his parents made him learn their mother language, even though they lived in San Diego.

70

Omar translated as quickly as he could into Kazakh, not wanting to incur the wrath of the ex-SEAL.

The Kazakh mercenary seemed to get the point before he was finished. Pulling out a fresh magazine from his chest rig, the Kazakh turned the magazine sideways, using it to depress the magazine release on his AK and pushing forward, unseating and dropping the empty magazine to the ground. Now he stuck the fresh one into the magazine well and rocked it backwards until it locked into place. Chambering the first round, he began laying down a suppressive fire while his buddy bounded forward to the next wooden barricade.

"Better," Rochenoire belted out, a rare word of encouragement.

It was the contractors' first day out on the range with their new charges, and so far they had been impressed. The Kazakh mercenaries were good, they just needed some polishing before moving on to more advanced material.

Jager was alongside the other Kazakh, yelling at him while they completed the stress range they had set up. Rochenoire couldn't help but think that Jager sounded like some kind of Reich's marshal, yelling with his German accent. Finally the Kazakh got into the prone and began sending rounds downrange into targets, cueing in Rochenoire's new protégé that it was time for him to move.

"Get up! Get off your ass, let's go!"

Omar snapped to attention, echoing the words in Russian.

It was nice to be working with military-grade explosives for a change.

The stuff he usually got left scars.

The table was covered with explosives and different types of charges he had constructed the night before. The Kazakhs had seemed apprehensive at first, not so much about working with explosives but about working with the Englishman who was to serve as their instructor.

Richie looked ten years older than he actually was, a combination of hard living and cheap cigarettes taking their toll. He hadn't spent a single day in the military, but the Kazakhs were quickly learning that he definitely knew what he was talking about.

"And this?" he said, pointing to an item on the table.

"PETN!" someone shouted.

"This?"

"RDX!"

"Good." He pointed to another.

"TNT!" several shouted. They were starting to like this.

"What about that one?"

"C4."

"All right then."

Richie grabbed an initiation system, twin green wires running from it and out onto the steppe.

"Direct your attention to the auto," he said, pointing to the rusting car hulk about three hundred meters out. The translator began relaying his instructions, but before he could finish, Richie had twisted and pulled the pins on the initiation system.

The car exploded, a shock wave kicking up dust in all directions. Richie frowned as something come loose during the explosion. He dodged to the side at the last moment, as the spinning car door came rolling end over end right past him.

"That is why you use 'P' in your demolition formula," he announced, shrugging off the near miss. "'P' for Plenty."

The Brit was familiar with both military and improvised explosives. The improvised part began when he was a young man blowing open safes in and around London. He had gotten his hands on military demo in places like Colombia and Liberia over the years, but truth be told, a fair amount of improvisation was used there as well. Typically, you don't use anti-tank mines to bring down a bridge.

He would train the Samruk mercenaries on basic

demolitions, to include breaching doorways and destroying enemy equipment. He would also spend extra time with a few who showed particular interest or talent, showing them everything from steel cutting charges to remote detonators, homemade explosives, and more.

"Now direct your attention to the paper targets out at one hundred meters."

The Kazakhs cringed, not knowing what shrapnel would come flying their way this time.

"If things go pear shaped you have to be ready to make a field expedient claymore mine. It can be built from a coffee can with some explosives, and scrap metal or nails or both as projectiles."

Richie picked up another initiation system, the green wires leading out towards the targets in the distance.

"Now watch this."

"Too slow. Push."

The Kazakh mortar section looked at the American with puzzled expressions.

Mendez moved his palms up and down in International Sign Language.

The Kazakh troops began doing pushups while Mendez lit up another Marlboro. Most of them had never seen a mortar tube before, but they were catching on fast. It was just a matter of saturation and building muscle memory.

"One round, HE quick," Mendez bellowed. "Deflection: two-six-five-two. Charge: six. Elevation: one-zero-six-two."

The 82mm gun crews scrambled to their individual tubes. The gun bunnies began dialing the data into their gun sights and realigning the mortar tubes on the aiming stakes stuck into the dirt behind him.

"Bubbles up! Fifteen seconds!" Mendez yelled, the translator repeating a little more sheepishly.

In the end he was to train the section on both 82mm and 60mm mortars, consisting of three tubes each. At the moment he would be running the fire direction center, or FDC, himself, but it was imperative to get gunners all the way up to team leaders trained to proficiency. He already had his eye on a former Field Artillery officer, in the ranks, to take charge when he was finished with them.

"Time!"

Mendez walked from tube to tube, looking down the sights with his good eye. The other had been taken out in Ramadi several years ago, leading to him being medically discharged from the Army. He had been a Special Forces Weapons Sergeant at the time and a mortar man in 10th Mountain Division before that. Thankfully, someone somewhere threw his name out there when contracts for Samruk International opened up.

"You aligned your sights on the wrong side of the aiming stake," he sighed. "Push."

"Steady, aim, breath, squeeze," Piet whispered. "You can't go wrong."

It was a ghost town.

Deckard called it his own Detroit. He had bought it for pennies on the dollar, or the tenge, as it was. Not far south of Astana, it was a sprawling, abandoned city, including government buildings, factories, residential areas, and even a school that had been picked clean by looters and ravaged by the elements since the collapse of the Soviet Union.

Perfect for urban combat training.

The Kazakh behind the Remington-made sniper rifle was a short stubby young trooper with a round face. He was taking to the

South African's training rather well. Despite some experience with the Russian Dragunov, he was already in love with the American-made bolt action rifle.

Infiltrating into the second story of the old factory under the cover of darkness, the Kazakh sniper had spent the rest of the night constructing his urban hide site. An old table had been scavenged to use as a shooting platform, his poncho hung behind him to prevent his body from silhouetting against the wall, and old curtains had been tacked over the window with a ragged hole slashed in the middle that was just wide enough to use as a loophole.

Nikita, along with the other sniper trainees, had come to respect the man they only knew as Piet. The truth was, no one seemed to know much more about him, and for the moment, no one was asking. He never raised his voice, like some of the other instructors; in fact he seemed to be trying to get them to relax and focus only on the task at hand. Young enough to be his son, Nikita also respected the man's seniority. It was clear that he had been soldiering for a very long time.

"Take your time. Fire when ready."

The Kazakh only understood about half the words he was saying, but somehow they were able to communicate. In only a week, Piet had built strong enough rapport with the men that he really only needed an interpreter during the classroom portion of their training.

On paper, the shot seemed easy, but in practice it was another matter. From the hide site he had to fire across two streets-- each street lined with buildings that acted as a wind tunnel-- an urban valley, then between several other buildings, and hit the steel target propped up in a second story window five hundred meters away.

Nikita settled into position, taking slow shallow breaths. Soon he was in almost a meditative state, focused on nothing but his target. Slowly he took the slack out of the trigger, the muzzle blast taking them both by surprise. He continued to look through his scope, but with the curtains waving back and forth, he couldn't see if he had hit the target or not.

Lowering his binoculars, Piet turned away from one of the other windows.

"Five o' clock, three inches," Piet said, drawing a human shaped target on the table with a pencil and showing the sniper where he had hit. The 7.62 round had struck the target three inches from the center of the target at the five o' clock position.

"That's a kill."

Deckard didn't own a suit and Adam left his at home, so instead the two arrived at the Sultan Ismail Train Station in American style outdoors clothes, looking like a couple sweaty vagabonds. Struggling in the humid air that permeated throughout Kuala Lumpur, or just KL as expats knew the Malaysian city, they looked at their map.

Today was the first day of the Defense Services Asia Exhibition and Conference, the kind of place shady arms dealers, the kids of Third World dictators, and intelligentsia liked to hang out.

Deckard had spent time in Malaysia years ago, spending almost a month at a staging area in preparation for a hostage rescue.

Adam insisted he had worked here a while back as well, as a telecommunications specialist or some such. Deckard had to wonder. They ran out into four lanes of traffic to get to the Putra World Trade Center where DSA was being held.

"I don't know about this, man," Adam commented under his breath.

"Yeah, me neither. Do you know where the hell you are going?" Deckard asked.

"It's through this brush," he replied, wading into something that looked suspiciously like triple canopy jungle. "But what I meant was DSA. You heard what happened to Max two years ago at this place, right?"

"Max Kishiro? I heard he fronted for the Agency, carrying several large arms deals on their behalf."

"Yeah. He got gunned down in an abandoned building not far from the conference center."

"I heard he got wasted, no surprise there," Deckard

commented, sliding down into some undergrowth. "You make a lot of enemies in that line of work."

"But do you know how it went down? He was meeting with the Deputy Chief of Science and Technology."

"Who?"

"The Chinese."

"No shit."

"Yeah, some people thought it was a tech transfer that went bad when Max tried to play fuck- fuck games with Wen and his boys. The real deal is that the Chinese were trying to stage a coup in Equatorial Guinea before a British firm beat them to it."

"Natural gas?"

"You got it. It was the son of a fairly notable politician who organized the whole deal on the Brit side. After the operation went to shit, Wen wanted any loose ends tied up, not wanting his name involved in any subsequent investigations."

"Damn."

"You said it."

Finally, they came out on a road leading up to the futuristic looking conference center. With over seven hundred companies from fifty nations represented, the expo acted as a barometer for what direction militaries in Southeast Asia and beyond would be heading in the next few years.

Adam began walking toward the front door with Deckard's shopping list in his hand.

He wasn't surprised by how dialed in Adam was in the intelligence community. He had started off in a black side commo unit in the Army that worked under NSA, before getting picked up by the Special Collections Service, or College Park as members called it. Before getting kicked out, he had learned Spanish, Arabic, as well as Pashto, and traveled all over the world. SCS mostly handled technical surveillance, which required him to be skilled in lock picking, safe cracking, cryptography, key impressioning, various bypass methods, and other forms of surreptitious entry.

Adam had even trained Deckard on a few systems when he

was with the Agency. A few years ago during the economic crash, Adam had found himself caught up in the real estate racket and went heavily into debt, causing him to lose his security clearance, and thus, his job.

The US government's loss was Deckard's gain.

The inside of the cavernous expo center was sprawled with vendor stands and displays, a GI Joe fantasy for generals and defense ministers.

Walking down the aisle, he spotted one of the items on his list.

On one of the display tables was what looked like a giant revolver, painted a dull matte tan color. Balancing its weight in his hands, Deckard examined the Milkor multi-shot grenade launcher. It fired six 40mm low-velocity grenades from a rotating cylinder and was accurate out to a hundred and fifty meters for a point target, such as a window or enemy combatant on a rooftop.

"How fast can you ship out twenty-four units?" Deckard asked the sales representative working the booth.

"As fast as you can fill out the paperwork," the balding man replied, with a smile.

"Hey," Deckard snapped his fingers at Adam who was inspecting an automated turret system at another stand. "Exchange information with this guy."

Moving on, Adam spent the next hour chasing after Deckard who acted like a kid in a candy store, placing orders with a dozen manufacturers for everything from shotguns for ballistic breaching, to MP5 submachine guns, to RPG kit bags to carry extra rockets.

Stopping for a twenty minute argument over whether the battalion should invest in .300 Winchester Magnum or .338 Lupua Rifles for their sniper section, they finally compromised by calling Piet back in Kazakhstan and letting him decide. Arguing for another ten minutes, the South African finally told them to place an order for the SIG Tactical Two rifle, with its modular barrels, if for no other reason than to stop the discussion in its tracks, which was probably just as well since the two of them were starting to draw stares from the expo patrons.

Finding a Virginia based company that made an assortment of grenades, Deckard next set about placing an order for flash-bang stun grenades. He was also sold on the company's 40mm High-Explosive Dual Purpose grenade that featured an internal shaped charge as well as a specialized propulsion device. The perfect grenade to fire from the Milkor launchers, once they shipped.

Also on order were a variety of specialty rounds, such as smoke, IR smoke for masking targets using night vision, non-lethal bean bag rounds, day-night marking grenades, flare rounds, and 40mm shotgun rounds, all of which were ordered by the pallet load.

Shaking hands with the company's chief executive and owner to seal the deal, the battalion commander turned to leave and saw a banner for a company called Special Security Solutions, or SSS for short. Deckard frowned. The booth was manned by two Eastern European men in black jumpsuits.

He had never heard of SSS, but they were advertising themselves as a private military corporation, like Samruk. PMCs were big business since the industry went corporate with the advent of the so-called War on Terror.

Deckard knew from experience that most of the firms out there existed as proxies for MI-6 and the CIA. Mostly, they put a disabled African American veteran as their own on-paper president since the US government offered special interest group priority when it came time to sign contracts. In the revolving door that was government service, everyone got rich at the taxpayers' expense.

The firms that didn't play ball got put out of business, quickly finding themselves tied up in legal litigation clear into forever while firms that knew the game and played by the rules were nearly given *carte blanche*.

A company like SSS was a different animal all together. Serbia was one nation that did not even bother with the appearance of regulation in regards to private military corporations. Some of them were on the level; others a haven for war criminals and thugs providing private security for crime syndicates the world over.

Turning away, Deckard knew that no matter how much people back home kicked and screamed, private security was going to continue to grow as governments and old institutions continued their descent into irrelevancy.

"I like their recruitment video," Adam quipped, at the hastily edited video of security guards in ninja outfits, firing guns overlaid with Serbian techno music that blared in the background.

"Maybe you can get a job application. You can use me as a reference."

"You'd do that?"

Rounding a corner, they walked into the section of the expo that had a few dozen military vehicles on display. Deckard and Adam split up, talking to representatives from a half dozen companies. They knew what specifications they were looking for ahead of time; it was just a question of who could deliver.

The Polish AMZ Zubr was interesting. Built upon a v-shaped chassis like the Mine Resistant Ambush Protected vehicles currently in service in Afghanistan and Iraq, it was armored against explosions and .50 caliber gunfire. Most importantly, it could be transported by C-130 military aircraft and be rapidly delivered in any theater of operation.

The drawback, Deckard thought, looking it over, was that it had an automated turret. The gunner sat protected inside the vehicle and essentially played video games on a monitor, trying to find and shoot targets. He knew the idea of leveraging technology against the enemy in place of focusing on hard training and discipline was an intoxicating one, especially for those employed by the Pentagon.

However, bottling troops up inside a missile magnet was not the direction he wanted for Samruk. Too many professional soldiers forgot that the most important part of maneuver warfare was to be able to maneuver.

Circling around a smaller armored car on display, he looked at the plaque that read 'Panhard Véhicule Blindé Léger' or Light Armored Vehicle. Remembering his days in Bosnia, Deckard recalled that the troops had dubbed it the Sarajevo Taxi, as it was so ubiquitous among the French troops stationed there.

Lightly armored, it featured four wheel drive, a manual gun turret, and was amphibious with a waterborne speed of five and half kilometers an hour. If they survived long enough, Deckard intended to make one company of the Kazakhs into a mountain company, another a mobility company, and the third a maritime company, to increase versatility. Taking a sales brochure, he made a mental note to keep the VBL in mind, but at the moment he needed something with more carrying capacity.

"Check this out," Adam called.

Looking up from the brochure, Deckard found himself looking at an Iveco Light Multirole Vehicle, modified by a third party, a UK based company, as an assault vehicle. He had seen the standard model which was built on the same frame as the Zubr but was instantly impressed by the assault variant.

It didn't float like the VBL but did damn near everything else. It featured armor plating and a v-hull like the Zubr and had an operational range of five hundred kilometers. Scrutinizing further, he saw that run flat-tires and the winch came standard. It also had a gun ring for a machine gun or grenade launcher, but what interested him the most was the assault variant package he was currently looking at.

The back of the vehicle had been lopped off, and in its place were eight seats sitting back to back, four on each side behind the gun ring where assaulters sat facing out. Arriving on the objective they would simply push off their seats onto the ground. While in transit they could return fire with their rifles or make use of several pivot mounts to place light machine guns on.

"I want one," Deckard said, smiling. "Actually, I want sixty."

Nine

Zhou Jinbao was the first to respond to the wanted ad on *zhantai.com*, but from the looks of three other teenagers he had already seen dropping USB drives around the district, he certainly wasn't the last. He often took odd jobs he found advertised online. Once he'd scored a high paying interpreter job, getting hired by a British business consultant who needed someone last minute. With a booming economy, China was now the largest English-speaking nation in the world, and Zhou was a part of that majority.

Strolling through the park, he took a moment to watch a group of pretty girls giggle at something as they passed a cellular phone around, laughing at something on the screen.

He didn't know what he had put on the USB drives he was placing around the business district and didn't care. He also didn't care why his directions were to place them around one specific building, inside if he was able.

Straightening the brim of his baseball cap, he moved on. Girls were scary sometimes.

After he had responded to the help wanted ad, his new employer had dropped a tidy sum of money into his Paypal account before instructing him to use it to go buy a dozen of the portable USB drives. With that completed, he was then emailed a folder of digital content to load onto each drive. Finally, he was to leave them for any random passerby to find near the Bao Corporate Building in the new district, Pudong.

Once he got back to his parents' apartment he'd report in. When his virtual boss was satisfied, he would be paid the rest of his wage.

Pushing through the glass doors and into the lobby of the Bao building, he ran right up to the front desk.

"Holy shit," he exclaimed in English. "I need to piss right

now!"

Several Bao employees looked on nervously as the security guard stood to his feet.

"We don't have any public restroom here. Head on out."

"C'mon," Zhou pleaded. "I have to piss. You want me to go right here on your desk?"

The security guard shook his head, muttering something about the kid's family lineage under his breath.

"Make it fast."

Zhou turned towards the restroom, smiling.

He made double for dropping the tainted drives inside the building itself.

Senior Vice President of Human Resource Management Henry Lu exhaled as his bladder began to empty itself. Another all nighter. Entertaining clients. Entertaining the ladies. Hell, yeah.

Looking down as he buttoned up, Lu noticed something on the tile, resting next to his shoe. Grunting, he bent down and picked up the USB drive. Walking out of the bathroom, he slipped it into his pocket, promptly forgetting about picking it up in the first place.

Three hours later, Lu sat at his work station browsing internet porn. He dreamed of someday traveling to America. That was where the women had the big cow tits like in the streaming videos he sat around watching all day. The thought reminded him about the USB drive he had found.

His cousin worked in computer repairs out of a small shop in another part of Shanghai. He'd told him all kinds of crazy stories. People would bring in their laptops to get them fixed, and he would find all sorts of wild pictures. Bored housewives playing with themselves. Teenage girls sending pictures to their high school sweetheart. Maybe he'd get lucky, too.

Looking back and forth, he saw that the coast was still clear and stuck the USB drive into his computer. There were strict policies against using your own data storage devices at work. The executives worried about employees selling corporate information to rivals. But what the hell did they expect them to do all day?

Clicking his cursor across the computer screen, he opened up the drive and scrolled through several pictorials. Boring. Straight Gonzo. Kid's stuff.

Yanking out the USB drive, he chucked it into the garbage can under his desk.

Senior Vice President of Human Resource Management Henry Lu had no idea what had booted up on his computer the moment he opened the drive.

"Son of a bitch."

"Are you through yet?"

"It's not me," Adam reiterated. "I got this kid in Sacramento hacking into the system."

"How much longer is it going to take him to crack it?"

"That's it," Adam said, running a hand over his bald head. "He's in."

"About time," Deckard said.

He was on his third cup of coffee.

"What do we have here?"

Adam's hands flashed across the keyboard, sifting through the information on the Bao Corporation's server farm. The keyloggers and other bugs that Deckard had installed in the Samruk office in Astana had quickly uncovered a connection between them and the firm in Shanghai. Unfortunately, they had had no way of cracking through the Chinese firewall until now.

All it had taken was a custom designed computer virus loaded onto some USB drives. Hire a couple kids on the Chinese version of Craig's List and let momentum, along with human nature, take care of the rest.

"Looks like a bill of sale," Deckard said, as he examined the data as it was projected onto the wall. "Phosphoramidites for nucleotides, A, G, C, and T."

"Let's see here, we got capping reagents and deblock. No way could they have a level four facility in the middle of a major city. The Chinese Government would never approve of it."

"I don't think this is a Chinese Government operation. What else is in these files?"

"Look at this," Adam said, opening another document, more data now flooding in from Shanghai. "Several units labeled A BAS 3900. Any ideas?"

"Yeah, we had to be trained up on how to recognize components of Weapons of Mass Destruction when I worked for the government. That thing is a DNA synthesizer."

The unit was only about the size of a large computer printer, but in the wrong hands it could reap levels of damage to society that defense planners still hadn't really wrapped their minds around. With a DNA synthesizer and the chemical components that had also been ordered, someone who knew what he was doing could download gene code right off the internet and build any specific DNA molecule the user wanted from scratch.

A Pandora's Box.

This particular model could be hooked up to a laptop from which a computer script writer could program the DNA synthesizer to build whatever he wanted. A simple bacteria harmful to humans would be fairly easy to construct. Once the bacteria was created, the user could use a gene gun to infect agricultural products. The newly constructed DNA would be attached to gold particles and blasted into the crops where it would enter the cytoplasm of the target cells.

A step up from that would be for a biochemist and a computer programmer to build an entire virus from scratch.

"Whatever this is about," Deckard said, shaking his head. "It's biological."

His thought was interrupted by the fax machine in the corner of the intel office kicking on.

"You got your hacker buddy in California faxing us documents as well?" Deckard asked, as paper got sucked off the tray and into the machine.

"Nope."

Getting up from his chair, Deckard threw his empty coffee cup into the trash and picked up the still warm papers out of the fax machine.

"Holy shit," he stuttered, flipping through the documents.

"What is it?"

"Our first field trip."

Ten

The MH-47 helicopters screamed through the night, the dull black finish on their fuselage blending seamlessly with the dark skyline.

The twin rotor blades cut through the air as they flew nap-of-the-earth, following the contour lines of the mountains as they rose and fell just a dozen meters above the surface, the pilots flying by instruments and night vision goggles.

In the belly of the six rotary wing aircraft, the passengers sat on the cold floor, front to back, loaded down with rifles, machine guns, ammunition, and grenades. The aircraft were completely blacked out, no one dozing off, due to a combination of pre-combat jitters and motion sickness as the helicopters rocked up and down.

The flight to the first combat outpost for refueling had been uneventful; now they were in a combat zone where pilots were subject to fire from surface-to-air weapons and small arms fire from guerrilla fighters from a dozen different factions vying for control over the rugged landscape below.

Door gunners on each side of the MH-47s leaned out into the cool night air, hands never leaving the minigun handles. Thousands of rounds were chained up and loaded through a feed chute leading to the internal magazine. A separate chute led down and out of the aircraft to eject links and hot brass.

As the foothills and mountains passed by, they spotted only the occasional walled compound, each family household an actual fortress with thirty foot walls and guard towers. There were no visible signs of life, no light amplified even through their image intensifying goggles. It was much too early for morning fires to be lit to warm the first kettle of chai, and electricity had yet to reach within fifty miles on their operational area.

Crew chiefs listened to their headsets as the mission commander in the lead helicopter put his men on notice. They clapped their hands to get the attention of their helicopter's occupants, letting them know that they were five minutes out.

Stretching arms and legs, the commandos pitched and yawed back and forth as the transport birds banked, taking evasive maneuvers and leaving nothing to chance. Using the side of the helicopter or each other for support, they pushed themselves up on a knee, preparing to move at a moment's notice, even as they were thrown about the aircraft.

The anticipation built as the rotors began to change their pitch. Some were nervous, afraid of the unknown. Others were eager to get on the ground because they had had to urinate for the last three hours. A few relished the opportunity for combat but would never speak of it.

Rapidly bleeding altitude, the black helicopters flared over a wadi that hadn't seen water in generations. The washout was created by ancient seasonal rains, creating the only area resembling a suitable landing zone for kilometers.

No one had been available to reconnoiter or secure the drop zone ahead of time, but during the hasty mission planning, the ground force commander had assured the senior pilots that in the event they couldn't land, due to unstable soil or rocky terrain, that his men would simply jump off the back ramp, dropping the final ten feet to the ground.

Leveling out, the pilots began to hover down to the ground. Coming in strung out in a file across the length of the wadi with valley walls rising on each side in pitch darkness required a degree of precision that the aviators had trained their entire lives for.

Closer to the ground, the combined power of twelve sets of rotors kicked up a cloud of dust that almost instantly browned out the pilots. Looking below, the gunners continued to guide them down to the ground as the rotor blades chopped at the dust cloud, creating sparks of light that could be seen in the green glow of their night vision goggles.

Gently, the wheels under the belly of the helicopters made

contact with the surface of the wadi. Hearing the news from the gunners and getting the okay from the pilots, the crew chiefs gave the order to disembark.

As one, the commandos rose to their feet and stormed down the ramp and into a twisting sandstorm. The dust swirled like a miniature tornado around the troops as they fanned out to security positions, hefting machine guns and mortar tubes with them.

Taking a knee and facing out, the troops were stung as sand beat at their exposed necks and faces. The line of MH-47s lifted off, hovering straight up and into the air before their noses dipped down, charging forward.

With the transport aircraft disappearing into the night, the commandos were left in the moonscape of Afghanistan in an eerie silence.

Platoon sergeants began giving orders in hushed voices, their men organizing into their squads, preparing themselves for movement.

It was going to be a long walk.

Fahran unrolled his mat, aiming it west towards Mecca, and began to pray alongside his peers, two young men he had grown up with in Kandahar. Learning by rote in the *madrassas* held little interest for the teenagers, and employment was easy to come by for someone as young and able as they were.

The boys performed the *salaat* as their fathers and father's fathers had, going back farther into antiquity then anyone could remember. Their words came from impassioned hearts that beat strongly in their chests, forming words long since committed to memory.

None of the boys heard the suppressed gunshots. The steel core bullets sought them out in the night, drilling them in the back of their heads, one each, ending the call to prayer. A dozen Kazakh mercenaries advanced forward, quickly securing the area as several Americans appeared carrying the silenced VSS rifles that had dispatched the small guard contingent.

The Kazakhs surrounded a hole in the ground and peered below, having no idea where the bottom was but hearing the rush of water below. One of their comrades dug into his pack and produced a steel wire caving ladder. Tethering the caving ladder off to a nearby boulder, they dropped it down the hole, the ladder uncoiling and splashing at the bottom.

Deckard moved forward while slinging his VSS rifle. Making a circular motion above his head, he pointed to the ground where the three bodies lay cooling themselves under moonlight. The mortar section moved forward, the first gun team setting in their base plate. In a few minutes the entire mortar section would be up and ready for fire missions.

Gripping the cold steel rungs of the caving ladder, Deckard took the lead, lowering himself down into the darkness. The *karez* was actually an ancient irrigation system dug below the water table that carried water to fields for agriculture, some of them dozens of kilometers away, in this case about ten klicks to the nearest village.

Hand over hand he descended, the air growing cooler below as the sound of the underground stream grew louder. His boots reached into the water, his feet feeling the frigid water seep in as he released himself and dropped into the thigh deep water.

Nearly slipping, he braced himself on the sides of the canal. Flipping down his night vision goggles, Deckard activated the infrared flashlight built into them to create some ambient light for the NVG tube to amplify.

Seeing nothing but cold water and cold earth walls, he looked up and gave two IR flashes, letting the team know that it was clear. Moving forward, he made some space, hearing the first squad carefully coming down the ladder behind him.

It was an opening gambit, one he preferred to a frontal assault that was guaranteed to end in a hundred percent causalities.

With the VSS compact assault rifle tucked into the pocket of his shoulder, Deckard edged down the waterway, struggling to see what lay ahead through the green tint of his night vision goggles. Taking point, he could hear the lead squad of Kazakhs gently sloshing through the water behind him.

It had been less than twenty-four hours since he had snatched the Operations Order off of the fax machine at his battalion's headquarters.

They had no warning or hint of it coming through his private channels, the hacks and bugs planted in the Samruk corporate offices. He wasn't even given the courtesy of a warning order to allow him to plan. But as he stalked down the dark tunnel, the former soldier knew that was, in fact, the plan from the beginning. Beta testing. Was Samruk combat ready, and was Deckard prepared to lead them into combat? The eleventh hour Op Order was designed to add more stress and urgency onto what was already an extremely challenging company level mission.

US Air Force C17 transport aircraft from Bagram had landed in Astana within hours. Most of the planning had to be done en route.

Using a pace count by keeping track of each time his left foot touched the slippery surface of the underground aqueduct, he knew he had already traveled four hundred meters. By the looks of the imagery he had studied at Bagram Airfield, the *karez* continued for kilometers. Hopefully they would find what he was looking for before traveling that far.

The only good news was that it would be extremely difficult to set anti-personnel mines in such fast moving water.

Listening carefully, he could tell the Kazakh mercenaries were falling behind. It wasn't entirely their fault; with minimal equipment there were not enough night vision systems to go around. At the moment there were no circumstances where he would allow visible lights to be used since they could compromise the entire operation.

Backtracking, he found the point man for the Kazakh squad and physically placed the commando's hand on the back of his desert fatigue shirt, ensuring that he had a tight grasp before continuing. The rest of the squad had a safety line that was tied around each soldier's waist, so there should be no further breaks on contact.

He had no one to blame but himself. Limited timetable aside, the planning and execution had been rushed to the point that he was leading the main element of the operation, a job normally belonging to a squad or platoon leader.

Proceeding slowly, all of his senses were strained to their limits. Maintaining a high level of alertness was a requirement in an environment this unforgiving. Subterranean combat was about the most dangerous thing Deckard could imagine, next to other enclosed tubular assaults such as a hostage rescue on an airliner or passenger train.

Eyes and ears detecting nothing in the darkness other than his own breathing and racing heartbeat, he picked up the pace slightly, leading the mercenaries forward. After counting off an additional six hundred meters, Deckard's hand ran off the side of the karez where the wall had been scooped out, creating a landing.

Reaching back, he released the Kazakh's hand and moved forward, the muzzle of his rifle tracking back and forth. Deckard stepped up and out of the water, onto the earth platform, scanning for targets. The ground was worn, indicating that the area was well traveled, however, no other signs of life were present.

Cursing under his breath, he wondered if his gamble had been a waste of time, foreplay before the inevitable.

Backtracking for the lead Kazakh, he helped him and the rest of the squad up onto the platform, whispering in Russian for them to establish a security perimeter. The Samruk mercenaries watched down the unexplored end of the tunnel while the rest of the platoon filed onto the landing.

Allowing red lens flashlights, they began searching the carved out portion of the karez. Footprints were quickly found. The faint tread of the type of sandals Afghans favored could be seen across the dirt floor. A couple observant Kazakhs turned up shell casings but thankfully no booby traps so far. Looking around, Deckard spotted a pool of water at the far end of the chamber.

"What's the deal boss," Frank said, coming up alongside him.

"Did your squad unroll the commo wire down here yet?"

"Yeah, they got the spool right behind us."

Sure enough Deckard could see one of the Kazakhs with his red light out, carrying a giant spool of WD-1A communication wire. It served the dual purpose of acting as a guideline for the mercenaries to move back and forth through the tunnels, as well as providing a way for them to talk to the mortar section back on the surface.

"Connect the field telephone and make sure that mortars are up."

"What about us?"

"I need to see what this is, before planning our next move," Deckard said, pointing to the pool of standing water. "I think this is a water lock, but I have to be sure."

"Like the Viet Cong used back in the day?"

"Yeah, low tech defense from an enemy introducing poison gas into the tunnel system or overpressure from explosives. The insurgent answer to American air power."

"Not a bad way to conceal hidden exits either."

"The *karez* systems are maintained by the communities that use them, but they are built by tradesmen who pass their secrets down from father to son. The same goes for any adjoining tunnels the Taliban may have forced them to build before the war."

"So who draws the short straw?"

"I'll do it, should only be a few feet underwater."

"Should be."

Deckard flipped up his night vision goggles, knowing he'd have to be careful not to crush them while underwater, and handed his rifle off to Frank. He was breaking a cardinal rule of getting out of arm's length of his primary weapon, but drowning because his rifle or sling got tangled on something in an underwater cave didn't appeal to him at the moment.

Slipping into the water, he involuntarily held his breath as the icy water circled his chest. Forcing a few deep breaths, he disappeared beneath the surface. The water was freezing cold and pitch dark for several claustrophobic seconds while Deckard clawed his way through the passage, emerging to take a massive gulp of stale air on the other side.

Pushing the NVGs down on the swing arm attached to the helmet mount, Deckard scanned back and forth. The Afghans who built the *karez* had their trade secrets, all right, and that extended to secret and hidden tunnels connecting various underground constructs. For instance, an emergency escape tunnel connecting a bunker complex to an ancient *karez* aqueduct.

Another deep breath, and he slipped back under the water lock, surfacing on the other side.

"It's good," Deckard said, squinting as Frank indiscriminately flashed his red light in his face. "We've got their egress route."

"How could you possibility have known this would be here?" Frank said, shaking his head.

"I didn't," Deckard responded, soberly, as he reached out, reclaiming his rifle. "It was an extrapolation based on the proximity of the *karez* to the bunker system."

"In other words, you pulled it out of your ass."

"Maybe. Have Third Platoon remain topside with the mortar section, and get Second Platoon down here to secure this foothold. We'll take First Platoon the rest of the way to the bunkers."

"Roger. We got comms with topside. Give me two minutes."

"Shouldn't take that long," Deckard said, motioning for First Squad to follow him through the water lock. Once on the other side, he helped the Kazakhs out of the water, all of them now soaking wet and freezing cold. Caves and underground passages kept the same cold temperature year round, regardless of what the climate was topside. At least the walls were wider and there wasn't any running water to complicate their footing.

Under night vision, he got First Squad together on a safety line before moving onto Second and Third squad. Frank was with

Second Platoon in the *karez,* and Sergeant Alexander would be at the rear, the platoon sergeant pushing his men forward. Finally Alexander came through the water lock with another spool of commo wire, trailing a line behind him back to the *karez* so the point element could maintain communications all the way back to the surface.

Glancing at the luminescent hands on his wrist watch, Deckard knew they had less then six hours of darkness left. Special Operations helicopters only flew at night, so if the assault went on into daylight hours, then they were stuck out in the hinterlands for an additional twelve or more hours until the next period of darkness.

Deckard forced himself to remain calm. Getting overly excited wouldn't make the situation better. There were a lot of moving parts, a lot of contingencies, and a million things that could go wrong. So far they were on track, even if somewhat behind schedule.

Proceeding cautiously, Deckard noted that the tunnel was better built with wide smooth walls that had even been cemented over in some portions. The Kazakhs shuffled behind him in the dark, following the crazy American into god knew what.

The tunnel more or less continued on a straight azimuth for another half kilometer before forking off in two directions. One passage continued straight towards the mountains where the objective was located; the other looked like it led to a dead end.

Halting the squad, he again took the lead, moving slowly while on lookout for any signs of danger. Straining his eyes through a dimly lit, green-tinted world cast by his night vision device, Deckard literally ran into the haphazardly constructed staircase. Suppressing a grunt of frustration, he looked up the rock carved stairs. They led up to the ceiling. The entrance seemed to be covered over at the top with wooden planks and something else, maybe a carpet.

Moving back, he ordered the Kazakhs to secure the intersection in his still stunted Russian. The mercenaries complied as best they could, still unable to see anything. Moving down the ranks of the platoon, whispering Alexander's name, he found the platoon sergeant and moved him up front. Alexander possessed one of Samruk's much sought after night vision systems, and Deckard pointed out to him the fork in the tunnel before showing him the staircase.

"Worth checking out," Deckard whispered.

"Da, da," he nodded.

The American pointed to the suppressor on the VSS sub-assault rifle and then pulled out a Ka-bar fighting knife identical to the one each commando carried.

Alexander nodded his head, the message clear. Keep it quiet.

Once in the alcove and away from the main passage, Deckard again allowed red lights to be used. First Squad quickly lit up the area, so they could see what they were doing. They untied their safety line and followed Deckard as he led them up the stone staircase. Feeling the material between the wooden planks at the top of the stairs, he confirmed that it was simply the underside of a carpet. A simple but effective way to conceal another hidden entrance to a cursory glance from the other side.

Keeping watch on the concealed entrance with his silenced rifle, Deckard pointed a finger at the wood and carpet covering the top of the stairs. Alexander ushered his men forward, and they climbed up, brushing past their commander.

They shifted the planks out of the way as carefully and quietly as possible, but at that moment it sounded earth shattering to the group of mercenaries, knowing that compromise in this situation would mean almost certain death. They were completely blind to what was going on topside.

With the opening exposed, Deckard climbed up, hand over hand. He found himself in an empty room with mud walls and a dirt floor; it could be any house in Afghanistan, but this one had giggles and grunts coming from the adjacent room.

Hearing a boot drag across the dirt floor, Deckard looked back to see Alexander close on his heels. The platoon sergeant was no coward and wanted to lead from the front, Deckard thought. He probably resented him trying to take charge to begin with. That was a good sign.

Raising a single finger to his lips, Alexander nodded. They were in Indian country.

The two crept forward to the open doorway. Down on one knee, Deckard pivoted at the hips, exposing himself just enough for the night vision tube he wore in front of his left eye to clear the side of the wall and see what was going on in the next room.

He wished he hadn't.

Moving aside, he motioned the platoon sergeant forward to take a look. For better or worse he needed to know what the situation was before his men were thrown in the middle. Alexander peered into the room and was frozen for a moment as if he didn't believe what he was seeing before turning away.

He looked a little green around the gills, but maybe it was just the tint of the night vision playing tricks with Deckard's mind.

Tugging on the platoon sergeant's sleeve to get his attention, he held up seven fingers in front of his face. He wanted all of First Squad upstairs, then he pointed to the Ka-Bar again. The Kazakh nodded.

Deckard held out one finger and ran it across his neck.

Moments later, First Squad was assembled in front of him, AK-103s slung over their backs, fighting knives in their hands. Deckard started forward, but Alexander put a hand on his chest and took the lead, himself. Deckard let him.

The Kazakh mercenaries silently moved into the adjacent room. A half dozen aging AK-47s were propped up against the opposite wall, their owners lined up and waiting their turn with the group's house boy. The Taliban giggled and whispered to each other in Pashto while their comrade kept pumping away.

The Samruk soldiers were fairly shocked by this, but Deckard knew that this 'teasing', as the Taliban called it, was pretty much par for the course in this part of the world.

The mercenaries descended on the Taliban like wraiths in the night. Steel blades were sunk into throats and carotid arteries, final gasps of life escaping dry lips. The attack was short and vicious, the Taliban pool boy being quickly dispatched as well.

Wiping the bloody combat knives off on the Taliban's *dishdashas*, the blades went back into their sheaths before the mercenaries shouldered their AK-103s. It was only a two room house, so one by one the Kazakhs ascended a ladder onto the roof and secured the structure.

Pulling out a piece of paper Deckard had printed out moments before loading the entire company on the back of the MH-47 helicopters, he turned on his own red LED light to look at the satellite imagery. Peering out the windows and doing some rough terrain association under the moonlight, he was almost positive they were in the single standing structure outside the bunker complex which would place them halfway between where they entered the *karez* and the bunkers, themselves.

Stumbling back down into the tunnel, he found the Kazakh with the commo wire and field telephone. Unwinding the cable up the stairs, he then handed it up to one of the mercenaries pulling security on the roof. Climbing the ladder, Deckard connected the field telephone to the cable and spoke into the receiver.

"Anybody there?"

Rapid fire Russian greeted him on the other end.

Such was the language barrier.

"Mendez? Find Mendez!"

"Da."

Several moments passed.

"Yeah," Mendez came over the line. He was back at the 82mm mortar section.

"It's me. Look to your northeast."

"Uh, what am I looking for?"

Deckard reached into the front pocket on his chest rig and pulled out a flashlight. The IZLID was no normal flashlight, however. It was actually an infrared laser used by forward observers to mark targets for fast movers and attack helicopters. Flipping the switch on, he waved it around in the air.

"Is that you?"

"Yeah, we found a passage that led up into this house

99

halfway to the objective."

"Nice overwatch position."

"Mark it on your fire direction board. I don't feel like getting fragged tonight."

"I gotcha."

"Here is the deal. Push Third Platoon down the hole. Have Kurt and Chuck lead them, following the commo wire, and catch up with Second Platoon which is still down in the aqueduct. I want both platoons at my position ASAP."

"You got it."

"Is Piet there?"

"Yeah, he is here with his two boys."

"Tell him I want him up here as well."

"He'll be glad to hear that."

"We need them to take another roll of wire with them."

"Roger."

Hanging up the field telephone, Deckard turned towards the objective and began to scrutinize the mountainside. Mulavi Ibrahim Khalis, or MIK for short, had dug his organization into the mountain several years ago. The warlord needed a safe haven from American air power and had found it in the Hindu Kush mountain range like many before him.

The mountain was riddled with a labyrinth of spurs and draws, each lined with stone bunkers, caves, tunnel entrances, and mud huts. A nightmare for ground troops to enter, and almost assured that a blood bath would be the result.

The real objective was MIK's underground bunker complex where he stored the opium before having it transported north to Tajikistan for entry into Russia and Europe. More importantly, in Deckard's view, was that somewhere down there would be the high value targets themselves, MIK and his lieutenants.

These types of subterranean structures represented a strategic puzzle for military planners. An enemy base dug into a mountainside with two thousand feet of overburden on top of it was considered essentially invulnerable to any conventional munitions. Ruling out a nuclear strike, the next best option was to use cannon fodder, foreign troops by their rationale, in this case Samruk International.

Luckily, Deckard had a few tricks up his sleeve. A Gettysburg charge at a well dug in and defended enemy was the last thing on his mind.

Unfortunately, none of that brass at Bagram Airbase had seen fit to enlighten him as to what the strategic value in all this was. MIK and his Islamic Jihad Faction sometimes trained and communicated with the Taliban and Al Qaeda but was really just a band of smugglers and bandits financed by drug money and extortion rackets.

More like Al Capone and less like Osama Bin Laden.

Pushing negative thoughts aside, he used his time to study the surrounding terrain, rethinking and revising the plan of attack.

Deckard was still examining the microterrain features when a hand came down on his shoulder.

"Eh, boss," Piet whispered. "Got Second and Third stacked up below." The former Recce held one of Samruk's Remington bolt action rifles and wore the web gear he had made for a job in Angola years ago.

"Good. Get the platoon sergeants and advisers up here."

The South African disappeared below.

A minute later Kurt, Chuck, Frank, Adam, and Richie, along with sergeants Alibek and Kanat, followed Piet up the ladder.

"Here is the deal," Deckard began. "Frank. Richie. You guys are with me. We continue the assault with First Platoon as planned. The rest of you look here." He leaned over the edge of the roof and lit up the terrain with the IZLID, so they could all see with their night vision goggles.

"I want the rest of you to infiltrate, following this microterrain feature," Deckard continued, highlighting a washout divot in the ground with the infrared laser. "You should be able to get down in that small wadi and follow it to the mountainside. Once you are in position, we have Mendez with the mortar section start hanging rounds.

"When you get a splash, that is the signal to assault. First

101

Platoon from below, Second and Third apply fire and maneuver tactics as you see fit, walking mortar fire in front of you. Piet, you take your boys and position them wherever you can best support the assault."

"Any comments?"

"Limit of advance?" Chuck asked.

"Line of exploitation," Piet corrected.

"Same thing," Deckard said. "The bunker entrance. I'll mark it as soon as we arrive. Try not to get baited any further, use indirect fire instead."

"Got it."

"A little luck and the enemy will be so confused trying to fight in two directions at once that the assault will be over by the time they figure out how to react. How long do you need to get into position?"

"Three quarters of an hour," Alibek said through his heavy accent.

"That's when we initiate. See you on the other side."

Rounding up the security element on the roof, Deckard and Alexander linked up with the rest of the platoon in the tunnel. He had one eye fixated on his watch. With the numbers ticking down, he picked up the pace, striding down the tunnel alongside the platoon sergeant.

Another seven hundred meters by his pace count, and the tunnel began to slant upwards. They were getting close. Deckard slowed down, now more wary of pressure plates and trip wires laid out as an early warning device.

The floor continued to ramp up at an angle as the two point men tiptoed forward. By nine hundred meters deep, the night vision tube was able to amplify a light source somewhere farther ahead. At first it was just a pin prick of light, but it began to glow brighter as they closed the distance. The escape tunnel came to an end at a stone wall, rocks piled one on top of the other leaving gaps between where the light showed through.

Flipping up his NVGs, Deckard squinted his eyes looking through the cracks. On the other side of the wall, he caught the silhouette of someone as they passed into a doorway. Beyond the wall was another corridor, this one lit up by a series of naked light bulbs wired along the ceiling. Entrances branched off the main corridor to other portions of the bunker.

The objective itself was a piece of cake. The Samruk commandos had been drilled over and over again on urban combat drills. Clearing hallways and rooms was nearly second nature to them at this point. The real problem would be breaching the wall in front of them.

Deckard did some calculations in his head. Taking the wall down manually would attract attention. The narrow confines of the tunnel would be turned into a shooting gallery. An explosive breach in the same narrow passage would probably kill them with over pressure.

The Samruk commander looked down at his watch.

Fuck.

Fuck, we're cutting this close.

Staying low, the entire platoon moved like ducks in a row through the sandy bottom of the wadi. Afghanistan's notoriously deadly terrain did little to dissuade the Central Asian mercenaries. The Kazakhs didn't mind it at all, especially after being soaking wet and freezing in an underground passage.

Adam looked up from his watch.

They emptied out into a draw, leading right into the mountainside where the two platoons halted, looking a little confused at first. The two platoon sergeants got to work getting squad leaders to rally the men and lead them up the military crest of the draw, preventing them from silhouetting themselves against the night sky.

The former spy moved at the rear of the formation with Piet and his two snipers. The South African scanned his surroundings until he found what he was looking for. Tapping Adam on the shoulder, he pointed out a rocky outcropping to their flank that provided a field of fire over most of the mountainside.

Adam nodded and Piet separated from the formation with his two snipers. They would occupy the terrain feature to provide overwatch and precision fire when the time came.

The Kazakhs suddenly stopped in their tracks, causing Adam to refocus his NVGs to see what was going on up front. Now he saw what the problem was. Kurt Jager had halted the formation. Alibek was about to take them over the crest in a single file.

The fact that Kurt spoke adequate Russian was nothing short of a miracle on this mission. Adam could converse with Afghans fairly well but was completely lost with Kazakhs.

Scheisse.

Kurt looked up from his Omega watch and began giving orders under his breath. If Alibek had led the troops forward in a single file, they could easily have been mowed down by a single machine gunner. Having the entire formation execute a left face meant they would creep forward in a skirmish line to their assault positions.

If they were compromised and made contact, they would now be much better situated to return fire and maneuver a flanking element, if need be. Now on line and facing the objective, Kurt led the way as they crested over the ridge. The Kazakh sergeants were talented, but the truth was that the entire unit was out of their element on an operation such as this.

The former GSG-9 Counter-Terrorist stalked forward, attempting to keep a low profile against the moonlit sky. Struggling not to kick loose any more rocks and debris then absolutely necessary, he still couldn't help but think they sounded like a herd of elephants. Cresting a second spur that ran down off the side of the mountain, the enemy fighting positions were now in view, and within range of small arms fire.

Giving the hand and arm signal to halt the troops, Kurt stopped the formation and brought Alibek up alongside him, pointing out enemy bunkers and mud huts sure to be occupied by guards. A few words of Russian passed between the two soldiers before Alibek moved back among his men, positioning them behind proper cover and pointing out priority targets.

Hearing footsteps behind him, he turned to see Kanat and Chuck moving both Weapons Squads with their PKM machine guns to the high ground in order to provide suppressive fire when things went hot. Apparently Piet had already broken off from the main element to scout out his options. Whatever the case Kurt trusted the judgment of a man who had been soldiering practically since he was born.

Watching the machine gun teams get into the prone position behind their guns with assistant gunners alongside, Kurt knew they had to get set in place fast. They were all running out of time.

Time and darkness.

"I just want you to know that there is fuck all I can do about it," Richie said, pointing a finger in his chest. "I told you, you bloody Yank, this is shit det cord from India."

"It was all that was available on short notice," Deckard hissed, trying not to raise his voice. "You've improvised with worse in the past."

"I just want you to know whose fault this is when it all goes pear shaped."

"Hurry the fuck up and get it set."

Turning away from the breach point, Deckard walked down the line of Kazakhs stacked in the tunnel. Three squads now broken down into six assault teams to clear rooms, weapons squad would secure the halls. Simple, or so it seemed.

"Frank?"

"Yeah?"

"Where is that field telephone? I need to talk to Mendez."

Frank hooked a thumb back in the opposite direction down the tunnel. "Back that way five hundred meters or so, I think," he replied, shrugging his shoulders.

"What the fuck?"

"Shit, man, that spool only has so much wire. We ran out, hooked up the phone, and left it there as the next best thing."

"Holy shit, you didn't feel it was pertinent to tell me that?" This is like dealing with SEALs, Deckard thought.

"Well, it is now."

"Alright, whatever, run down there and tell Mendez to fire on the target reference points in exactly seven minutes."

"Yes, Massa," Frank answered, setting the timer on his watch. "I'll stand by until he hangs the rounds then catch up with you."

"See you then."

Deckard walked away shaking his head. This is the price you pay when SATCOM and FM radios are hopelessly back-ordered and you have to resort to World War Two era communications.

"Mida, mida!"

Mendez turned around, recognizing his name in Kazakh dialect. As per common sense, the worst soldier in the mortar section got assigned to monitor the field telephone. This guy couldn't lay on a mortar system if his life depended on it. Thankfully, the rest of the section was full of fast learners.

"Yeah," Mendez said, holding the receiver to his ear,

fighting the urge to light up a cigarette.

"Hey, it's Frank."

"What's up?"

"The boss wants you to fire up the TRPs in, hold on," Frank paused for a moment, "exactly three minutes."

"No shit?"

"No shit."

"Okay, better keep your head down."

"It's not me you need to worry about."

Mendez passed the telephone back to his make-a-wish foundation soldier and consulted his Fire Direction Center board.

"Gun One."

All three gun teams jumped to their feet. It was time to work.

"Five rounds, HE Quick. Deflection-"

"Three o' clock, three hundred meters," Piet whispered, one eye fixed on his target through the magnification of his Leopold scope. "Three boogers behind the stone wall. AKs. Looks like a DShK mounted behind the wall as well."

"Da," Nikita and Askar answered in unison.

The Kazakh snipers lay side by side the South African watching, unblinking through their sights. With the proper night vision not having arrived in Astana in time, they were reduced to duct taping the standard PVS-14 NVG tubes to their sniper scopes to see at night. It was primitive, but effective. When their American commander had seen their improvised night scopes he had remarked to them, *if you can't duck it, fuck it.*

"Quarter value wind, right to left. Hold a heavy quarter on him."

They breathed shallow breaths.

In the distance they could see the insurgents up close and

personal through ten-power scopes, watch them laugh amongst themselves and smoke cheap Pakistani cigarettes. They'd spent weeks training, and now Piet would observe his students under combat conditions. No one would shed a tear for dead terrorists, but it would be a blow to his ego if they missed the shot.

"Steady," he whispered, not expecting a reply. By now they were focused, breathing and body position already relaxed. They watched their targets and waited.

Somewhere behind them, Piet heard the retort of three mortar tubes as 82mm high explosive rounds shot into the air on trajectory for enemy positions to their front. Through the green tint of the night vision, they saw the reactions of the insurgents as they looked back and forth for the source of the distant sound.

Piet turned the knob on his Motorola radio. Open channel traffic would be used, once things went overt. If he remembered the correct data from his days as a young gun bunny in the SADF, he estimated a time of flight of about twenty-five seconds.

He had to adjust the knob as the Kazakh squad leaders jumped the gun by a few seconds and Russian chatter came over the net. Then he realized he might be a few seconds off as the HE rounds slammed into enemy positions on the mountainside, detonating as they made contact with the ground, one after the other.

Nikita and Askar gently squeezed the triggers on their rifles. Piet watched their targets disappear behind the wall, impacts to their chests knocking them backwards. Before they could transition to secondary targets, the support by fire line opened up, muzzle flashes lighting up the night as six PKMs went cyclic.

The entire mountainside was lit ablaze.

The vibrations caused by exploding mortar rounds shook dirt loose from the ceiling.

"Do it."

Richie pulled the pins on the dual primed initiation device, setting off the double strand of detonation chord taped in a circle around the stone wall. Deckard had personally supervised to make sure that this time P was not applied to the breaching charge.

The overpressure was intense. The assault teams bore down with earplugs firmly in place, the force of the explosion knocking most to their knees and a few off their feet. Deckard slammed one boot down on the floor and pushed off, sprinting fifty meters to the breach.

Sure enough, the charge had crumbled the stone wall. The rocks having been stacked on top of each other without any mortar being used meant that it didn't take much. Glancing back to ensure the assault teams were on his heels, Deckard stepped through the breach. The blast had taken out a few bulbs in the hallway, leaving him in the shadows.

One of the insurgents leaned out of a doorway down the hall, investigating the blast just in time for Deckard to gain target acquisition with the VSS rifle. Two rounds center mass dumped him on the ground for someone to clean up later.

The Samruk assaulters stepped through the breach, stacking up along both walls. Deckard took the first door on his left, tossing in a FMK2 hand grenade. A few seconds later the combination of recrystalized hexogen and TNT exploded, turning the grenade's metal body into fragments that shot out in all directions in a fifteen foot radius. Flowing into the room before the smoke dissipated, Deckard cleared the right corner, the Kazakh behind him clearing the left.

As the rest of the assault team entered and cleared their sectors, several Afghan terrorists struggled out of their cots with blood streaming from their ears. Breaking down their sectors of fire, the assaulters fired two rounds apiece from their AK-103s into the enemy before they had a chance to reach for dusty pistols and rifles.

Deckard joined the Kazakhs in a preliminary search of the room while grenades were detonated outside by other assault teams. Kicking over beds and overturning carpets produced nothing of immediate interest.

Lining up on the door for an organized exit, Deckard was about to call them out into the hall, when one of the PKM gunners opened up. A few screams later, and one of the Kazakhs yelled to the machine gunner pulling security down the corridor. The gunner yelled something back, and the stack flowed back into the hall.

Stepping over several fresh corpses, the assault team leapfrogged past another team clearing what looked like a kitchen area and lined up on the next available doorway. With the second man in the stack preparing another frag grenade, the gun team picked up their machine gun and ammunition, coming up alongside to provide cover fire as needed.

The assaulter winged the fragmentation grenade into the room and waited. Without warning, one of the insurgents came running through the door, trying to avoid the blast. The lead Kazakh slammed the muzzle of his AK into the Afghan's chest, knocking him back through the door as the grenade detonated.

This time Deckard was the last in the stack and patiently followed the mercenaries as they took their points of domination inside the room. Striding through the door, he felt like the entire room was flashing in slow motion. The muzzle flash of an enemy's AK-47 blinked like a disco strobe light in the dark as he blasted away, 7.62 rounds spraying everywhere. Deckard sidestepped out of the door as quickly as possible, the Kazakh standing to his flank dropping to the ground like a marionette that had its strings suddenly cut.

The remaining assaulters turned their guns on the muzzle flash, emptying magazines at the threat. Riddled with bullets, the insurgent was punched backwards by the hail of gunfire. As the mercenaries secured the room, Deckard moved to evaluate the injured assaulter. No need, he realized. The enemy's shots had caught him in the face and neck.

Deckard made a mental note that this room needed to be searched and marked for demolition. The walls were stacked nearly to the ceiling with wooden crates showing dust-covered Cyrillic writing. He recognized most of them as being ammunition crates, mostly for PG-7 rocket-propelled grenades and 7.62x39 AK rounds. Others he wasn't so sure about. Blasting the stanchions that ran down the center of ammunition depot would probably do it.

The commandos quickly took turns loading fresh magazines into their rifles before Deckard yelled out to the machine gun team.

"Coming out!"

"Da!"

Back in the corridor, Deckard glanced down the hall. The barricaded entrance to the bunker complex at the end would lead outside. He was surprised how fast they were clearing and advancing through the complex, even with six assault teams leapfrogging each other. Collectively, his team cringed as another group let loose a grenade across the hall.

Reaching over and grabbing the PKM gunner to bring him down the hall with them, Deckard was preparing his assaulters to take the next room, when an Afghan calmly walked into the middle of the corridor from the room at the end of the hall.

Everyone shouldered their weapons just a moment too late as the terrorist leveled an RPG-7 launcher in their direction and pulled the trigger.

Chuck Rochenoire had lived his life by some very simple words.

When in doubt, shoot from the hip and go with what you know.

Hence the six lines of green parachute chord, tied to the web gear of each PKM gunner on the support by fire line. After all six guns went cyclic on the target area for fifteen seconds the former SEAL yanked the strings, signaling them to cease fire.

Next he pulled the string tied to the first gunner and let him fire for five seconds before pulling the string tied to the second gunner. When gun two fired, it was the signal for gun one to shut down. After another five seconds he tugged on the string tied to gun three, and the process continued all the way down the line as they swept the enemy with a powerful base of fire. Chuck would continue to use the 'dopes on a rope' method until the machine gunners gained more experience. Eventually they wouldn't need him or the parachute chord to dump huge amounts of coordinated fire on the enemy.

With their barrels beginning to glow in the darkness, the titanium frame Russian machine guns were proving their worth, alongside the gunners themselves. Assistant gunners reloaded and readied fresh belts of 7.62x54 rimmed ammunition during down periods. Meanwhile, each gunner actively tracked targets, carefully using the red arc of his tracers to walk his fire less than a dozen meters in front of the advancing assault line.

By the time the enemy was out from under the onslaught of machine gun fire, the assault line composed of two entire rifle platoons would be right on top of them.

Chuck was laughing on the inside.

Kanat grabbed the rifleman, pulling him backward to stay

parallel with the rest of the assaulters on line with each other. Some of the mercenaries were getting over excited and scrambling ahead of their comrades, sending the platoon sergeant into fits of rage, barking corrections as the assaulters stalked forward.

Arriving at the first of the enemy positions, the platoon sergeant reached into his pocket, retrieving a chem stick. Snapping it mixed the chemicals inside, causing it to glow bright orange. Hurling it across the objective, he gave the signal to the support by fire line to shift fire.

Seeing the tracer fire move from their immediate front to lay suppressive fire deeper into the objective, the platoon sergeant yelled to the riflemen to sweep and clear. Second and Third Platoon advanced forward, individual squad leaders taking change and clearing stone pill boxes and mud huts built into the side of the mountain, finding plenty of fresh corpses created by mortar and machine gun fire.

In between the rapid bursts of PKM fire, individual rifle shots could be heard as the Kazakhs double-tapped downed enemy combatants, assuring that the dead were truly dead.

Kurt Jager terminated a brief conversation with Chuck over his Motorola radio and ducked as a grenade exploded, showering him with rock and debris. More rifle fire was exchanged in the distance. Having established a foothold within the enemy's fortified positions, they would now wait for weapons squad to displace themselves to somewhere that they could better support the assault. The objective area was simply too big to be adequately covered by a static support by fire line.

Kurt yelled to several Kazakhs and pointed out where he wanted them to pull security until Chuck arrived. Taking cover behind a dirt berm, the mercenaries almost immediately began taking enemy fire. Stepping over the bodies of several insurgents that the sniper team had eliminated before they arrived, Kurt moved to a DShK heavy machine gun mounted on a tripod.

Thankfully, the enemy had been deprived of the opportunity to use it against them, but now he had to act fast.

Reaching into his cargo pocket, he pulled out a flex linear

113

charge he had made out of detonation chord, deciding to improvise a bit to destroy the machine gun before moving on. The last thing they needed was an insurgent getting behind them as they continued to clear the area and man the 12.7mm Soviet cannon.

Kurt wrapped the door charge around the barrel and affixed the time fuse in place. He was just about done with the square knot when he heard someone shout in Pashto.

A single shot cracked in the darkness.

The German shuddered, expecting an impact.

Turning, he saw an insurgent on the roof of a hut ten meters away pitch forward over the edge and crash into the ground below, taking a long dirt nap.

"Watch yourself," Piet's voice said over the radio.

Kurt shook his head, finishing the preparation of the explosives as Chuck and his PKM gunners came shuffling toward him, ducking their heads as green tracer fire crisscrossed the night sky.

"Chuck, glad you could make it."

"Wherethefuckarethesemotherfuckers?"

"We should keep three guns on our right flank, so we can hold the high ground. Detach the rest of the guns to the assault squads for immediate support by fire. The terrain looks rough ahead."

"Got it," Chuck said. "I'll take the three gun teams and leave the other three with you, so you can explain it to them."

Kurt nodded in agreement.

Chuck Rochenoire policed up his men and headed uphill, eyes already scanning for a new place to station his men for the duration of the assault.

Turning away from the DShK, Kurt began speaking in Russian to the remaining machine gun teams, knowing that lost time meant the assault lost momentum. Seconds later, the Kazakhs acknowledged their understanding and began to break off to find individual squads.

Standing up, Kurt was about to call Chuck over the radio, when something heavy rolled between his feet.

They stared like idiots as the rocket propelled grenade soared over their heads, leaving a faint plume in its wake. The PG-7 anti-tank projectile continued on its path, spiraling down the corridor before smashing into the wall on the far side of the escape shaft they had entered from and exploded.

In the narrow confines of the bunker, the pressure was overwhelming, knocking the mercenaries off their feet as more shrapnel was flung over their heads. Struggling back up, the Afghan dropped his RPG-7 launcher, looking as surprised as his opponents were. The confusion quickly turned to anger as the Kazakhs sighted in and sent a barrage of fire into him.

The terrorist was practically turned into a sieve by the time it was all over.

The Kazakhs were still checking faces and testicles with their hands to make sure everything was still there in the aftermath of the blast, when Deckard started yelling and forcing troops back to their feet, grabbing them by the collar.

As near as he could tell, the bunkers were more than half clear, but a glance back at the remaining mercenaries told them they were taking casualties in the process. If they lost the initiative for even a moment and the enemy was able to launch an effective counter attack, it was all over for the Samruk men. They had nowhere to retreat but to a tunnel that was impossible to defend from.

"Doorway left! Doorway right! Go!"

The assaulters surged forward.

More grenades were hurled into the uncleared rooms, simultaneous explosions jarring Deckard's fillings. The American jumped in the nearest stack, moving into the next room. Inside, two insurgents were sprawled out on the ground, lifeless eyes staring at the ceiling. It seemed that the FMK2 grenades were worth the ridiculous invoice Deckard had been given for them.

A third terrorist attempted to stand, but was quickly put back down by shots from three AK-103s and Deckard's VSS rifle. Outside, the staccato bursts chattered back and forth. The rumble of explosions shook the walls, showering them with debris. Deckard whistled. The chamber was packed to the gills with poppies ready to be processed into opium.

Another assault team bounded past as they exited through the door to move deeper down the corridor. Deckard was stepping out into the hall, when Frank literally ran into him with a sheen of sweat coating his face.

"We got him," Frank panted. " Khalis. MIK, and his boyfriend, too."

"Oh, well," Deckard lamented. "At least he died doing what he loved."

Frank snorted.

"Make sure you get a picture of him and DNA."

"That's fucking disgusting, I'm not doing that shit."

"I mean a blood sample, you fucking idiot-"

Screams were suddenly drowned out by gunfire.

Kurt Jager slowly opened one eye, then the other, before lifting his head up off the ground.

When the grenade rolled between his feet, the former sergeant had leaped to the ground, covering his head with his arms and hoping to avoid the inevitable blast. It never came. Looking at the Soviet pineapple grenade, Kurt reached out and picked it up. Pulling the pin, he hurled it back at the enemy.

The explosion rewarded him with the satisfying smell of sulfur. It permeated through the air, alongside the screams of dying insurgents.

By now Chuck had reset the support by fire line. The

machine gun teams opened up, holding the triggers down, significantly reducing the amount of incoming enemy fire as the insurgents were again forced to the ground to avoid the wall of lead cutting through the air above them.

Knowing it was time to move, Kurt pulled the pin on the initiator, beginning the burn sequence on the time fuse.

Alibek and Kanat could barely be heard above the gunfire, but the men got the message and once again began to advance. Jumping over the sand berm, Kurt and his adopted squad moved with one of the PKM gunners bringing up the rear. The terrain quickly narrowed into a single winding path that clung to the side of a cliff. He suspected it was much the same for the other squads as they cleared laterally, sweeping around the mountainside from one enemy position to the next.

During a break in machine gun fire, he heard something sliding down the cliff face and halted the squad. Pressing up against the side of the crumbling earth wall, the mercenaries watched as the bodies of two insurgents slid off the cliff, flailing like rag dolls, recent victims of Chuck's machine gunners in a kill zone somewhere above them.

Inching along the path, Kurt rounded a bend and found himself face to face with another sandal-wearing insurgent with a Mosin-Nagant bolt action rifle in his hands. Both gunfighters brought their weapons into play, Kurt beating him by a wide margin and drilling the man with three shots into his chest. Dropping his rifle, the insurgent slid off the cliff to be reunited with his comrades somewhere below.

A little more cautious now, the squad moved forward, all too aware that they were channelized along the mountain trail with nowhere to go, a suicidal leap of faith down the mountain excluded.

Back at the stronghold they had left behind, the charge set on the DShK exploded. Combat created a strange kind of time distortion. It seemed like they had been on the trail for an hour already, but in reality there was only a minute of time fuse to burn before the charge went off.

Rounding the next bend in the trail, Kurt afforded a quick glance around the turn before exposing himself. Sure enough, there was a sandbagged fighting position, three insurgents present and manning a ZSU-23 anti-aircraft machine gun. Nestled into the mountain face, it was out of the line of fire of Chuck's PKM crew.

Leaning back, he whispered in the lead Kazakh's ear, explaining the situation and plan of action in Russian before telling him to pass the information back to the rest of the squad. Hopefully it didn't result in a game of telephone where the tail gunner in the rear got a story about Genghis Khan's army sitting in a foxhole.

"Piet?" Kurt whispered into his handheld radio.

"The boys are a little busy. We got buggers crawling all over the mountain."

"Can you handle a few more?"

"Where are you?"

Kurt flipped on the infrared strobe light strapped to his assault rig.

"I just switched on my strobe."

"I've got you. Whole squad lined up on there, huh?"

"Look to your left from my strobe."

"A couple gun barrels in there, I think."

"Two barrels, one gun. A ZSU."

"Ah."

"Three bad guys, too. Give me a moment to get ready."

"Make it fast. Nikita is the only thing stopping the squad below you from being overrun."

Kurt palmed one of his grenades. Holding down the spoon, he yanked the pin.

"When you're ready," he said, keying the radio with his free hand.

Almost immediately a single shot thundered out from Piet's bolt gun. His concealed position in the rocks gave the remaining the enemy little hint as to where he was located. The survivors began shouting in excited Pashto as Kurt lobbed the Argentinean grenade into their fighting position. Half a second later, Piet fired

118

a second shot, cutting off the Afghan's conversation; a second after the grenade detonated ending any notion of it.

"*Tausend dank,*" the German called back.

Piet responded with something in Afrikaans that Kurt couldn't understand.

Moving in, the squad rapidly captured the insurgent position, finding it occupied by two corpses shot through the head and another riddled with shrapnel. Kurt put the PKM gunner facing forward to take on any new threats while he decided their next move.

Without any more explosives he did the next best thing to disable the massive anti-aircraft gun. Detaching the linked 23mm rounds, he lugged them to the side of the cliff and hurled them over.

Muzzle flashes were lighting up the night, tracer fire flying in every direction. So much gun powder was in the air that it wafted in with a nauseatingly sweet smell that seemed to stick to their sinuses.

A barrage of RPG rockets streaked over their heads.

Kurt wondered how much farther it was to the bunkers.

Chuck winced as one RPG whooshed just a few feet over his head before the second rocket hit the ground in front of the firing line, raining shards of rock down on them. While trying to blink his eyes and see through the toxic cloud left in the anti-tank round's wake, a third rocket exploded and threw him on his back, everything blinking out, going dark.

Coughing and wiping dust out of his eyes, the former Navy SEAL felt like he was moving in slow motion, his mind struggling to keep up with his surroundings. His hands ran over his body, out of instinct more than anything, checking for holes. Forcing himself to focus he looked at his hands but didn't see any red.

Looking back he remembered where he was.

A single PKM gunner was holding down the trigger, sending a constant volley of fire down range while the two other machine guns lay silent. Despite the nearly blinding flame shooting from the muzzle of the lone PKM, Chuck found it strange that he couldn't hear anything.

Arm over arm, he high crawled forward until he laid his forearm down on something hot. Retracting his arm in pain, he saw that he had crawled on top of one of the PKMs or what was left of it, the receiver hopelessly bent by a rocket propelled grenade.

Closer now, he saw the bodies of two gunners and one assistant gunner. The remaining AG was rolling back and forth holding his face. There was nothing Chuck could do for him at the moment. If someone didn't start putting more fire down range, they'd have more dead and dying friendlies on their hands.

Manning the remaining PKM, Chuck conducted a functions check on the weapon, his mind struggling to remember the procedure. Racking the bolt back and forth a few times was the best he could manage under the circumstances. Digging through the dead AG's kitbag, he found what was left of the 7.62x54 linked bullets.

To his right the remaining gunner ceased fire, smoke coming off the barrel as the Kazakh was also sent digging around for more ammunition.

Chuck slapped the fresh belt in the feed tray, slammed the feed tray cover closed, and racked the bolt to the rear.

Looking down the iron sights, he targeted an insurgent in the distance, only visible as a silhouette under the moonlight, but the outline of the RPG-7 was clear enough. The tube primed with a fresh rocket.

Pulling the broken wooden stock tight into his shoulder, Chuck went cyclic.

Adam ducked back behind the boulder as AK-47 rounds kicked dirt into his face.

Lower on the side of the mountain from Kurt's squad, they had found themselves in relatively open terrain, even if it sloped at a vicious angle, making it difficult for the troops to maintain their footing. Only a few lonely boulders and shallow depressions offered them any cover as the insurgents hammered them, apparently determined not to lose any more ground.

"Right side! Bound!"

On taking fire, the squad broke down into two assault teams. Adam and his team leaned out from behind the rocky outcropping and fired on the enemy positions. It looked to him as if the muzzle flashes of several enemy rifles had blinked out permanently but he wasn't sure.

The second assault team leaped out from the depression they had lain prone in, sprinting forward to a pile of rocks that had gathered at the base of the cliff to their right flank. Meanwhile, their only PKM gunner moved up behind them, searching for his own position.

Once Adam heard the automatic fire of the PKM, he signaled to his men that it was time to move. With their counterparts laying down suppressive fire, the team ran forward, bullets still kicking up geysers of dust around their feet.

When they collectively huddled behind the only boulder in otherwise open ground, Adam was relieved to see they had all made it, even if one young kid's face was covered in blood from god only knew what. At least he was still on his feet.

On each side of the boulder, a Kazakh got in the prone while another took a knee beside him. Leaning out from behind cover, they fired high and low. When one of the kneeling mercenaries went dry on his AK and had to reload, Adam pushed him back, taking his place. They continued to sweep gunfire at known, likely, and suspected, targets until the PKM gunner came up behind them, moving Adam and his buddy out of the way.

The gunner went cyclic again while the other fire team found relief in a nearby ditch created by weather erosion. Finding their new positions, the assault team joined the AK fire stitching several insurgents across the middle, weapons falling from lifeless hands.

"Let's go," Adam ordered taking the lead.

His team rushed forward, finding another small gully created by rainwater; it was knee deep at best. By now incoming fire was reduced to the occasional crack that sent dust showering down over the edge of the ditch.

"Grenades!"

The Kazakhs looked back and forth, not understanding until he pulled an FMK2 grenade from his chest rig and pulled the pin out. Tearing through chest harnesses, the Kazakhs primed their own grenades and waited for Adam's command.

Five frag grenades arced through the night, coming down on top of the bastion. Explosions knocked down haphazardly built stone walls and tore the insurgents limb from limb.

Amid the pained screams coming from their front, the other assault team made one last bound before the entire squad formed a skirmish line and stalked across the enemy position, double-tapping bodies to make sure, while in a few cases delivering a final *coup de grace*.

Halting the squad, Adam ran down the assault line, physically lifting them up and placing them where he felt they could best pull security in case of an enemy counter attack. Finding the kid with blood gushing down his face, he pulled out some gauze and began wiping his head down, looking for the source of the bleeding.

They turned in unison, as it sounded like strikes of thunder were slamming into the side of the mountain.

Deckard sunk the blade into the terrorist's throat until it stopped at the hilt.

Cutting through the thick muscles around the neck was somewhat more difficult than most people expected. Slicing the rest of the way through the enemy's carotid artery, Deckard grabbed him by his *dishdasha* and cast the insurgent aside.

The Kazakh who had been pinned underneath the insurgent got to his feet.

He looked pretty good for having a near-death experience or two.

With Frank distracting him, some of the assaulters had gotten spread a little thin. By the time he caught up with them, one of the mercenaries had already been sideswiped and taken to the ground.

Down the hall, assault teams looked back at him, giving the thumbs up. The bunker complex was clear. Finally.

"Alexander! Medic!"

The platoon sergeant came rushing forward, his right hand covered in blood. Pulling out a pair of medical shears, Deckard grabbed the Kazakh commando by the arm and sliced off his shirt sleeve. Alexander grunted, just now noticing the shrapnel wound on his forearm that was pumping a steady flow of blood.

Deckard began applying a field bandage while glancing up at Alexander's bloodshot eyes.

"We need security," he said, nodding. "Security. Casualties? Bullets?"

"Medic, yes."

Securing the bandage with its metal fasteners, Deckard patted the sergeant on the shoulder.

"Go."

The platoon sergeant took off, making sure his men pulled security rather than just standing around. Barking orders, squad leaders began to report in with any injuries their men had sustained and how much ammunition had been expended. Deckard already knew they had several fatalities.

"Frank?"

123

"Yeah," the Army veteran said, sticking his head out a door.

"Start collecting whatever you think is relevant."

"Already on it." Then as an afterthought, "We got a couple prisoners here, too."

Evidence exploitation was specifically not included in the Operations Order. They were supposed to kill and destroy everything they found. Scorched earth. His handlers didn't want him collecting up hard drives and documents, much less interrogating anyone.

They wanted him in an intelligence black hole and it wasn't his place to ask questions. He had other ideas.

"Shit, how the hell did that happen?"

"Guess they missed a couple guys during the initial sweep who had tried to hide."

"Remember that for the AAR."

Alexander came stomping back. What followed was an impossible to follow dialog, for any casual observer, that took place in English, Russian, and sign language, but the point was made. The troops expended about two magazines each. There were seven injuries, two dead. The platoon medic was working on the most serious injury.

Motioning for the platoon sergeant to lead the way, Deckard followed him to a critically wounded Kazakh, lying on the ground in the insurgent's kitchen area. The American stood back, silently observing.

The casualty had been shot through the abdomen, the bullet punching straight through his chest, leaving a ragged exit wound. The commando gasped, struggling to breath. Using the plastic packaging from a field dressing, the Kazakh medic taped it over the exit wound before pulling out a fourteen-gauge needle and carefully sticking it between the second and third mid-clavicle line below the collarbone.

A whoosh of air escaped from his chest cavity, a successful tension pneumothorax treatment that decompressed the chest cavity. As if someone had waved a magic wand, the casualty began to breath normally again. If the medic was able to keep his patient alive all the way to the field hospital in Bagram, Deckard would make sure both the medic and the former Green Beret who trained him received a bonus.

Deckard turned around, examining the other casualties that had been consolidated in the kitchen for triage and treatment. Some cuts and non-life threatening gunshot wounds; the five Kazakhs would survive. It was the final casualty that concerned the Samruk commander.

"Richie, what the fuck?"

"Bullocks, you bloody bastard," he gasped.

"That's a real gusher you got there."

The demo expert looked down at the mostly cauterized burn across his shoulder.

"One of those fucking barbarians of yours got too close when we were clearing a room," he spat through clenched teeth. "Got caught with his muzzle flash."

"Hold on a sec," Deckard said, sympathetically. "Let me help you with that."

Reaching down, he grabbed Richie by the ear and painfully dragged him to his feet.

"Does it feel better now?"

"I'll slot the whole lot of you wankers!"

"We don't have time for you to start sandbagging on us. Gather up whatever demo you distributed to the platoon. I want a line main down the corridor. You can probably find enough mines and rockets in the stockpile they have here to sympathetically detonate and bring the roof down. Got it?"

Richie stormed out of the kitchen, ego bruised, but reputation still about par for the course.

Back out in the hall, Deckard grabbed several Kazakhs who were standing by for further orders.

He had no way of knowing the status of the assault topside, but it was time to open the bunker doors and find out.

125

The only way left to go was up.

One of the Kazakhs leaned against the cliff face, making stirrups with his hands.

Putting a hand on the merc's shoulder to steady himself, Kurt stuck a booted foot in his hands and sprung upwards, searching for and finding purchase on a rock sticking out of the dirt. Scrambling up, he found himself on an embankment that looked to offer an easy way forward over open terrain.

Leaning over the edge, he gave his squad the thumbs up to begin climbing up.

Offering his hand, Kurt helped the next Kazakh up the slope, preventing him from sliding back down. Grabbing him by his belt, the German's bicep flared as he lifted and flung him onto the embankment. The Kazakh stood up, dusting himself off, when the hand of god seemed to swat the mercenary right out of the air, literally tearing him to pieces.

His face now splattered with his comrade's blood, Kurt rolled out of the way as large caliber rounds tore apart the ground he had occupied a fraction of a second before, churning up a cloud of dust in their wake.

The noise was deafening, twin barrels chewing apart everything in their line of fire. What had become merely sporadic bursts from the support by fire line now ceased completely, the assault's momentum lost.

Kurt rolled right, finding concealment if not cover behind a few rocks piled on top one another. Stealing a glance at the enemy's hard site, he confirmed what he already knew from sound alone. Another ZSU-23, so named for the dual 23mm anti-aircraft cannons, now turned on unarmored ground troops to ruthless and morale-depriving effect.

With its crew spinning the gun turret's wheels, the cannon rotated, raking the side of the mountain with fire, causing both platoons to find immediate cover or be taken apart like a holiday turkey. The ZSU was roughly one hundred meters away over sloping but open ground. A frontal assault was out of the question.

"Piet," Kurt called to the sniper team leader on his radio. "Do you see that other ZSU?"

"No, the elevation is too high. We can't see it from here but can sure as hell hear it."

Kurt considered his options. At any moment the ZSU gunners were liable to see him, and he didn't have any illusions about a few rocks protecting him from twin streams of 23mm bullets.

"Mendez, this is Kurt. Fire mission, over."

"Kurt, this is Mendez. Fire mission, over," the radio crackled.

"Grid mission," Kurt said, looking down at a topographical map. "42S 1350 7595." He rattled off the most accurate grid possible under the circumstances. Reaching into the pocket sewn onto the shoulder of his fatigue jacket, he retrieved the Silva compass he had carried since his orienteering days as a teenager. "253 degrees."

The compass only read degrees, so Phil would have to convert the number to mils for use by the mortar teams. Really it was the least of his problems. The anti-aircraft gun chopped away at the mountainside with a hailstorm of automatic fire.

He had a fat finger trying to read digits and analyze terrain features in the dark with just a small red lens flashlight. At any rate he was definitely into the red with this one.

"Danger close. Anti-aircraft cannon, no overhead cover."

"Roger."

The pause seemed to go on forever while he waited for Mendez to get his guns aligned.

"Shot, over."

"Shot, out."

"Splash, over."

Kurt's jaw tensed. There was a certain margin of error when using mortars at over a klick away and having them land right in front of you. He was only a hundred meters from the intended target.

The 82mm HE round went wide, landing to the right of the ZSU-23. Kurt blew out his cheeks. Not that he didn't have faith in the mortar section or anything.

"Splash, out. Left two hundred meters."

It was hard to adjust fire at night with limited equipment. He could have Mendez fire an illumination round first to light up the area, which would give him forty seconds or so of light to make adjustments, but in the meantime who knew how many hidden mercenaries he'd be buddy fucking if the light revealed their positions and subjected them to more than half a minute of fire from that cannon?

He'd just walk the rounds laterally until he got them behind the gun and then walk them in.

"Shot, over."

"Shot, out."

"Splash, over."

The mortar round exploded smack dab behind the ZSU.

"Splash, out. Drop fifty meters. Fire for effect."

"Drop fifty. Fire for effect."

While the mortar tubes could be heard bellowing in the distance, the rounds themselves didn't whistle as they soared overhead.

Three 82mm mortar tubes hung ten rounds apiece in rapid succession, the high explosives detonating all around the ZSU, rocking the gun and its crew with blast after blast that lit up the night, casting spooky shadows across the rocky ground.

By the time Phil and his boys were done, there probably wouldn't be enough of the bad guys left to soak up with a sponge.

"Let's go, lift that cross bar," Deckard ordered, stepping forward to help the five Kazakhs struggling with the heavy wooden beam. With a final grunt, the six of them were able to lift the beam from the metal braces it sat in and drop it on the tunnel floor.

The twin metal doors sounded like nails on a chalkboard as they were pushed open. Deckard gave the halt sign to the Kazakhs with a closed fist and began walking towards the mouth of the tunnel. Linking up with friendly forces in the middle of a firefight had an exceedingly high probability of some kind of blue on blue incident going down. Friendly fire usually wasn't.

Confronted with a series of ninety degree turns, he snaked through the passage, which was wide enough to drive a truck through. The turns were designed to prevent Uncle Sam from launching a cruise missile straight into the mountain fortress through the front door. Feeling his way through the darkness, he could hear the occasional *crump, crump, crump* of mortars.

The fight wasn't over yet.

Turning the last bend, Deckard could see the mouth of the tunnel and flipped on his radio just in time to hear someone who sounded like Mendez making a transmission. It was coming in garbled and undecipherable, due to him still being underground.

The ground shook hard enough to knock Deckard to his hands and knees. His first thought was an earthquake, until he registered thirty or more mortar rounds striking a position that couldn't be more than fifty meters from where he stood.

As the tunnel flooded with dust, a supporting beam jutting across the ceiling fell free, shaken loose by the onslaught outside and landed with a crash just inches from Deckard's head.

Coughing and spitting out dust, he snapped a green chem stick and tossed it outside the mouth of the tunnel, giving the all-clear signal.

"Any station on this net," he choked out, "this is Samruk Six."

"Hey, O'Brien. This is Kurt."

Apparently call signs had fallen by the wayside during the fog of war or something.

"You see my green chem?"

"*Scheisse.* Is that you?"

"Yeah."

129

"Are you okay? There was an anti-aircraft gun right next to the opening of the tunnel. I didn't even know it was there until you mentioned the chem stick you just threw out."

"I'll live. Move up and secure this area. As soon as that's done, I need you and Adam in here."

"Roger."

"Got it," Adam's voice came over the net.

Standing at the entrance to the tunnel, Deckard watched sunlight creeping over the horizon, casting long shadows across the mountains. It created a panorama that looked like a Nicolas Roerich painting. The infiltration and assault had taken all night. With pilots unwilling to fly into such a hotly contested area during daylight, they were stuck out in the hinterlands until nightfall.

Motherfucker.

Reconsolidation and reorganization took an additional forty-five minutes. Deckard knew from past experience that it would take some time to get their act together with the entire company spread out over difficult terrain. All troops had to be accounted for. Wounded needed to be identified and treated. Dead needed to found and gathered in a centralized location.

After writing the final numbers down on an index card, his eyes seemed frozen on the figures. Twelve dead, twenty-three wounded. Most of the wounded were ambulatory, but three, including the sucking chest wound he had observed earlier, were urgent surgical.

Sliding the card into the front pouch of his assault rig, Deckard knew the mission was far from over. Not until the helicopters set down at Bagram Airfield would he even begin to let his guard down.

Looking over his shoulder and down the corridor, he could hear the muffled sounds of Adam interrogating the two prisoners in a side room. The walls of the hallway were littered with empty crates and what looked like oversized sardine tins, all three platoons having replenished their AK magazines from the enemy stockpile. Richie directed the several Kazakhs assisting him in setting the charges, linking them off the line of detonation chord running down the hall.

Piled at the mouth of the tunnel were several crates of recovered 82mm mortar rounds.

"Richie, how long?" Deckard shouted down the hall to him.

"Five minutes," Richie shrugged.

"Kurt," he said, walking into the kitchen area that had been converted into the casualty collection point, "do me a favor and tell the platoon sergeants that I want all three platoons moved out of here. Find some fortified areas outside to hunker down in until nightfall and move the dead and wounded there. We're going to demo this place in ten minutes," he said, adding a buffer to Richie's estimation.

"No problem," Kurt said looking up from one of the wounded Kazakhs he was tending to.

"How is Chuck?"

"Concussion. He'll be okay in a few days. When you suffer that kind of blast, your brain gets bounced around and bruised pretty bad. That's why he looks drunk right now."

Looking across the room, Charles Rochenoire did indeed look like he'd been on all-night bender, and if Kurt had not vouched for the salvo of RPG fire he was in the middle of, Deckard probably wouldn't have believed the concussion story.

Supposedly, a Kazakh corporal had found Chuck wandering around the mountain absentmindedly with a PKM, firing at any rocks or sandbags that looked at him the wrong way.

"I also want Third Platoon to carry those recovered mortar rounds down to Mendez and then reinforce the mortar section."

"That's a hike."

"I don't want to leave him out there by himself all day. If need be, he can collapse back to our position. I don't like splitting our forces in half, anyway."

Moving back outside, Deckard took a knee as Third Platoon came pouring out behind him, carrying the crates of mortar rounds. The men looked tired but motivated, several of them walking wounded. Deep down he knew they were better then he deserved.

"Mendez," he said, keying the radio. "I'm sending Third Platoon down to you with a resupply."

"Ah, okay," the mortar section leader paused. With the sun cresting above the horizon, he probably hadn't waited a moment longer to light up a smoke. "Cool, I'll be waiting for 'em."

"Roger, out."

Deckard watched Third Platoon as they made their way down the mountain on the donkey paths, the mercenaries growing smaller as they got farther away until they looked like a line of ants. By then First and Second platoon were emerging from the bunkers, carrying the dead and dying on improvised stretchers. Chuck stumbled along with them incoherently. Frank brought up the rear. His assault pack was overflowing with potential intelligence sources he'd found on the objective.

"What have you got?"

"A laptop, a few hard drives I pulled out of computers, bunch of documents, a couple Thuraya satellite phones, took down serial numbers off of everything including the lot numbers off the ammo crates."

"Don't let that pack leave your sight. I want you and Adam all over that shit as soon as we get back to Astana."

"Right on."

"Alright, get up there and assist Kanat and Alibek for now."

"Groovy."

Frank grunted, following the Kazakhs up to another fortified area they had found.

Deckard moved back inside, personally checking each room to ensure that no one was left behind. All he found were the bodies of insurgents with flies crawling across their lifeless eyeballs.

"Adam," he said, finding the ad hoc interrogation room. "Move those two jokers out of here with the rest of the company.

This place is about ready to go."

The two prisoners had had their hands tied with some rope as they were not carrying flex cuffs or other conventional restraints. One of them was a grimy looking creep; the other an older guy with a beard.

"Alright," he responded momentarily, switching from Pashto to English. "Too bad. I'm about done with these guys. We could just leave them here and drop the roof on 'em."

"I can give you a few more minutes."

"Nah, I'll get them out of here."

"Have it your way."

Adam led the two Afghans out at gunpoint while Richie was uncoiling time fuse towards the entrance.

"Is this shit going to work?"

Richie gave him a *what the fuck* look.

"Awesome."

"You ready, boss?"

"Do it."

Richie turned the pins on the fuse igniter, and with a snap and fizzle, the time fuse began to burn.

"Three minutes," Richie announced.

"Three minutes until detonation," Deckard announced over the net as they cleared the tunnel entrance.

Following the same path as the two platoons, they climbed past the wreckage of the ZSU-23 that Mendez had mortared. Distracted, his eyes were drawn to the ridge line above them. They had good coverage from where they were but no vantage point at the summit of the mountain.

"Piet?" he called into his radio.

"Yes?"

"Think your snipers can cheat forward up to the top to the ridge and give us eyes on the other side of this hill?"

Static hissed over the radio.

"Yeah, give me a minute to get the boys moving."

"Roger, let me know when-"

Deckard's words were cut off as gunfire smacked the

133

ground on his flanks, the muzzle flashes clearly announcing the enemy gunfire from the ridge above them.

TWELVE

Unblinking dilated eyes fixated on the flat screen television.

The incoming feed was displayed in black and white with data plates arrayed along the edges of the frame, showing azimuth heading, altitude, wind speed, time on target, and other critical data. Fifty-something crazed Islamists flooded down the side of the mountain, clashing with Kazakh mercenaries and their American compatriots.

Flashes across the screen showed the exchange of gunfire, the Taliban gunmen taking the brunt of it as the Kazakhs fought back with a vengeance. Rockets shot through the air, some creating a splash to great effect as seen by the forward looking infrared system on the unmanned drone's observational camera package.

Larger impacts walked across the crest of the mountain, devastating the platoon of *mujahedin* fighters. Below, Hilux pickup trucks ground to a halt at the base of the mountain, each vehicle disgorging another small army of fighters. Just then, the entire mountain shuddered as the bunker system was collapsed by explosives. A dark pillar of smoke poured out of the tunnel's mouth.

His heart beat faster as the firefight raged on.

The footage fizzled across the screen for a moment before returning to normal. The drone circled overhead at twenty thousand feet, its sophisticated cameras zooming in close enough to see individual soldiers. With MIK gone, the Taliban knew there was a power vacuum and wanted to fill it, regardless of the foreign invaders who had done them the favor of disposing of their rival.

The disruption of the live feed distracted him for a moment. Losing focus, his heart rate began to return to normal. During the

135

height of the insurgency in Iraq he was able to watch every night, watch the various Army units trade fire with terrorists as they raided house after house. Some days he was lucky enough to see an IED blast kill some of the blood bags riding in the vehicles. Now he had to savor these moments.

It wouldn't be enough to watch a recording. There was nothing like watching death in real time.

His pulse quickened again, endorphins coursing through his bloodstream. The battle reminded him that this was foreplay compared to what was coming, what he was creating. The great culling would come, and his new plaything on the screen, fighting for its life, would be an instrument of that harvest.

Kammler swallowed hard.

The Gulfsteam 550 banked, finding a new heading toward Eurasia.

"Hey boss," -the drone was also intercepting all radio traffic coming from down below- "I know this isn't the time, but I don't want to move these guys again. The younger prisoner is a foot soldier, but it turns out the old guy is MIK's number two, his brother actually. What do you want me to do with these clowns?"

"Do 'em." It was the voice of the man he had met at the Grove. O'Brien.

On the plasma screen a flash of gunfire could be seen independent of the ongoing firefight.

"Done deal," the other voice answered back.

Kammler took a deep breath, forcing himself to relax.

This O'Brien was special. Another dumb animal to be expended, yes, but an animal with its uses. He was resourceful and ruthless; the Afghanistan mission had been a testament to that. He took the big risks, expecting the big payday.

Chuckling, he was unable to help himself.

O'Brien was so much more interesting than the swivel chair generals they propped up in front of Congress from time to time. They dazzled the powerless bureaucrats with dialect and baffled them with bullshit, so that meanwhile, the real work could be done.

Having his consultancy firm do a thorough background

check on Mr. O'Brien, they found that real work he had done. After an unremarkable military career, other than a bad conduct discharge, he had been picked up by one of the hundreds of fronts Kammler and his close associates used as needed. He ran with several death squads in areas troublesome for the IMF and World Bank before being picked up by a talent scout for wet work. Assassinations and bombings from what he understood, but it wasn't like they kept records.

Yes, if the pawn survived, O'Brien would be given an offer he couldn't refuse. A place in a highly structured system. Even after the collapse, some level of enforcement would be necessary.

Otherwise, he would have to be disposed of, along with many others who would know where the money was and where the bodies were buried. If he did a good enough job, Kammler decided he would put his name in the hat to replace their current operations manager, Chad Morrison, who seemed to be rapidly outliving his usefulness.

As the gunfire died down on screen, he leaned back in the leather seat.

According to murky details his intelligence experts uncovered in far corners of the globe, this O'Brien character quickly rose through the figurative ranks of corporate hit men, having contained several situations for a recent sitting President whose sloppy lifestyle threatened his administration. Thus was the cost of doing business, Kammler knew. Only the heavily compromised could be permitted into the Oval Office, so that leverage was there when he needed it.

That was one way to get the job done.

One of the others was to act as a proxy for extended international negotiations for the President, who himself was acting on policy decisions arrived at, not by Congress or his own Cabinet, but by the round table groups and foundations that Kammler Associates ran in the first place. In the true architecture of power, presidents were just middlemen who read teleprompters for those who made the real decisions.

For a moment Kammler felt weightless as the Gulfstream

began to drop altitude.

The talking points for this negotiation were exceedingly simple. Force the heads of state into a corner, use treaties and threaten economic sanctions to make them prove a negative to the world. An impossible imposition, of course, but that was the point. When they failed, and they would, Kammler would use the media outlets to intensify the level of rhetoric against the Muslim nation. Scare the milk cows of the Western world into war.

It had worked over and over again, he himself only using the mechanisms of deception and control to send Americans to war since Vietnam, but there were many before him. It began not long after the American Revolution but did not start in earnest until the Kennedy assassination.

Later, when the wheels touched down on the tarmac, Kammler turned off the television set, the firefight dying down. There would be more to come before O'Brien would be able to pull his people out, but he had other priorities.

Besides, it was just a sidebar to the main event.

THIRTEEN

Deckard came awake with a start as the lights were flipped on.

Recognizing the voices that had entered his office, he remembered to breathe.

"Hey, wake up," Frank said.

Sitting up on his cot, Deckard squinted, the light hurting his eyes. With a sinking feeling, the memories of the last seventy-two hours washed over him.

"We have flights to catch in a few hours," Adam announced. "If we are going to make it to the airport in Astana in time, we have to do this now."

"No problem," Deckard replied, swinging his legs over the side of the cot. He'd been awake for nearly three days by the time he finally got the chance to lie down. After a marathon like that, five hours of sleep left him feeling like he had awakened from a coma.

Looking down, he realized he was still wearing his fatigue pants and dirty socks. He didn't even remember coming back into his office. Landing in Astana, he had men who needed to be transported to the hospital. Bodies that needed to be brought to a morgue until they could be claimed by family members, if they had them.

"Since we got back, we've been reviewing data we recovered on the objective," Adam told him. "From talking to MIK's brother, I confirmed that they were running a smuggling route into Tajikistan where the poppies would then be distributed to Russia and Europe. The refining into opium could happen anywhere along the way from Uzbekistan to Kosovo."

"Pretty much what we thought," Deckard said, resting his elbows on his knees.

139

"Yeah, but we uncovered more from several of the hard drives," Frank replied. "You'll never guess who was paving the way for them."

"You mean making sure the shipments made it past coalition checkpoints?"

"You got it. Human Terrain Teams."

"The social scientists that work for the Department of Defense? Aren't they anthropologists and shit like that?"

"On paper, yeah," Adam cut in. "They map the 'human terrain', basically studying social networks. They build tribal link charts to help coalition forces understand the local people they are interacting with."

"Sounds benign at best and just another money pit of a defense contract at worst."

"But get this," Frank interrupted again. "We made some phone calls; the defense contractor who fields the HTT teams is Global Systems Inc. founded by Carl Weiss. He kicked the bucket a few years ago, so now his son Neil runs the business."

"HTT isn't a huge step for them," Adam continued. "This company is sort of an umbrella that has sent teams all over the world mapping different ethnic groups under various pretenses, usually under the banner of one Non-Governmental Organization or another."

"To what end?"

"Not sure yet, but we've uncovered a few clues. Turns out the Weiss family are a bunch of closet Nazis, going all the way back to their support for the Third Reich during the Second World War. Big supporters of the eugenics movement on both sides of the Atlantic."

"You mean racial hygiene?"

"A little more high tech, but yeah."

"This is bizarre. We started going after a warlord smuggling opium and found that they are connected to a US based firm that is mapping ethnic groups and had Nazi ties?"

"It gets better. Two HTT members in Afghanistan have died under suspicious circumstances in the last few months. Not corporate management types, but the scientists themselves. One was an anthropologist, and the other had a doctorate in political science. Officially, they are listed as dying from enemy action, but the family of one went to the press, calling bullshit. Some internet rumors surround the other death, but we can't be sure."

"They were going to go public, so someone took them out."

"Don't think it ends there. CEO Weiss, junior, and the late senior were and are members of the Council on Foreign Relations."

"I told you about our trio of employers. They are all heavily invested in CFR. Major stakeholders to say the least."

"Yeah, we're trying to figure out what that connection is, but it doesn't make sense."

"Think of it like this," Frank interjected. "We all know the Afghan Prime Minister is balls deep in the heroin trade. His brother is a warlord, doing most of the dirty work. The PM works for the US. I'm thinking our employers didn't like the competition they were getting from a rival CFR member."

"So MIK was a convenient beta-test for Samruk. Two birds with one stone, exactly the type of thinking you'd expect from the owners of mega-corporations who live on the interest created by their interest."

"We've also been tracking some atmospherics that may or may not be related," Adam added.

"What have you got?"

"Strange shit. A lot of smart weapons being moved in and out of Diego García. Maybe nuclear, but my sources don't run that deep. There have also been transactions of unusually large amounts of gold bullion in the last few weeks. Mostly out of the US to China and India."

"Sounds like the CFR goons getting on a war footing."

"What have you gotten us into?" Adam asked. "I need to know you're not in over your head here."

"We all are, but this is going to work."

"How can you know that?"

"Because no one has ever done this before. "

"Christ," Adam remarked, shaking his head.

"Anything else?" Deckard asked, standing up and stretching his arms.

"One other thing. Global Systems Inc. also fields a subsidiary called Information Technologies LLC out of Singapore. As near as we can tell, the entire company consists of three ex-CIA psychologists."

"Some kind of PsyOps deal?"

"Mind fuckers," Frank said, nodding.

"But we're not sure what they're up to yet," Adam finished.

"Let me know when you find out who they are targeting."

"Yeah, we need to get moving. We're heading-"

Deckard stopped him by holding up a hand.

"Don't want to know."

Unable to fall back asleep, Deckard went out for a run just as the sun was creeping across the horizon. None of the Samruk troops were out and about, most still asleep. Deckard had ordered them to grab some chow and hit the rack. They'd spend the next few days refitting and resting before being put on pass for a long weekend.

As he ran down the dirt road, Deckard's thoughts drifted to the events that had transpired in Afghanistan. After taking the objective and being denied extraction, they spent the day fighting off wave after wave of Taliban fighters. The Kazakhs were strong and knew how to soldier, but by the end of it, he was beginning to see the signs of battle fatigue and shell shock setting in. Getting some downtime was important in the following days.

Once nightfall came, Deckard called the Joint Operations Center in Bagram with an Iridium phone and coordinated for the pickup. Securing the landing zone several kilometers away, they'd moved the dead and dying first before getting the rest of the company into the Chinooks.

Most of the injured would be coming back to work over the next couple of weeks as their wounds healed. Others would need an extended stay in the hospital. He had already assured them that they would have a job when they came back. If they couldn't soldier, they could be trained as mechanics or work staff jobs.

Turning onto a side road, he could see their compound in the distance, the morning sun reflecting off the corrugated steel warehouse.

Twelve were coming back for their funerals. He had never felt so responsible and never felt as guilty as he did now for already contemplating how to replace them. They would recruit locally first, vetted relatives of current members, but he also wanted to bring in some more special forces types from stateside to make up for the lack of training in the other new recruits.

When the boys woke up, they'd clean weapons and confirm that all equipment was accounted for. If there were any losses, like a machine gun turned into scrap metal by an exploding rocket, they would have to be replaced. On the plus side, they managed to smuggle fourteen RPG launchers out of country right under the noses of the military police at Bagram Airfield.

Feeling his muscles begin to loosen up, Deckard picked up the pace spending the remaining distance back to the compound thinking of comments for the after action review in the afternoon.

Minutes later he arrived at the compound and took his first shower since getting back from Afghanistan. It was bad enough that he could smell himself from across the room. Thinking about the AAR and the meetings he needed to have with the Sergeant Major and his Executive Officer, he knew he had a lot of work to catch up on.

He just hoped Adam and Frank would be able to work fast before their employers called his bluff.

FOURTEEN

Adam brushed passed the bouncer and into Klub X-Rated.

Douk-Saga hip hop music from Cote D'Ivoire blasted over a boom box in the corner of the club while the lithe forms of African girls hid in the shadows of the club, dancing for foreign men in country on business from South America. Adam snorted.

The entire place stunk of cheap perfume and shame.

He appeared to move in slow motion as the strobe light blasted on and off as he approached one of the men huddled with a local girl. When the girl looked up at him with wide brown eyes, the mercenary motioned her away. Having spent more than a day or two in the shady establishment, she knew it was time to leave, quickly gathering her things and moving to the opposite side of the club.

"Hey," the man said in accented English. "Get your own girl, I already paid for her."

"You got a date with me tonight," Adam said, pushing the man back down onto his seat.

"Shit," the Colombian said with recognition. "You didn't tell me you were coming."

"I'll be sure to call ahead next time."

Eduardo was in the drug business, and at the moment business was good, Colombian Special Forces having eliminated his competition several months ago, taking credit for *El Jefe* himself in the process.

The small sub-Saharan nation of Guinea-Bissau had perhaps the lowest per capita income in the entire world and a government that was easily bought and sold.

Combined with the island archipelago off the coast, it was an ideal stop on the underground drug railroad leading to Europe. Eduardo was a facilitator, making sure that the air drops and midnight landings off the coast went off without a hitch.

"We need to talk," Adam stated. It wasn't the first time they'd had words or exchanged information. A bag man was more like a freelance import/export agent than a loyal minion to a drug lord back in southwest Colombia.

"What do you have for me?" the cartel member said, smiling.

"A waiver. Help me out, and I won't have to put you out of business."

"Bullshit-" the Colombian jumped to his feet. "You come here to threaten me? I own this country, what the fuck do you do?"

"Take a seat, Edward," Adam ordered, glancing back at the bouncers. "This isn't a good time to be a drug lord, if you hadn't noticed."

"What the hell are you talking about?"

"I'm talking about Ramirez. I'm talking about Khalis. I'm talking about running product through Croatia instead of Greece and pocketing the difference."

Eduardo's eyes went wild, his face getting redder.

"I just want information."

"What kind of information?" the bag man said, taking his seat, attempting to calm himself down.

"You know the term *cui bono*?"

"Get to the point."

"Why was Ramirez killed?"

"Doing business with the wrong people."

"There are not a lot of *right* people in your line of work."

"Some are more wrong then others. Some believe that competition is a sin."

The Colombian wore a lightweight tropical suit, with a gaudy florescent tie hanging loosely around his neck. The slicked back hair and sunglasses perched on his head even after sundown completed the image, carefully cultivated to let everyone know exactly who and what he represented. Reaching into his jacket pocket, he palmed a pack of cigarettes.

"What does that mean?"

"Ramirez was an idiot," he said, shaking loose a cigarette from the pack. "There is a system, an order to things, but he was too stubborn too see that. He invested his money in real estate and businesses; the rest he kept hidden around the countryside. Millions of dollars. Billions. By the caseload. If you want to stay in this line of work, you have to be smart."

Eduardo flicked his lighter and inhaled on the cigarette. "Smart like me."

"What do you do different?"

"I keep my money in banks. The right banks," he replied, exhaling a cloud of smoke.

"You give the bankers a cut for laundering your cartel's money."

"Of course, this is how it has always worked. Haven't you ever wondered why some cartels in Mexico get a free pass while others have the entire Mexican army deployed against them? Unlike in the US, the border is tightly controlled on the Mexican side to protect the corridors. It is much the same for us. If you know your place, you will be allowed to operate. This is the price of doing business."

It was a long shot, but with the information Deckard had given him and what he had uncovered on his own, Adam intended to follow the money.

"What are the *right* banks?"

"The *gringo* kind," Eduardo laughed.

Frank climbed down the fold-out stairs and moved to the side of the Learjet, standing watch as the heat mirage rippled up from the asphalt airstrip.

As his principal stepped off the aircraft and walked toward the small terminal, he followed one step behind while the two other members of the Personal Security Detachment covered both flanks, keeping a sharp lookout as they approached immigration.

"Welcome to Nauru," the clerk manning the desk said smiling.

The American stepped forward, handing over all four passports to the customs official. It was a slow day for him as the plane from Brisbane to the island nation only flew twice a week. Being in the employ of United Bamboo and having access to one of their private jets certainly cut down on time spent waiting for flights to remote airfields.

As the three Taiwanese and one American stood sweating on the tarmac, the official quickly stamped the four passports before handing them back to Frank. He knew the deal. VIP's don't get dicked around with.

The protection detail moved in formation around Kao, heading toward the waiting Mazda van. Kao was a big name in United Bamboo, the largest of the Triads. Chen and Kenny were both made men in the organization that was as well known for counterfeiting and copyright infringement as drug trafficking and kidnapping.

Frank was just along for the ride, working out a deal with a fellow contractor to call in sick at the last minute and recommend him for the job. A perfect cover needed to infiltrate the world's smallest country.

Taking the key from the attendant, Kenny slipped behind the wheel while Frank held the door open for Kao. After Chen followed him in, he shut the sliding door and rode shotgun next to the Taiwanese bodyguard.

Pulling onto the lone road that ringed around the six kilometer circumference of the island, they passed a Chinese restaurant, which led to an exchange between the Taiwanese in their native language. Feeling like a fifth wheel, Frank could only guess what the conversation was about. Chinese immigrants operated restaurants all over the world, many of them a front for the Triads. Others were a front for Chinese intelligence. Many of them probably acted as a proxy for both.

Speeding by the turquoise waters, Frank was comforted by

the pistol riding in a shoulder holster under his jacket. Despite the tranquil setting he had a feeling he would need it.

After Western powers had raped Nauru of what little mineral resources it had, the islanders were left to fend for themselves with little if anything to bargain with. They found one avenue to quick cash in recognizing the sovereignty of small breakaway republics and semi-autonomous zones on the international stage, such as Nagorno-Karabakh, in exchange for cash payments. They were also one of the first to join the "coalition of the willing" in support of the US invasion of Iraq.

The other method devised by the crafty island government was to set itself up as a tax haven. Foreign investors could deposit money tax free, even open their own banks on the island. No questions asked. The new policy had made the island republic the host of a constantly revolving cast of shadowy figures from dozens of countries.

This shady character's presence seemed almost preordained. The son of a city councilman in Taipei, he had been photographed soliciting a prostitute. The picture was splashed all over the hot sheets the following morning, so the Nauru job was just what Kao needed until the heat died down back home.

Passing a dilapidated-looking concrete bunker built by the Japanese during the Second World War, they spun in front of the main doors of the island's only hotel. Several other vehicles sat idling, tough guys in dark suits and shades smoking cigarettes as they waited for their own benefactors to arrive.

Doors swung open as the delegation climbed out of the van and strutted into the lobby. When the uniformed woman behind the desk saw the Taiwanese, she tried to hand Kao the key to his room.

Snatching it from her hand, Chen walked off to scout out the room and conduct his security checks while the crime boss signaled to Frank that he wanted a drink.

"The boss likes Johnny Walker Black," he told the receptionist.

Nodding, the woman quickly disappeared into the back

148

room.

Frank looked back at his temporary boss.

The islanders must have had run-ins with United Bamboo in the past. They were the largest crime syndicate in Asia, next to Yamaguchi-gumi of Japan, operating through ancient and complex business schemes that the average man or woman in the Orient knew better than to cross.

When the woman reappeared, Frank held his breath. She was holding a glass of Scotch on the Rocks. He couldn't remember if Kenny had told him if Kao liked ice or not. Breathing a sigh of relief, Frank watched the crime boss smile at the receptionist as he took a sip from the glass.

Kenny shouted from around the corner, giving them the all clear. Chen began following Kao up to his room, pointing Frank back to the van.

"Bags."

Frank mumbled something while walking back to the third-hand Mazda van.

At the moment he was part of a growing fad, or a victim of one, as it were. Any Asian businessman of stature was hiring men with Western features as subordinates to fill their staff requirements in the rapidly expanding Chinese economy. Not to be outdone, the Taiwanese seized upon the status symbol as well. This included Triad mob bosses occasionally hiring round-eye bodyguards, especially when conducting business with foreigners.

The disgruntled employee lifted the bags from the van, hoping that the embarrassment was worth it and glad that none of his pals were around to witness it.

Looking up from his computer screen, Deckard held his phone to his ear while distracted by a knock at the door.

"Come in."

Pallets of ammunition were beginning to flood in on a weekly and then daily basis. The mercenary soldiers had been firing even more ammunition than he had forecast, which was well in excess of what an infantry battalion would consume. As commander he had no complaints about the current levels of expenditure, but now he had to dispatch a detail back to the capital to facilitate another pickup.

The door opened and one his interpreters walked in, closely followed by one of the Kazakhs in his woodland fatigues. Deckard terminated his call with a diesel fuel supplier in Russia, motioning for the two men to take the seats in front of his desk.

"What's up?" Deckard asked.

"Lev asked to speak with you," the interpreter announced. Kevin was a second-generation Russian-American, his parents having made sure he went to the best schools. He had obtained a degree in chemistry and lived comfortably in San Diego until getting laid off by the chocolate company he had worked for. With the economy hit hard he had been forced to find new avenues of employment, this time making use of his bilingual background rather than his scientific one.

"He would like to resign."

Deckard frowned.

"Is everything okay?"

Kevin translated, Russian being spoke between them for a moment before the interpreter turned back to Deckard.

"He says that he respectfully wishes to break his contract early and is willing to accept a penalty, but he feels he can no longer be a part of the company."

"I'm willing to accept his resignation if this is really what he wants, but did he give a reason? If he has family problems, we can work out a period of leave for him."

More Russian exchanged between the two.

"No, he says that combat was more frightening then he could have imagined. He says that he hasn't slept right since getting back to Kazakhstan. He has a family to take care of."

Now he could place the Kazakh soldier. Lev was in

Alexander's platoon when they had taken down MIK's bunker. He was the one who had been taken to the ground by an insurgent, until Deckard showed up.

"Tell him that this is somewhat normal. Many soldiers have this type of reaction to their first time in combat."

Lev said something in Russian, shaking his head back and forth.

"He says this isn't true," Kevin translated. "He says that you weren't afraid at all. You didn't care of you lived or died, he says."

"Please," Deckard began to explain. "I was afraid as anyone else."

Lev and Kevin looked at each speaking back and forth while Deckard waited.

"He doesn't believe you."

Maurice kicked, churning the water behind him as he rolled over and into a backstroke.

The sun hung low in the sky casting the clouds in brilliant orange, red, and pink hues. Warm water rippling over him, he stopped swimming and allowed himself to float while the sun continued its descent toward the horizon.

Not bad for a dead man.

Not bad at all.

A smile crossed his lips, thinking about the sunset, thinking about how he had found himself on a remote island in the Pacific Ocean. Fate was a funny thing, he thought, soaking in the remaining sunlight. A criminal indictment in New York had sent him strolling down a path that allowed him to shrug off his bitch of an ex-wife and schedule himself for a permanent vacation.

The New Yorker had many jobs over the years. Investor, stock broker, currency speculator, and investment adviser were all positions he had held over a forty-something year career. He'd even been a chairman of NASDAQ for a time and held a membership at the Council on Foreign Relations. Everything was going great until it wasn't anymore.

Tranquilo, that was the word. That was what he had found at Nauru.

Maurice had been busted by the Feds for running the largest *ponzi* scheme in world history. After driving several businesses into the ground as a young man, he had found himself with a equally young and very pregnant bride. There was more than one way to make a living as it turned out, and being golfing buddies with the guys at the Securities and Exchange Commission didn't hurt. Everyone else couldn't or wouldn't confront what many secretly knew. Why would they when so much money was being made by his investors?

The clouds moved slowly overhead, giant cotton balls flush with color as the sun sunk toward the sea. Nauru was a nice place, if tainted by the people who actually lived there. Still, it beat a life sentence in a federal prison. He had a bid in to buy an island in French Polynesia, so this hideaway was really just a stepping stone to more permanent fixtures.

Yeah, everything was going great until some prick in a competing investment firm dropped dime on him to enough people in the SEC, FBI, and Treasury Department that they couldn't ignore the warning signs anymore and moved in. He had been put on house arrest while they finished conducting their investigation, ankle bracelet and all. While he was cooling his heels on the Upper East Side of Manhattan, the Feds were seizing his assets, the ones they could find anyway.

Flipping over he began lazily swimming back to his bungalow. It was a squat one story home painted blue and green that sat right on the edge of the shore, the waves washing right up to his deck at high tide. It was spartan compared to his old apartments, estates, and mansions, but he couldn't complain.

As he got closer to trial, his lawyers told him in no uncertain terms that his goose was cooked and he needed to enter into a plea bargain with the Feds if he didn't want to spend the rest of his life in a federal pound-you-in-the-ass penitentiary. Then as he prepared to turn state's evidence on every other crook he knew on Wall Street, a guardian angel arrived.

Of course his fellow Council on Foreign Relations member was a little overweight and he had never heard of a guardian angel who smoked Cuban cigars, but the deal he had offered was a lot sweeter then what the Feds were promising.

Not able to take it anymore, he committed suicide.

Or at least a stunt double did. Kammler hadn't told him who the guy was, and frankly he didn't care. With a handful of medical officials and police officers bought off, he had been put on a private jet out of the country that night. The islanders were more than willing to accept a white guy with a brand new passport and no history whatsoever. He wasn't the first and they knew he wouldn't be the last.

Winston Churchill had called them the High Cabal. Dwight D. Eisenhower had called them the Military-Industrial complex. Whoever the hell they were, Maurice was damned glad he was a member because they looked out for him, knowing he could bring the whole house of cards down with him if he ratted on the hyenas infesting the financial sector.

Reaching the shore he stood up, trudging through the thigh deep water.

The whole damn house of cards, he laughed to himself.

It was a lie he knew, the things they said about him in the papers. There was an even bigger *ponzi* scheme then his, and it was called the global economy.

Walking towards his bungalow, he squinted trying to ascertain if he was seeing correctly.

"What the hell do you think you're doing?"

Some clown was sitting on his lawn chair, drinking his beer, and listening to his stereo right there on his front porch overlooking the ocean.

"Just having a beer," the younger man said. "Lighten up, Maurice."

The former stock broker swallowed.

"I don't know who you think you're talking to. I'm Wesley-"

"According to your new passport, I know. But it turns out the rumors about your death being faked weren't just rumors. One of your lawyers had a few details and didn't mind some money getting thrown his way."

"Mother-"

Frank grimaced as Maurice's pasty white breasts swung back and forth as he began to shout.

"Don't blame him, he just put us on the right path. It was one of your bankers in Argentina that finally led me to your vacation getaway in Nauru."

"And you are?"

"Private security contractor," he answered, swallowing a swig of beer. "My boss gave me a few hours off. He thinks I'm banging out a prostitute, a pastime near and dear to his heart."

"Son of a bitch," Maurice growled, reaching for the intruder.

"I don't think so," Frank said calmly. Somehow as Maurice had reached for the interloper, Frank had slid a hand under his shirt, drawing a pistol. Maurice didn't know what it was called, just that it was small, black, and deadly. "Have a seat," the mercenary said reassuringly.

Eyes drilling into the stranger, Maurice cautiously sat down in the lawn chair next to him before turning as they both looked out across the ocean just as the last sliver of sun disappeared.

"Isn't this nice," Frank commented. "I knew we could be buds."

"What do you want?" Maurice asked, nearly choking on his words, his world crumbling around him. Again.

"Just wanted to have a talk."

"About what?"

"About twenty billion, the twenty billion the Feds never found out about."

"You want my money?"

"You're offering?" Frank asked with a raised eyebrow.

"I'm no danger to anyone out here."

"You are, even if you don't know it." The commando shifted in his seat, "I want to talk about your offshore accounts and what you know about DNA synthesizers."

FIFTEEN

Mousa Zerktouni was one of five separate names attached to five separate lives committed to his photographic memory.

The Mousa alias was French-Moroccan. The others were British, French, Saudi, and Indian. He spoke the languages that accompanied each name, each identity. Each had an entirely different life that went along with the name. Families, schools, lovers, career highs, and personal lows. They were all seared into his mind with laser precision, his recall tested regularly by his handlers.

His fingerprints were not his but had belonged to a Chinese cadaver and were surgically grafted into his fingers one by one, allowing him to bypass the biometric systems in various airports without raising any red flags. Likewise, his face had undergone numerous reconstructive surgeries, making it nearly impossible to ascertain what his real age was.

He was deniable, invisible, and if need be, expendable.

The dark skinned man was a weapon to be used as it suited his benefactors, despite his realization that ultimately he was tool, if a useful one. He had compromised himself and his soul to the point that it was too late by the time he understood what he had done. Now he had a family as closely monitored as he was, virtually held hostage without their knowledge.

Steering the boat towards the shore, he kept the last vestiges of daylight to his back as he cut the engine and let the waves guide him towards the beach. He'd carefully studied the relevant sea charts and knew precisely where to dump a body overboard where the current would make sure it was swept away for good.

Usually he was used for completely deniable operations. In those cases not only would the assassin remain undiscovered, but

156

the methods used would be likewise undetectable. Most of the time, the fact that a murder had taken place would never be discovered, the death being attributed to a drug overdose or suicide. A few times, a surgically altered doppelganger had been inserted to take the target's place after his execution.

Other times a message was sent with, say, an icicle dipped in curare and jabbed into one of the target's kidneys. In still other cases, a target could be eliminated with a portable defibrillator the size of a pack of cigarettes that would induce heart attack. A variety of poisons were also made available to him.

Every tool has its use.

Ricin, slipped into the food of a federal investigator. A single shot placed to the back of the head of a political organizer. By his count he averaged five to ten kills a year, only being called in when they wanted the job done right.

As his mind wandered, he began to wonder if they had others like him. Other assassins deployed across the globe, their families with invisible daggers swinging over their throats, just like his own.

It was dark by the time he dropped into the water and dragged the small boat up onto the shore. For this assignment no elaborate measures or exotic weapons would be necessary. From the limited information he had been provided, he could infer that the target was already dead and buried on paper. Now they wanted him physically dead and his body disappeared.

It felt somewhat sloppy to him. Normally he disposed of bodies with industrial grade acid, used for burning through metal at construction sites. In other instances he had to improvise by bribing employees at fish paste plants. He had used a wood chipper in one of his first assignments, an experience he was not keen to repeat any time soon.

There were a number of irregularities with his current mission, but it wasn't his job to ask why.

Stalking across the beach, he arrived outside the house and pulled his suppressed .22 caliber pistol from its holster. With the suppressor and the subsonic ammunition, he could effect a nearly silent kill.

His hand froze on the door handle.

Through the screen door he heard voices.

Complications.

"There were multiple shipments," a gruff voice said in response to an unheard question. "Some of them were decoys, like the one in Denmark. Others were funneled eastward."

"Where?" A younger voice.

"Shanghai and Singapore. I don't know where the final product was to be assembled."

"It's not a product; it's a weapon, so stop beating around the bush."

"They know someone is onto them but don't know who. For now they are writing it off as the cost of doing business, but who knows for how long? I'm sure they are actively looking for you."

Mousa clenched the latch and eased it open, his target making the decision for him. Any confederates were to be sanitized as well. He found himself in a small kitchen with a half-sized refrigerator and electric stove. A six pack of beer sat sweating on the counter, one bottle missing. The voices continued from somewhere deeper in the house.

"What are the vectors for transmission?"

"I don't know, I've been cut out of the loop, but it could be anything. The water supply is something they've looked at in the past."

The assassin edged around the corner, looking into the living room.

Maurice stood talking, singing like a canary. Sweat rolled down his face in droves as he talked to a man still obscured behind the wall. He was revealing information for the first time that he had tried to convince even himself that he didn't know. Mousa knew what he had to do. His family had already been inoculated against what was coming, and so his loyalty had been bought and paid for.

Taking careful aim at the target's head, he sighted in just

below the earlobe and stroked the trigger a half dozen times in a blindingly fast succession that he spent hours a day training for. The multiple shots blasted from the small pistol fast enough to appear as a single shot that plowed into the target, toppling him to the floor with a hollow thud.

Before he could shift his weight on the balls of his feet and target the second man, two bullets tore through the drywall above him and shattered the beer bottles sitting on the counter, spraying glass and foam in all directions.

The assassin cursed.

A professional.

Frank fired two snap shots from the hip before assuming a two-handed modified weaver grip on his pistol. Dark colored glass spun across the kitchen floor as he moved forward.

When a shoulder and half of a face appeared from behind the wall, he changed direction in mid stride, strafing towards the wall as several bullets coughed from the gun in the assassin's hand. The ex-soldier returned fire a second time, the blasts rendering him temporarily deaf, his shots reducing the door frame to splinters. Preparing to fire through the wall again, now knowing the shooter's position, he heard the killer's footsteps bounding back through the kitchen over the ringing in his inner ear.

Spinning on his left foot, he faced the second entrance to the kitchen as the door was flung open. The assassin rushed forward, eyes wide with surprise at being confronted face to face. Frank squeezed the trigger, his shot grazing the side of the assassin's head and taking off most of his left ear.

Recoiling in pain, his attacker darted to the side, firing just a moment too late as the American mercenary took hold of his wrist in a vise-like grip. Frank fought to bring the Glock 19 back into the fight as assassin reached for his wrist as well, wrenching

Frank's gun hand away from him.

As the two jostled back and forth for control, the silenced . 22 caliber pistol spat bullets that whizzed through the air with each trigger pull, punching holes in walls and demolishing a television set. Only a quick shift at the hips saved Frank as the assassin attempted to knee him in the groin in a bid to gain the upper hand. With the last shot expended, the assassin's pistol went dry.

Releasing his wrist, Frank struck his attacker with an open palm to the face before pushing him into the wall, sheet rock caving in under their weight.

Dropping the .22 to the ground, the assassin launched his own attack, a chop of his hand hitting him that instantly numbed Frank's wrist, causing him to lose control of his own firearm. The Glock went skidding across the floor.

The dark-skinned man pivoted and dived for the pistol.

Bringing a knee above his waistline, Frank stomped down on the assassin's hand just as his fingers wrapped around the pistol's grip. Screaming with new pain, the killer flung himself back around, blood leaking from what was left of his ear; he slammed down in a hammering motion at his leg.

Frank yelped as a blade sliced a shallow line through his calf muscle, a small knife appearing in the assassin's hand from somewhere in the folds of his clothes.

Trying to get back to his feet, Frank ignored the pain and delivered a second kick to the assassin's face before bending over and dropping his heel down hard on his knife hand. Bones cracked as he came down, placing his knee on his attacker's neck.

The assassin thrashed under Frank's weight as he gripped the Glock and shoved the muzzle under the would-be killer's chin.

In that last moment, he was unable to determine if he saw resentment or relief in those dark eyes.

The 9mm round blasted through the assassin's skull, splattering the wooden floor with bone fragments and brain matter before his head dropped to the ground like a paperweight.

A friend had once called the city-state Disneyland with the death penalty. Adam shuddered to think what would happen if he was charged for espionage in a country that put such a premium on law and order.

Singapore was a Southeast Asian enclave of mixed ethnic groups, complicated investment schemes, and cutting edge technology. Stretching out on a narrow peninsula, Singapore acted as a choke point from the Indian Ocean into the Pacific, connected by the Malacca straits. High tech mercantilism existed comfortably alongside low tech piracy.

Billed as a luxurious tourist attraction at the southernmost tip of the Asian continent, Sentosa Island endeavored to attract wealthy expatriates with low tax rates, bank privacy laws, and modern conveniences. Taking the cable car in earlier in the day, Adam noticed that the fauna of the island may have been beautiful, but he couldn't ignore the black water washing up on the artificial beaches or the oil refineries on the nearby mainland.

Waiting for nightfall, he pitched a small rock, sending it arcing through the darkness where it bounced end over end into the landscaping in front of the target building.

The wireless data harvester, or slurper as it was called in the technical surveillance field, rolled close enough to the entrance of Information Technologies LLC that it would be able to pick up data as soon as employees began coming to work in the morning. The artificial rock was packed with expensive electronics that were capable of sucking data right out of the air, especially with people now so dependent on wireless networks.

The Colombian in Guinea Bissau had led him to a Turk in Ankara, who had in turn led him to an incarcerated Russian in Thailand. He got deeper and deeper, finally coming full circle, back to the Global Systems subsidiary in Singapore. Pooling information with Frank and Deckard, they realized that there were still a lot of blank spaces in their intelligence map regarding the

161

enemy's order of battle, but the emerging picture chilled them to their core.

The slurper was disguised as a rock by coating the device with a plastic resin and airbrushing it a suitable grayish brown color. The battery would keep it operating for nearly a week while it harvested information from wireless routers, cellular phones, and any other devices that came within range. Addresses, telephone numbers, passwords and more would be sent to a repeater installed down the street before being bounced via satellite to one of Adam's encrypted email accounts.

They knew that several former CIA psychologists operated out of the Singapore office. Now it was just a question of discovering what they were doing there.

Opening his netbook, Adam connected to his own wireless network, quickly establishing contact with the repeater now synched up with the slurper lying next to the building. The screen already displayed some data, most of it, of course, useless.

Sighing, Adam began walking towards a cafe he had spotted earlier.

He had work to do.

Sixteen

The cavernous hanger sitting in an empty corner of Astana International Airport was now packed with sixty Iveco assault trucks, many still packed with plastic wrapping over the seats and partially incomplete with gun turrets and other components unassembled.

British mechanics and welders combed the hanger as the clang of metal on metal echoed throughout the open spaces and sparks flew into the air.

Deckard and Sergeant Major Korgan oversaw the delivery and installation of critical vehicle assemblies as they examined the trucks with the foreman from the British firm that produced them. The trucks had been put together *in situ* back in the UK, with only smaller components needing to be furnished and put together after transport.

Samruk's commander drank another gulp of coffee from a Styrofoam cup. He had been managing on only a few hours of sleep a night. The combat training had been completely turned over to his contractors, who were quickly working themselves out of a job. The Kazakh mercenaries turned out to be quick learners.

Once the umbilical cord was finally cut, he'd keep some of the Western mercenaries on the payroll to teach specialized courses in advanced communications, technical surveillance, and certain infiltration techniques. Of course they could also break their contract and sign on as soldiers, provided they were willing to accept a change in role and work under a Kazakh sergeant.

In a matter of hours the trucks would be completed, and he'd need the contractors to begin a new program of instruction that covered mobility training. Tactical off-road driving was a skill like any other, one that soldiers needed to acquire.

The Sergeant Major climbed up on the hood of one of the

assault trucks and watched a welder use an oxy-acetylene torch. Korgan muttered something barely audible over the construction underway.

"He wants to know what the welder is doing," Deckard told the foreman. He had been learning, as well, his Russian gradually improving beyond the level of a chimpanzee.

"Welding on the brackets," the foreman said, pointing to the metal ammo can holders. "It will move with the entire turret, but this is just the mounting bracket for the can. You can have the links feed from whichever side you like."

Deckard had familiarized himself with the vehicles, from front to back, and grilled the sales managers before placing the order. He'd even called the CEO and the senior engineer in the UK to get their assurances faxed to him on paper. Thankfully, they had delivered, if barely meeting the deadline stipulated in the contract. Over the years he had seen plenty of defense contracts and arms deals go bad.

The trucks were lined up in the hanger, like a legion of hulking Roman soldiers, waiting for orders.

They came painted in a kind of dull tan color that was pretty much standard for NATO forces operating in the desert. He would have them repainted as necessary.

The front end was fairly standard in appearance, looking like an Iveco LMV with armor plating and bulletproof glass made out of layered polycarbonate thermoplastics that surrounded the cab. Inside, the driver and passenger would sit with a communications suite between them. The metal rack with the mounting brackets was in place even if the encrypted radios themselves hadn't arrived yet.

On the front of the trucks was a heavy duty winch, dual visible and infrared headlights for driving under night vision goggles, and several antennas.

Directly behind the cab was the gun turret, fitted with a rotating ring that the gun pedestal itself rested on to provide three hundred and sixty degree coverage by the machine gunner. The gunner was left standing, unless he improvised a strap to sit on while the turret was rotated manually by depressing a lever. Storage space was provided for a half-dozen cans of ammunition.

Behind the gun ring were eight seats made of bulletproof ceramics that sat back to back, four on each side facing outward. The metal struts that also supported the gun turret ran over the top of the seats, providing some overhead cover, in case of rollovers and additional storage space, probably where most squads would place the spare tire. Running along the sides of the truck were two long storage compartments where the assaulters' boots would rest while seated. The metal shelves could house additional ammunition, fuel and water cans, military rations, or other mission-specific equipment.

Seat belts were provided as Basic Issue Items along with tow bars, tow straps, and jacks, but how the men used and carried them would be left to platoon SOPs and the recommendation of Deckard's instructors.

On each flank was an additional swing arm that could mount machine guns for the assault team to utilize while in transit, providing even more firepower. For the time being each pedestal would be fitted with a PKM machine gun, at least until they got their hands on something heavier for the gun turret.

The back of the truck provided some more storage space for recovery equipment and metal stirrups for any hangers-on.

He had seen lots of military vehicles over the years, but these were the most versatile assault specific trucks he had encountered. Four wheel, all terrain, day/night, long range, and with an emphasis on offensive capabilities, they even looked nasty.

While the welder continued his work, they watched another technician installing a larger antenna on the back of the truck. The jammer it connected to inside the cab created a twenty five-meter electronic bubble around the truck, preventing any signals from reaching any potential remote-detonated improvised explosive devices they might encounter. On the other hand there was not much they could do about command-detonated IEDs other than use tactical convoy formations and mount an effective counter attack.

With the final shipment arriving less then twelve hours ago,

165

they would soon have enough trucks operational to have the entire battalion outfitted, with an additional three medical evacuation vehicles, one going to each company.

Korgan lit up a cigarette, blowing off industrial safety standards, but that was how they rolled and no one was going to say anything to him about it. The foreman glared enviously for a moment, then back toward Deckard questioningly. Finally, he lit up one of his own.

Deckard grinned.

He loved it when a good plan came together.

"To use a proper ramming technique, you need to slow down to about ten miles an hour."

The Kazakh mercenaries, turned students, huddled around the sand table with open note books.

"As the driver slows down, he needs to look out over the center of the hood to make sure he is on target with the rear quarter panel of the blocking vehicle."

Gordan demonstrated the desired result on the sand table. Lines had been drawn out in the sand to represent roads. Two toy cars were used to show the friendly assault truck and the enemy vehicle blocking the street. This was one of the few techniques Deckard had forbade the ex-Special Forces Team Sergeant from actually training the men hands on. The cellophane had just been peeled off the trucks, and the mechanics were not to earn their pay quite yet.

"If possible, make contact with the lighter end of the vehicle. The trunk will be easier to push, with the engine being the heavier portion in the front. Now at the last moment, just as you make contact with the blocking vehicle, accelerate and push through the blocking position."

On the sand table he showed them how the blocking

vehicle would spin around and out of the way, allowing the assault truck to power through and clear the blockade.

"Do you have any questions?"

The former Master Sergeant had taught the Kazakhs the Standard Operating Procedures on the sand table, having eaten up most of their morning covering down driver drills, down gunner drills, recovery drills, bailout techniques, and much more, breaking each drill down into easy-to-digest steps with model cars and plastic army men.

It may have looked amateurish, but the classes were not designed to insult the intelligence of the Kazakh soldiers. The same training methods were applied when teaching the soldiers of First World armies.

"No questions?" The translator repeated his request while he watched them put away pens and paper.

"Good, pack up and go see Kurt."

Sitting down beside the recently completed barracks, Gordan gulped down some Gatorade as the Samruk soldiers began moving out with their NCOs to the next training station. The battalion would spend the week doing circuit training, moving from one station to the next.

They would be given a basic familiarization with the trucks and the recovery equipment by Richie, practice actual recovery methods of damaged vehicles with Kurt, and conduct driving training with Mendez and Chuck, both on and off road. Next week came live fire drills, reacting to ambushes and IEDs, as well as conducting night driving training.

As the next group arrived around the sand table from Richie's station, Gordan set down the Gatorade bottle.

"The first subject we will cover here is pre-mission checklists," Gordan began.

Five assault vehicles glided slowly and silently over cracked asphalt, running off battery power as they neared the objective.

Wind howled across the steppes, blowing through the brick buildings. A door slammed shut repeatedly somewhere in the distance, echoing through the empty streets.

Stopping, the assault trucks rocked gently on their suspension, and rubber soles of combat boots slapped against the street, quickly moving into squad formations. The mercenaries left the trucks behind, manned by the driver, gunner, and truck commander riding in the shotgun seat.

Splitting into two elements, the platoon moved down both sides of the street in columns, pulling cross coverage above on the buildings opposite of them, rifle muzzles sweeping across open windows and rooftops. The senior sergeant stepped it out with his men trailing behind as he led them towards the objective.

Moving tactically down three blocks, the assault squads followed their platoon sergeant as he made a left-hand turn down one of the side streets, the infiltration route having been briefed and reviewed hours before.

Reaching the objective building, the platoon sergeant halted the men and called forward the lead squad. All three squads were similarly outfitted with their standard kit, as well as specialized equipment for gaining entry. Individuals in each squad carried metal pry bars for manual entry as well as sawed off shotguns for ballistic breaching.

On this objective they needed to flood the building with as many assaulters as fast as possible, calling for a demolition breach with a dual-primed flex-linear charge, constructed by the mercenaries during the planning stage of the operation.

One Kazakh pulled security on the door while another rolled the charge down the left hand side of the door, sticking the explosive in place by its adhesive. Defeating the hinges was often easier than trying to blast through multiple locking mechanisms on the other side of the door.

Trailing out from the end of the charge were two plastic

tubes, which the security man placed a foot on to hold in place while the other mercenary unrolled the shock tube back to safe position. Once the ignition system was attached to the shock tube, he signaled for the security man to run back and join the stack of assaulters behind him.

Inside the plastic tubes was a coated filament core that when ignited by the device in the breacher's hand, would stimulate a chemical reaction, shooting down the tube at 7,000 feet a second. Standing next to the breacher, the platoon sergeant began the countdown over the assault frequency.

"I have control," Russian words chirped over a hiss of static. "Five, four, three, two,-"

The last number was never heard as several things happened at once.

For a microsecond, the shock tube flashed bright blue in the night as the chemical reaction took place, two blasting caps setting off the detonation chord in the flex-linear charge and searing the wooden door in two.

Four blocks away, the drivers idling by in the assault vehicles heard their platoon sergeant's cue over the radio and turned over their engines.

Three assault teams rushed forward in their stacks, flowing through the doorway, stomping over what was left of the door.

The shouts of squad leaders were drowned out by flash-bangs exploding throughout the structure, bright flashes casting shadows in the night. Several gunshots rang out as the assault trucks spun around the corner and surrounded the building, effectively isolating it from the rest of the town with machine guns pointed outward and locking down the streets.

A few more bursts from the Kalashnikovs could be heard above sergeants giving orders before one of the squads unceremoniously ushered out a man who had been blindfolded and handcuffed, loading him onto one of the assault vehicles.

The hostage.

Taking up security positions around the truck, they waited as the platoon sergeant consolidated his element and prepared to exfiltrate off the objective.

Deckard was impressed.

Watching from a nearby rooftop, he monitored the assault along with his Sergeant Major and Executive Officer.

The Kazakhs had made extraordinary progress in an exceedingly short period of time. Long hours of training had paid off. As he had predicted, the Kazakhs were nearly at the same level of competency commonly associated with the elite troops of more developed countries. The mercenaries were loading onto the assault vehicles, when the cell phone in Deckard's pocket began to buzz.

Looking at the phone's screen, the text message from Samruk's corporate offices alerted him to stand by for an information dump.

"I need to get back to the office," he announced to Sergeant Major Korgan and the Serbian second in command.

Deckard tossed Korgan his radio. They could communicate with the platoon sergeant, simulating orders from headquarters sent down to the platoon as would happen during actual combat operations.

"Have them hit the follow-on objective, then IED the convoy on their way out of the city," Deckard said, referring to the faux-explosive device loaded with pyrotechnics. Roadside bombs were the new reality and needed to be trained for, whether their next mission took them to Sudan or Iraq.

Deckard had a feeling he would find out where that mission would be sooner rather than later.

SEVENTEEN

Two hours later Deckard stood before the assembled battalion leadership.

Once again his fax machine had spat out certain doom.

"Alpha Company will be the main effort for this operation," Deckard told the audience. Quick glances passed between Alexander, Alibek, and Kanat. The platoon sergeants knew they were going into the breach again.

"Terrain varies, consisting of central lowlands covered in thick jungle as well as steep central highland mountains. Hardball roads exist around natural centers of gravity for the local population and deteriorate to unimproved roads as they move out into less populated areas. Rivers and streams wind through the entire region, meaning we need to be prepared for river crossings.

"Situation. Enemy Forces: the Chinese-speaking United Wa State Army consists of approximately 20,000 armed men and women divided among eight divisions. Two divisions are deployed along in the south; this will be Charlie Company's area of operations, designated AO Tiger. The remaining six divisions are stationed near the border with China. Some of these forces will be motorized; others will conduct foot patrols from fortified compounds only.

"The enemy will be armed with locally produced AK-47 rifles, as well as M16s purchased from the black market in Thailand and Cambodia. The UWSA is also known to possess RPK, PKM, RPD, and DShK machine guns, along with SPG-9 recoilless rifles and RPG-7 rocket launchers. Expect enemy compounds to be protected by mortars and Chinese-made Type 77 and Type 54 heavy machine guns, as the UWSA is now conducting arms deals through China rather than traditional black market venues in the region.

"The UWSA has also procured HN-5 man-portable surface-to-air missiles from the Chinese, which is a reverse-engineered Soviet SA-7A. This is the same anti-air platform that scored forty-two kills against Russian forces in Afghanistan, including Hind helicopters. It has also been used successfully against civilian fixed-wing aircraft in Rhodesia by ZIPRA terrorists, a C-130 in Iraq during the Gulf War, and a Blackwater operated Mi-8 helicopter in the more recent Iraq War. This needs to be carefully considered in regards to our arrival and departure from country by fixed-wing aircraft.

"Recently, the UWSA has been engaged in conflict with the host nation government after a twenty-year ceasefire agreement fell apart. Previously, they had been working with the junta to fight against other competing factions. The ruling junta changed its policy in regards to ethnic armies like the UWSA, wishing to absorb them into the regular military as border guards. The UWSA violently opposed this policy shift.

"When the junta attempted to raid a UWSA weapons factory, resistance broke out against the government troops, resulting in hundreds of casualties and displacing tens of thousands of civilians. This low intensity conflict persists into the present.

"Meanwhile, the UWSA continues its illicit trade in y*aa baa* methamphetamine pills, having abandoned heroin, due to y*aa baa's* ease of production. It is estimated that they operate approximately fifty drug labs and are the largest narcotics producers and traffickers in The Golden Triangle. Most of these factories exist in the southern end of UWSA territory while the weapons factories, headquarters, and centers of commerce exist in the northern end, designated AO Leopard, where Alpha and Bravo companies, will operate.

"The enemy's most likely course of action is initial shock and disorientation after first contact, giving our platoons a narrow margin of time to exploit after having achieved speed, surprise, and violence of action. Recovering from initial surprise, the UWSA's leadership will attempt a counter attack where they are able to move reinforcements into the area.

172

"The enemy's most dangerous course of action would be quickly and effectively calling in and massing a large number of armed guerrillas against Samruk forces and overrunning our positions with superior numbers and using their knowledge of local terrain to their advantage.

"Friendly forces: None.

"The junta has proved to be a ruthless dictatorship, violently waging a genocide against various ethnic minorities and suppressing any popular dissent. Ethnic opposition armies exist throughout our area of operations. Do not engage any of them if you don't have to, or we'll find ourselves fighting the entire countryside.

"To the south, we have Task Force 399 in Thailand, consisting of Thai Special Forces advised by American Special Forces teams. Do not attempt any cross-border engagements.

"Fire support will be provided by our mortar section. No Close Air Support, artillery, or medical evacuation will be given to us for the duration of this mission.

"Mission: Samruk International conducts special operations missions against the United Wa State Army in seventy two-hours in order to disrupt and destroy enemy forces in AO Tiger and AO Leopard located in The Union of Myanmar, previously known as Burma."

Deckard dismissed the NCOs and advisors, having finished briefing the Operations Order and giving the men a timeline to adhere to. In an hour he expected a report from subordinate leadership, after they conducted an initial inspection of men, weapons, equipment, and vehicles.

Stepping into his office, he saw a giant black penis drawn on his dry erase board. Apparently Chuck was feeling better after his Afghanistan debacle. It was a good thing because he needed everyone at peak performance for this operation.

"Djokovic!"

The Serb meandered into Deckard's office with his ever present scowl.

"I need you to handle this," he said, giving the Serb a handwritten list of equipment. Additionally, I need a five man detail. They can be drawn from the troops we have recovering from injuries, if need be. As long as they can carry boxes and crates a short distance and provide static security, they should be fine. I don't want to take operational men away from platoon sergeants who need them."

"Why me?" the second in command questioned.

"Because Korgan is busy with other tasks. I need you to do this."

Snorting, Djokovic spun on his heel and stormed out of the office, not even trying to hide his disdain.

Deckard shook his head.

I'll take care of you later, pal.

Somewhere above the jungle, an airplane buzzed through the night.

The Short 360 had been leased in Seychelles, the pilots contracted out of Germany, and its cargo loaded in Sri Lanka. With the seats tossed into the Indian Ocean during the initial flight, the seven passengers sat on the floor amid the cargo strapped down to the belly of the aircraft.

The pilots were Turkish, hired through a firm in Leipzig. Both had logged hundreds of hours of so-called *deep water* or black flights for numerous intelligence agencies. The pilots guided the aircraft, making an initial pass to insure the landing zone was clear of obstacles. They had learned to expect forklifts in the middle of runways or rioting crowds firing at them on final approach.

The jungle airfield was little more than a mud airstrip with a few modular structures around it. Large craters at the west end of the airfield looked like miniature divots from above, the additional landscaping a gift delivered by RAF B-54 bombers over sixty years ago.

The pilot yanked on the yoke, taking the plane into a nearly suicidal button hook and dive straight down towards the airstrip. With the passengers hanging on to anything they could grasp, the pilot pulled up on the controls at the last moment, the wheels touching down gracefully, everyone breathing a sigh of relief.

Powering down the twin Pratt and Whitney engines, the Turk pulled to the side of the runway next to one of the outbuildings. The passengers already had the side door open and began passing boxes and bags out as soon as the 360 came to a halt.

The cargo accumulated in a large pile on the side of the runway while five Kazakhs and two Americans downloaded the equipment. In a couple minutes they were finished, one of the Americans signaling to the pilot with a thumbs up.

With the pilot backing the Short 360 onto the airstrip, the co-pilot ran to the rear of the passenger compartment and closed the door before returning to his seat. Cranking the engines, the pilot spun the airplane around and shot back down the runway, lifting off and disappearing into the night just as abruptly as it had arrived.

The advance party had been successfully inserted into the operational area.

The Kazakh men began loading the cargo onto several handcarts that they had liberated from Jaffna Airfield, until the wheels began to sink into the mud. Ultimately, the two Americans assisted them in carrying the gear into one of the corrugated metal buildings.

Inside, Dr. Nick Van Fleet gave directions in the unpacking and setting up of the field hospital.

Known as "Nick the Dick" by his co-workers, he could be a

diligent taskmaster. Many considered him arrogant, while he thought of himself merely as self-confident. The former Special Forces medic had gone to med school, becoming a surgeon as he neared his fortieth year.

Many would have taken Deckard's one AM phone call with horror, but he jumped at the chance. The most fun Nick got to have these days was driving his Porsche at death-defying speeds around the hairpin turns of Muholland Drive near Hollywood.

Andy was a recently discharged Special Forces medic himself, and would act as an assistant when casualties arrived sometime after combat operations commenced just hours from now.

He had been assured that casualties would, in fact, arrive.

Several stretchers and an operating table were unfolded and put together, areas to triage patients established, surgical tools and medications positioned and accounted for. The impromptu field hospital would render any and all lifesaving treatment to casualties before evacuating the men back to their home station.

Deckard hadn't been willing to tell Nick where that home station was, but looking at the faces of the men he had sent to help provide security, he could hazard a guess.

His old friend had told him that he'd be earning his rather substantial paycheck for services rendered before the fun and games ended.

Jean-Francois walked into the hanger, wearing cut-off camouflage shorts, Jerusalem cruisers, and sporting the kind of sideburns that get good men killed in combat, according to Sergeant Majors the world over. He wasn't a conventional soldier, and having walked across the Astana airport from the civilian terminal, it was apparent to him that this was not a conventional military unit.

176

The hanger was packed with tan colored assault vehicles loaded down with weapons and ammunition, with individual rucksacks strapped onto the sides. Kazakh mercenaries jogged back and forth carrying out their assigned tasks, loud voices filling what little empty space was left inside. Green and brown jungle uniforms were washed but well worn, combat boots broken in, and weapons were handled with comfortable confidence.

These guys looked like they were wired pretty tight.

Definitely not the type of Mickey Mouse operation he had half expected.

Behind him trailed two other former military men he had flown in from London with. During the flight, conversations had been guarded as they felt each other out.

"Ah, replacements," a voice boomed from across the hanger. "Love me some fresh meat!"

A big black guy with dreadlocks motioned them over.

"Where did you come from?" the big guy asked, tossing Jean-Francois an AK-103 rifle.

"London."

"I know that, dickhead. I mean, what outfit were you in?"

"The Legion. 2REP."

"Jesus, you probably won't make it back," he muttered. "What about you two?"

"I was with Force," the former Marine with a high and tight haircut announced.

"Recon? Yeah, you're fucked, too. How about the other guy?"

"Operational Mobile Reaction Group," the Polish mercenary said in stunted English.

"GROM, huh? Holy shit, I'm really going to have to talk to the boss about this. This shit ain't right."

The trio of new recruits looked sullen, the former Marine looking down at his toes.

"I'm just fucking with you guys-" the giant black man burst out laughing. "You people take this shit too seriously," he said, handing the other two men their rifles.

177

"You might want to clean the cosmoline off those things before we hit the ground, and by the way, you are actually here to replace mercs who got smoked, so I don't expect you to last long. Until then you can call me Chuck."

Reaching behind him, Chuck effortlessly lifted a nylon kit bag filled with gear and winged it at Jean-Francois. Catching it, the Frenchman was almost dragged to the ground by its weight. Tossing two more bags to the others, Chuck crossed his arms in front of his muscled chest.

"Hey, boss!" he yelled again. "The new guys just showed up."

Standing by the hanger door with a finger buried in a subordinate's chest, another American turned towards them. Speaking in Russian, the soldier he was addressing turned and ran off as the commander approached them.

The only thing Jean-Francois saw was his eyes.

They'd seen things, and for some reason he didn't want to know what.

"You made it in time. We should be wheels up in a few hours-" the mercenary leader looked at the Polish recruit. "Good to see you again, Leszek. I was hoping you would take our offer."

"Good to see you as well D-"

"It's O'Brien now."

"I understand." The ex-Polish commando hadn't known he was signing on with an old friend until now.

"All of you were vouched for by existing team members, so that says something, but I don't know all of you personally. Square away your gear and do what you're told. That's the best advice I have for you since you missed rehearsals and mission planning. Don't die in the next twenty-four hours, and you might see your first paycheck."

Turning away, he looked over his shoulder to Chuck. "Escort them to their platoon sergeants."

"No problem."

Chuck led the way, dropping the American and the Polack off with a Kazakh wearing sergeants stripes on his uniform. He

178

introduced himself as Shasha, with Bravo Company. Luckily for them the former GROM commando had a working knowledge of Russian and was able to translate for the American.

"Isn't that special?" Chuck remarked at their handshakes. "C'mon, Picasso," he said, motioning for the Frenchman to follow. "I know somebody who wants to talk to you before I introduce you to your new boss."

They stopped on the other side of the hanger where four trucks were lined up, front to back as a single unit, the platoon they belonged to making final adjustments to various straps and oiling machine guns.

"Wake up," Chuck bellowed, throwing a ratchet socket he found on the ground at one of the mercenaries asleep in the driver's seat of an assault truck.

"Huh?" he said, rubbing his eyes.

"Your buddy is here."

The American struggled out of the driver's seat with a groan before stretching his arms.

"Sorry, JF," Frank apologized. "I just got in a few hours ago."

Jean-Francois' eyes widened in recognition.

"Who do you think got you this job?" Frank said, seeing his expression. "You were pretty good in the woods back in the Congo, as I recall."

"That's why? I would have expected you to recruit Delta Force guys, or Chuck Norris, or someone."

"I heard about you drifting around. Liberia, Sudan, and then I heard about you hanging out with Karen rebel fighters in Burma."

"Six months ago. We were ambushing the SPDC as they tried to come in and flatten Karen villages."

The State Peace and Development Council was the Orwellian-named regime that routinely sent in the death squads to ethnically cleanse the Karen minority in southern Burma. Murder, rape, child soldiers, and land mining Karen villages after attacks were all on the SPDC's shopping list.

179

"Exactly, and I got to thinking, this is just the kind of guy we need. Did you learn any Burmese while you were in country?"

"I had to, I was training the villagers to defend themselves."

"How about Chinese?"

"Very little."

"Well, more than me anyway."

Both men turned towards the open end of the hanger, hearing the sound of six monstrously large cargo aircraft screaming down the runway one after the other.

"Where are we going again?"

Frank smiled knowingly.

Eighteen

The massive Antonov-125 cargo carriers came in low and slow, one behind the other as they approached Nansang Airfield in southeast Burma.

The Ukrainian-built aircraft were scrubbed clean, engine decals missing, airline stencils fabricated, serial numbers non-existent. The six airplanes had been completely rebuilt at a little-known airfield in Colorado by mechanics and engineers who worked for a shadow air force that specialized in deniable missions.

With the An-125 being the second largest cargo carrier in the world, behind its big brother the An-225, it was difficult finding reliable pilots with hours on airframes of a comparable size. Most of the pilots and crew were sheep dipped from US military service and employed by front companies after giving up their duty positions on the C-5 Galaxy military transport airplane. A few other crew members were repatriated members of the Russian Air Force.

Air pirates.

Soldiers of fortune.

It was the world's second oldest profession. Unlike the oldest, they didn't earn their pay on their backs, but sometimes a soldier for hire had to question his career choices. The *condottieri* were mercenary captains fighting on behalf of the Italian city-states as far back as the thirteenth century, and while the players had changed, the job remained much the same.

Today, private military corporations existed on the global stage, hiring themselves out when and where strife existed. They were war's entrepreneurs.

With the aircraft blacked out, the troops felt like they had been swallowed by a leviathan, trapped inside the dark belly of a

181

metallic beast. Deckard sat on the hood of one of the assault trucks, wearing a radio headset that allowed him to follow time hacks called out by the pilots.

"Ten minutes out."

In the past someone like him would have found himself trapped between warring barons, heartless Venetian banking cartels, and the papacy. Now it was a labyrinth of ethnic-based autonomous militias, non-governmental organizations, and the death throes of a Western empire.

Burma was the home of many peoples who had historically resisted any and all forms of governance, to include the ruling military junta. The Kachin Defense Army, the Kachin Independent Army, the Myanmar National Democracy Alliance Army, the Pa-O National Army, the Shan State Army, and the United Wa State Army were just a few of the tribal militias that existed in the region, not including state-based actors. The SPDC, Task Force 399, and Chinese intelligence were sure to be thrown into the mix as well.

Examining his map with a red lens flashlight in his hand, Deckard mentally overlaid the dubious territorial boundaries of each militia.

In the near future the very notion of a state would become obsolete, hemorrhaging credibility and forcing local people to look for local solutions. Burma, Somalia, Nigeria, Germany, and even the United States would carve itself into enclaves, each with its own private security contractors hired to maintain stability and enforce laws.

In his travels, Deckard had seen the future, and it wasn't pretty. Societal breakdown and reorganization was no longer a far-flung idea restricted to the impoverished world or abstract futurist predictions, but one already becoming a global reality.

"Five minutes," the pilot informed him over the headset.

The present was rapidly catching up with future.

"Five minutes!" Deckard yelled, waving his hands to get everyone's attention. No one could hear him above the sound of the engines but understood when he held up five fingers.

The assault vehicles were ratcheted down to the floor of the aircraft with heavy duty nylon straps. The ratchet straps would prevent the trucks from rolling around and crushing someone while in flight, but the Kazakhs needed to be ready to pop them the second they hit the ground.

Wheels screeched as the plane finally set down on the runway. The mercenaries immediately popped off the ratchet straps and quickly rolled them up before stowing them in the storage compartments on the trucks.

We'll need them for the trip back, Deckard thought to himself, cynically, if any of us make it back.

As the An-125 peeled off the runway and onto the parking apron, the next cargo carrier was coming in right behind them. Everyone was still holding their breath. If their operational security had been compromised and someone was waiting at the end of the runway with one of the anti-aircraft missiles they had been told of, then this mission could be over before it began.

Sliding its massive frame into position, the pilots announced they were set, even as the rear ramp was opening. Deckard put the headset aside and ordered the Kazakhs to drop the second portion of the ramp into place. Two metal struts bridged from the end of the ramp the rest of the way to the ground, clanging loudly as they landed.

Drivers turned the ignition, starting their engines, gunners already in place and assaulters quickly taking their seats. They were primed, butterflies in their stomachs, wondering what to expect in the darkness outside.

Headlights remained off as Deckard motioned for them to disembark and begin rolling down the ramp. The first assault truck bounced as it maneuvered from the first section of the ramp and onto the struts before rocking again as it hit the tarmac. A few dozen trucks regurgitated themselves out of the airplane before Deckard followed the last vehicle out on foot.

The final assault truck halted, and several Kazakhs got out to help Deckard remove the struts and slide them back inside the aircraft. The entire sequence of events had been rehearsed again and again with the trucks sitting inside fuselage mockups made of plywood back in Kazakhstan.

Five other Antonovs were now lined up perfectly on the parking apron alongside them as they unloaded a battalion's worth of vehicles. A few minutes later, the entire unit was on the ground. As platoon sergeants and company commanders took over, the pilots were already turning and preparing to take off. They'd be hanging out somewhere more secure until Samruk called for exfil.

Meanwhile the vehicles were getting lined up on the side of the runway in a quick staging area for accountability before beginning movement. The three companies had been split up among the six aircraft, so it was important to make sure everyone was in the right place. The difficulty in not having officers was that Deckard, Korgan, and Djokovic had to split up and act as company commanders for the duration of the mission.

Just as the last Antonov lifted off, Deckard initiated movement. Illuminated by an overcast moon, the mercenary battalion skirted around the edge of a small village before cutting onto the main road junction.

The combat operation called for a complete blackout. Drivers drove, looking through night vision goggles with infrared headlights turned on to help them see at night. The PKM gunners in the turret had the best field of view and could help the driver navigate, relaying directions by radio.

At the intersection the battalion silently split off. Alpha and Bravo Companies took a right heading north on National Highway Number Four while Charlie Company, being led by Djokovic, turned left on Highway Forty-Five.

Keeping a good separation between vehicles, Alpha and Bravo crept up to fifty miles an hour on the straightaways, making good time for the moment. It was important not to drive faster than they could see, especially when driving with night vision goggles on. With the driver deprived of depth perception, an obstacle in the road could quickly lead to disaster.

The central lowlands made for pretty easy driving, with gently rolling terrain and fairly well built roads. Only occasionally did they have to slow down to snake back and forth down a ravine to cross a bridge over a river. The high rate of speed also kept the commandos riding in the open air rear area of the truck cool from the humidity.

"Band-Aid One, this is OB-One. Radio check, over," Deckard said, keying the truck's encrypted radio hand mic from the passenger seat of his truck.

"OB-One, this is Band-Aid One. I read you, Lima Charlie; how about me?"

Dr. Nick the Dick was supposed to be ready to accept casualties the moment the main element hit the ground if need be.

"I got you, Lima Charlie. What is your current status, over."

"We're green and waiting for your call, over."

That was a call he seriously didn't want to make.

Piet scanned the scenery as it flashed by.

Leaning back in his seat, he took grim pleasure in the knowing that while he was exposed in the back of the assault vehicle, at least if he were shot, the round wouldn't go through his chest and kill the guy sitting behind him, thanks to the bullet-proof ceramics of the seats.

The .300 Winchester Magnum sniper rifle sat resting on its rubber padded stock between his feet. He'd spent the last few weeks with his six man sniper section out in the steppes, getting familiar with the new rifle and collecting data for their log books.

Craning his head around, the South African looked through the assault truck's rear window at the guy in the passenger seat, eyeballing the back of Djokovic's head.

Jean-Francois leaned back in his seat, the Kazakhs sitting next to him holding their AK-103 rifles close. The air smelled fresh after recent rainfall, reminding him that monsoon season had already moved in.

He was still assigned to Alpha Company, headed north with the battalion commander.

Speeding through the disputed Shan State, he could see thatch-roofed villages nestled into the jungle through his night vision goggles. It felt good to be back. Previously he had been farther south in the Karen State, battling it out with the Burmese Government's death squads.

In 1950, Chinese nationalist forces, sponsored by the newly formed Central Intelligence Agency, invaded the Shan State in eastern Burma. Their reign of terror included tax collection, forcibly conscripting local men into their so-called secret army, and forcing the Burmese to grow poppies.

This resulted in the Burmese Government forming an alliance with Shan warlords to fight back against the Chinese insurgents, using military equipment purchased with opium money. And thus began the Opium Wars, a low intensity battle that had never really ended, with one faction or the other struggling for control over the poppies and the convoys that carried them to the surrounding nations.

With the current leader of the UWSA, Saya Peng, indicted by a grand jury in Brooklyn, New York and facing mounting international pressure, including a second conviction in absentia in Thailand, he had finally been convinced by the ruling junta to stop trafficking the poppies. Peng forcefully relocated thousands of the Shan civilians south several years ago, setting up factories and beginning to produce *yaa baa* methamphetamine pills instead of farming poppies. Being of Sino-Burmese lineage and well connected to the underworld on both sides of the border, he easily obtained the necessary precursor chemicals from China.

After sixty years, no one could imagine the Shan without a narcotics-based economy.

Frank had filled him in on the rest during the flight.

The UWSA had grown stronger then the junta's military under Peng's leadership. When Peng refused to unify his people with the government forces, they sent in troops to disastrous effect. The junta was left with little option. Acknowledge and cede authority to Peng, or attack once more, this time with newly acquired chemical weapons from North Korea, an option that would have brought down even more heat on the regime from the United Nations.

This was where foreign mercenaries entered into the picture. Some entity, somewhere, had cut a backroom deal with the Burmese government.

Frank had assured him that this mission wasn't part of some kind of ethnic cleansing on the SPDC's behalf. They were taking down an exceedingly violent drug cartel, but his old friend had still tap danced around who had hired them.

Looking at his watch, he saw that Charlie Company would be reaching their Area of Operations soon. Gripping his own AK a little tighter, the Frenchman knew this mission was going to get ugly fast.

Nineteen

Djokovic was getting pissed.

The little brown mercenaries were little better than Roma, or even Albanians.

"What is problem," he hissed into his radio.

The entire convoy had pulled to the side of the road, gunners in the turret of each vehicle covering to the left and right on the alternate side of the one in front. It had been about an hour and a half, and they had just entered AO Jaguar. So far Charlie Company was well within the timeline, but the Serb wanted to clean house and make it back to the Pickup Zone well before Deckard.

Deep down he was still bitter about the last mission. After leaving him behind to mind the troops while the commander took Alpha Company to Afghanistan, he felt perceptions towards him change. Although assured otherwise, the Kazakhs knew there had to be a reason why he was not brought along. He could see it in their eyes.

He would prove how wrong they were.

Charlie Company would rack up a body count like he hadn't seen since Srebrenica.

"Sierra-Five, this is Sierra-Mike One." It was the one called Adam.

"Why are you stopped?"

"A truck belonging to Sierra-Two has a flat. Must have picked up a nail or something. We're good on run flats, but we need to let them do a tire change before we start hitting targets, over."

Djokovic gritted his teeth. Second Platoon needed to learn how to drive.

"Make it fast, out."

He could even hear the American's condescending tone over the radio.

Five minutes later Charlie Company was rolling again.

Reaching another fork in the road, the company split up, this time into platoons for the final leg of their infiltration before raiding individual objectives. First and Third Platoons went right, with the company's medical evacuation vehicle and the mortar section attachments. Second Platoon, headed left down national highway number five.

Gordan would be sticking with Second Platoon as they hit a series of drug labs in their assigned section of the AO. Adam, Piet, and Mendez would be at the XO's disposal, along with the rest of the company.

Driving through the rolling jungle terrain, Djokovic's element slowly made their way downhill. One false move under the night vision goggles and one of the trucks could go over the lip of the road and roll a few hundred meters to the bottom, probably landing upside down in the river.

Reaching the bottom of the hill, the convoy rolled over a metal frame bridge, the waters below dark and uninviting. The men knew it was almost game time. A few hid nervous shakes with nervous laughs, chuckling alongside their buddies in the back of the trucks.

Minutes seemed like hours until finally they came into a valley, lights illuminating a distant village. The Serb spoke into the radio, halting the convoy once more.

The mortar section got off the trucks that they had been cross loaded onto and began moving out with their 82mm tubes, base plates, bipods, and an assortment of mortar rounds. With the area around the village being deforested, the entire section was able to fit comfortably between two draws, trailing down from a nearby mountain, for better security.

Leaving Mendez and his section behind, the two platoons took the convoy off road, leading deeper into the forest towards people who would rather be left undiscovered.

"Sierra-Five this is Mike-One. Guns are up, over."

"Roger," Djokovic responded to Mendez's transmission. Not that he cared. They were going in with or without indirect fire. If a few mongrels died taking the objective, they would just train new ones.

At the base of the hill he could see a checkpoint that guarded the only access road up to the target. This checkpoint consisted of a sandbagged pillbox with some orange cones put across the road. The Executive Officer laughed. He'd seen Muslims manage better defenses.

Rolling up to the checkpoint, the two guards on duty looked on with eyes bugging out of their heads, mistaking the convoy for the SPDC with some new toys. The machine gunner manning the turret on Djokovic's truck opened fire, stitching the pillbox back and forth, the bursts of gunfire echoing through the valley, as bullets tore apart sandbags and flesh alike.

The Serb had another laugh. The truck's driver looked at him curiously.

Driving over the cones, the convoy twisted its way around hairpins turns, increasing in elevation as the trucks climbed up the side of the hill. As the trucks cresting the summit, the front gate came into view.

With the headlights switched off, the driver slowed the truck down before ramming through the flimsy wooden gate, tires cracking the branches and wooden planks in half. First Platoon drove straight into the middle of the garrison, guards finally waking up in their foxholes and bunkers, searching for flashlights.

All five trucks commenced firing as the Serb gave the order to initiate. PKM machine guns and AK rifles ripped through the garrison, tearing apart thatch huts and digging into bunkers constructed with logs and sandbags. Many UWSA militia men died in their sleep, never knowing that they were under attack.

The surrounding camp was lit up by muzzle flashes, a foot of fire spitting from the barrels of the automatic weapons that traced fire back and forth across the compound. The assault teams jumped off the trucks to begin their attack. Moving into squad formations, they came under some sporadic fire, the militia men finally mounting what seemed like a half-hearted counter-attack.

On the next hill over, Djokovic could see high explosive rounds impacting just short of another drug lab. A driver called in corrections to the mortar section over the truck's radio, walking the rounds in until finally they fired a shake and bake mission.

First, they hit the drug laboratory with another HE shot as a spotter round. Next, they fired a red phosphorous round that burned across the hill in a nearly perfect circular pattern, immediately igniting the precursor chemicals used to manufacture methamphetamine.

The resulting secondary explosions ripped through whatever was left of the compound. Pieces of wood spun through the air with long wisps of flame chasing after them.

At a distance, Djokovic couldn't hear the screams but could still imagine them crying out as they burned alive. However, he did hear Third Platoon's guns somewhere deeper in the jungle. They must have just hit their own target, the next garrison over, just a few kilometers away.

Swinging open the door, he stepped out into the slaughter, a stray bullet ricocheting off the door as he closed it. The Serb ducked behind the truck as Adam came up alongside to help direct the troops.

Two assault teams were kicking in doors and entering the huts while the third was in the prone, preparing to throw hand grenades before clearing a trench line on the eastern side of the compound. The PKM gunners in the vehicles continued to lay down a steady wall of lead in the direction of the few shots that rang out in opposition.

Suddenly two of the Kazakhs from Third Squad were thrown to the ground as a grenade detonated, spewing dirt and debris into the air.

"Fuck! Fucking fucks!" Djokovic growled. "What are they doing?"

The assaulters got to their feet and continued to advance with their comrades, lobbing grenades of their own into the trench. While their buddies provided suppressive fire, two mercenaries lay parallel to the trench, feet to feet, before rolling in and firing rapid bursts. Having established a foothold, the rest of the squad followed in after them.

The XO muttered something in his native tongue, his words drowned out by another explosion while he fished through his pockets for a cigarette. Lighting up, he exhaled a cloud of smoke, looking towards Adam with words unspoken as his head exploded.

A single gunshot rang out through the night.

The Serb lay motionless, his head pulped beyond recognition as if a firecracker had gone off in his brain.

Keying his hand mic, Adam announced to the platoon that he was assuming command.

Piet racked the bolt, ejecting the spent shell casing from his sniper rifle.

Occupying one of the haphazardly built wood and mud bunkers, the South African had lain down on top of the still warm body of its former occupant, his body torn apart with machine gun fire.

Sliding the sniper rifle's bolt home and chambering another round, he scanned for fresh targets.

TWENTY

Deckard cursed under his breath.

After being on the road for six hours, Alpha and Bravo Companies had finally split up at their last check point. Driving cross country for the next couple hours, his company alone had suffered two flat tires on the winding dirt road leading towards the Chinese border.

Standing by his vehicle, he watched the Kazakhs through his PVS-14s. Using a tow strap, one truck successfully yanked another out of the mud, the recovery vehicle promptly becoming stuck itself.

They had made allowances for the effects the monsoon would have on the unimproved roads in their timeline, but that didn't make the situation any less frustrating.

The newly freed vehicle pulled ahead of the truck stuck in the mud, its tires spinning wildly, slinging mud behind it, before the driver accepted that four-wheel drive alone wasn't going to let him creep out of the watery pit. Dropping off the back of their vehicle, the Kazakhs ran another tow strap back to the hard point under the immobilized truck's bumper and locked it in place with a steel clevis, preparing to repeat the process.

Meanwhile he was receiving updates over the radio as Bravo Company crossed phase lines towards their own objectives. He noted that they had experienced similar mobility issues, including a rollover. Soon they would be arriving at their assigned objectives to the north. Meanwhile Charlie Company was already calling in OPSKEDS, or operational code words, to indicate that they were pulling off their objectives, mission complete.

Initial reports stated that Charlie Company had three men killed in action, ten wounded, and had successfully eliminated six drug laboratories, three UWSA garrisons, and took out a few enemy checkpoints as well. Adam had assumed command with Djokovic among the dead.

At least something was going according to plan.

Now he could only hope that the element of surprise hadn't been completely compromised. The enemy or a spotter planted among the locals could have called north, alerting Peng and his remaining militiamen.

Deckard could have held Charlie Company back and had each company strike simultaneously but the odds were that someone would be compromised somewhere, effectively denying the entire battalion an edge up on the enemy, rather than just one or two companies. It was a tactical decision and like most, there was no one hundred percent solution.

The assault truck's wheels found purchase as the tow strap tightened and the lead vehicle helped pull them out of the mud. Deckard climbed back on his truck, just as the convoy began moving. The roads were only getting more rugged the deeper into the bush they traveled. At times the mercenaries seated in the back of the trucks were leaning out over a sheer drop as the trucks skirted right along the edge of the road.

Unfortunately for them, a helicopter infiltration wasn't always feasible.

Twenty One

Green tracer fire arced over Sergeant Major Korgan's head.

Leading from the front, he high crawled forward as someone launched a flare into the night sky, shadows shifting as it slowly descended to the ground by parachute. Bravo Company's Second Platoon cautiously crawled up behind him.

Every handful of terrain became critical to the mercenaries as they inched forward. With the infiltration team compromised, the dismounted support by fire line initiated, using the traverse and search method to hose down the UWSA weapons factory, 40mm grenade launchers entering into the flurry and pounding the objective with high explosive rounds. It kept the enemy distracted, but the heavy machine gun sent shivers down the Kazakh's spines as it fired just inches over their heads, causing them to hug dirt.

Over a small dimple of ground, Korgan could see the top edge of triple strand concertina wire silhouetted against the sky. Sliding into a mud-filled pit, the Sergeant Major stole a glance backward before ducking, a fresh burst of machine gun fire searching him out, sending large clumps of earth into the air.

First Squad was right behind him, the others slowly making their way forward on their bellies, attempting to find their own way forward to the enemy's perimeter. The men knew from training and rehearsals that each squad had to address the terrain and enemy to their own immediate front. With Korgan finding a way to the front lines, the other squads would probably follow his lead rather than continue to explore other paths through barbed wire and booby traps.

Somewhere inside the enemy compound, mortar tubes thundered.

First Squad squirmed into the pit with the Sergeant Major, huffing and trying to catch their breath. Korgan noted that the chest rigs they wore made it somewhat difficult to low crawl while under enemy fire, but that was an issue that would have to be dealt with at another time.

At the moment, the massive Chinese Type 54 machine gun spat a glowing fireball of burning powder, leaving no mystery as to the gunner's position, 12.7 bullets ripping across the front lines. First Squad lined up on his left while Second Squad was now crawling in on his right. The platoon carried the needed breaching equipment in satchels and assault packs.

"First the breach, then grenades," Korgan yelled in Russian between machine gun bursts.

The troops nodded or gave a thumbs up, indicating that they understood the plan of action.

Heavy gloves and wire cutters were carried only as a backup. Even with friendlies laying down a suppressive fire, there was no way they would maneuver across another fifteen meters of flat terrain up to the concertina wire and simply cut through it. Not while the Type 54 was hammering them.

Two of the Kazakhs carried an Anti-Personnel Obstacle Breaching System or APOBS. The mercenaries quickly deployed the two hard plastic carry cases, opening them and attaching the needed components. The mud was making their work more difficult than it should have been, but they were not deterred. The Chinese machine gun paused to reload before again reminding them of their urgency.

"Set!"

With the APOBS ready, the men of Second Squad readied hand grenades.

By now Third Squad was coming up right behind them.

"Fire," Korgan ordered.

The APOBS launched from its tube with a whoosh, a small rocket carrying a guide line angling into the air before a drogue chute at the end of the rope began to catch air. With drag provided, the rope arched downwards and lay over the three rolls of concertina wire. The Type 54 continued to fire blast after blast at their position, oblivious to what was coming.

The nylon rope the rocket had carried was strung with over fifty fragmentation grenades, all of which detonated simultaneously. The explosion shook the ground, easily slicing through the concertina wire and detonating a dozen anti-personnel and anti-tank mines buried in the soil under its path.

The Second Squad grenadiers jumped up on their knees and flung their grenades directly at the Type 54 sitting in its sandbagged fighting hole. Several grenades bounced off the sandbags and exploded harmlessly, but one managed to roll inside the pit right under the tripod that supported the heavy machine gun. After the last explosion, the entire platoon was on their feet, combat boots stomping through the mud and spilling through the breach in the perimeter.

First Squad immediately stormed the machine gun bunker, only to find the gunner and ammunition loader on their last breaths; the fragmentation grenade had done its work. The mercenaries helped expedite the process, delivering mercy shots.

"Shift fire," the Sergeant Major ordered, keying up his radio.

The support by fire line, buried in the jungle, shifted their barrels, now firing behind the objective to cut off the escape of any UWSA militiamen who decided to cut and run. The weapons factory itself looked like it already lay half in ruin, with one wall and part of the roof collapsed from the barrage of 40mm grenades.

Second Squad brushed past him, heading for the enemy's mortar pit, Third Squad moving on what was left of the factory. Korgan ran to catch up with Third Squad as they neared the collapsed wall.

At that moment, Second Squad dumped a few more fragmentation grenades into the mortar pit then chased the blasts, rolling into the trench before the earth had even settled. AK fire lit up the night as the squad swept through, killing off the mortar team. Next, they would rig the stockpiled mortar rounds for demolition.

Stepping over the rubble, the Sergeant Major moved into the factory with Third Squad. He'd seen action with the Kazakh

Special Forces, chasing around drug smugglers and the like, but never anything this intense. His heart rate was climbing to nearly ninety beats a minute, his chest thumping hard.

Muzzle flashes blinked from the far side of the factory floor. Several hold-outs lay in wait on the opposite side of the building. They had probably been taking refuge inside from all the external gunfire.

Korgan took cover behind a pile of steel billets, 7.62 rounds sparking off the metal as he returned fire.

The squad found their own cover behind a lathe used in the manufacturing process. In fact, the lathe looked to be the only machinist piece in the warehouse, the rest of the construction being done the old fashioned way, by hand. One of the muzzle flashes winked out as another mercenary fired back, but it was quickly replaced by two more.

Korgan left his position and bounded forward between several wooden tables and ducked behind a metal handcart. Third Squad began creeping forward on their own terms, finding their own way to close the distance. One mercenary would provide cover while the other bounded, working in two man teams.

The UWSA gunmen caught on and decided to find cover as well, two of them flipping over a table and taking a knee behind it. Sergeant Major Korgan shouldered his AK-103 and drilled the table with 7.62 rounds, punching through the flimsy wooden tabletop. The UWSA gunmen dropped to the ground, AK rifles that they had probably helped manufacture clattering alongside them.

Stalking forward, Korgan passed rack after rack of AK-47s- there were enough to arm a battalion of soldiers- and rows and rows of the Burmese rifles, cloned from Chinese models, which were in turn copied from the classic Soviet design. They were not only arming themselves but probably neighboring militias. Maybe the entire region.

Someone was planning an offensive.

As the squad closed in, one of the Burmese militiamen panicked and jumped to his feet, spraying automatic fire with his

198

rifle pointed towards the Kazakhs in only the most general sense of the word. One squad member, the youngest looking of the group, placed his own accurate fire on target as the enemy gunman's shots went wide. The Burmese doubled over, trying to hold in his intestines even as they slipped through his fingers. The young Kazakh fired once more, this time striking him just above the ear, peeling off the top of his skull.

The newly made corpse fell to the floor, the bowl shaped portion of his skull still connected to his head by a narrow strip of skin.

One of the supposedly dead Burmese suddenly launched at Korgan the triangular shaped bayonet under the AK-47, narrowly missing his abdomen as the Sergeant Major twisted at the hips to avoid it. Undeterred, the militiaman sprang on the Kazakh, pushing him into a nearby table, metal tools rolling off the edge and paper schematics flying into the air.

Momentarily stunned, Korgan lost his grip on the foreguard of his rifle. Seeing an opportunity, the Burmese decided to grab at his AK and wrestle him for it, his own apparently out of ammunition or jammed. Reaching out with his non-dominant hand, Korgan grasped something on the table and swung it as hard as he could.

The solid steel billet caught the UWSA gunman just above the eyebrow, splitting the skin. The militiaman dropped to the concrete floor like an empty coat, dead from a fractured skull. Korgan looked at the billet in his hand, blood and skin now stuck to the corner of it.

Shrugging his shoulders, the squad looked back at their Sergeant Major with a few nervous laughs.

As Korgan tossed the billet aside, it struck the ground just as the factory's windows imploded, sending triangular shaped pieces of glass everywhere under a torrent of gunfire.

Frank crept through the jungle, spotting the dirt road ahead.

Down the road, Second Platoon was currently engaged with the weapons factory. In the distance they could hear the vicious firefight. It sounded like a good one as tracer fire skimmed through the air and mortar rounds exploded somewhere deeper in the jungle.

Farther east, Third Platoon would be moving on the ammunition plant, but from the sights and sounds in that direction it seemed that their fight hadn't kicked off yet.

In the opposite direction, the road led to the northern Shan State, where some ten thousand UWSA troops were garrisoned. They had the arms and the vehicles to react to Bravo Company's raids on the arms factories, as well as Alpha Company as soon as they hit Panghsang in less than an hour. If those troops successfully mobilized, the fight was effectively over; Samruk would be encircled and overrun.

With the road identified, he quickly cross-referenced it on his map, to make sure that they were at the right place. It had been hard going after leaving the vehicles behind with a security detachment and moving through the bush on foot. Burma did not consist of dense triple canopy jungle, but it still made for some unforgiving terrain.

Convinced they had arrived, he motioned the troops forward. The platoon edged up in a column, Sergeant Sasha placing his men on an ambush line alongside the road, making sure they were behind adequate cover. When the UWSA reinforcements began moving, they had to be ready.

First Platoon's task was to set up a mechanical ambush on the road, to cut off and ensure those reinforcements never arrived to interfere on the other objectives. Riflemen, grenadiers, and others armed with Afghan procured RPG launchers would provide backup.

The shadows of five Kazakhs moved down to the road and began emplacing Claymore mines. The curved anti-personnel mines were not called *red vapor mist machines* for nothing. While riflemen and RPG gunners found their positions, the demo team stuck the Claymores into the ground on their metal legs, making sure they pointed towards the road.

Although Frank referred to them as Claymores, they were not actually the American-made mines but the Yugoslavian copy that was easier to procure on the open market. Called the MRUD, it contained a TNT-based explosive with 650 ball bearings that acted as shrapnel. The mercenaries diligently placed the mines with overlapping sectors of fire, to make sure the enemy did not escape the intended kill radius. Ultimately, nearly two dozen of them would be daisy-chained together. Sasha would maintain the detonator, or clacker as it was called, to initiate the ambush.

With the Kazakhs in their platoon sergeant's capable hands, Frank decided it was time to find his own position. The firefight had been raging at the weapons plant for ten minutes or so. By now someone had certainly placed a phone call north. Troops had been woken from their cots and were probably already loading vehicles.

Heading out, Frank heard someone grunt and realized he'd stepped on one of the ambushers.

"Shit," he whispered. "Sorry."

"S'okay," the prone man answered in English.

"Who the hell is that?"

"Roger," the voice whispered back.

"Who?"

"One of the new guys."

"Oh, I'm glad you're still alive. Hold on a second."

Backtracking, the American found Sasha and spoke into his ear. They got along just fine but there was still something of a language barrier between them. Finally understanding, Sasha nodded his approval and Frank moved back to Roger.

"Hey, let's go."

"Where to?" Roger asked.

"We're going to go provide security up ahead."

"Gotcha," the other American said, standing up.

The two moved into the foliage, looking for a decent

vantage point. Finding a good lookout point near a copse of trees, they got down to the ground, providing overwatch on the road. From there they would call Sasha on the radio and give him early warning when the enemy convoy neared.

Resting on their stomachs, Frank looked back and forth for signs of danger. Finding none, he set his AK down beside him and pulled out a silver-topped can of Copenhagen snuff. Tapping on the lid a few times, he pulled out a pinch of dip and stuck it in his lower lip before offering the can to Rogers.

Accepting it, the former Force Recon Marine threw in a dip as well. Once your body dumped any initial adrenaline that flooded your system in combat, you had to find a way to stay awake during long patrols. The Copenhagen definitely gave the two of them a slight buzz, to keep them awake but despite it Frank still felt himself nodding off.

After running himself into the ground all over the South Pacific, he had made it back to Astana just in time for another combat op. After familiarizing himself with the operations order, the best he could do was grab a few hours of sleep on the flight into country.

"Hey, Roger."

"What's up?"

"Talk to me man, I'm falling asleep," Frank said, squirting dip spit between his teeth.

Chuck planned on keeping this thing quiet as long as he could get away with it.

With Second Platoon providing a fireworks show that offered distraction for the militiamen occupying the ammunition dump, he was going to make a stealth infiltration. The Burmese were running around, trying to figure out who was doing all that shooting at the weapons factory eight kilometers northeast, rather than watching their own perimeter.

Careful reconnaissance had told the former SEAL that the ammo factory was surrounded by a trench line with a bunker every couple of hundred meters. In front of the trench was coils of concertina wire to tangle up anyone trying to sneak up on them. Luckily for Bravo Company's Third Platoon, one thing you can always count on with any military operation is somebody fucking things up.

Crawling forward, his large frame blended into the shadows, his jungle fatigues matching the surroundings, and face covered in green camouflage cosmetics. With his AK-103 in one hand he crawled forward arm over arm nearing the bunker he had been aiming towards for the last quarter of an hour.

Somebody had definitely fucked the pooch on this deal. While the other bunkers appeared to be placed properly, this one was dug in just above the military crest of the hill that the enemy base rested on. In this position, the hill sloped and fell away in front of the bunker, and whoever manned it could not see down the edge of the hill, creating dead space in the defender's field of fire.

Thanks to this error, Chuck was able to crawl right up to the concertina wire unobserved. The plan of attack had been worked out with the squad members before they began to infiltrate. Using several sticks collected and cut to size, they used the 'v' notch naturally created where the stick forked to hold up the rolls of defensive wire to form a gap. Somebody had forgotten to stake the wire down properly.

The twelve-inch gap was plenty for Chuck to take the lead once again and crawl under the wire. Somewhere nearby, they heard the thump of mortar rounds, mixed in with sporadic bursts of machine gun fire. Squirming through the wire, he spotted several anti-personnel mines. They were the large circular variety that the Russians made and the Chinese copied.

It was all military *laissez-faire*, Chuck figured.

Clearing the wire, he paused for a moment and listened as a gentle breeze cooled the sweat on his forehead. No rustling, no clicking of gun metal. So far so good. Then again, he had lost a few decibels since Afghanistan.

Hooking around, he continued to low crawl, pawing at the grass with his free hand until he found what he was looking for. Sliding his Ka-Bar from its sheath, Chuck cut the wire used to command detonate the mine from the bunker, then turned back around to find the wire leading from the other mine he spotted.

After few minutes of careful, deliberate movement, he found and cut the second wire.

Back at the newly formed gap in the wire, he motioned the Kazakhs forward. They would form the assault element when needed. The support by fire element had been in place from the beginning, monitoring the infiltrators' progress in case of compromise.

Creating as low a profile as possible, Chuck had his ear pressed into the ground as he inched forward up to the edge of the trench line. UWSA commanders shouted inside the base in Burmese and Chinese alike, rallying the troops. None of them seemed to have a clue as to what was going on right under their noses.

Silently lowering himself into the trench, Chuck found himself kneeling in mud. One by one, the Kazakhs began flowing in behind him. When a squad's worth had arrived, he moved in a crouch, staying low as he approached the first bunker.

The perimeter bunkers were haphazard, made with locally procured materials, like logs and mud with some sandbags. Overhead cover was crafted with medium-sized tree trunks, the gaps filled with more sandbags.

With his eyes already adjusted to the limited visibility of the darkness, he could see into the bunker. The guard was watching to the rear, fascinated by the red and green tracer fire buzzing through the air from the nearby firefight rather than watching his own sector of fire. His AK-47 lay next to him, unattended.

No wonder they had gotten this far undetected.

Slinging the AK, he drew his fighting knife once more and closed on the sentry, prepared for the grim realities of combat.

The guard wore the same olive drab uniform as all the UWSA militia, his head bobbing under a mop of jet black hair. Chuck clasped a hand over the guard's mouth as he tried to cry out. Drawing the blade to his neck, he froze. The Burmese guard continued to fight back against Chuck, but it was to no avail as he was nearly three times his size.

The sentry couldn't be more than twelve years old.

Chuck sheathed the knife, and quickly set the child soldier in a chokehold. In moments the kid passed out, falling limp in his hands like someone flipped off a switch. Easing him down to the muddy ground, he secured the boy's hands and feet with flexible plastic handcuffs.

Drawing the blade again, the Kazakhs looked on as Chuck cut a strip from the boy's oversized uniform. He was already waking up as the American tied the knot on his gag.

The Samruk mercenaries might have been rough around the edges, but they certainly weren't in the business of killing children, even if others had no qualms about putting a rifle in a little boy's hands.

The ex-SEAL wondered what he would do if another child soldier fired on him at some point. He preferred not to think about it.

With a foothold secured they would now begin the next phase of the plan.

Sabotage.

Chuck looked to the Kazakhs, all three squads now occupying the trench and bunker. Somebody was in for a nasty surprise if they stumbled upon them. The assaulters ducked as a flare went up. A radio crackled in the background as a UWSA officer tried to reach a superior- someone, anyone to tell them what was happening.

As the flare began to sputter and die, Chuck looked above the edge of the trench and visually identified the ammunition plant. The AK's were manufactured on Second Platoon's objective, the ammunition for the rifles being made on theirs.

It was a long rectangular building set in the center of the

compound, made of salvaged sheets of aluminum. Several more sentries were stationed at the entrance, on high alert with all the commotion. Deciding on the best avenue of approach, Chuck pointed the building out to the Kazakhs.

Another flare went up. One of the perimeter guards started shooting at ghosts on the other side of the compound. They were getting spooked.

Indicating that he wanted Second and Third squad to remain in place until he called them up, he had them pass up all the satchel charges to First Squad. He'd be taking them into the ammo factory, himself.

Gripping the AK, he watched, waited, until the flare fell into the jungle and disappeared.

Jumping out of the trench, he took point, Kazakh mercenaries loaded down with explosive charges trailing behind.

"And, you know, bro, I was totally shocked that Phoebe had a husband," Rogers said, shaking his head.

"Well, that shit makes sense," Frank muttered. "She was always the weird one. But then Chandler came out with that whole thing about having a third nipple."

"Shit, yeah. That was strange, but what about them finding out about Joey being in a skin flick."

"But not actually *being* in a skin flick."

The two mercenaries chuckled.

"That was the same one where Ross was asking Rachel for sex advice," Frank continued.

"Yeah, and she totally bullshitted him about-"

"Oh, fuck."

"What?"

"Are those headlights coming this way?"

Squinting, they could see several sets of headlights turn

into several dozen as they grew closer.

"Hell, yes," Frank said, keying up his radio. "We're on, Sasha. Looks to be about twenty-five trucks."

"Da," his voice answered back.

Hunkering down, the only noise heard was the engines of the approaching cargo trucks as the two mercenaries spat Copenhagen juice on the jungle underbrush.

Moments later, the two-and-half-ton trucks rumbled by their position, the back of each truck loaded to capacity and bristling with combat troops, rifles pointed in every direction.

With the convoy disappearing down the road, everything was still for a moment.

Then the earth shook.

Sergeant Sasha depressed the clacker.

Twenty-four Yugoslavian claymore mines had had their backs removed by the demolition team. Small amounts of the mine's TNT explosive had been extracted, and then detonation chord had been substituted and strung from mine to mine, daisy chaining them down the entire length of the linear ambush. The center mine had a blasting cap inserted into it with the clacker attached by a wire.

The mines exploded, shredding human flesh, shattering glass, and pock marking steel. The awful sounds of the dead and dying filled the sulfur-laced air with their screams. The ambushers opened fire with machine guns and assault rifles. The RPG teams had rockets primed and laid out next to them, firing shot after shot in rapid succession.

The lucky ones were killed in the initial blast; the less fortunate UWSA irregulars were left wounded, only to suffer the gunfire and anti-tank rockets that slammed into the wreckage of the trucks. The fuel tank on one of the surplus cargo trucks ignited, lifting the back two tires clean off the ground in a brilliant fireball.

Another truck skidded through the mud with two burst tires, before rolling on its side. As it slammed onto its flank, the dead militiamen riding in the back were flung into the air.

After a full minute, the onslaught was completed, and Sasha called for a ceasefire over his radio. They listened for the sounds of anyone left alive. Moans and groans sounded ahead of them on the road. Someone was yelling for help in his native tongue. Sasha was distracted by something out of place in the trees above him.

The light produced by the burning truck illuminated the woodline and allowed him to discern what he was looking it. It was a human torso thrown into the trees, intestines unraveled behind it and strung through the branches.

"Assault!"

The ambush line picked up and moved forward to finish the job.

Chuck took aim at the nearest sentry and milked the trigger, the Kazakh next to him doing the same a fraction of a second later.

The two sentries collapsed, head shots making sure that they never knew what hit them. Closing the distance, a First Squad trooper opened the heavy steel door to the ammunition factory and held it for Chuck to drag the two bodies inside. The UWSA gunmen guarding the compound were now so spooked by all the shooting going on at other objectives that they were shooting at ghosts outside the wire and sending up flares every thirty seconds.

Two shots were not enough to alert them to what was actually happening under their noses.

Pulling the corpses inside, the mercenaries shut the door, posting one man as a guard. Through the windows running along the warehouse, they could see shadows darting back and forth. Full-blown panic was taking hold of the militiamen at this point, fear eating them from the inside out.

Chuck could now see the equipment needed to manufacture the ammunition laid out in an assembly line fashion. There were furnaces for melting lead, with various sized bullet molds, presses, and boxes full of spent shells for reloading, but what was most interesting were the drums full of magnesium phosphate, used in the production of tracer rounds, and drums of white phosphorus, for making incendiary rounds.

The ex-SEAL felt like he had just scored the winning touchdown of the Super Bowl.

"Go to work."

The Kazakh mercenaries fanned out while one man watched the door. Chuck assisted in the placement of the satchel charges. Several of the twenty pound satchels were spread around the fifty-five gallon drums of explosive chemicals. The squad hurried, placing other charges around the presses and other machinist tools used for production.

"Sergei," Chuck whispered to get the Kazakh's attention. The troop guarding the door looked back at him.

"Are we clear?"

The mercenary cracked open the door and peered out to make sure their route back to the trench line was unobstructed. Looking back, he nodded his head to the big American.

"Everyone ready?"

Seven sets of eyes drilled into him, ready to go.

"On three," he ordered. The satchels had one minute of time fuse on them and needed to be initiated simultaneously. It wasn't the most precise way to use explosives, but it would get the job done. If anything, this much demo was overkill.

"Three, two, one-"

The Kazakhs pulled the pins on the fuse igniters, beginning the burn sequence on the time fuse. Lining up on the door, they flowed back outside, Chuck moving out last to make sure no one was left behind.

Like race horses out of the gates, the squad ran at full speed back towards the trench where their comrades lay in wait. Each of them had plenty of motivation to put distance between themselves and the factory as their lungs burned, chest rigs bouncing back and forth full of grenades and spare magazines.

They were half way to the trench when another flare shot up into the sky.

Popping once it reached altitude, the flare illuminated the squad, and they came under fire a heartbeat later. Staccato bursts of machine gun fire searched them out. The militiamen occupying the other bunkers sent gunfire in three hundred and sixty degrees, crisscrossing the entire compound. Tracers skipped by, missing them by inches, stray bullets kicking up dirt at their feet.

The mercenary squad ran even harder, their strides eating up the ground in front of them.

The Samruk soldiers crouching in the trenches returned fire, shooting at the other bunkers. One mercenary cut loose, blasting one of the outbuildings with a RPG that exploded into the wall and collapsed it. First Squad dived back into the trench, Chuck sliding into home and falling on top of another one of the mercs.

"Everyone down!" he yelled.

The Kazakhs ducked as Chuck fired his own red pin flare into the air, signaling the support by fire line. Four PKM machine guns fired on automatic, sweeping the objective with 7.62 rounds for several seconds until the ammunition plant exploded, turning night into day.

The explosion blew the factory's roof sky high, throwing debris everywhere as the C4 ignited the phosphorus and magnesium. The fireball rose into the air like a miniature mushroom cloud, finally burning off into a thick plume of dark smoke.

Most of the platoon had to pick themselves up and out of the mud, the blast having knocked them off their feet; then they hit the ground again as debris began raining back down to earth. Hot pieces of metal hissed as they fell into the muddy puddles.

Chuck glanced back in the bunker. The twelve-year-old kid was still squirming against his restraints, trying to yell through the gag secured over his mouth. He looked back at the flaming wreck that had been an ammunition plant until a moment ago.

"Damn," he said, shaking his head. "This is your lucky day, kid."

Twenty Two

Liora turned her cell phone over in her hand, wringing it in her pants pocket.

For the first time, she cursed her high scores on placement exams, the ones that earned her a potentially career making opportunity, working out of the nondescript building just outside Tel Aviv. She had looked forward to conscription, but if she got caught now, well, she knew Shin Bet would make sure she never saw the light of day.

Ignoring inappropriate glances from her male co-worker, she excused herself to use the restroom as she set her headset down and got up from behind her station. She didn't know what he was looking at with all of her buried under her ill-fitting olive drab uniform.

Whatever.

With all the action popping off tonight, she had to hurry before the brass started showing up.

Unit 8200 was the Israeli answer to signals intelligence analysis. They took the information gathered by the Urim signals unit in the Negev Desert and rendered the intercepted data into actionable intelligence before delivering the intel packets to the Israeli Defense Forces and Mossad.

As a girl she had read lots of science fiction, quickly growing bored with school work, but even she was shocked by some of the technology she'd been exposed to since she started working at the unit. They tracked everything going through the air in four continents, not to mention underwater, Mossad units having installed taps on underwater communications cables that linked the Middle East to Europe by way of Sicily.

They monitored Inmarsat, commercial satellite communications, used direction finding stations to track maritime

212

shipping, and listened in to diplomatic traffic between embassies. That wasn't even including mobile SIGINT platforms that flew orbits over the Palestinian territories day and night.

Making sure the coast was clear, she ducked into the female restroom and locked herself in a stall. Officially the building was a Faraday cage that stifled civilian cellular signals. Realistically, a girl with an IQ well into the genius range finds ways to piggyback on existing military systems.

Flipping open her cell phone, she made the call.

The Iridium phone rang again and again amidst the chaos of the field hospital.

A stainless steel bowl filled with bloody medical instruments fell to the ground with a crash while patients wailed in pain.

Nick muttered something under his breath in frustration.

He'd lost two patients.

The filled body bags lining one of the building's walls didn't let him forget that fact.

He didn't know the mercenaries personally, but like a sniper missing a thousand meter shot, it was a blow to his professional ego. The former Special Forces operator turned surgeon wasn't used to losing. Not a life, not a drag race, not a video game, not anything.

The Kazakh on his surgery table had stepped on a landmine, a toe-popper, with just enough sauce in it to take off his foot up to the distal tibia and strip away a good portion of the soft tissue around his lower leg. Thankfully, his teammates had been well trained and immediately applied a tourniquet to their injured buddy's leg, or he would have bled out in under a minute.

Nick treated the casualty for shock, administered antibiotics, and was now putting a nerve block around several key

213

nerve clusters in the limb to ease the pain. In the past, such a procedure would only be conducted in the sterile medical setting of a hospital. Combat had a way of shifting priorities.

Using a large gauge syringe, Nick went into what was left of the amputated limb and injected a combination of lidocaine and epinephrine. The bulbous sack of painkillers would rest against the nerve endings, slowly diffusing across them to relieve the casualty's agony until he was received in a proper facility.

The injured mercenary looked a lot better than when he had arrived at the field hospital but the men waiting in triage didn't sound so hot.

"Let's get this guy moved," Nick stated gruffly.

The Kazakhs assigned to his detail moved in and transported the casualty off the gurney to make room for the next guy who had been waiting on deck, another kid, this one with a serious looking stomach wound.

Stripping off his surgical gloves, Nick found a towel and wiped the sweat off his brow. If the rest of the battalion got chewed up as bad as Charlie Company he was in for a long night. Bringing over a sterile set of medical tools, Andy was still on assist. Setting them down, he bent over to clean up the tools that had been dropped to the floor.

Nick immediately set to work on the gutshot mercenary as the detailed men brought him over and set him on the table.

Setting the blood and gore-covered tools to the side, Andy thought he could hear something above the racket and went looking for its source. He found the phone sitting on top of a tan colored assault pack. It was the Charlie Company commander's satellite phone.

The new CO and another guy with a sniper rifle slung over his shoulder were talking to each other in hushed tones in the corner of the building.

"Hey," Andy said, getting their attention. "Someone's trying to call."

The balding commander walked over and took the phone from him.

214

"Thanks," he said, repositioning the phone's antenna.

His green camouflage uniform was splattered with bits of bone and specks of blood. He stank of cordite and death.

"Hello," Adam said, taking the call.

As the voice on the other end spoke, his eyes grew wider.

Twenty Three

Panghsang became visible as the mercenaries neared the Chinese border, light puncturing through the darkness, providing the only respite from the jungle they had seen in hours. The medium-sized town sat on a fishhook-shaped piece of land that jutted into China, creating a type of unadministered autonomous zone on the Burmese side of the Shweli River. The UWSA used Panghsang as their center of operations. The Chinese took their cut of the profits and allowed the outlaw town to service the vices of visiting Chinese citizens.

Methamphetamine, gambling, and transvestites were all on the menu, alongside a variety of endangered species in a handful of restaurants. Everything was for public consumption, and the public was plenty hungry.

For the moment it was peaceful. The sounds of insects could be heard above the low rumble of the convoy's engines.

The Iveco trucks rolled through the darkness until the dirt road leveled out. It was the only road that serviced the town from the Burmese side. Passing between jungle foliage and the muddy river, the mercenaries drove into the town, encountering no resistance. The road forked at the first main intersection.

"Phase line red, phase line red," Deckard announced over the radio.

The final phase line was a control measure established during mission planning, a signal that launched the three platoons to their individual targets.

Third Platoon broke off from the rest of the convoy, heading towards the narrow bridge that connected Burma and China, while the other two platoons split up and continued to their objectives deeper inside Panghsang.

With the trucks reducing speed to a slow roll, two snipers

216

jumped off the back of one of Second Platoon's assault vehicles and disappeared into the night. Driving down darkened streets, Alpha Company continued to weave its way through the confusingly chaotic town.

Deckard rode up front with First Platoon. According to the target packet Samruk had received, Peng divided his time between the casino and the local whorehouse. He was hoping to catch the UWSA leader unaware, but had Third Platoon sealing off the bridge just to make sure he didn't escape. Besides that, bridges worked both ways, and he wasn't looking to square off with The People's Army anytime soon.

"Left turn, left turn onto objective road," he transmitted over the net.

The driver turned at the corner, taking them onto the target street. A few blocks down, they could see the flourescent lights and a crowd gathered outside one of the buildings.

"That's the casino," Deckard told the driver. "Hit it!"

The driver stepped on the gas, gunning it down the street. The other four assault trucks accelerated to keep up with the lead vehicle as they rolled right up to the front door. As rehearsed, his vehicle pulled to the far corner of the building and stopped, each vehicle taking a different corner and isolating the building.

No one came on or off the objective without their say-so.

Mercenaries hopped off the trucks, forming up into assault teams as they rushed the door.

That was when the first gunshot echoed through Panghsang.

Nikita panted, trying to catch his breath while looking back and forth for a way up. Having run several blocks down the street after getting dropped off, they needed to find a good vantage point. Time was running out.

"This way," the sniper said, slinging his rifle diagonally over his back, barrel up to prevent damage to the crown.

With Askar watching the streets, Nikita climbed up the cross members of a rectangular wrought iron telephone pole, quickly making his way up. There was always the chance of electrocution with the rat's nest of wires that served as the town's power grid, but the thought barely brushed across the surface of his mind. Reaching the top, he stepped off onto the adjacent rooftop, two stories high.

Taking a knee, Nikita provided security, watching down the road until Askar scrambled up the telephone pole and joined him. Helping his teammate over the lip of the roof, they jogged together to the opposite side.

Their primary target was impossible to miss. The cellular phone tower, or base station transceiver, as Piet had lectured, was the tallest freestanding structure in Panghsang. Extending the bipod legs on their SIG Blaser Tactical Two rifles, they gained target acquisition, sighting in on the transceivers mounted along the outside of the tower.

The earbud connection to his radio crackled in Nikita's ear.

"-urn left, this is the objective road."

The Kazakh exhaled, letting it out and taking calm, deliberate breaths. Long hours behind a precision weapon had taught him that a bolt action rifle nearly shot itself. All he needed to do was not screw up.

"Seven hundred meters," he whispered, as not to disturb the rifle while his cheek rested on the stock.

"Roger," Askar confirmed.

He was already dialed in to five hundred meters on his scope, so that if he had to make a quick shot, he could improvise some hasty range estimation and offset his sights, aiming high or low. Now he came up seven clicks on the scope's bullet drop compensator for a more precise adjustment.

"Is that the right building?" It was Second Platoon coming over the radio on the other side of town.

"No, it's the next block down," someone responded with a

halting German accent.

"Half value winds-" Nikita observed the leaves on the trees downrange moving ever so slightly.

The wind would have very little effect on the .300 Winchester Magnum round as it flew on a nearly flat trajectory to its target. The bullet was so powerful that it was advertised as having the same amount of kinetic force when it hit a target a thousand meters away as a .357 magnum did if you stuck it in a bad guy's chest and pulled the trigger.

"That's the casino," their commander said over the net. "Hit it."

"Let's do this," Nikita announced, pulling the butt stock deeper into the pocket of his shoulder. There were two rows of long rectangular transceivers on the top of the cell tower. Nikita aimed for the one on the upper left while Askar shot for the lower right.

Both fired simultaneously, working the rifle bolts straight to the rear after the first shot. The SIG's innovative design did not require the shooter to rotate the bolt in any fashion but merely pull and then push it back forward to chamber the next round, making for much faster combat reloads.

With his eye never leaving the scope, he observed the .300 winmag round blast the transceiver into several pieces, Askar's shot having the same effect. Rapidly firing, the two man team worked across the cell tower until each transceiver had been disabled.

With the primary task completed, the snipers moved to opposite corners of the building.

The Universal Night Sight attached in front of the scope illuminated the town in a creepy green color. It could have been designed to show black and white, but the human eye could detect more detail with the green tint. Nikita scanned the rooftops, identifying the casino three hundred meters away. Askar was on the other side, watching Second Platoon's objective.

Suddenly, shadows appeared on the roof, running towards the edge to ambush the convoy on the streets below.

It was time to deny the enemy the high ground.

Deckard pointed to the front door, his other hand gripping his rifle, directing his men into the casino.

"Go!"

The assault squads pushed through screaming civilians and made entry through the double doors, the sounds of slot machines emanating from within.

A gunshot cracked in the darkness.

Deckard looked up just in time to lunge out of the way.

The would-be trigger man went face first into the pavement, his teeth skipping across the street and bouncing off Deckard's booted foot. Edging backwards he looked up, the neon lights on the building preventing him from seeing into the darkness above.

Spraying the lip of the roof with a hasty burst of fire, he continued backing towards the protection of one of the assault trucks, his shots taking out segments of the neon bulbs. Another shot sounded, another body collapsed forward, this one down with arms hanging limply over the edge of the roof. His H&K G3 rifle smashed through another neon sign on its way down before landing on the sidewalk amid a shower of orange sparks.

The SIGs were a good choice after all, Deckard reflected.

Running back across the street, he pushed through the door and into another gunfight.

The casino floor opened up into rows of electronic gambling machines and craps tables, civilians hugging the floor while bullets were exchanged back and forth. The Kazakh mercenaries strong walled the huge interior space, lining up on the nearest wall and firing deeper into the room. With the gamblers wisely removing themselves from the line of fire, the casino's bouncers went down in a fusillade of fire.

Scanning his sector alongside his men, Deckard shifted his rifle barrel as a side door was thrown open and the security team came pouring out. One mercenary brought down the last man through the door by a snapshot, the others taking cover wherever they could.

First Platoon did the same, ducking behind chirping pachinko machines. Bullets cut in every direction, shattering glass mirrors, slot machines, and tearing apart the card tables. One of the Kazakhs dropped, taken down by a spray of autofire. The man next to him moved in front to provide cover fire for his comrade, when he was hit as well.

Deckard spotted one of the UWSA men peering from behind the roulette table, his AK barrel sweeping towards another of his mercenaries. Placing the red dot in his reflex sight on the shooter's forehead, Deckard squeezed the AK-103's trigger, putting a bullet between his eyes.

Finally, a squad leader hurled a flash-bang across the room. Thankfully, he was situationally aware enough to realize that using a fragmentation grenade would have killed the casino's patrons in the process. The stun grenade went off, temporarily blinding the nearby security guards. Another two shooters jumped out from behind slot machines, having avoided the stun effect, when the flash-bang suddenly detonated a second time, then a third and fourth, wrecking both hearing and sight.

The nine-banger continued to do its job, the Kazakhs gaining the upper hand for precious few seconds. A few of the gunmen staggered to their feet, shocked into incoherence. One ran, another began firing wildly.

The Kazakhs had distance from the flash-bang and forewarning on their side, leaving them able to take a more measured response. Long hours of training settled nerves, muscle memory executing the rest, just like hundreds of drills out on the range. The mercenaries carefully aimed and fired, and the nearest two gunmen fell, sprawled on the floor with lifeless eyes. Another stood next to the banger as it continued go off again and again, completely dazed until someone shot him in the chest.

221

The panicked shooter held down the trigger on his AK-47, sweeping the entire parlor with gunfire. A line of auto fire crept across the wall, tearing through one of the Kazakhs before the crazed man's magazine went dry. Deckard leveled his own rifle on target, double-tapping him in the face.

Shaking like a French soldier, the last security man bailed out the backdoor, 7.62 rounds chasing him on the way out but failing to land on target. As the door swung shut on its springs, they heard the rattle of machine gun fire out on the street. One of the assault trucks isolating the casino had taken care of the retreating gunman.

"Stairs, right!" Deckard said, attempting to get things moving again.

First and Second Squad moved towards the staircase that led up to the offices while Third Squad secured the casino floor, ushering civilians out both exits. The platoon medic moved in to treat casualties.

Jumping in the stack, Deckard followed the assaulters up to the second floor. First Squad was just reaching the top when a grenade flew through the air and bounced off the wall next to him.

Kurt Jager stepped over a body, triggering a burst into a stocky guard brandishing a pistol.

Disco strobes flashed everywhere, Canto-pop blasting over a stereo system, the whorehouse rapidly being taken down by the numbers as it was flooded with assaulters.

The scant intelligence Samruk had received with the Operations Order had placed Peng in one of two locations within Panghsang's exotic nightlife. The casino or the whorehouse; it was a toss-up, so they crashed both parties at the same time.

Killing Peng was instrumental to the dismantling of the UWSA. Of Chinese origin, not a whole lot was known about the elusive figurehead of Burma's largest narco-militia. No known family, didn't carry a cellular phone, paranoid, and with a large entourage of bodyguards, but no one seemed to know much more about the Golden Triangle's most prolific narcotics producer.

Second Platoon had stormed through the front door, executing the bouncers before they could reach for weapons, and hit the lounge, securing the ground floor in seconds.

The party came to an abrupt halt. Second Squad flexcuffed the bartender and secured the liquor cabinet while Third Squad went for the stage and rounded up the prostitutes. First Squad lined up the whorehouse's customers, to see if any of them matched the photo they had of Peng.

This is starting to look like a B-grade porn, Kurt mused.

Thankfully, someone kicked over the stereo and unplugged the strobe lights.

The platoon sergeant took charge, directing one squad to evacuate the girls and continue to secure the ground floor while the others began working their way up. The remaining twenty Kazakhs flowed upstairs.

Reaching the landing, the German mercenary saw the hall lined with private rooms, the doors covered with bed sheets tacked to the walls. This was where the action happened. The Kazakhs proceeded with gusto, apparently curious as to the goings on up in the second floor.

Four assaulters stacked on one entrance and pushed through the stained bed sheet, moving inside. Screams sounded from inside, not the high-pitched voice of a female prostitute but coming from the mercenaries themselves.

More yelling in Russian ensued before the curtain peeled open and a squat Chinese man in business attire stumbled into the hall, fumbling to buckle up his pants. Looking up he made eye contact with Kurt, paused for a moment, and then ran down the stairs.

Behind him, a deceptively tall woman walked out as the curses in Russian continued. Huge breasts were literally mounted to her chest, the product of a plastic surgeon's careful work. Kurt frowned as she strode past him in high heels, now noticing the penis dangling between her legs.

Other, more natural born women and their patrons were ushered out of their rooms. The men were cross-checked to make sure none of them were the High Value Target, or HVT, before cutting them loose as well. So far they had no positive matches.

Kurt spun, hearing someone scream somewhere down the hall. Storming down the corridor, he found which room it had come from. Inside, four Kazakhs were struggling to get a naked man under control as he thrashed back and forth. Flinging one commando off his back, the Burmese man pushed another squad member into a chair, knocking them both over. The other two attacked, one going for his legs and taking him to the ground while the other tried to secure his arms.

The crazed look in the man's eyes told Kurt that he was most definitely sampling the UWSA's product, the methamphetamine sending him into a frenzy. With what appeared as super-human strength, the drug addict managed to fight back, taking a bite out of one of the Kazakhs and kicking free of the other.

The drug left the man feeling no pain, allowing him strength that was well beyond the threshold of normal men. The mercenary who had been bit in the shoulder stumbled off in pain, while the others readied a counter attack, preparing to take him down. Kurt let them tackle the meth head again before stepping in.

Tightening his grip, Kurt slammed the stock of his rifle into the addict's face. The junkie screamed before focusing in on the German with wild eyes. Lunging towards him with bared teeth, he almost broke free of the Kazakhs' grasp a second time. Kurt struck again, this time holding nothing back.

The second blow stunned him, but Kurt didn't stop there, following up immediately and pounding at him a third and fourth time until he fell to the floor permanently. His blows had caved in the addict's skull, leaving him in a pool of his own blood.

Unfortunately for him, the methamphetamine addict had left them with little choice. The mercenaries had tried to restrain him rather than using lethal means, but the man had jeopardized the safety of the team with his drug-fueled frenzy.

Shouts echoed throughout the second floor as Russian voices called out that all rooms were clear. Back out in the hall, a commando stood guard on the narrow stairwell leading up to the third floor. Looking up, Kurt saw a heavy steel door which looked to be secured with multiple locks from the inside.

The front to the building hadn't even been that secure, other than a few bouncers, probably half asleep until the platoon arrived. For an internal door it was definitely out of place.

What the hell was up there?

"Bollocks," Richie cursed, fumbling with a stick of C4.

The demolition team was left over exposed in the middle of the bridge while they wired explosives in place.

The bridge only afforded them enough space to drive a single vehicle halfway down, to provide some semblance of cover fire if needed. A short walk twenty meters or so to the opposite river bank marked the far western boundary of the People's Republic of China. A lone Chinese border guard watched from the other side, occasionally shouting at the demo team but not daring to do much more.

On the Burmese side, four more assault trucks from Third Platoon waited, guns pointed towards China, just in case. Richie and the two engineers he had trained felt like fish bait, hung out to dry on the bridge that linked the growing superpower to the Third World.

It was called a Bailey bridge, an invention developed out of necessity during the Second World War. The trusses were prefabricated and trucked into position to be assembled by hand, no special machinery needed. Bailey bridges had the advantage of being easy to build, the ability to span about sixty meters of river,

225

and able to support commercial trucking.

The Kazakh engineers worked the trusses on both sides of the bridge while the retired safe cracker reached between the wooden planks to gain access under the bridge where he could find the sway braces. The long metal rods connected underneath the main structure, forming an X that maintained the bridge's rigidness. Using the same type of plastic flexcuffs for securing prisoners, Richie ziptied one-pound sticks of plastic explosives to each sway brace in his section, maintaining control of the leads that primed each charge.

Leaving the Kazakh commandos to their task, Richie retrieved his roll of detonation chord off the nearby assault truck, glancing up at the gunner who was eyeballing Red China nervously.

"Fucking cunt," Richie muttered under his breath.

He hoped all this trouble was worth it. Apparently the boss thought the Chinese might try to chase them into Burma. Gunfire was already raging inside Panghsang, the other two platoons going to work.

Unreeling the det chord, he strung it out in a circle around his charges before cutting the line with his folding blade and tying each end together in a square knot.

By now, the two engineers had finished their work and came to him with the leads to their own charges. They had placed one-pound charges between the channels on each truss and half-pound charges on each piece of diagonal bracing in their section of bridge. According to his calculations, it should be enough to bring the bridge down.

The three man demolition team tied their leads into the round main that Richie had laid out. With all ten charges tied into the det chord, Richie set about stringing a dual primed British junction into his system to detonate all of the explosives simultaneously.

The British mercenary had the entire system rigged, when the first gunshot sparked off one of the trusses just a few meters away.

The PKM on the assault truck belted out a long burst, stitching the Chinese border guard on the other side from crotch to chest, the Type 56 rifle he had carried falling silent. Not willing to waste another moment, Richie pulled the pins, starting the burn sequence on the time fuse.

Now you've done it.

Muzzle flashes from the Chinese side announced that they had in fact kicked the hornet's nest. Turret gunners in all five trucks fired back, dumping lead into Chinese territory. With gunfire now flying in both directions across the Shweli River, the demo team jumped on their truck.

Richie had cut a full two minutes of time fuse to give them plenty of time to make it to the minimum safe distance. If the truck broke down on the bridge after they initiated, they'd need every second of it. The ex-con's phobia wasn't based on irrationality, but rather experience. He bore the scars to prove it.

The driver threw the vehicle in reverse and stepped on the gas. The machine gunner let it rip, the muzzle flash illuminating the bridge as the truck lunged backwards. Bullets coming from the Chinese side rang the side of the truck like a cowbell, as well as slamming into the metal struts of the bridge on both sides.

The driver came too far to one side, scraping a long streak of paint along the bridge before arriving on the Burmese side of the river. Cutting the wheel, the driver pulled the truck behind a small stone wall for cover, the turret gunner rotating his machine gun back on target.

Now it was a full blown fire fight, the border guards being joined by the Chinese military, if the amount of incoming fire was any indication. Richie looked at his watch. Another minute until the bridge blew, but it might as well have been another hour while in contact with the enemy. They had to stay in position to make sure the job was done before seeking cover deeper in Panghsang.

The Chinese troops could always commandeer one of the flat keeled junks moored at the docks and put men on their side of the river, but they would be without heavy armor or heavy weapons, not to mention conducting an illegal border crossing.

The premise of the entire mission was that the Chinese would not be willing to instigate an act of war over their assault on Panghsang.

So much for that idea.

"Keep those guns up!" Richie screamed at the PKM gunner, now in the middle of reloading. Of course he didn't understand a word of English.

Loading the metal link belt into the feed tray, the Kazakh slammed down the feed tray cover and held down the trigger, flame belching from the barrel. The rest of the platoon had dismounted from their vehicles and shot at any enemy muzzle flashes in their sector.

Richie reached into the back of the assault truck and freed one of the Mk14 grenade launchers. The Milkor looked like a jumbo-sized revolver, loaded with High Explosive Dual Purpose 40mm grenades. Flipping on the holographic sight, he adjusted it for one hundred and fifty meters, far enough to hit the deepest enemy positions. There must have been a barracks nearby with the amount of shooting coming from the Chinese side, increasing by the second.

On the far bank he could see the bursts of enemy fire coming from behind the low wall that surrounded the border check point, the Chinese troops turning themselves into a linear target that Richie was more than happy to service.

Sighting in, he rapidly depressed the trigger, walking the barrel from side to side as he fired. The 40mm grenades made a hollow *pop, pop, pop,* as they spiraled out of the barrel and armed themselves as they arced across the river.

The explosives flashed as they made contact, devastating the Chinese lines.

Down at the other end of the convoy, one of the commandos launched an RPG. The rocket whizzed across the river and struck one of the enemy fortifications, spitting the remnants of sandbags and at least one human being into the air.

Steel cross members snapped, the explosion deafening them, as the C4 detonated. Richie stole a glance over the stone wall he had taken cover behind. Amazingly, the Bailey bridge was still standing, the plastic explosives having failed to completely sever the trusses.

Motherfu-

Richie squinted through the darkness as a pair of headlights came into view. In between the gunfire he could barely make out the rumble of an engine.

Then the Type 63 Armored Personnel Carrier came barreling down the bridge towards them, the heavy machine gun mounted to the roof aimed directly at Richie.

Deckard put his shoulder into the stack of assaulters in front of him and drove them forward, pushing them up the stairs as hard as he could. His legs acted like pistons; for all he knew, he was pushing his teammates into enemy fire and certain death. At the moment, death just seemed more certain with a grenade landing somewhere at their feet on the darkened staircase.

On cue, gunfire erupted at the top of the stairs. The squad on the steps behind him had turned and bounded down, while the other half of the stack had continued up. Up or down, options were limited.

Reaching the landing at the top, Deckard was thrown into the wall, the blast jarring his senses. The grenade demolished most of the wooden stairwell, a mercenary unlucky enough to be caught in the explosion screaming amid the chaos.

Everything seemed to move in slow motion.

Deckard struggled with his rifle, trying to find the correct grip, his hands felt like they had heavy gloves on them. He was vividly aware of the carpet in front of him being torn apart by enemy gunfire. Shouldering his Kalashnikov, Deckard searched the office he now found himself in, the Kazakh mercenaries to his left and right shooting on automatic.

An angry face with a flat nose appeared from behind a desk, a Skorpion machine pistol in his hands. Still on his knees, Deckard fired a single shot, catching his would-be executioner under the chin, a spray of blood turning aerosol in the air as he recoiled backwards.

Standing on shaky feet, he scanned the rest of the office. Desks and tables were laid out, along with some cots for people needing to sleep it off after a long night. A half dozen bodies now added to the interior decoration.

"Over here," an accented voice shouted in English. "This one is still alive."

Deckard looked down the ruined stairs, a gap now separating them from the ground floor. Below, the medic was attending to the commando caught in the grenade blast. His observation from afar told him that it didn't look good, a pool of crimson spreading beneath that Kazakh even as the medic attempted to get a tourniquet into place.

Turning away, he saw the Frenchman holding a captive militiaman pinned against the wall, the UWSA man's shoulder a bloody mess after acting as a bullet sponge during the firefight.

It was Jean-Francois, the new guy that he had met just hours earlier before leaving Astana. He didn't know much about him, but Frank vouched for the former legionnaire. Apparently, JF had *his shit in one sock,* as Frank had put it.

"That isn't Peng," Deckard told JF.

Wishful thinking.

JF spoke in Burmese to his prisoner. They continued back and forth for a moment as the commander stood by.

"This is his accountant," JF said, looking back at him.

"Where is the HVT located?"

The Frenchman continued his interrogation, his voice raising as the accountant stammered and then hesitated. JF shoved his thumb into the gunshot wound on his shoulder, causing him to wail in pain. Not as much pain as their teammate downstairs but enough to do the job.

With sweat pouring down his face, the UWSA bag man

spilled his guts.

"About five kilometers from here," JF translated. "A hilltop."

"Defenses?"

It didn't take as much prodding this time.

"Massive perimeter wall. Several large structures inside, mansions for Peng and his associates. Underground tunnels and bunkers, about a hundred men on his security force."

The bag man rambled on, words coming freely now.

"Damn," JF said shaking his head. "He says the compound cost sixty million USD to build. I guess he'd know if he is Peng's money man."

"Tell him he's coming with us," Deckard snorted. "And we don't like liars."

When JF told him, the accountant looked like he was ready to shit ten different kinds of bricks.

"Let's get the casualties packaged," Deckard said, keying his radio. "We'll cross load them into the Medical Evacuation Vehicle when we rendezvous with Second and Third platoon. I want us off this objective in five--"

His next words were cut off as the entire casino shook on its foundations, ceiling tiles rattling loose and falling on top of the mercenaries from above.

The cutting charges burned through the solid steel door, sending a thin line of liquefied metal punching into the frame, slicing through the locking mechanisms, and allowing the door to fall to the floor with a heavy clang.

The Kazakhs fanned out through the top floor of the whorehouse, moving systematically from room to room. The first few were empty, so the mercenaries continued moving on. Fresh screams drew Kurt's attention, another meth addict maybe.

Another problem he would rather not have.

Stepping into one of the rooms at the end of the hall, he was shocked by the scene he had stumbled upon. Four Kazakhs stood along the wall, guns pointed forward and shouting orders. Next to one of the windows, a Chinese man held a woman hostage, a screwdriver pressed into her throat.

The bedroom was filthy, even with the plastic sheets covering the floor. The place stank of death. A video camera attached to a tripod lay on its side, someone knocking it over in the commotion. Laying on the plastic tarp was the eviscerated body of another young woman, lifeless eyes staring into oblivion.

From the looks of things, she had had her fingers sliced off and her intestines spilled in front of her before her tormentor slashed her neck from ear to ear. The evidence made clear why a heavy steel door separated the third floor from the rest of the building.

Snuff tourism.

The Chinese man stood in his boxer shorts, snarling as he jabbed the screwdriver deeper into the woman's skin, drawing blood. The woman cried for something, anything, in a language none of them understood. Her breasts had been badly burned, the results of the torturer putting out cigarettes on her chest.

"Slingshot, this is Oscar Two," Kurt said, into his radio speaking in Russian.

"Oscar, this is Slingshot," Askar's voice came over the radio.

"Top floor, fifth window on your left."

"Confirm, top floor fifth window. My left."

"Roger."

The Chinese sadist yelled at them in rapid fire Cantonese, no doubt warning them to back away or he'd kill the woman.

"Which one," Askar asked.

"The taller of the two, on your right-hand side."

"The taller one on my right."

"Wait one."

Kurt began pushing the Kazakhs towards the door, waving

his hand to the Chinese hostage-taker. The mercenaries resisted at first, preferring a showdown, but the look in Kurt's eyes told them he was serious. Pushing them out, the former GSG-9 commando stood alone in the door. He didn't want any friendlies learning a difficult lesson in terminal ballistics.

"Ready?" the radio hissed, the precision marksman now chomping at the bit.

Kurt depressed the transmit button on his hand mic.

"Do it."

Glass shattered and the Chinese man pitched forward as if hit in the back of the head by a baseball bat. Of course, it was merely a sympathetic reaction, the .300 winmag bullet having cored through his skull and exiting through his forehead in a spray of gore. Gray white matter painted the wall to Kurt's side.

The corpse fell on top of the Burmese woman, the screwdriver rolling across the plastic sheets.

Kurt covered the distance in two large steps, with the Kazakhs right behind him. Flinging the lifeless body away, they dragged the woman to her feet and carried her out of the torture chamber. Eyes wide, she was too shocked to cry. The German mercenary gritted his teeth.

They were too late to save her companion, her brown eyes staring up at him.

Turning away he keyed the mic again.

"Good shot."

It sounded like a thousand nails on the world's largest chalk board.

The bridge strained under the weight of the APC, struts stretching and groaning in protest. The Chinese soldier in the gunner's hatch swung the DShK towards Richie, aiming down the flip-up rear sight at his chest, thumbs pressing on the butterfly trigger.

With a final screech of twisted metal, the bridge hinged where the explosives had partially cut through the metal braces and cross bars. The armored vehicle dropped as the bridge fell away from under it, the gunner bracing himself to no avail. The treads made contact with the dark water below, displacing enough liquid to cause waves to rush and lap at both sides of the river. The gunner jumped out from behind his machine gun a moment too late, the vehicle taking on water and lurching to one side.

Finally, the APC barrel rolled in the river, dragging the gunner down to the bottom with it.

Trying to catch his breath, Richie eyed the bridge, an entire section now missing, sunk underwater. The Kazakhs and the Chinese eyeballed each other for a moment, guns silent, trying to process what had just happened.

Gathering their wits, the Kazakhs commenced firing.

Deckard hurtled across the gap in the stairs that the grenade had blown wide open. Landing with bent knees, he rolled forward over his shoulder before coming up on a knee with his AK at the ready.

His men on the ground floor coughed and swatted at the smoke that now permeated through the casino. The platoon medic leaned back, having protected his casualty's body during the explosion. Reaching for a pill pack full of antibiotics, he resumed his work, unfazed by the combat all around him.

Sprinting forward, the former soldier searched for the source of the explosion, following a trail of debris. He burst into the security room, his barrel tracking multiple people, all turning out to be his own men. They looked up at Deckard with Bambi eyes.

Between them, he could see a heavy vault door had been

thrown open by the charges they had set. Grabbing the nearest commando by his collar, Deckard pushed him into the wall.

"What the hell do you think you're doing setting off demo without telling anyone?"

The Kazakhs shrugged back at him, knowing they were in the wrong.

"Goddamned pirates," Deckard grunted.

The vault door had been part of a walk-in safe that the casino had used to secure their profits, swindled from visiting Chinese businessmen and locals spending hard-earned narco-dollars. Fanning away the foul-smelling smoke, he walked inside the vault, the bank robbers at his heels.

The room was lined with shelves that overflowed with hard currency, stacks of yen, euros, and dollars bundled together. Bags and cases of gold coins and bullion were shoved into every crevice of the vault. Dollar signs were in all of their eyes as they scanned the hoard.

"I'll be damned," Deckard whispered.

TWENTY FOUR

Alpha Company's assault trucks sat a little lower on their suspension as they drove out of Panghsang, the spoils of war secreted in them were even heavier than expected. Since they were on a professional vacation to Southeast Asia, the mercenaries had seen no reason not to give themselves a hardship bonus, payable in gold bullion.

"Is your Iridium on?" Adam asked over the satellite communication system in Deckard's truck. He was wrapping things up at the field hospital, the Turkish pilots already flying one exfil flight for casualties back to Singapore.

"Yeah, I got it right here."

"Standby for a phone call. You are going to want to take this one."

"A phone call from who?"

"One of my sources."

Just then the satellite telephone Velcroed to the console in front of him began to ring, the display lighting up with a number he didn't recognize.

"Is that it? I hear something ringing?"

"Yeah it is. Catch you later."

"Out here."

Deckard set the hand mic down and tore the Iridium telephone off the dashboard.

"Hello?"

"Uh, hi. I was asked to report to the person reached at this number."

Deckard frowned.

A woman's voice. She sounded cute, too.

"I'm listening."

"Uh, well, look, you guys have to stop shooting up the

Chinese border."

"Who the hell are you?"

"I'm not good with names. I'm only talking to you as a favor," she said, sounding put off.

"Okay." Deckard couldn't do much about that over the phone. "Go ahead."

"Some guys, I guess your guys, just shot up a platoon of Chinese Special Forces troops on the border. Are you trying to start World War Three over there?"

Jesus Christ. Richie.

"Anything else?"

"Yeah, I've been doing traffic analysis, and right now they are waking people up in Beijing and putting several military bases on alert. They're calling up people up at my place of employ as well. I hope you know what you are doing."

"We'll be out of here before it comes to that."

"You might want to reposition your UAV in the meantime to watch the border until you leave. That's my opinion anyway."

"What UAV?"

"Uh, the one orbiting over your convoy at ten thousand feet."

Nice.

"You got a make and model on that thing?"

"The Chinese have looked at the radar cross section and think it's a Global Hawk, or at least the same platform. American-made for sure, and using crypto that we've never seen before. Neither have the Chinese, from what we've intercepted."

She was young, spent some time in the States, but Deckard could detect the Israeli accent. Almost certainly a conscript. Adam must have had something big on her in order to persuade her to break this many national security protocols.

"What about Peng?"

OPSEC was a joke at this point. This twenty-year-old kid straight out of commo school knew more about his operation then he did.

"He thought the SPDC had taken down his drug labs to the

237

south but then when he got a call about the weapons factories getting hit, he bailed for his fortress. We've had a lock on his cell phone for the last few hours. He's calling in every favor he has."

"Looking for an exit strategy."

"He knows you guys mean business."

"His compound?"

"Imagery is still working on that."

"Anything else I should know?"

"Yeah." She even had a cute laugh. "Tell your friend I said, 'hi'."

Adam.

Son of a bitch.

The five guards at the checkpoint were quickly reinforced, tripling their manpower in preparation for the foreigners they knew were coming. Magazines were loaded, charging handles racked, grenades were laid out next to fighting positions within easy reach. From behind cement barriers they watched the road for headlights, listened for the sound of engines.

The UWSA militiamen heard the sound of the rocket being launched, but could not locate which direction the sound came from. Rocket-propelled grenades slammed into their position, shrapnel tearing through several of Peng's proletarian guard. The survivors flung themselves to the ground as 40mm grenades began raining down.

The HEDP rounds struck the concrete and exploded a fraction of a second later, crumbling the bunkers. Before anyone could react, the enemy's assault trucks were on top of them. The militiamen never heard the engines, never saw the headlights.

Drivers closed the distance, wearing their night vision devices with only infrared headlights on, leaving no sign visible to the naked eye. Engines had been switched to recon mode, on electric power to reduce sound.

One of the guards looked up cautiously, only to find himself staring down the barrel of a machine gun as the first truck drove by. The PKM gunner unleashed a burst of fire into the bunker before driving out of range, the second truck replacing it and repeating the maneuver.

The entire A/co convoy drove up the road, firing into the bunkers as they flashed past.

At the top of the hill, reinforced steel doors were swung shut at the compound entrance, heavy crossbars lowered into place. Guards rushed down the walkway along the top of the twenty meter high wall, guns at the ready.

Richie ran forward as gunfire pounded the compound's walls.

PKM, RPG, and AK fire hammered away on both sides, Samruk and the UWSA equally unwilling to offer any quarter to their opposition. Struggling with the weight of the explosives in his hands, he zigzagged, trying to avoid gunfire, right up to the side of the modern day castle.

Slamming the forty pound platter charge on the concrete wall, one of his engineers came up behind him with a prop stick. The hydrogel on the contact side of the charge would stick to nearly any surface, but due to its weight, they needed the wooden board to make sure it remained in place.

Concrete chips rained down around them, the autofire tearing away at the wall above them. The assault trucks were confined to one dirt road, giving them a hard time as they tried to get as many guns in the fight as possible. The best that platoon sergeants could manage was to line up on the grassy area at the mouth of the fortress, putting suppressive fire above the demo team. All it would take was a slight pause in the shooting and the militiamen would start dropping grenades on Richie and his engineers.

The platter charge was already primed, shock tube back-stacked in a roll for immediate deployment. Once the prop stick was in place, the trio dashed back to the trucks, trailing shock tube behind them. Taking cover behind one of the vehicles, the British demo expert attached the initiation system to the tube.

Richie had quickly assessed that trying to breach the metal doors would be a disaster. It was probably secured with steel I-beams, and they had no idea what was on the other side. If they had any sense about them, the UWSA would have pulled a bus or a dump truck behind the gate. Bypassing the main entrance altogether was a far better course of action.

Passing the M81 fuse igniter to one of the engineers, he began a hasty countdown over the radio; they were getting pounded with gunfire while they sat on the road.

"I have control," Richie said, his words high-pitched and riding high on adrenaline. "fivefourthreetwo-"

The Kazakh engineer twisted and pulled the M81's pin, sending a flash of blue riding down the shock tube. Forty pounds of C4 plastic explosives pushed the metal plate on the contact side of the charge straight through the reinforced concrete wall, collapsing the structure under its own weight.

Burmese gunmen standing on the catwalk along the inside of the wall were blown off to fall and be crushed on the ground below, a few getting buried under the rubble. With the gunfire temporarily halted, First Platoon rushed forward and into the smoke. They were determined to crawl through the breach, even if they had to find it by hand.

Through the haze Richie saw a bright blue light, a chem stick left behind by one of the assaulters to mark the breach point where the wall had collapsed. A fresh round of shooting broke out on the other side as the assaulters made it inside the compound. Meanwhile, Second Platoon ran towards the blue marker, ready to back up their comrades.

Slinging his rifle off his shoulder, Richie looked back,

waving Third Platoon forward.

The smoke was beginning to clear as his platoon scrambled over the pile of concrete blocks and metal rebar. Inside the compound, First Platoon had occupied Peng's ornamental garden, ringed with an artificial stream, using it as cover to lay down a base of fire on the mansion while Second Platoon moved forward.

With the mansion suppressed, Second Platoon moved in a wedge formation headed straight for two oblong wooden buildings on the nearside of the compound. RPG-7 gunners loaded and fired rockets that drowned out the first part of a transmission coming over the radio.

"-ance on the main building. Do you copy?" It was Samruk's commander.

"Say again, over," Richie yelled into his hand mic.

"Third Platoon, advance on the main structure. Confirm?"

"Hit the main building, roger."

"We'll shift fire as you close the distance, out."

Finding Kanat, he pointed the platoon sergeant towards their new objective. Nodding, Kanat gave the hand and arm signal to his men to move in a column up along the far side of the mansion. Feeling like redcoats in the Revolutionary War, third platoon was able to mass their fire as soon they were engaged by the enemy.

Taking effective fire, Third Platoon hit the ground, gunmen in the first and second stories of the mansion shooting from deeper in the rooms to try to avoid First Platoon's onslaught. Rushing to remove themselves from open ground, they advanced forward, half the platoon remaining stationary to put more fire on the target while the other half rushed forward. The technique was called bounding overwatch and was designed to keep the enemy engaged while advancing tactically.

Needless to say, rushing forward nearly into First Platoon's tracer fire was somewhat disconcerting, but no matter where the unit moved, front, back, or side to side, no available options guaranteed you wouldn't eat a bullet.

It took four bounds of shooting and maneuvering before

they reached the mansion. First Platoon shifted fire while Third stacked up and prepared for entry. Reaching into his bag of tricks, Richie slammed a door charge on the front entrance.

Taking a squad with him, Deckard backtracked to the breach site. Third Platoon was effecting an entry into the mansion, while his platoon redirected their base of fire. They would follow on, moving to the objective, once Richie established a foothold, but first they had to get the gate open.

The UWSA had further obstructed the way by parking a bulldozer behind the compound's entrance. Climbing over the mud-covered treads, Deckard noticed that the obstacle would have been somewhat more effective if they had removed the keys from the ignition.

Twisting the key, Deckard revved the engine to life and backed the heavy machinery out of the way. Running forward, a squad of mercenaries unlocked the gate and swung the doors open. Now Alpha Company's assault trucks came pouring through, locking down the compound with automatic weapons pointed in every direction.

With the immediate area secure, Deckard got on the radio, ordering First Platoon to cheat forward up to the mansion. From Peng's garden, the Kazakhs were supposed to move in a wedge formation with good separation between each individual soldier. In reality it turned into more of a bum rush as they ran for the entrance.

Deckard sprinted after them, trying catch up with his platoon.

Inside, the mansion opened up into a large central room that was in absolute chaos. A fountain in the center of the lobby was shot to pieces, water rippling across the floor. The dead bodies of two Kazakhs from Third Platoon lay nearby, blood mixing with the water in a pinkish hue.

Richie was crouched behind what was left of the fountain, his men swapping fire with Peng's shooters on the second floor balcony above and from doorways on the ground floor. With First Platoon scurrying across the lobby like ants flowing from an ant hill, the Samruk troopers quickly established fire superiority.

FMK grenades were hurled at the militia holdouts, four Kalashnikovs hosing down each enemy position. Marble bannisters and wooden door jams were reduced and destroyed under the barrage. With the initiative back on their side, Second Platoon cleared the east wing while First Platoon cleared the west wing of the mansion.

Moving from room to room, squad members carrying shortened Remington 270 shotguns ballistically breached interior doors, kicking them open before assault teams entered and engaged the enemy, single and multiple shots cracking off as they cleared down the long halls.

The mercenaries had hit a snag.

Having cleared the ground floor, they discovered the stairway down into the basement, the landing opening up on a concrete slab leading to the entrance to Peng's underground fortress.

Richie pushed the Kazakhs aside, examining the vault door. Whistling, he walked back and forth, looking at the grouting the door was set in. His eyes probed, searching for any weaknesses and finding none. The safe room was more of an underground bunker.

The door itself was reminiscent of some of the barriers he had encountered in England or France, seriously high-end stuff. The door would be loaded with layers of ball bearings or metal chips to prevent drilling, the metal itself including layers of copper and aluminum designed to transfer heat and interfere with cutting torches.

If his suspicion was correct, and sometimes it was, a gas ejection device would be placed between barrier layers. In civilian settings they usually included non-lethal tear gas, but in this situation it was more likely to be a nerve or blister agent.

"Maybe an explosively formed penetrator," he remarked with his hands on his hips.

"Not on your fucking life."

Richie jumped, on hearing the voice appear from nowhere. Turning, he found Deckard standing behind him, covered in sweat, grit stuck around his neckline and the corners of his eyes.

"I told you to bring down that bridge, not start a shooting war with the world's largest military."

"Couldn't be helped, boss."

Deckard sighed.

"We need to identify Peng, which means you can't put a plasma jet through that vault door and incinerate everyone beyond recognition."

"You got it all wrong--"

"Use the thermic lance instead. You can still frag everyone inside after."

Richie stormed off, mumbling something, heading for the stairs.

Deckard held his radio to his ear, listening as Alexander with Second Platoon gave the word that they had cleared the barracks, encountering limited resistance.

Suddenly the mansion rattled, something buzzing overhead.

"Fast movers," Deckard announced to no one in particular.

Bounding back up the steps and into the hallway, Deckard ran for the door while screaming into his radio. "All units, get under overhead cover!"

Stepping outside, Samruk's commander looked into the night sky. The first pass was just to get a lay of the land. With the second, they would be going hot.

"Everyone get indoors now. Leave the trucks where they

244

are. I want--"

Flashes streaked through the sky. The ball of fire began falling towards the earth, splitting into two sections before burning out on its trajectory to the ground.

He couldn't be sure, but had a feeling that he had just witnessed a UAV, probably a Global Hawk, getting shot down at ten thousand feet.

Looking down, he keyed his hand mic.

"Anyone find the armory? Report."

"No."

"*Nyet.*"

"*Nyet.*"

"Nah."

"*Nyet.*"

"*Nein.*"

"Probably behind this door." Richie.

"Make it fast. I need some of that hardware up here if intel is correct."

"Got it."

The Chinese Chengdu J-10 fighter jets came in low and slow, strafing Peng's compound. The first J-10 let rip a burst of twenty-three millimeter cannon fire, the massive bullets tearing up the terrain before crossing over one of the assault trucks. Several mercenaries who hadn't evacuated fast enough were cut down by the jet's stream of fire.

Now anyone left outside understood the urgency, sprinting for the mansion and the barracks as the second J-10 came in right behind the first, firing up another one of A/co's trucks, detonating something on board. The vehicle was quickly consumed in a blaze, bullets cooking off in the flames sounding like firecrackers.

Whether the Chinese were pissed about Richie's indiscretions and were seeking revenge, or Peng had called in a favor, using some piece of dirt on the PRC as leverage, the rationale seemed irrelevant at this point.

The fighters were circling around for another pass.

Richie walked towards the vault door, his hands covered with heavy gloves, face shielded with a darkened welding visor.

Burning through nearly two inches of steel a second, he pressed forward holding the thermic lance by its pistol grip, the other end connected to an oxygen bottle. The vinyl covered rod made up the actual lance. Inside were steel and aluminum wires that, when infused with oxygen from the O2 bottle and charged by a twelve-volt battery, burned at over ten thousand degrees.

The lance created a superheated plasmic cone that was enough to burn through any barrier in seconds, rather than spend all night wearing through dozens of drill bits.

Moving the lance from one attack point to the next, sweat beaded on Richie's forehead, even as cannon fire swept the compound topside. They could feel the gunfire reverberate through the mansion. He was moving as fast as he could.

"Richie, what the hell is going on down there?" his radio nagged him, the voice on the other end sounded stressed.

Gritting his teeth he hoped for the tear gas rather than a fast acting nerve agent.

Deckard dove for the ground as 23mm fire ripped into the UWSA's headquarters. The Chengdu fighter came in along the fortress' long axis, shooting up another assault truck, the barrage of fire walking across the lawn and into the mansion itself.

Large caliber bullets tore open the roofing and smacked into the stone floor before the jet broke off, circling around for another pass.

"All stations on this net," Deckard said into his radio "triangulate fire approximately a hundred meters in front of the jets the next time they make a pass at us."

To Richie's delight it was just an Oleoresin Capsicum based gas that was ejected from the vault's fail-safe mechanism and not mustard gas or something worse. The OC stung his face, burning his eyes with some of the worst pain he'd felt in recent years. The tears flowed down his face freely as he hyperventilated in the narrow confines of the basement.

Pushing the thermic lance through the blast plate on the door, he managed to disable the final locking bars. Trying to blink away the tears, he spun the valve shut on the oxygen bottle and set down the lance. The Kazakhs moved forward with scarfs and bandanas tied across their faces against the OC gas and attached a tow strap to the handle on the composite metal door.

With eight men on the other end of the strap, they managed to yank the door a few inches ajar with the first heave. From inside they could hear shouting in Chinese, the actions on pistols and submachine guns being racked.

Another heave and the door was pulled farther open, this time leaving about a foot of space. Two mercenaries ran up, each tossing a nine-banger through the opening as gunfire began slamming into the vault door from the inside.

Giving a final tug on the tow strap, they got the door fully opened, just as the flash-bangs began to go off. Two squads were already on standby and rushed through the door. Stacked in a column, they pushed forward like Roman legionnaires in a phalanx, desperate to get into the fight.

The first assaulter through the door immediately went down under a hail of gunfire.

Jean-Francois ran for the assault truck and jumped up on the side. His boot catching on the side of the truck, he stumbled before righting himself. Slinging his rifle, he reached down to the pivot mount and yanked the retaining pin out that held a PKM machine gun in place.

The stench of gasoline invaded his nose, the tank punctured from one of the previous gun runs.

The sound of jet engines grew near.

The J-10 opened fire with its 23mm cannon, JF firing his own weapon, careful to lead the aircraft by a wide margin by watching his tracer fire. It was one of those instances where tracers were of vital importance, but of course the enemy could follow their trail right back to him as well.

Several other streams of fire sprayed in front of the Chinese fighter jet, the Kazakhs having the same idea and recovering their automatic weapons from the trucks during a pause in the chaos. The others joined in, firing their AK-103s from doors, windows, and anywhere else they were able to take cover.

Someone must have begun scoring hits, the pilot probably hearing the impact against his fuselage, because suddenly he yanked on his controls. The J-10 arched up and away, attempting evasive maneuvers to avoid the ground fire.

Shouts of elation went up from the mercenaries, proud and relieved to have driven off the enemy.

Sadly, their celebration was short-lived as the second J-10 came in on approach, nosing directly towards JF's position.

Four members of Second Platoon came stomping up the stairs and down the hallway. In their hands they struggled with two rectangular dark-green wooden crates which were carried by attached rope handles. Setting them down in the lobby, they stepped away as Deckard kicked open one of the lids with the edge of his boot.

As advertised, a HN-5 anti-aircraft missile launcher sat in the crate in pristine condition.

"We have them cornered in their bunker," one of the Kazakhs reported.

"Peng?"

"We are looking."

Grunting, Deckard yanked one of the missile launchers out and shouldered it. One of the older looking Kazakhs handled the second HN-5. Sometimes he forgot that their Central Asian home country was once a Soviet satellite state, many of them having grown up around Russian weapons platforms.

"Let's do this," he told the Kazakh.

Stepping outside, they screwed the thermal batteries into the front end of the launch control unit attached to the missile tube itself. With the HN-5s on their shoulders, they used the iron sights on the tubes to target the approaching J-10, while they waited for the electrical supply and internal gyros to stabilize.

Deckard milked the trigger halfway while sighting in on the Chinese fighter jet. He was the first to get a solid IR lock, the control unit buzzing and blinking red.

"I got him," Deckard said, ordering the Kazakh to stand down.

As the jet swooped over the compound, he took up the rest of the slack in the trigger. The missile launched, the booster burning out before it left the tube. The rocket engine initiated, the four stabilization fins unfolding simultaneously.

With the HN-5's seeker locked onto the jet's IR signature, the missile flew at over four hundred meters a second, eating up the distance in a heartbeat.

Jean-Francois rolled the dice and lost, the two hundred round belt having been exhausted by holding down the PKM's trigger, leaving him with nothing but a smoking barrel.

The J-10 closed in.

Cannon fire spat from the aircraft, large caliber rounds tearing up the ground and headed straight for him. The former legionnaire winced a moment before the anti-aircraft rocket smashed into the side of the jet.

The impact fuse on the missile detonated the fragmentation warhead, lighting up the J-10's reserve fuel tank and separating one of the wings, sending the rest of the jet spinning out of control. Separate streams of fire flashed out in the night as the wreckage crashed into a hill behind the UWSA compound.

The second J-10 coming in behind tried to pull up, the pilot having seen what happened to his partner. He popped chaff and flares just a moment too late as a second HN-5 missile snaked right up the jet's tailpipe and exploded, blowing the aircraft out of the sky.

With the back end taken out, the aircraft folded on itself, wings blazing, the fuselage engulfed in flames. The pilot never had the chance to eject as the enormous g-forces hurled him back and forth before the entire jet separated and fell to the jungle below like miniature meteorites.

JF set the machine gun down, remembering to breathe.

Deckard turned towards the Kazakh as he dropped the still smoking launch unit to the ground.

"Talk to me about promotions when we get home," he told the mercenary.

Deckard's business model promoted positive performance.

Shaking his hand, Deckard could have sworn he saw a smirk on the trooper's face.

Peng cursed his misfortune.

He had gotten his ducks in a row a long time ago, greased the right palms, played by the rules, and now he was left in ruin. The Sino-Burmese gangster had so much dirt on so many Chinese bureaucrats that he wielded a disproportionate amount of power that stretched far beyond the small autonomous zone he had carved out of the jungle to freely run his narcotics business from.

If the information he had was revealed in the Chinese press, dozens of officials would instantly walk home and commit suicide, knowing that there was no such thing as a not-guilty verdict in a Chinese courtroom. That was the kind of power that allowed him to wake up generals in the middle of the night and have fighter jets deployed against his enemies.

Waging war against the Burmese Government might be off-limits, but gunning down foreign mercenaries was another matter entirely.

Straining his entire body, he managed to push open the trap door at the top of the ladder he stood on.

They had watched the entire assault via closed-circuit television cameras hidden throughout his compound. Sixty million bought a lot, but apparently not invulnerability. The foreign mercenaries brought down the reinforced concrete walls, fought their way inside, and had the audacity to burn their way into his inner sanctum.

Seeing the red glow of some strange type of cutting torch slicing through the supposedly impenetrable vault door, Peng had decided it was time for him to utilize his fall back plan. He abandoned his bodyguards just as the door was being hauled open, slipping behind a bookcase that moved on well maintained hinges. Disappearing into the darkness, he had heard the firefight rage behind him.

It was a four hundred meter long underground escape tunnel, the first structure he had built, even before the walls went up. The contractors came from Hong Kong, recommended by a Triad boss and trading partner of his. It was the backup plan for the backup plan.

Emerging into the terraced central highland fields, Peng actually felt relieved. He'd been fighting his whole life. The UWSA leader took a deep breath of fresh air, palming the pistol tucked into his pants and freeing it, just in case.

Every day for decades, he had to respond to one emergency or another. Uniting warring ethnic groups, playing others off against each other, fighting it out with the SPDC every few years, blocking Triad attempts to edge into his market. It was exhausting and he wasn't getting any younger.

In a strange way he had been provided with a way out. Untapped offshore bank accounts were hidden all over the world, bulging with narco-dollars. He'd spend his final days in Mauritius or someplace drinking whiskey and taking a different woman to bed every night.

Kicking the trap door shut, he smiled as he walked towards the Chinese border.

A quick swim across the river and he would link up with some of his customers. If they wanted access to his cash reserves, and they would, his people would be more than happy to issue him a brand new passport and a one way plane ticket.

Smiling, he never heard the shot that thundered across the terraced paddies.

"Target down," Nikita said, racking the bolt on his sniper rifle.

Twenty Five

"We are entering an entirely unique period of history, one unlike any era of the past. In the near future, power will be drawn from new centers of gravity, the very idea of the state quickly becoming obsolete. Old mechanisms, old systems of vertical integration, will give way to non-state actors. This will be a complete paradigm shift, not just in the political and economic arenas, but a shift in social dynamics as well. This will be a change in energy itself. Complete deinstitutionalization will take place in the coming decades. As the state bleeds credibility and legitimacy, new centers of population will turn towards the multinational corporate conglomeration, the guerrilla organization, the terrorist group, the privatized army, or other free agents. Crime and war will blur. Citizen and soldier alike will be thrown into direct competition with every single human being on the planet.

"While the old paradigm will persist deeper into this century, it will become increasingly irrelevant. The old powers still attempt to shape the geopolitical landscape, but this new energy will outpace any monopoly on state violence. While the Global South continues to construct federations to stand against Western influence, a new type of undeclared global insurgency will rise in the place of these old powers."

Jarogniew looked up from the podium. The participants seated around the stage were hanging on his every word, large eyes searching for insight from the world's mapmaker.

"Thank you," he finished, taking a sip of water as the audience politely applauded, not sure how to respond to the world's subject matter expert on international strategy telling them that their life's work would be crashing down around them in the coming years.

His words had been frank and candid.

The former presidential advisor had made his career with brutal honesty. Some ignored his words, to their detriment. Others just stared in disbelief, convincing themselves that he had not, in fact, meant what he had just said, that somehow they had confused his message.

Shaking themselves back to reality, Council on Foreign Relations members lined up to ask questions. Jarogniew set down his glass of water, nodding at the little worm of a man at the front of the line.

"My question," he said, clearing his throat, "is that as we find our way forward, what are the main challenges we face in creating this new style of global governance?"

"Yes, the main challenge we face in achieving this goal is the global political awakening that is now taking place. While in the past only the elites were permitted into certain intellectual circles and given a say in society, we are now in a time of advanced communications technology that allows individuals to attain a level of connectivity like we have never seen before.

"Only the elites participated in the first Renaissance, knowledge such as philosophy and mathematics was a carefully guarded secret, restricted to Pythagorean cults and the like in more ancient times. Today nearly everyone has access to every single word ever written, and ideas propagate much faster today, whereas a mental reshuffling would require a hundred years during the Middle Ages.

"This leads to human beings the world over casting aside their previous status of political inertness, now becoming awakened, activated, and joining in a struggle for a new type of personal freedom or an older kind of ethnic self-determination. This awakening triggers social turbulence that transcends sovereign borders and is the most significant threat to the construction of global governance."

"Uh," the suited man stammered, "thank you."

Most of them thought they understood what he was saying.

Jarogniew smiled a vicious smile to an oblivious audience.

The time was now.

For hundreds of years the power elite, the anointed ones destined to rule mankind, had used a system of incrementalism, slowly changing paradigms and archetypes, humanizing the mechanical and dehumanizing the living. Injecting insanity into the collective unconscious, making the masses pliable, and ultimately useful as serfs working the cotton fields of a dying global economy.

However, his fellow elite failed to identify their own shifting status in the grand hierarchy.

They occupied the gilded halls of academia, manned the round table groups, and staffed the foundations, the men who pulled the invisible puppet strings tied to the alleged seats of power. They belonged to a kind of shadow government, invisible custodians that most were subconsciously aware of, even if programmed cognitive dissonance told them otherwise. This farce was falling apart before their eyes.

Jarogniew sneered as he watched the rain water streak down his limousine window.

Bohemian Grove, Council on Foreign Relations, Chatham House, Club of Rome, The Trilateral Commission, The Bilderberg Club. They had all served their purpose, managing global order as the monarchy and the Lombardi cartels had before them.

Mostly they were just old men, playing at Byzantine power games while the world passed them by. The awakening would crush them, rising up like a phoenix in the coming years, ending absolutism once and for all.

He had seen it in his mind's eye long ago.

Over a decade had passed since he had sat his own faction down for a private meeting, creating what they internally called The Council of Three. They were the capstone of the pyramid. If they didn't act now, bypassing incrementalism for something more drastic, they would all lose control over everything, *everyone*, forever. Their great work would be left unfulfilled.

Disgust for his elitist minions fading, Jarogniew's face crested with the familiar smile, the animalistic intensity glowing in his eyes.

Drawing together and compartmentalizing various experts and controllers, they had dusted off old plans and put together new ones, utilizing control grids already in place, innovating and inventing new ones as needed.

For well over a hundred years, true scientific progress and knowledge had been concealed from the public, for their own good of course. The greater public was only exposed to the third tier of scientific knowledge; governmental programs classified as Top Secret/Secure Compartmentalized Information were allowed access to Tier Two tech. Only those supranational entities who worked at a level darker than black knew about Tier One.

Tier Two had instituted various eugenics programs for the last hundred years, continuing into the present. Social anthropologists had combed the globe, categorizing and cataloging various ethnic groups. In the modern hospitals of the Western world, each child's blood was taken at birth, logged in massive paper databases before the advent of computers.

These data inputs had allowed them to design the perfect virus, guaranteed to prune the world's population by at least ninety-five percent. All of it was very under the radar, and had to be, since the last eugenicist who had blown off incrementalism had sensitized the world to the concept of racial hygiene.

The public had already been primed. The previous year's swine flu had been intentionally introduced into the populace, its strain was novel, or without any pedigree. The so-called H4N7 had carried the precursors for what was to come. It carried with it a stealth virus that had entered into the masses' genomes and would lie dormant until the time was right. The genetic engineering involved was several generations ahead of anything the public was aware of.

Once the biological trigger was released, the two strains

would combine with each other, forming a binary biological weapon. The oncogenes in human DNA would then be switched on, stimulating uncontrollable cellular growth, causing a cancer that would literally eat the body from the inside out.

With customary thoroughness, The Council of Three had experimented with human subjects to ensure that the binary virus killed in hours, or at most a few days, once activated.

Using advanced game theory- numbers crunched with quantum computers using all variable inputs- they had planned the collapse of civilization. From day zero through day thirty, when the holocaust would be more or less completed. Every event was planned, structured, and war gamed.

Even as the world's population ticked down to an estimated hundred million, The Council needed to prevent an all-out nuclear apocalypse and safeguard critical infrastructure that they would need in the aftermath to build their new society.

The eaters and consumers could be difficult little devils, especially in the midst of an apparent species-wide extinction, so special measures needed to be taken to prevent them from doing any more damage then they'd already done.

Project Snow Beam circled the earth in geosynchronous orbit, sophisticated detection systems scanning for the launch of intercontinental missiles which would be shot down moments after exiting their silos, if it came to that. Yes, the Chinese were still playing target practice on old weather satellites with their ground-based lasers, but Jarogniew was convinced that the risk of interference had been appropriately mitigated.

Soon they would hit Day Zero Minus One. The Council along with high level minions and servants would then occupy safe zones and armored redoubts, safe from societal collapse. Key strategic assets would be moved into place. Samruk International and others would occupy centralized hubs, such as Denver Airport, to respond to contingencies.

On Day Zero the trigger virus would be released and quickly identified by various departments of health. The media would roll out preplanned press releases. The United States would use cold war era defense plans updated for the war on terror, instituting Continuity of Government. In effect, America would be placed under martial law, the President declared dictator for the duration of the emergency.

With all three branches of government operating from secret bunker complexes in the Virginia Mountains, The Council would allow them to manage the crisis, to a point. COG would help contain and isolate trouble spots around the country, easing the process as best possible.

Twenty-seven threat fusion centers would be operational, until eventually overrun or the operators themselves were killed off by the virus. Their stated function was to guard against terrorism, but in reality they were always designed to spy on and monitor the American public, cracking down on anyone who threatened the establishment.

On Day Sixteen the President would be assassinated in his underground bomb shelter, Congress and the Senate would have nerve gas piped into their bunkers. In effect, The Council was the shadow government's shadow. They would move in to run key systems, once the situation had gone critical when the government was at its weakest. To the very few outside observers left, it would all seem to be done in a very spontaneous but organic manner.

The military and police forces would be quickly exhausted, expended on futile attempts to save the public amid the riots and irrationality. While the public self-destructed, The Council would send in its enforcement arm to protect key areas. Dams, bridges, airports, and other infrastructure needed to be preserved for the elite.

Of course no virus was a hundred percent lethal. Some would isolate themselves in remote areas, safe from the transmission vectors the virus would travel along. Others would have freak immunities to even the most cleverly designed virus, nature's way of safeguarding the human species from such pandemics. Some of these loners would roam the world's wastelands, others would gather into tribal groups, and some would form terror cells which would eventually attempt to strike out at the elite.

Day Seventeen would mark when The Council would send its mercenaries out to preempt any such efforts. Lone survivors would be executed; larger groups would be brought back to collectivized camps for more efficient processing. Of course Council members and those in their employ would be inoculated against the virus on Day Zero Minus Two.

The population would continue to plummet, ticking down to about one hundred million. Over six billion would perish when all was said and done. It had been a serious debate within The Council; a few extremists wanted them all eliminated, but eventually cooler heads had prevailed. Jarogniew had managed to convince the elites that they still needed warm bodies, at least enough to work the fields for another couple of decades.

Day Thirty would mark the end of Phase One, the population sufficiently reduced and the beginning of their great authoritarian society.

Some of the old cities would be restored, but mostly new cities with entirely new methods of architecture and advanced technology would rise from the ashes. What was left of the public would be forced into crowded city states, travel restricted to the elite and their servants. Super highways would connect some of the megacities; others would be placed in the center of jungles or tundra, and only accessible by tilt rotor aircraft.

Cities would divide the pruned population by age and work group. Children would be raised in massive communes to insure emotional sterility. Their minds would be dulled by mass education, encouraged to believe that everyone is the property of everyone else, and promiscuity and petty entertainment would replace so-called human values.

The serfs would live and work together in large labor groups. Shuffling to and from the factories, they would serve the barons who oversaw the city-states, their overlords. Each worker would be tagged with a subdermal RFID chip that controlled what resources they had access to and when.

The new scientific dictatorship would use the RFID chips

to channel the workers into a cashless society that would work for virtual currency. Like the monetary system of one of today's video games, the public would never see actual currency or hard assets. Credits would be assigned to each user's RFID chip, to be redeemed for basic provisions and methods of entertainment at the city canteen.

The scourge of private property would finally be abolished; babies would be born when authorized, with millions of dollars of virtual debt hanging over their heads. The population would be permanent indentured servants, trained to love the very servitude that enslaved them.

Pervasive throughout the new city-states would be a panopticon of technical surveillance features. Millions of cameras would be placed on the streets, in places of employment, even in the barracks where the workers lived. Microphones would be planted everywhere, supercomputers monitoring every conversation for key words, hints of threats that needed to be silenced.

Biometric scanners would be ubiquitous, so common that the worker bees would soon grow jaded to their very presence. Fingerprint and iris scanners would be used for identification everywhere they went. Other scanners would function on computer programs connected to the spider web of cameras that would measure each person's gait and mannerisms. Other systems would measure the pattern of veins in a worker's hand or arm for more advanced forms of control.

Brain scanners would be set up at key choke points such as subways and bus stations. The second generation Functional Magnetic Resonance Imaging devices would measure actual brain waves and signatures, literally reading people's thoughts. Third generation devices would be hand held.

Such crude behavior modification would be necessary only until several generations of children, genetically engineered to be servile and impotent, were brought online. Afterward, any remaining survivors from Day Zero would be culled as well. With new technologies in hydroponics, aquaponics, and alternative energy, like cold fusion, brought to the forefront, automation would increase exponentially, the need for human capital reduced once again.

The elite would be protected by private armies, of course, but the public needed tending to as well.

With the population herded into strategic hamlets, they would now be administered by teams of experts, mid-level minions who would, in return for their services, be granted access to a slightly higher quality canteen for material goods.

Mobile sterilization teams would scour the city-states for unauthorized pregnancies. The teams would be manned by a representative from the central authority, two program officers from the city itself, two junior officers, and a small support staff. After the first round of forced sterilizations, the number of mandatory abortions necessary would decline dramatically, but the situation would still be closely watched.

Armed enforcers would be omnipresent. Armored thugs would tote a variety of non-lethal weapons designed to inflict maximum pain compliance. Long range tasers would shock resistors at distance, firing along energized ion trails, and sonic resonance systems would lull them to sleep. Eventually, malcontents would be taken for rehabilitation or destruction, depending on the severity of the offense.

The watchers at the city-state level would of course be watched by high level commandos deployed by the true architecture of power. The hunter/killer teams would be armed with Tier One technology, constantly on standby to lead sharp point operations that would crush anything that looked at the power brokers the wrong way. Mostly, they would be deployed to keep the low level barons in line.

It was expected that The Council's top-level assassins would compete for the chance to lead the elite teams. Kammler had called him just hours before his speech to give him an update about Burma. Peng was eliminated as expected. O'Brien had once again surpassed expectations, his ruthlessness ensuring that he had a place on the H/K teams.

However, there were many fail-safes, a virtual division of power to guarantee The Council's grasp on power and absolute control. Artificial intelligence systems would create a simulation of every system on the planet, creating a separate node for each individual with cognitive profiles gathered from surveillance systems and in-depth screening. The supercomputer would predict events before they happened, giving forewarning to the elite. Troublemakers would be rounded up before the thought of trouble even occurred to them.

It was called Project Leviathan. Its sentient intelligence would compute numbers into infinity in the blink of an eye. Predictive programming, precognition, and more were all possible. Human beings would be reduced to biological androids, not a moment of their lives left unplanned or unscripted.

Jarogniew was brought back to the present as the limousine came to a halt in front of the United Nations building. He had several more meetings scheduled for the day. Much more work to do before Day Zero.

The Council of Three controlled the past, present, and future.

Their great work was the alchemy for total control.

Twenty Six

Deckard walked to the entrance, automatic doors parting to allow him through.

Astana's brand new hospital was getting broken in the hard way, the casualties of war coming in on stretchers. Others were getting wheeled into a separate area with white sheets covering still bodies. Nick was shouting at doctors and nurses, twin veins in his neck stretching like garden hoses as anger took hold.

It had been a long plane ride home, the longest of Deckard's life, sitting alongside the body bags. They had finally touched down in Kazakhstan an hour ago. Most of the troops were on their way back to the compound to hit the newly installed showers and then rack out in the bunks.

As the chaos swirled around him in the emergency area's waiting room he felt it again, the crushing feeling that hung over his head. He had never lied to himself about who he was or what he did. Deckard liked war, loved it occasionally. Combat was the only time he ever saw people for who they truly were, a place where anyone can be a hero or a coward, or both at the same time. War was the only time you saw the world for what *it* really was.

With societal constructs removed, the truth became apparent, obvious even. Compared to war, any other job was just punching a time card.

He intrinsically understood that the mercenaries he commanded were grown men who had made their own decision, freely and with full knowledge of potential consequences. They hedged their bets because the pay was good, or signed up looking for some action after their military career. When you play big boy games you play by big boy rules, and any one of them could have been the guy coming home as a corpse.

For some reason, this time that notion didn't make him feel

any better.

"Mr. O'Brien?"

Snapping out of it, he realized he was supposed to respond to that name. Deckard turned around. A balding man wearing a suit and tie was standing in his way, peering at him through thick rectangular glasses.

"Yeah," Deckard said, his hand inching towards the Glock 19 strapped to his hip.

"Your benefactors have sent me to speak with you."

"Regarding?"

"Just a job interview."

"Not happy with my performance?"

"Not at all, but this is a different kind of job they have in mind," the suit replied. "Now, please follow me."

Glancing across the lobby, Deckard could see Nick pushing a doctor aside and treating one of the Kazakhs himself. He was in charge here, no doubt about it.

"Adam," he said into his radio. "I'm going to need a few minutes. Personal business."

"You okay?" his new second in command asked.

"Yeah, I'm cool."

Adam was still outside, helping to unload casualties from one of the trucks.

"But I'm going offline for a few."

"Got it."

Deckard was dealing with the type of people who were not used to refusals. He was in too deep to turn away now. Besides, one well-dressed prick was hardly a threat.

"This way," the man said, adjusting his glasses.

Leaving the scene in the emergency room behind, Deckard was led down the long, empty halls, the sharp stench of sterilizers used by the cleaners stinging his nose. Cutting around a corner, they climbed a set of metal steps to the second floor. The halls were completely silent, abandoned.

Following colored lines painted on the floor, the suited man continued to lead him through a maze of corridors.

"What is this all about?" Deckard finally asked, looking around suspiciously.

"As I said," the mystery man droned. "Just an interview."

They walked through another set of automatic doors, Deckard's eyes frozen on the words above the entrance: *Department of Neurology.*

Footsteps rounded the corner behind them, the commando turning to see a trio of trigger men striding up from behind. Middle Eastern looking, wearing bootleg American clothing with knock off sunglasses perched on top of their heads. MP-5 sub-machine guns rested comfortably in their hands. He studied them carefully with just a glance, and they eyeballed him right back.

Hezbollah by the looks of them, flown in from Lebanon. Hopefully, they didn't recognize him. Deckard grimaced, knowing that he was none too popular in that part of the world.

Three more terrorists walked from a side room and took position to their front, effectively boxing them in. There was no turning back now.

Deeper into the empty hospital wing they crossed the final threshold, Deckard realizing what was happening with a shock. The placard on the door announced that they were entering the fMRI clinic. He had never been through the process himself, but had heard the stories about psychological torture sessions carried out on high level NSA and CIA officials.

The Islamic fundamentalists waited outside, standing guard, while Deckard and the suit went into the changing room. Lockers lined the walls, a hospital gown already laid out for him.

"The fMRI emits a magnetic resonance thirty thousand times stronger than the pull of gravity," the mystery man stated. "It is required that you get changed and leave behind all metallic objects. Walk through that door as soon as you are finished and we will get started."

"What about the shrapnel in my leg?"

"What shrapnel?"

"A souvenir from Burkina Faso a few years ago. Won't the MRI yank it out?"

"Probably. Luckily for you, we are in a hospital. We have people on staff who can attend to you if it rips out a vein or artery."

Ouch. Sounds painful.

"Please hurry, Mr. O'Brien. We have people waiting and our time is valuable as I'm sure is yours."

The suit exited the changing room, the door sliding shut with a click, leaving him alone under humming fluorescent lights.

Cursing, Deckard took his AK-103 off its sling and set it down. The rifle was filthy with mud but had held up just fine when he needed it. Next, he pulled the Glock out of its holster to lay it down next to the rifle. It was also thick with carbon and covered in dirt, yet no one had complained about the handgun's performance.

Shrugging out of his combat rig, Deckard laid it on the floor as well. The AK magazines in it were empty; the pouches that had held fragmentation grenades were hanging with loose flaps, empty as well. The cylinder shaped pouch that had held a thermite grenade was hanging open too. He had used the red colored device that had been inside to burn Peng's mansion to the ground.

Still other pouches held a water bladder, pistol magazines, sheathed combat knife, escape and evasion gear, a handheld GPS system, garrote wire, night vision monocular, and other tools of the trade.

Dumping his gear he did a quick circuit, opening the locker doors and finding nothing inside. Two were locked. Squatting down he unzipped the main compartment on his combat rig and retrieved his lock pick set. Going to work on the locked door, he placed the tension wrench in the lock and applied light pressure while flicking the tumblers with a raking tool.

Deckard knew he had to work fast.

The tension wrench turned, the lock opening. Inside were a pair of slippers and a white lab coat hanging on a hook. Rifling through the pockets he turned up nothing but lint and a ballpoint pen.

Peeling off his fatigue jacket, he cast it aside, where it

landed with a plop in the corner of the room. The sweat and grime was setting in with the stench of rotting food.

Going to work on the next lock, he held his breath, hoping to find what he was looking for.

He was nearing the drone zone. Awake for nearly three days straight, the former soldier was having trouble concentrating. The bright overhead lights seemed to pierce his skull, his recall fading, making everything more difficult. The simple five pin lock would have been child's play under any other circumstance, but now he was struggling just to apply the correct level of pressure on the metal tools in his hands.

Looking over his shoulder, he expected the goon squad to rush in at any moment, forcefully dragging him out, and holding him down while the MRI scanned his brain.

Finally, the lock popped open. Flinging the door open, Deckard tore through the clothes he found inside before his eyes froze on a bottle resting on the top shelf. Snatching it in his hand, he looked at the label on the pill bottle.

Bingo.

"Mr. O'Brien." The suit pushed open the door irritably. "Please, we don't have all day."

Deckard was just finishing tying the drawstring on his medical gown.

"Sorry about that," he replied with a nervous smile. "I smell like death warmed over."

"This way, please," his new handler responded flatly while holding the door open for him.

"Thanks," Deckard grumbled as he passed by.

Immediately his eyes went to the doublesided mirror that stretched across the far wall. Quickly shifting his gaze to the fMRI machine that took up most of the room, he walked towards it.

Swallowing hard, he was pretty sure he was screwed. Although he wasn't a doctor, he could read the label on the side of the machine.

It was a Siemens 3T Magnetom. He might not be familiar with the specific machine, but he did know that 3T stood for three Teslas, a unit of measurement that indicated that this was the most advanced type of model available, offering the highest resolution brain scans.

Nowhere to hide. Not even in your own mind.

"Please lay down on the table now."

Deckard sat down on the cold slab hesitantly.

The functional Magnetic Resonance Imaging device worked by measuring the blood oxygen level dependence, or BOLD level in the human brain. Stimulation would cause the blood flow in the brain the change. Certain neural pathways would be activated, and the neural cells themselves would demand more glucose to consume, increasing the blood flow to that portion of the brain.

The 3T Magnetom would create an extremely powerful magnetic field that would measure the inner working of the mind based on BOLD levels and show a three-dimensional model of Deckard's brain on a computer monitor. As stimulus was provided, experts could analyze which parts of his brain were active and when.

The thought of a high tech mind fuck disgusted him, but it was too late, with too much at stake to blow it now. He'd do his best to spoof the system. If that didn't work, all he had at his disposal was a small fiberglass knife hidden in his sock. Not only were they reading his mind but had also found a way to make sure he was disarmed, all of his hidden party favors left with his fatigues and combat equipment with no metal allowed in the room.

Once he was lying down, the suit came up beside him and fastened several straps around his face to prevent Deckard from moving and throwing off their readings.

"Very good," the spectacle-wearing man commented almost to himself.

Sliding the slab forward on its rollers, Deckard's head was

now inside the machine as it hummed steadily, someone on the other side of the mirror starting it up.

"Try to relax, this should only take an hour or so."

"Fucking hell!" Deckard screamed as several small metal fragments were torn from his calf muscle, ripping flesh before sticking to the side of the fMRI machine.

The suit calmly walked out and returned with heavy bandages.

"I'm sealing your wounds with medical glue. Keep an eye on it over the next few days. We don't want you getting an infection."

"You're all heart, thanks."

The door slammed shut leaving him alone. The half dozen Arabs who stood guard outside were probably confiscating his equipment in case things went bad.

Suddenly the speaker system came to life, the suit's calming voice speaking in his ear.

"Your name is Jake O'Brien."

"Yes," Deckard answered.

"Mr. O'Brien, please shut up. Your response is not necessary, just listen and stay still."

They didn't need him to say anything, just measure his BOLD levels in response to each question. The fMRI would take one scan a second, it was a variation of an event-based MRI that would essentially read his mind.

"Your name is Jake O'Brien," the voice repeated.

Several seconds passed allowing time for the scans. Like a polygraph, a series of control questions would be asked to establish a baseline. Precedents had to be formed, sample scans indicated, so that when the real questioning began, they could determine what his mind looked like when it was told the truth and what it looked like when it was told a lie.

"You were born in Raleigh, North Carolina."

What the technicians running the lie detector test didn't realize was that he was working under alias and all of their control questions were lies from the get go.

"Your mother's name was Whitney Shepard."

Deckard breathed normally and allowed himself to relax, making no attempt at subterfuge. The more convoluted the results the better.

"Your father's name was Danny O'Brien."

The questions regarding Deckard's false past continued for what seemed like forever, but was probably only twenty minutes or so. After covering his supposed childhood and military career, they finally began getting around to recent events.

"You are the battalion commander of Samruk International."

It was a struggle to keep his eyes open. He was completely exhausted and the grilling wasn't making things better.

"You did not conduct combat operations in Burma."

Some negatives were occasionally thrown out to mix things up a little.

"You were involved in the murder of Stevan Djokovic."

Deckard began reciting his seven times tables in his head.

"You plotted the execution of your Executive Officer."

Seven times seven equals fifty...no, forty nine.

"You personally led the assault on a casino in Panghsang."

"You allowed a situation to develop that resulted in the death of Stevan Djokovic."

They kept coming back to Djokovic, once again confirming that he had been a plant inside the battalion. They were suspicious. No doubt, Djokovic had sent them scathing reports about Deckard before he was killed.

The questions kept coming, harder and faster then before, trying to trip him up.

"You will follow any orders given to you."

"You will not disobey your instructions."

"You have no moral objections to ordering your men to certain death."

"You ordered two prisoners executed in Afghanistan."

"You ordered the murder of Stevan Djokovic."

"You were born in Raleigh, North Carolina."

"The assault of the UWSA headquarters was successful."

Deckard blinked hard, getting confused as the minutes dragged on. The baseline questions may have been invalid, but his guard was lowered due to exhaustion. He had one fail-safe, the one that was keeping him artificially calm.

"You fired on the Chinese military in Burma."

Popping a couple of Valium pills in the changing room, they had taken effect just minutes later and would alter how his brain responded to questioning. With the basic physiology of the brain altered by the drug, the entire results of the tests would be skewed and invalid. The drug contained active benzodiazepines, which created a number of effects, including sedation, muscle relaxation, as well as anti-anxiety. With the Valium running its course, the blood oxidization levels in Deckard's brain would remain at a fixed rate regardless of the probing questions he was subjected too.

"You never question the validly of the orders you receive."

At least that was what he speculated.

"Your mother's maiden name is Shepard."

Two cognitive psychologists, two statisticians, and three MRI technicians poured over three-dimensional models of Deckard's brain from behind the double-sided mirror. What they discovered was as frustrating as it was bizarre.

The imaging was fed through a computer system that then displayed the graphical representation of the subject's brain while statements were given or questions asked. Different colors would show up on the three-dimensional model brain, indicating which neural pathways were currently active.

The team was the best in a very elite field of medicine and science. Usually they were tasked to evaluate high-ranking members of intelligence agencies or corporate executives of the

Fortune One Hundred set. Billions of dollars and vital national security secrets rested on their shoulders on a daily basis.

In ten years they had never failed to identify a traitor or corporate spy. Zero false positives. Federal raids of the suspects' homes and property after the team's confirmation always validated their findings.

Tension filled the room. They were closing in on two hours, longer then they'd ever spent with a single subject in the past. The data shown on the computer monitors was opaque, strange, insane even. They were assured that the subject was a highly capable military commander, but the readings said otherwise.

Based on the scientific evidence alone, their subject was being told lies and truth all at the same time. They had only seen this sort of thing in medical studies performed on schizophrenics at mental hospitals.

One of the statisticians rubbed her hands nervously.

Who was he?

What was he?

Finally the lead psychologist, a PhD from Harvard University, hurled the paper readouts in his hand across the room.

"Fuck."

Twenty Seven

"In other words Peng fucked them," Frank summarized. "Just like Ramirez and Khalis."

"Hold on," Deckard said, rubbing his eyes. They sat in the S2 shack, or what passed for it inside Samruk's warehouse headquarters. The intel section had come a long way, with flat screen HDTVs mounted to the walls for presentations and laptops set up as workstations, but it was still just a glorified plywood cubicle.

"So JF finished interrogating Peng's accountant before we left?"

"Yeah, and he told us that Peng had had a falling out with his people across the border in Thailand. Drug money from the Golden Triangle is traditionally laundered through South East Asia to American and European banks located in Australia. The Western banks were demanding a bigger slice of the action, so Peng started looking to the East, towards China specifically."

Deckard had only managed a few hours of sleep so far and was still trying to process the information. The ache in his leg wasn't helping.

"So the Burma mission was a consolidation, but of what? Wealth and power, but then the next question becomes, to what end? Why now?"

"Someone wants to bankroll a huge amount of money and fast," Frank replied. "I'm afraid of what the end game might be, but it must be something big."

"When I first took over the battalion, they had these guys doing nothing but cordon and search operations to conduct gun confiscations," Deckard said, rubbing the sides of his head. "It was weird."

"What are you thinking?"

274

"I'm afraid to say it."

"You think this has all been preparation for something else."

"I think the fringe benefit for our employers has been a consolidation of wealth, but they have a wider goal in mind as an end game," Deckard said, shaking his head. "Sergeant Major?"

"Da."

"Give me a SITREP on the battalion."

"All companies are conducting command maintenance today. Statements of loss are being compiled as we speak. I will have them for you within the hour."

"Initial damages?"

"Seven vehicles were rendered non-recoverable during the mission. Six were destroyed by enemy aircraft, a seventh from Bravo Company drove over a landmine on the way back to RV at the field hospital. All weapons are accounted for except one missing AK that Charlie Company lost when someone accidentally dropped it in a river."

The material losses seemed superficial compared to the dead.

"Killed and wounded?"

"Seventeen killed, twenty-four wounded. Of those twenty-four, eight are still in the hospital with long recovery times. The others should be back to work as soon as they get stitches removed or recover from concussions."

"What about the dead?"

"Funeral arrangements are being made with families of the local men. Bank accounts are being established for families who don't have them so life insurance payments can be made. Tomorrow, the body of the only non-local will be flown back to the United States. Roger Llewellyn. He was killed in the truck that ran over that land mine."

"He was the former Marine that Adam brought on board," Deckard cursed under his breath. "Keep me updated."

"Of course," the battalion's senior NCO stated. His entire report was from memory. He knew everything that was happening in his battalion.

"What do we have for atmospherics?" Deckard asked, changing the subject.

Frank looked down at his notes. Atmospherics were general intelligence points, usually regarding a specific area or country. Today they had to take the entire global situation into account if they wanted to predict where they would be sent next.

"Gas prices back home just hit five dollars a gallon. The spot price on gold is up to two thousand. Almost twenty percent unemployment, with riots breaking out in Atlanta and Los Angeles."

"Heading for hyperinflation."

"It looks that way," Frank continued. "Several states are reacting by putting the National Guard on alert, but get this, CDC is telling state governments that they need to start stock piling bodybags."

"The left hand isn't talking to the right, typical government bureaucracy. Somebody knows what is going on and is jumping the gun. If the Center for Disease Control is getting in the act then this thing is going to be biological."

"It is," Adam said, standing in the door with a handful of papers.

"What do you have?"

"I finally wormed my way into the servers in Singapore."

"The Information Technologies servers?"

"Yeah," Adam nodded. "Look at this," he said, handing Deckard the stack of papers.

Flipping through the printouts, he browsed the headlines printed from major American and European newspapers, his eyes narrowing to slits.

"What the hell is this, Adam? Two hundred thousand dead? Plague claims fifty thousand in Aspen, Colorado. Paris reduced to a ghost town? Look." Deckard pointed to the flat screen in the corner of the room that was constantly tuned to a twenty-four hour news channel. "I'm not that out of the loop. If this was real they'd be reporting on it rather than covering some celebrity's wardrobe malfunction."

Adam's hands shook as he spoke.

"Check the dates."

Deckard turned back to the stack, his eyes growing wide as he examined the dates tagged to each article.

They were all dated to next week.

Deckard shoved his hands into his pockets as he walked into his office, his mind racing to understand what he had just seen.

Looking up, snapping himself out of a trance, he saw a stranger sitting in the chair beside his desk. The Kazakh stood, flatting out invisible wrinkles in his suit with his hands.

"Who are you?" Deckard demanded in Russian.

"Kareem Saudabayev, Ministry of Justice," he answered in British-accented English.

"I don't recall any appointments with the Ministry of Justice. How did you get in here?"

"I was allowed in by the corporate CEO of Samruk International. He is standing outside with dozens of law enforcement officers as we speak. He assured me that you would not be confrontational as this is merely a legal function and you are not a shareholder in the company."

"What the hell is this about?"

The government official popped open his briefcase on Deckard's desk and handed him a sheet of paper.

"Under the law I have to physically present you with this legal summons."

Deckard frowned, studying the Cyrillic text, but remained unimpressed.

"Under Kazakh national law you are under suspicion of operating a private military company without license, running a military training center, smuggling illegal weapons and military

277

grade equipment, training local and foreign troops without government supervision, engaging in mercenary activities, espionage-"

"Hold it right there, Kareem." Deckard had heard enough of the power play to get the gist. With Djokovic dead, the old men at the Grove had decided to sic their puppets in the Kazakh Government on Samruk and on him. They wanted total control and oversight on everything they did, nothing less would be acceptable.

The Ministry of Justice official cleared his throat.

"You will be permitted to continue your business until a trial date can be established, but with government supervision. All facilities and operations are being officially nationalized as we speak."

Deckard waved his finger at the Kazakh bureaucrat while walking behind his desk. Powering up his laptop he punched in his pass code, quickly accessing a number of servers located in the four corners of the globe.

While Adam probed the enemy's databases in Singapore, Deckard had been doing the same with Samruk's corporate office ever since his break-in.

"Mr. O'Brien, please come with me so we can get the relevant paperwork in order. Then you will be able to meet with your new counterparts in the Ministry of--"

"Tell me, Kareem," Deckard said, spinning the laptop around so he could see the screen. "What do you make of this?"

The screen flashed, a grainy but unmistakable video of the Ministry of Justice Official meeting with Samruk's CEO in their corporate offices. Kareem watched himself on the recording discussing a variety of issues with the corporate leader, ranging from bribery to murder.

Deckard punched a button on the keyboard and another video popped up. This one showed the CEO on the phone in his office. Overlaid on the video was the voice on the other end of the phone, taken from a separate tap on the line. The voice was unmistakable, it belonged to the President of Kazakhstan.

They were talking about liquidating the Kazakh National Bank and turning the reins over to shareholders in the United States.

"I've got it all, Kareem," Deckard said, pausing the video. "Hard evidence. Government collusion with Samruk's corporate leaders to assassinate bankers and journalists who are not on board with your program. Selling Kazakh mineral wealth to European nations dirt cheap in exchange for kickbacks. Funny money Washington consensus loans with the IMF. Plans to eliminate ethnic minorities so you can build a new oil pipeline. It is all here."

The Ministry of Justice official looked like he was about to be ill.

"Don't even think about playing your games with me," Deckard warned him. "I've got these video archives encrypted and uploaded to servers all over the world. Each archive is on a timer, counting down to zero before it automatically emails itself to hundreds of thousands, if not millions of random e-mail addresses. If I don't intervene at specific times to stop it, then these files fall into the hands of people who will make you and your government famous, and not in a good way."

Kareem pitched back and forth on his feet, as if he was about to pass out.

Deckard walked back from around his desk, grabbing him by the sleeve and helping him stay upright.

"So here is the deal," the American said, leading him to the door. "You call off the goon squad and head on back to the capital. Tell your bosses that you talked me into whatever you were supposed to talk me into. Lie to them. Whatever, I don't care. Stay out of my hair and I won't be a problem for you. Got it?"

Now he had that thousand meter stare.

"Do you understand?" Deckard said, shaking him by the arm.

The Kazakh bureaucrat swallowed hard, nodding his head from north to south but refusing to make eye contact with him.

"I knew you would see things my way."

279

Deckard pushed him out the door. Kareem tripped and stumbled, nearly smashing face first into the outer wall of the supply room before recovering. Looking back at Deckard with wide eyes, he turned and ran.

"Who the hell was that?"

Deckard turned, seeing Kurt Jager standing at the other end of the hall, pushing a handcart loaded down with crates of ammo.

"Nobody important," Deckard muttered.

Downing the final mouthful of coffee, Deckard tossed the cardboard cup into the trash.

The worm viruses that Adam had infiltrating the enemy's computer databanks had continued to feed data back to them. The sheer volume was staggering and left them trying to drink from a fire hose. They were now entering twenty consecutive hours of intel analysis and mission planning.

"Hey, boss," Frank said from across the table. He waved a circular can of smokeless tobacco at him. The dip provided a buzz that helped keep you alert, but he'd quit that stuff a long time ago.

Schematics and printouts covered the table, the dry erase boards were filled with scribbles, notes, and doodles that they had used to explain ideas to each other with. Note books were held open with mugs of coffee, and empty soda bottles were a refilled with brown dip spit.

They had been attacking one problem after the next, readjusting as Adam brought in fresh information every few minutes until he had finally exhausted the hard drives in Singapore.

"You sure?"

"Fuck you," Deckard said, grabbing the can of Copenhagen.

A projector displayed a satellite image of a small island in the Pacific Ocean.

This is really happening.

Even after reading the news articles, it still seemed surreal, enough to make a person doubt their own reality. Maybe that was what the enemy was counting on. Engineered cognitive dissonance on a massive scale as they turned the planet into one big global snuff film.

Tapping out a pinch of dip, he packed it into his lower lip, spitting the excess into the garbage can.

The Center for Disease Control preparing for death on a global scale, gold bullion mysteriously transferring between countries, large shipments of weaponry being moved offshore, the National Guard being mobilized. All the periphery information suddenly made sense.

Kammler. Jarogniew. Hieronymus.

It was clear that they had been planning this for years. The news articles had been written by their psychological manipulators to help ease the public into its extinction. They didn't want everything collapsing all at once, no; the wars and strife could damage the environment or destroy infrastructure they wanted for their own purposes.

A global pandemic. Once activated, it would only take a few weeks before it chewed through the world's population. Deckard's eyes darted to his troops. They didn't look up from their work. They couldn't allow it to happen. He had known from the beginning that he was being hired for something sinister, but this was beyond anything he could have imagined.

It was finally time for Samruk to go off the reservation.

The mission they had in mind was ridiculous in complexity, extremely difficult in terms of logistics, and a final assault that was next to impossible, no matter what angle they attacked it from. They'd be going up against layers of security and the most highly trained and experienced soldiers in the world.

"O'Brien," Adam said, looking up from his laptop. "There is one aspect we haven't discussed."

"What is it?"

281

"The most reasonable option. We go after their families."

"Killing children isn't acceptable."

"We don't have to kill them. We just have to make them think we will. Send a small team stateside and grab a few of them up."

"These are the most ruthless people in the world," Deckard replied. "Psychopaths like this can hardly be bothered with anyone's well-being other than their own."

"Is that your final answer?"

"It is."

Frank turned the satellite phone over in his hands, knowing he was playing Russian roulette with his friends' lives.

Once again they needed to find replacements, warm bodies to take the place of those killed in action. He knew that of the friends he called, nearly every one of them would show up and be standing plane side, ready to go in twenty-four hours. It didn't matter what the reason was, not really. When you had saved each others' lives more times than either of you cared to count, they would be there for you when you needed them.

That didn't make him feel any better though. Roger had gotten pulped by that landmine as they pulled off their objective in Burma. In fact Samruk's mercenaries were dropping like flies. At this rate every one of them would be a salty veteran after just two or three missions with the unit, probably taking a hundred percent casualties before long.

The ex-Ranger's thumb hovered over the phone's keypad, wondering who he would be condemning to death. Pushing aside his guilt, he punched in a thirteen-digit number and pressed send. The call went through, bouncing off a satellite before connecting in the United States.

"Hello?"

Adam was frozen in place as his heart beat wildly. Gently, he set down the phone, terminating the call.

"Who was that?" Deckard asked.

Moments ago he'd interrupted mission planning and got the immediate leadership together for an emergency meeting.

"My source in the SIGINT business," Adam replied. "This is getting crazy."

"Okay," Deckard said, sitting down. "In the last hour General Lancaster was killed in a car accident outside the beltway, and I just found out that Admiral Whitcomb died in a hospital, supposedly of food poisoning, last night."

"Former National Security Councilman Dale Werbacht was found shot in his bedroom by police this morning," Frank added.

"Lynn Chapman was found by his wife floating face down in their pool forty-five minutes ago," Adam said in monotone.

"What did you just say?" Deckard blurted.

"Lynn Chapman is dead, it's under investigation--"

"Holy shit," he said, leaning back in his chair.

"A friend of yours?"

"Lynn was providing top cover for me for the duration of my time with Samruk. I had been working for him. Hell, he was the one who got me face time with those creeps at Bohemian Grove. I didn't know what he was getting me into at the time."

"Who was he?" Frank asked.

"He worked on the fringes of the National Security Agency. He often piggybacked his own missions on non-officially funded operations. Lynn was one of the good guys. He even served with my dad in 'Nam."

"What the hell is going on?" Adam wondered.

Deckard rubbed his temples, trying to take it in.

"They're killing anyone in the system that might be able to

intercept and interdict their plans. Anyone who could have the wherewithal to put the pieces together and interfere with this pandemic they have planned."

"Does this mean your cover is blown?"

"Probably not, all the backstops are still in place, and knowing Lynn he would have a fair amount of redundancy built into his system. Then again, if they go digging deep again, they might find some cracks."

Just then the fax machine clicked on with a whirl.

The three mercenaries looked in its direction as it warmed up for a moment before spitting paper onto its tray.

With dread filling his gut, Deckard stood and snatched the paper printouts. It was another Operations Order. He flipped through the pages looking for the second paragraph.

"Mission," he read aloud, Frank and Adam's eyes drilling into him. "Samruk International relocates to Denver International Airport, fully operational, with all personnel and equipment needed to conduct sustained combat operations in the continental United States. All maneuver elements will be prepared to execute time-sensitive special operations missions, cordon and search operations, civilian internment and relocation, and other tasks, as directed by Higher Headquarters in accordance with local conditions and emerging threats."

They had just been ordered to go to war with the American public.

TWENTY EIGHT

Footsteps echoed across the floor, reverberating through empty space. Obsidian was inlaid into the marble floor, forming a black sun wheel, stylized rays of dark light branching out from the center. Situated in the heart of the underground compound, the black sun formed the most ancient of archetypes.

The very Void of Creation.

Hieronymus crossed over the antediluvian symbol, a single pillar of light shining down from the oculus and reflecting off ebony rock. The circular room was cloistered with various pillars, each a different style, originating from ages long forgotten. Some of the pillars were caryatids, shaped in human and non-human forms, idealizations of man throughout the ages; others were of creatures from before recorded time. The imagery was buried deep in the subconscious of man, but known to make the uninitiated ill with just a glimpse of their visages.

The entrance to the next chamber bore stone reliefs that displayed an owl on one side and a deified woman bearing the features of a bird of prey on the other.

The warrior woman was named Lilith in some cultures, Inanna or Ishtar in earlier civilizations, and went by yet another name in time immemorial. To the Babylonians she was massless and able to assume any form at will. Hieronymus knew her real name and true purpose. She was nothing less than the gatekeeper of initiation into the Order of the Black Sun.

The Order maintained the hidden knowledge of mankind's true origins, the truth of a fabled land long lost beneath the sea. Human civilization was not a progression of development but rather a legacy inherited from those who came before. After man's fall from grace, Lemuria sank beneath the waves. Humankind migrated to the Ancient Near East, a series of despotic rulers conquering the souls of man and rendering them pliable ever since.

Just as the useless eaters had been given mass religion, many members of the elite had been given a secret doctrine to help them feel like insiders. It was something that allowed them to view themselves above the people they were expected to subjugate. Soon, they too, would be led into the Charnel House of Time.

Most of the symbolism had been used by his family for hundreds of years having double or triple levels of meaning. One level for the masses, another for initiates, and finally the third, which held the true secrets to the architecture of power. The third layer was held in reserve by several powerful families and passed down through the mystery schools. They prevented the truth from losing its power through overuse, misinterpretation, and blatant abuse by those unworthy of its hidden energy.

Since recorded history the esoteric and arcane had been kept hidden, for use by only those properly indoctrinated. Otherwise, control would be lost, the grimoire welded against man taken from them for all time.

Perception was reality and they were the self-appointed perception managers, the invisible governors who provided the handrails for a domesticated populace.

Crossing the threshold, the old man shuffled into a room with a black and white checkered floor. The inner sanctum was dimly lit, the large subterranean hall seeming to stretch on forever, disappearing in the blackness somewhere beyond.

Standing in front of the Leviathan, Hieronymus clenched his fists. He felt *it* ripple through his body. Thousands of years had led to this moment. Tomorrow was Day Zero. The beginning of the end for humanity. The beginning of a new future for those who occupied the capstone of the pyramid. The coming of a time when they could enjoy the empty, wide open expanses the earth had provided for them.

At ninety-four years old many thought that he would never live to see his new order realized, but beneath the flowing black robe his skin was pulled taunt with thick layers of muscle. The best nutritionists and doctors had cared for him from the beginning. Human growth hormones were carefully administered, artificially restarting his life cycle over again from a chemical standpoint.

With the breeders wiped out by his plague, he could finally bring a new line of long-suppressed occult technology to the forefront. Life extension technologies would ensure that he and those he selected would survive to carry on their ambitions for hundreds of years, until such a point came that technology rendered life as currently perceived irrelevant and their species evolved into something altogether different.

Oh, a portion of humanity had been there before, in a time long forgotten. Prior to The Fall, a race of optimally functioning people had existed even more powerful than he.

Before him Leviathan purred, electronic hums idling by, waiting patiently for work. A small field of databanks were interconnected, containing solid state data storage, enough to contain every piece of information that had existed, into infinity as near as occult scientists could tell. Centered in the core of the data processing center was the brain, a quantum computer that was not supposed to exist. For the moment it was isolated, underground, and quarantined from the outside world.

The supercomputer made use of the bizarre effects of quantum entanglement, manipulating information laterally across the time domain to provide any calculation, any function, faster than the human mind could comprehend. The effects were so unbelievable, so shocking, that several of the world's preeminent scientists had to be condemned after working with Leviathan. Hieronymus made sure they stayed in solitary, pumped full of pharmaceuticals, not that anyone would believe them anyway.

In the darkness of their cells, they whispered to themselves that the computer made the calculations in the past, before the data was even inputted into the system.

He could have had them disposed of, but found that they made far better pets; they bore testament to The Order's agenda, the coming amalgamation. Their feeble minds were literally driven insane, unable to comprehend what he had known since

287

Leviathan's inception. It wasn't science but black magic, drawing on the power of the black sun. It channeled the power flowing from the reality that geometrically unfolded itself from the Void.

The artificial entity called the United States Government was allowed to run a parallel but far inferior project called Main Core, making use of more conventional technologies. Still, it had served its purpose, monitoring enormous swaths of the eaters simultaneously.

Power consumption, financial systems, infrastructure, political opinion, psychological trends, and much more were cataloged by Main Core and filtered through its periphery systems. Closed-circuit television camera systems from London to New York to Basra were monitored. Cell phone conversations were listened in on for key words and exact coordinates to that person's location, triangulated and tracked. Social Media networks and other websites compiled massive amounts of data hourly.

All of it was added up into an aggregate, one that when processed through the computer systems could be used to predict the future with a fair amount of accuracy. When the collapse was initiated and the US Federal Government was eliminated on Day Sixteen, Main Core would be taken offline if the chaos hadn't knocked it out already.

On that day, Leviathan would be unleashed on the planet. Tapping into dark fiber and redundant systems put into place years prior, it would keep the world running, and running by Hieronymus' rules. The earth's resources would be quickly calculated and redistributed as he saw fit, and Leviathan's systems would maintain Total Information Awareness, an all-seeing eye that never blinked. Silently, it would monitor what was left of the cattle.

The puppet master grinned, watching his creation, blinking red lights flashing as it waited in the darkness. Hieronymus inhaled sharply. It knew he was in the room.

After the cleansing, the world would be redesigned in his image. Singapore would explode into a metropolis of technology-manufacturing with serfs assembling the tools the elite required.

Meanwhile, the planetary regime would establish a massive spaceport just outside the capital of Kazakhstan. The elite themselves would peer down on their subjects from heavily fortified enclaves and towering skyscrapers. True technological progress would be unveiled, harnessing energies yet unrealized.

In a few decades the terraforming of the planet Mars would begin and two decades after that the first human-led superluminal space travel would take place. Channeling ancient, esoteric energies, they would create craft that moved faster than light itself, exploring the vastness of space.

Remote viewers had already made contact with no less than five extraterrestrial consciousnesses in their galaxy alone. Gliese 581 had been transmitting signals at least since the elite's scientific foundations and societies had begun listening. The data contained in the transmission had been decrypted by Leviathan, but the message remained obscured; the occult scientists remained baffled by the language and manner of speech.

It was no matter. It would be no more than forty years before they made first contact.

Assessments would be carried out; the alien planet's mineral and sentient life forms would be calculated and cataloged. Then the harvesting would begin once again. The alien species would be subjugated and used as slave labor until they were rendered useless by further technological advancements. Planned extinction would come next.

There would be one remaining thorn in his side and that was the elite themselves.

Their will to power, the need to conquer and kill would never be quenched. Not by the global culling, nothing would satisfy those elites who operated near his own level. After the pandemic they would war with each other, sooner rather than later in Hieronymus' estimation.

Leviathan concurred.

Weapons, conventional and non-conventional had been prepositioned and secreted away in caches across the globe, hidden for later use by Jarogniew, Kammler, and many others. They thought their contingency plans remained clandestine, but in truth nothing remained a secret from him.

Deeper in the hall, resting alongside Leviathan were all manner of officially non-existent weapons. Directed energy, psychotronic generators, geoengineering, radionics, and orthogonal frame rotational weapons were already at his disposal. In the aftermath of the culling, around Day Thirty the weapons would be fired upon his fellow elite, not to mention at least two other factions he expected to survive his apocalypse in China and Japan.

He alone would have first strike capability, hitting hard and fast the moment the elite let their guard down as they attempted to consolidate power after the plague.

Letting his hands rest on the composite plastic cube that housed the supercomputer, he let out a laugh that resonated throughout the great hall. The cube was now nothing more than a mental placeholder, a receiver at best. The calculations and processes were done elsewhere, inside the infolded electromagnetic space all around them.

Turning away, he walked from the cavernous hall. He could feel Leviathan disengage from him, the mental link severing as the computer, or being, or whatever it was, noted his absence and went back into meditation.

Back in the initiation room he changed from his robe and back into his customary fitted suit and loafers. Without bothering to glance back at his work, Hieronymus left Lilith and the others behind, boarding a heavy freight elevator.

With a push of a button he began ascending to the surface. Minutes crawled by, the darkness interrupted by the occasional service light. When the elevator came to a halt, he stepped off and sat down on an electric golf cart. Powering the cart down the long corridor, a gust of cool air brushed across his wrinkled face. Motion detectors activated banks of overhead lighting as he sped down the tunnel. Behind him a series of heavy blast doors slammed shut. Leviathan would be running the compound in his absence.

With the final blast door swinging shut, Hieronymus

squinted in the natural sunlight, continuing to drive down a dirt road. Behind him a bulldozer rumbled up to the twelve ton door, pushing dirt over it. The work crew in charge of concealing and sanitizing the area was already taken care of. The activation agent to the binary virus was laced into their catered lunch. They would be dead before they ever stepped off the work site.

Hieronymus remained stone-faced as his private jet came into view. The engines were already warmed up, the pilot waiting for him to arrive. Pulling up alongside, he put the golf cart into park and walked towards the open hatch. As he climbed the steps, the cold Colorado wind tossed his gray hair. The old man couldn't help but smile.

The black stork was on its way.

TWENTY NINE

Burning bridges never felt so good.

Deckard braced himself against the fuselage of the aircraft, gazing out the small portal as they flew high above the clouds. It had taken a long time to get to this point, with everything riding on the line. Good people had died. His people.

His only source of relief was in knowing that the best he could hope for was a pyrrhic victory. If they failed, none of them would be around to experience the results. Squinting, Deckard could barely make out masses of land somewhere below. Swaths of earth, farmed by and lived on by human beings. Slowly, he shook his head.

Billions dead.

He wouldn't let that happen.

His fingers brushed against the grip of the Kimber 1911 automatic sitting snugly in his holster. He had forgone Samruk's standard issue Glock 19 opting to carry his personal weapon. The Glock was a fine gun, but tonight he wanted the extra knockdown power provided by the .45 caliber round.

Shifting his gaze, Deckard saw Pat sitting on the grated floor of the Antonov, preparing his gear for what was waiting for them on the other side of an hour or so. The pilots didn't know it yet, but Samruk International was on a collision course with the most powerful men in the world.

They had as much money as printing presses could produce at their disposal, hundreds of private security contractors, and the most high tech weapons and equipment imaginable waiting for anyone who crossed them.

Samruk's sole advantage lay in the fact that they were doing something that had never been done before.

In hours they had stripped their headquarters, packing

everything onto the half-dozen Antonov's that arrived back in Astana hours after they received the Operations Order. All vehicles and weapons were strapped down; the contents of their offices were palletized and loaded to take with them for extended operations.

Officially, Pat was still on convalescence leave from Delta Force after his ordeal in Colombia. Frank had reached out to him for help. All he had said was that it was something Deckard and the old crew were all on board with.

The Master Sergeant didn't need any further explanation. As the Russian cargo planes were warming their engines, preparing to lift off in Astana, Pat came running up to the ramp. Red in the face and out of breath, he threw his gear bag onto the plane and was helped on board.

Pat expertly reassembled his AK-103, making sure that key points of friction were lubricated, before obsessively examining his kit for a third time. He was no stranger to the realities of combat and knew that survivability depended largely on setting the conditions for success before ever stepping onto the battlefield. He continued his preparations, despite Deckard having told him that everything came down to a roll of the dice.

Turning back to the window, Deckard's jaw tightened.

They were now over the Pacific Ocean, the six huge aircraft transporting the entire battalion to Denver International Airport.

It was time to roll the dice.

"What does that thing do?"

"Lower the landing gear," the black operations pilot answered, more than a little annoyed by his backseat flyer.

"What about that dial?" Chuck Rochenoire asked.

"Fuel gauge."

"And what about that?"

"Why don't you take a seat already," the copilot said. "We don't need any war tourists upfront."

"You got me all wrong," Chuck said, smiling as he pressed his Glock 19 pistol into the nape of the pilot's neck.

"Hey, what the hell!" the copilot screamed, before reaching for the .38 Special tucked under his jacket.

"Halt," Kurt Jager said, grabbing the man's wrist in an iron grip, his own pistol shoved under the copilot's nose.

Sergeant Major Korgan tossed the curtain aside that served as a partition between the cockpit and the cargo area, immediately pointing his pistol at the navigator.

"Now you reorient on new set of coordinates," he said in heavily accented English.

Unbeknownst to the flight crew, a similar scene was taking place on each of the transport aircraft at that moment. Samruk mercenaries were raiding the cockpits, effectively staging multiple simultaneous hijackings. They could already feel the shift under their feet as the massive airplane changed its heading, the pilots given little choice at gunpoint.

Making wide lazy turns the aircraft shifted onto azimuth, heading to the Southern Pacific Ocean.

THIRTY

A low-pitched hum in the distance was the only warning before the dark shadows came into view. They flew in low, landing gear skimming just feet above the choppy ocean waters.

With Johnston Atoll almost entirely blacked out, the pilots flew under night vision goggles, relying on the few beacons that were lit. The passengers of the first flight bounced off the cold metal floor as the wheels made contact with the runway, the pilots immediately throwing the levers to apply thrust reversers and speed brakes to slow them down before they ran off the other end of the runway.

On the ground, black-uniformed gunmen frowned and pointed at the unexpected arrivals as one plane landed after another. Dozens of different aircraft had been flying in and out for days, all intended to be under the radar, but at least those had been announced to the ground crews so they could prepare for the arrival.

Peeling off onto the parking apron, the massive Russian airplanes dropped ramp, tan colored assault trucks disgorged themselves and spilled out like locusts, accelerating across the covert airbase. Splitting into platoon-sized elements, the Kazakh mercenaries rushed for their individual objectives.

With defense systems finally being brought online by the control tower, a dozen Phalanx anti-aircraft cannons swung into position to confront the final Antonov on approach. The last Samruk aircraft almost made it to the tarmac and out of the offensive radius of fire before the guns opened up with cannon fire shooting through the sky.

The radar-guided Gatling guns locked onto target and immediately began pouring on long bursts of twenty millimeter tungsten steel armor-piercing rounds. Multiple streams of fire chopped through the aircraft's wings and fuselage, sending it bursting into flames. Tilting to one side, the aircraft dipped down sickeningly, then rotated into a vicious angle until its wings were nearly vertical, trailing flame behind them.

When the Antonov slammed into the concrete that made up the artificial island, the subsequent explosion briefly turned night into day. Flaming wreckage rained down on the northern side of the atoll, the revolting smell of burning jet fuel invading the mercenaries' noses.

Deckard noted the losses in as detached a manner as he could from the back of his assault vehicle. Half of Charlie Company was gone. Kazakh comrades and old friends, Piet and Gordan, were the first casualties. Grimly, he acknowledged that this was just the opening salvo.

Much worse was to come.

Bravo Company trucks screamed down the tarmac, swerving to avoid large chunks of burning wreckage as they sped towards the hangers.

Johnston Atoll sat in the Pacific Ocean, south of Hawaii and had been continuously expanded throughout the Cold War. Stretching from atop its base on a coral reef, the military base sprawled out over fifty square miles. Used for nuclear testing until the collapse of the Soviet Union, it was then maintained for the storage and decommission of the military's aging chemical weapons stockpile. Finally in 2004 the atoll had been completely stripped of buildings and officially shut down.

Unofficially, it had been reopened just days later under the auspices of several intelligence agencies and rebuilt into a covert staging ground. A black site.

The lead vehicle jerked, the passengers holding onto their seats and other handholds to avoid being thrown out, as enemy gunfire caught the driver by surprise. Green tracers skipped across the concrete, searching for them. Turning their turrets to face the enemy, the PKM gunners fired back in the direction of the enemy's muzzle flashes.

Still speeding towards the hangers, individual Kazakhs seated in the back of the vehicles laid down a volley of fire with their Mk14 grenade launchers. The result was a combination of machine gun fire and bursts of forty millimeter HE grenades.

The mercenaries were closing the distance quickly while delivering at least semi-accurate suppressive fire. It looked like they were going to make it, when a bright orange streak flashed through the air. It skipped off the pavement and detonated somewhere behind them. The next anti-tank missile came hurdling straight towards the center of the convoy as they drove in a wedge-shaped formation.

One of the drivers saw it heading for him and yanked on the wheel just a moment before it exploded next to them. The mercenaries were peppered with debris but otherwise left unharmed except for one Kazakh who was thrown off the back of the truck.

Seconds later, Bravo Company overtook the remaining guards and encircled the hanger complex. Dead security contractors littered the ground, some crying out in agony. The mercenaries were under orders to take as many alive for questioning as possible. No executions would take place, not yet.

Alpha Company kept a large degree of standoff, hanging back to avoid close combat. The three brick and stucco buildings that served as barracks were in the process of getting hammered by both direct and indirect fire.

The barracks housed the support personnel that maintained the facilities on the clandestine base as well as the private security contractors, the hired goons standing by for whatever dirty work needed to be done. On seeing the size and scope of the facilities, Frank knew that he was seeing a mirror image of Samruk International. A parallel group who would serve similar purposes after the plague was released on the world.

From a defensive position behind a concrete bunker, Mendez's mortar section was dropping round after round down their tubes. The 82mm mortars crashed through the roofs, blowing out windows, and devastating the enemy as they crawled out of their beds and shrugged into their clothes. Samruk never gave them a chance to resist.

With the upper floors quickly consumed in flames, the atoll personnel were left with little option but to attempt to escape out of doors and windows alike. They chose to die by automatic gunfire from the Samruk mercenaries, rather than perish by fire.

None of the participants gave much thought to which fate was worse, only which was faster.

Sergeant Major Korgan cursed through his teeth.

Somewhere behind him a ten thousand gallon JP-8 fuel blivet exploded into a miniature mushroom cloud, fire rising along a massive pillar into the night sky, casting long shadows across the airfield.

Deckard was diverting resources from Bravo Company to their position to help, but it wasn't coming fast enough. With half of Charlie Company incinerated during infiltration, their task was made twice as difficult.

Gunfire from the enemy's M4 rifles pinged off the belly of the capsized Serbian armored personnel carrier they were taking cover behind. Inside the tin can they could hear the occupants screaming and thrashing around, trying to figure out what was going on outside.

Richie was cooking up an explosive, an incredibly destructive method to crack open the APC. Thankfully, a low ranking Kazakh acted faster, producing a gas can from one of the assault trucks and pouring the flammable liquid into the crack where the hatch met the chassis on the armored vehicle. Most of the mercenaries smoked so one of them quickly flicked a lighter and set the gasoline ablaze.

The occupants threw open the hatch in short order, smoke-producing fire invading the confines of their vehicle. Surrounded, the contractors were pummeled by the Kazakhs and stripped of their weapons and equipment while the firefight sputtered out and restarted all over again.

Korgan recognized their language and features. He had seen them before. They sounded like the late Executive Officer Djokovic. Serbs. Shoulder insignia on their uniforms identified them as working for a company called Special Security Solutions.

A large caliber shot cracked above the noise of the battlefield.

One of Samruk's snipers was engaging the airfield's control tower from an assault truck parked a few hundred meters away. The .300 Winchester Magnum rounds thudded into the tower's Plexiglass windows. The shots penetrated, spider webbing the rest of the glass although it stubbornly refused to cave in.

Meanwhile, five more assault trucks rushed up to the side of the tower and came to a screeching halt. Any guards that remained standing were quickly cut down by the assault force as they moved towards the entrance to the airport's electronic nerve center.

One of the mercenaries ran for the door and slapped a charge on it. Seconds later, the explosives tore the door off its hinges, the assault team gaining entry.

The firefight was sputtering and winding down when the hanger doors began rolling open.

It had taken a few minutes for someone to figure out how to get them open, but not much was really locked or otherwise secured with everything on the island heavily guarded until now.

Adam crossed the threshold with the huge doors still rolling open. His eyes scanned across dozens of different aircraft illuminated by powerful overhead lights. Most of them were military models. Cargo aircraft and fighter jets, including the new model of the F-22 Raptor. Hard cases filled with the tools and diagnostic equipment needed for long term maintenance were left alongside the walls, someone clearly thinking ahead for the long haul.

Surrounded by Kazakhs, he moved deeper into the hanger. Coming face to face with something that his mind struggled to comprehend, his brain skipped a beat, trying to decide what he was seeing.

"Holy shit."

Someone uttered a response, Adam shaking his head, trying to catch up. Deckard walked passed him, a Kalashnikov cradled in one arm.

"What did you say?"

"Aurora."

"Aurora?"

"That's what they call it," Deckard said, motioning to the black craft.

Adam was still trying to piece together what he was seeing. It looked like something literally out of this world. Roughly triangular shaped, it resembled a black porpoise designed for aerial flight. The nose of the aircraft, where the cockpit was located, was slightly bulbous, and tiny wings swept out on each side. It certainly didn't look like anything designed for use by human pilots.

"What is it?"

"The result of a thirteen billion dollar no-bid contract," Deckard answered. "The Air Force's last manned spy plane."

300

"But--"

Deckard held up a finger as someone began transmitting over their radio frequency.

"--objective Hammerhead secure," a German accented voice said over the net.

"Kurt took down the control tower," Deckard said to no one in particular.

Another hiss of static came over the hand mike.

"--Objective White is secure."

"This is Six," Deckard responded. "Where is it?"

"Bunker Number Two."

"Prep it for demolition immediately. I want an ETA as soon as possible."

"Roger."

Deckard released the handmic and took a deep breath.

"They found the trigger virus," Adam said, voicing their thoughts.

Samruk's commander nodded, "The catalyst."

"And this thing?" the intel specialist said, pointing towards Aurora.

"Obviously they are planning on a war with whoever is left after their depopulation holocaust is complete. Looks like we pretty much fucked up that part of their plan already."

Deckard craned his neck, looking around.

"What is it?"

"They probably have the strategic bombers and attack helicopters in another hanger."

"But what is the purpose behind Aurora?" Adam asked. "I worked in intel and I never even heard of this thing."

"You've seen the high resolution pictures it took before. You were just told they came from spy satellites to help keep the project compartmentalized. This baby was developed about ten years ago to help fill in the black spots not covered by our satellite network. Also, as you know, those satellite orbits are monitored and highly predictable. Training areas get sanitized and sensitive equipment gets stored under over head cover when US spy

301

satellites come in for a look, so they built Aurora as a counter."

"I've never seen anything like it."

"That's because there isn't anything else like it anywhere. It actually functions in contrary of several known laws of physics. Conventional scientists would never believe it exists even if told about it, which has helped keep it secret. Aurora operates in the mesosphere where there is extremely little oxygen and most anti-missile and anti-aircraft systems are ineffective. Aurora exploits that defensive gap by utilizing a plasma funnel in front of the intake valves to increase the intake of air."

"What?"

"That's what I said. This is a spy plane, but theoretically other models could deliver nuclear or other hypervelocity weapons on targets; that or drop out of orbit to put a free fall team over enemy territory."

"And you know this how?"

Something came in garbled over the radio before a voice could be recognized.

"Objective Thrasher secure. Two WIA, one KIA, two prisoners."

"That's it," Deckard said before keying his mic. "All stations on this net; this is six, consolidate all prisoners at hanger seven."

Individual platoons began calling in to acknowledge Deckard's orders.

"So tell me again how you got read on to something like this?" Adam reiterated.

Deckard paused as the affirmatives coming in over the net slowed down.

"I wasn't," he answered. "I was responsible for recovering the project's chief engineer."

"Recovering him from who?"

"The North Koreans who had kidnapped him in Pensacola."

Adam stood slack-jawed, shaking his head in bewilderment.

302

"You have no idea who you are fucking with," the handcuffed enemy mercenary spat, coughing flecks of blood onto his lower lip. "No idea."

Deckard was unimpressed.

While his men were preparing the next stage of the operation, he oversaw the interrogation of prisoners to gain an edge up on what they would find at their next objective.

The man kneeling on the tarmac in front of him was American. He didn't know him by name, but Adam had recognized him from a previous operation during his military days. The Serbs had been brought in to provide the numbers and muscle. Former Delta Operators had been brought in to provide leadership and take care of tactical decision making.

They were aware of the virus. He had already told Deckard as much. Along with their families, they had been inoculated against it. Their families had been moved to several designated safe areas on one of the less populated Hawaiian Islands.

"You think I'm kidding," the ex-Army Sergeant said getting overconfident. "Check out what we got in Bunker Six," he said with a laugh.

"Wait one," Deckard said, kicking him hard in the stomach for good measure.

The Special Operations traitor buckled over, coughing his guts up on the tarmac as Deckard turned to speak with Adam who was stepping out of an assault truck even before it came to a full stop.

"This is it," his intel specialist said, handing a small bottle to Deckard.

Turning it over in his hand, Deckard frowned. It was nothing more than commercially available aspirin that could be found at any pharmacy.

"This?"

"Yeah, they have thousands of crates of this stuff in bunker two."

"This guy says that the 727 on fire over at the far end of the airfield was in the process of fueling up just when we arrived," Deckard added. "They planned on taking this stuff out in hours."

"I agree. We didn't have to force our way into the bunker. It was already open with several forklifts abandoned by the transport crew when Richie found the place. They were moving this out when we showed up."

Deckard's jaw clenched.

After everything he had seen and experienced, he was still shocked by the disregard these people had.

"When people started taking this stuff thinking it was regular aspirin, the trigger molecules would combine with the dormant strains hidden in that swine flu last year."

"Then it would go airborne. You remember the documents we recovered from Singapore."

"Tens of millions dead."

"And that was slated to happen tomorrow."

"Escalating to billions in a few weeks."

Deckard looked out into the sea. The atoll itself sat atop a coral reef, the rest of the reef hooking around forming a lagoon. In the center, several dozen naval ships were anchored, waiting for a war that he was determined to prevent from happening. In the distance he could see the dark shapes of his men paddling smaller boats out into the lagoon to claim the larger ships.

Another vehicle pulled up, Kurt Jager stepping out to report in next.

"Did the tower get a warning out?" Deckard asked.

"No, survivors told us the tower was empty when we arrived, the crews were not due to show up for another thirty minutes when that 727 over there was scheduled to take off. Two of the air traffic controllers managed to get into the tower once we hit the ground, but it looks like our snipers took them out before they could transmit anything of value."

"Good work."

"Although we heard over the radio that they did see that fireball when the fuel blivet went up."

"Shit, they're close." Deckard did the math in his head. Due to the curvature of the earth they had to be within twenty five miles. "What did you tell them?"

"I had one of the survivors get on the radio and tell them we had an industrial accident. We are not sure we can contain the fire, so we are moving critical personnel and systems to their position."

"You think they bought that?"

"Sounds like it," the German shrugged.

"Next I need you to get one of the radar dishes operational and figure out exactly where they are."

"Already got men on it."

It was better than any of them could have hoped for.

"ETA?"

"We should be ready to move to our follow-on objective in thirty minutes, provided we can get at least one of those ships operational. We only have a few guys with that type of training. A few prisoners have also volunteered to help with a little extra persuasion."

"Bunker Two will be ready for demo in ten minutes," Kurt said, looking at his watch.

"I guess that leaves just one more thing," Deckard said, yanking his 1911 out of its holster.

Sticking the toe of his boot under the captured mercenary's chin, Deckard pushed him over onto his back, sending him off on another fit of coughs and gags.

Kneeling, he pressed the barrel against the side of his head.

"What is in Bunker Six?"

305

THIRTY ONE

A lone ship crashed through the waves.

White-capped swells slapped against the hull, rocking the ship from side to side on its keel, its nose arching upwards, almost vertical before suddenly dropping down into the cold spray. In the distance a storm approached. Lightning flashed through the sky, seen but not heard, not yet. The crew grimaced, knowing that the rough waters were only a preface.

Flanked by two Zumwalt class destroyers, a super-cruise-liner sat hulking in the water, its massive size unaffected by the roll of the ocean waves. The name across the side of the ship read, Crown of the Pacific.

The smaller ship powered right up to the stern of the super-liner. It flashed the correct IFF signal, the meeting prearranged. The Phalanx cannons retrofitted onto the civilian cruise ship remained silent as they scanned the horizons.

Chad slammed a quarter ton of weights onto the ground.

The steel plates crashed loudly, the bar flexing in the middle before rebounding back into the air for a moment.

"Chad Morrison, please report in," the speaker system repeated a fourth time.

With one large vein threatening to pop right out of his neck, he snatched up a nearby telephone receiver and spoke into it for a few seconds. Snarling, he slammed the plastic phone into the wall, breaking it in two. He was too busy to deal with bed-wetters, no matter how much they paid.

Throwing a towel over one shoulder, he wiped his face off while walking out into the corridor.

Chad had been hired under the euphemistic banner of Physical Security Specialist. What that meant was that he was the man overall in-charge of security on the one and a half billion dollar super-liner, the largest ship ever built. To simplify further, it was his job to kill anyone on ship who didn't belong there and ensure that his employers didn't die in the process.

Even he was overwhelmed by the size and scope of the ship. It had been purchased just a month prior and ran half a kilometer from bow to stern. There were over a dozen decks, shopping malls, clubs, and five star hotels. It was a floating city and a high class one at that. That wasn't even getting into the rushed modifications made just before their current voyage.

After getting kicked out of Delta, he had managed a small private military corporation startup, running operations from Iraq to Afghanistan, even a few in the Philippines and in Latin America. His true employers were several steps removed, but it was always understood that he operated under the umbrella of Western intelligence agencies, guaranteeing that he'd never run afoul of the law regardless of how messy the job might get.

He was doing just fine at throwing the company's earnings away on cocaine and prostitutes before being made an offer he couldn't refuse. He and his men had received the vaccinations.

Stepping into the control room, he looked more than just a little out of place in sandals and a cut-off t-shirt.

"What is the problem?"

"The GPS trackers just went dark," one of the Pakistanis said looking up from a console.

Buried in the heart of the ship, the control center made a half moon shape of desks where flat screen computers hummed. The wall displayed a projection of the earth with a timer ticking down to zero. The perfect place to manage the end of the world.

"Check sonar."

"Sir?"

"Do it," Chad growled back.

He thought he had settled the issue an hour ago. Some idiot, undoubtedly one of the Serbs, had been smoking by the fuel point and set half of the atoll ablaze. Now the surviving contractors on the island needed to displace critical equipment off the island and onto the Crown of the Pacific before the rest of the island was consumed by the fire. Critical equipment meant the contents of Bunker Six, which the GPS trackers had been attached to.

The technician across from him swallowed hard.

"What is it?" Chad demanded.

"Um, all three units are stationary," the Pakistani said with wide eyes. "Fourteen thousand feet below the surface."

Turning red in the face, it took what little self-discipline he had not to rip the skinny Paki's head off. All three units. It was no accident.

Whoever was arriving at their stern had just dumped three nuclear weapons over the side of their ship.

Deckard was too exhausted to be surprised anymore.

Richie had worked fast, cutting into Bunker Six with the thermic lance, the horsepower provided by a dump truck they found on the base, helping them pry open the doors the rest of the way.

Inside were three Mk174 tactical nuclear weapons of the type that had become almost legendary in intelligence circles. The United States and Russia were the only two nations to have successfully miniaturized nuclear weapons to the extent that they could be carried in a suitcase. They were the prized possession of both countries' nuclear arsenals.

Such weapons could be smuggled into an enemy country via commercial air travel or even strapped to a military free-fall parachutist to deliver to a key target. These three were the latest models, with a yield of twelve kilotons apiece.

A military base run by mercenaries. Black project spy planes. Suitcase nuclear weapons. The old men at the Grove that owned a controlling interest in Samruk, and in Deckard, also owned the United States Government, National Security Council and all.

Their cargo boat bobbed and dipped in the ocean as heavy lines were thrown down to them from the stern of the super-liner. Samruk's mercenaries grabbed the ropes and secured them to hard points along the side of the ship, mooring the two vessels together.

As this was done, Deckard ordered the nukes rolled off the side of the ship.

They had been his best shot at using a Trojan Horse to get close to the super-liner, and since he wasn't coming under fire from the two destroyers, it appeared to have worked. The nukes themselves were in hard cases with multiple redundant systems. They would be safest at the bottom of the ocean until the US Navy could recover them at a later date. There was no way he was going to risk having them fall back into enemy hands.

Deckard watched the three metal cases splash and disappear beneath the dark waters.

His men fired several stunted, suppressed gunshots, killing members of the super-liner's receiving party.

It was time to go to work.

Thirty Two

Charlie Company stalked the shadows, moving deeper into the artificial valley created by a dozen decks stretching straight up on each side of the boardwalk. With the reception party eliminated, there was nothing standing in their way as they made their infiltration.

The steel canyon was a novelty of nautical engineering. Both sides of the ship were packed with luxury cabins for guests and crew alike, the center left open for attractions and commercial shopping. The area near the stern of the ship was designed to look like an old-fashioned boardwalk, wooden planks artificially aged, metal rusted over with fresh paint. In the center, a vintage merry-go-round spun, lights flashing across their faces in the night.

The Kazakh walking point fired, VSS rifle coughing sub-sonic rounds. Another Serbian contractor and a couple out for a late night stroll were drilled with SP-9 bullets. Deckard's orders were clear. Both men and women were here for a specific reason, to lie in the lap of luxury while they perpetrated a global genocide. Children who had been brought along would be spared, but the wives were guilty by association. It only would have taken one of them to blow the whistle, and the curtains would have fallen on any notion of a planned global extinction.

Somewhere inside the cabin areas to his flanks, Deckard could hear muffled gunfire. Alpha and Bravo Companies were moving up the sides through the living quarters of the ship. They would be tasked with clearing the cabins, room by room, deck by deck. Take care of business and move on.

Meanwhile they would move straight up the middle, searching for the enemy's operations center. It wasn't the best plan, but a well laid plan could not wait until tomorrow.

The two surviving platoons from Charlie Company weaved

310

their way between the various park rides and concession stands, headed towards the bow of the ship. At half a kilometer, they were in for a walk.

There was no warning when the inevitable happened.

An explosion rocked the boardwalk, knocking over a food stand, spilling popcorn that crunched under Deckard's feet as he moved to cover.

Gunfire erupted from the dozens of balconies that looked down on the boardwalk, as well as from the top deck. The mercenaries were immediately and effectively caught in a U-shaped near ambush. Both rifle fire and grenades rained down on them, shredding wooden facades into splinters and shattering glass.

Taking fire from three sides, there was nowhere for the Samruk mercenaries to take effective cover, even as they desperately tried to duck behind the carnival rides, only to be shot at from an opposing angle. Taking a knee behind what was left of the popcorn stand, Deckard shouldered his AK and let loose a burst at the first balcony he had seen a muzzle flash from.

At this point the mercenaries could fire in almost any direction. Sweeping his muzzle laterally, Deckard shot bursts into balcony after balcony, not pausing to confirm that any of his shots had met their mark. They needed fire superiority and fast.

A burst of return fire answered back, stitching across the wooden planks to his side. Tucking his shoulder in, Deckard rolled to his right, just out of the cone of fire that smashed into his former position.

Bouncing back to his feet, the former soldier expected a second burst to tear apart his torso, when the ship vibrated under his feet. Just several seconds after the enemy initiated, the platoon assessed the situation, Mk14 gunners firing with reckless abandon into the balconies. The HEDP grenades shattered through the glass doors and reached deep into the suites behind the balconies, detonating with a thump somewhere inside.

A severed hand flopped down next to Deckard. Looking down at it for a fraction of a second, he then noticed his empty magazines. Strangely, he could not remember reloading despite the two magazines that lay between his feet.

The grenadiers laid it on heavy, the cylinders on the oversized revolvers spinning as they exhausted their weapons of ammunition, devastating the enemy in the process. With the enemy occupying an elevated and covered position, Deckard knew that the counter fire would buy them a few seconds at most.

"Move," he yelled, his voice nearly drowned out by gunfire. "We need to move!"

A Kazakh rifleman to his side leveled his rifle and fired several rapid shots into one of the balconies. His efforts were rewarded, an M4 rifle fell from lifeless hands, spinning through the air and crashing through an umbrella stuck through the center of a table at the dining area.

Moving to the next target, the mercenary fired again, just as an enemy somewhere above put a well-placed round at the base of his spine. The Kazakh sprawled out on the ground, crippled. Deckard slung his rifle, reaching for him as the injured trooper attempted to sit up with a severed spinal chord.

Another burst stitched him across his chest, killing him.

Out of options, Deckard leaped over the corpse and sprinted for the glass doors at the end of the boardwalk.

Somewhere a grenade exploded, the overpressure washing over the mercenary commander and toppling him over. Deckard rolled into a plastic garbage can, knocking it over and covering him in refuse.

A squad's worth of mercenaries had taken cover behind one of the carnival rides and were able to lay down a suppressive fire. From their position, they delivered accurate point shots on the multitude of places where the enemy presented himself from. It was a giant game of whack a mole, the moles seeming to multiply by the second.

The plastic trash can was plucked away by enemy shots that searched out Deckard as he rolled away and staggered to his feet, coughing and gagging on the sulfur smell that hung in the air.

Then a Samruk merc got a machine gun back on line, quickly joined by a second.

Grabbing several stunned and disoriented platoon members, Deckard pushed them towards the exit, his hoarse words falling on ears deafened by gunfire and explosions. They found their own cover in a wooden stand constructed for one of the carnival games. Seeing their comrades, more survivors quickly joined them.

Looking across the boardwalk back toward the stern of the ship, all he could see was camouflage-clad bodies.

"Move to the doors," he said, keying up his radio.

The other group of mercenaries firing from behind the tilt-a-whirl were oblivious to his transmission.

"Anyone on this net, respond," Deckard said frustrated.

Their communications were being jammed.

One of the grenadiers pushed him aside as the carnival lights flashed in a moment too surreal to comprehend. With his weapon reloaded, the Samruk trooper got back on target, whacking more moles as the muzzle flashes appeared on the balconies to both sides.

Looking towards the source of the grenade fire, the other group of mercenaries spotted Deckard and saw him pointing towards the doors. Finally someone took charge of the group, and they ran towards the exit while Deckard's group went heavy with rifle, machine gun, and grenade fire to cover their movement.

No one bothered to actually open the doors. The pane glass was shattered all around them, leaving only empty frames for the Kazakhs to lunge through. As they neared the doors, Deckard started grabbing shoulders and pushing troops in their comrades' direction. They were so fixated on targets that they were losing situational awareness.

In a firefight, with adrenaline pumping, body sweating, your vision was constricted down into a small periscope.

Pushing the last few Kazakhs towards the shattered doors, they ran at full speed across the open area with enemy fire nipping at their feet. Ducking through the exit, they met up with the second group, already barricaded behind a concrete container filled with small trees and exotic plants.

They were trading fire with more enemies now to their

immediate front.

Regardless of the threat, there was nowhere for them to maneuver to but straight ahead. The enemy had the high ground, occupied their flanks, had them channelized, and would no doubt soon encircle them by coming up on their rear from the boardwalk in seconds.

The park area of the ship resembled the boardwalk area as it was an open air attraction in the center of the ship with cabin decks stretching up on both sides with the addition of hanging gardens. The difference was that this area was a mock-up of a city park with elaborate landscaped gardens. Cafes and restaurants lined the sides. It was a natural enclave in the middle of a steel ship.

Joining the other group, the former soldier saw that C/co was now reduced to platoon strength or less.

They wouldn't last much longer.

Peeking from between two palm trees, he saw the opposition bounding through the vegetation and across the walkways, closing on them. In the severely restricted confines of the ship, flanking maneuvers were out of the question.

Deckard flinched as the concrete planter chipped away next to his face, the opposition drawing a bead on him.

The flash of movement he had seen confirmed his fears.

They were wearing a mix of military fatigues and civilian clothing, plate carriers strapped across their chests, tattoos covering forearms, M4 rifles with shortened barrels for ease of movement. They weren't Serbs but Americans. Ex-Special Forces working for the highest bidder.

Having sized up the situation, he knew they needed to take the initiative. It was now or never.

"Half of you go right," he said to his group. "The rest of you follow me to the left. Bound forward until we clear the park. Don't stop for anything," he instructed them in Russian.

To his side, Jean-Francoise nodded his understanding, the Frenchman picking up what he was laying down. Checking the load left in his magazine, the former legionnaire rocked it back into

314

place in the Kalashnikov's receiver. It looked like some shattered glass had sliced up the side of his face, a half mask of blood coating the skin, but otherwise he seemed to be holding up well.

Without another word spoken, the group of Kazakhs moved around the planter and engaged the enemy. While the team flipped over tables and chairs, moving through one of the outdoor cafes, Deckard led his group down the left-hand side.

Coming under fire the moment they stepped from behind cover, Deckard knew they were in trouble. One Kazakh was struck down, his screams ignored amid the confusion of the firefight.

Moving a half dozen strides, Deckard dove to the ground behind a circular metal kiosk situated between a cobblestone path and a copse of tropical plants. 5.56 bullets were blasting apart the displayed advertisements inside the display case as JF came up alongside him. Two Kazakhs took cover behind the concrete lip created around the winding path, while two more knelt next to some palm trees.

The enemy shooters were drawn from the ranks of American Special Operations units, battle-hardened veterans of the wars in Iraq and Afghanistan. They came on aggressive, placing accurate fire on the mercenaries. These weren't Third World tribesmen or some opium militia.

Looking down his sights, Deckard spied one of the enemy gunmen pop up, bounding forward on the path ahead. Stroking the trigger, Deckard dropped the gunman, arms flailing in the air as he dropped his rifle. He had once been one of them, but Deckard knew that when you play big boy games, you play by big boy rules.

They had decided to stand with the enemy.

JF ripped a burst of fire across the park, missing his mark, but keeping the enemies' heads down for a moment. On their right, they could hear the other group fighting and dying. Seizing the moment, the mercenary commander leaped to his feet, staying low as he stalked off the path and slipped into the foliage ahead.

The others came in behind him; the dense jungle in the center of the park had been allowed to grow freely. Even if it was

315

only a narrow patch of vegetation, they would take every inch of cover and concealment that they could get.

With the firefight continuing to rage on the other side of the park, Deckard was able to cheat his group farther forward, taking advantage of the overgrown area. He had to shake off the unreality of it. Recorded bird calls sounded from a speaker system, mimicking a real jungle. Stepping carefully between tentacle-like tree roots and oversized ferns, he waited until the first enemy came into view before shouldering his rifle.

The Hispanic looking ex-soldier wore jeans and a sleeveless shirt under his body armor. A ball cap was perched on the top of his head as he swiveled back and forth, scanning for targets. Stepping across the artificial stream that gushed across the center of the park, he must have detected something and turned, looking in Deckard's direction.

Deckard shot first. The double-tap punched him in the face, penetrating the cranial vault. The Special Operations veteran was dead before he hit the ground.

That was when hell broke loose all over again.

Deckard's team went prone as a hailstorm of gunfire chopped through the foliage above their heads. Crawling forward, the entire element got parallel with each other and began selecting targets. Deckard fired on a big guy with slicked-back hair who was running down one of the paths, attempting to advance over easy terrain.

His first shot slammed into his plate carrier, the body armor easily absorbing the impact but staggering him back a few steps. Deckard's follow-up shots were better placed, striking him in the chin and cleaving away half of his jaw bone.

A grenade exploded to his side, peppering one of the Kazakhs with debris as blazing hot shrapnel tore through the leafy growth just inches above them. On his other side, JF shifted toward an enemy who was kneeling behind another concrete planter. The mercenary was sweeping his muzzle through the forested area, making bold corrections to seek out their positions with a flurry of 5.56 tungsten penetrators.

The Frenchman milked the AK's trigger and the merc collapsed, the side of his skull emptying its contents across the cobblestone in a crimson smear.

The lull in fire lasted for scant seconds but was enough time for Deckard to roll forward. Dropping into the rocky depression that the artificial stream flowed through, he came up on a knee.

A flash caught his attention, another grenade exploding, this time inside one of the restaurants.

More American mercenaries poured into the park from multiple entrances. Carbines and light machine guns were tucked into their shoulders, trigger fingers curled and ready.

Using the depression as cover, he popped up and delivered a double-tap, his reflex sight centered on an enemy's face, before ducking back down. He did so in the nick of time as automatic weapons fire crisscrossed the space he had previously occupied. Staying low he changed positions, moving laterally, sloshing his way upstream.

The Kazakhs slithering into the stream behind him, Deckard tore a fragmentation grenade off his chest rig. Pulling the pin, he hurled the bomb into a circular area created by manicured hedges with park benches inset under them. The grenade bounced and rolled into the sitting area where a mercenary with a Ranger scroll tattooed on his forearm and a heavily muscled man holding a belt-fed machine gun were firing from sporadically.

The grenade blasted the two freelancers. The former Ranger was blown backwards into a wrought iron gate outside a restaurant, killed instantly by the impact. The machine gunner was actually thrown into the air, both arms cleaved off his torso and sent flopping into the stream.

Glancing down, the Kazakhs grimaced as the clear water flowed around their shins, now tinged with red.

"Bound!" Deckard ordered.

Stepping out onto the path, he pivoted at the hips, changing his direction mid-stride.

His muzzle was already creeping upwards as he felt as

much as he saw something in his peripheral vision. Squeezing the trigger, a two round burst crashed into a Serb standing in one of the balconies overlooking the park.

Both shots shattered through the glass banister, taking the Serb low in the pelvis. Pitching forward, the Eastern European fell through the shattered glass. Flailing through the air, his body screamed through the wooden latticework over the dining area of a bistro, toppling tables and chairs underneath with a wet *thwack*.

Shifting again, Deckard pointed his rifle at a camo-clad shooter farther down the path.

The buzzcut American brought his M4 into play almost simultaneously with him. Pulling the trigger, the hammer in Deckard's AK-103 struck on an empty chamber. All out of quarters in that video game, he thought. No way would he be able to snatch his side arm out of its holster in time.

With a snarl, buzzcut pulled his weapon in tight, trigger finger flexing, when he suddenly fell to his knees. A half dozen AK rounds pounded into his unprotected side, the exposed area under the armpit.

Spinning, Deckard saw the second group of Kazakhs emerge from a restaurant. They had ducked into it and moved through the facade, using it as cover to get deeper into the park. Smart move. One of them nodded to Deckard, his barrel still smoking.

The sound of shattering glass drew their attention back to their front.

The staccato bursts of machine gun fire drove them back down to the ground. A trio of general purpose machine guns had been moved into position behind the glass doors at the end of the park. A wall of hot lead streamed over their heads, the grazing fire designed to chop soldiers off at knee height. Once again, they had stalled.

Both groups of Kazakhs began to maintain cross coverage, pulling security on the balconies as more and more Serbs popped out of the cabins, making another attempt to dominate the high ground. Behind them, Deckard could hear occasional gunshots crack. Advancing soldiers attempting a recon by fire, shooting at suspected positions that his men might be occupying.

They had been cut off and encircled.

Chuck shotgunned the door jamb a final time, the buckshot devastating the locking mechanism before he reeled back and slammed a size fourteen boot into it. The cabin door flew open, bounced off the wall, and was in the process of slamming shut again as an assault team of Samruk mercenaries pushed through to clear the room.

Gunfire emanated from within as the former SEAL moved on to the next door, another assault team stacking behind him.

Bravo Company was moving fast. Three decks of passenger and crew cabins had already been cleared. Adam was one deck above, and Sergeant Major Koran one deck below. Ship seizures had been Chuck's bread and butter when he had been in the Navy, but the scale involved in this operation was ridiculous.

The idea of using an entire SEAL team to take down a single ship was pretty much unheard of. Tonight they were using an entire battalion and it still wasn't enough. The Crown of the Pacific was mind-boggling in size.

Shotgunning open the next door, he stepped aside, letting the Kazakhs go to work. Screams sounded inside.

It was grisly work.

It was a slaughter.

They were technically non-combatants. Not soldiers or officers but puppet masters. They were bankers, CEO's, foundation members. The world's self-appointed elites.

The floor tilted at an angle beneath his feet. The waters were getting rough outside.

Chuck shucked the Remington 270 shotgun once again.

Grisly or not, the work would get done.

THIRTY THREE

Deckard was considering exactly how fucked they were, when something in front of him moved.

At the far end of the park, just in front of the glass doors was an oval-shaped bar surrounded by stools and a few tables, all of which were now lowering and disappearing. Crawling forward, he barely believed what he was seeing.

The entire bar was on an elevator platform.

With the bar slowly sinking downwards, Deckard reached for his chest harness, pulling free a smoke grenade canister. Yanking the pin, he threw the cylinder over the bar where it landed and rolled next to the glass doors. Thick white smoke sprayed from both ends of the grenade with a hiss, obscuring the machine gunner's line of sight.

For the next thirty seconds they would be firing blind.

Motioning for the Kazakhs to follow, Deckard took the lead. He scrambled forward on hands and knees, still attempting to stay as low as possible with machine gun fire traversing and searching for human targets.

Pushing off the ledge, he fell down towards the bar before landing on the balls of his feet. The remnants of Charlie Company didn't need any prodding to escape from the hell zone they had been trapped in. The strange layout of the ship had ended up saving their lives. He never would have suspected that there was an elevating bar in the middle of the ship, where patrons could grab a refill while moving to a lower deck.

Trying to catch his breath, Deckard loaded his final magazine into his Kalashnikov.

White smoke continued to obfuscate the view above them as the elevator platform touched down. Coughing and hacking, the mercenaries found themselves surrounded my neon lights and deep hues of blue and purple. The deck underneath the park was a two-tiered shopping mall.

"Let's go," Deckard said. "Fan out, they'll be here any second."

Leaving the elevator, the ten man squad was all that was left of an entire company. They spread out in a wedge-formation, walking down the promenade, headed deeper into the bowels of the ship.

Music greeted them from each shop they walked past. The scene was hyperreal, a bizarre exaggeration of a regular shopping mall, with flashing lights and deeper colors splashed on the walls. There were more bars, restaurants, designer clothing stores, video game arcades, music shops, and whatever else for wealthy Americans to indulge upon.

Walking briskly towards the atrium, they could see at the end of the mall. The mercenaries scanned their sectors, wary of threats. A news ticker scrolled across a LED screen as they passed, the text reading something about Hollywood.

Deckard took some solace in the fact that life was continuing as usual elsewhere in the world. If the plague had been released, the news would have been reporting on the articles Adam had shown him, prepared and ready to go months in advance. Instead, the news was covering some celebrity's latest panty shot.

At the end of the mall, one of the elevators stopped at their floor, and the doors pinged open, revealing a quartet of mercenaries who were bristling with weapons. This time Deckard's crew acquired the upper hand as the entire squad raised their weapons in unison. Sparks flung in every direction as the elevator was turned into a death trap. Kalashnikovs rattled, actions cycling back and forth, sending 7.62 bullets scorching through human bodies.

For a moment everything was quiet.

The elevator attempted to close but the doors shut on a bloody arm before retracting back open. Muzak was piped through the mall's sound system, ambling on in the large empty space.

A half dozen elevators pinged, doors sliding open,

contractors ready for a fight.

The Samruk mercenaries dove to the ground. A fresh fusillade of gunfire stormed through the shopping mall. Taking cover wherever they could, Deckard found himself behind a clock tower situated in the middle of the mall with another Kazakh. Others took refuge behind a bar and concrete tree planters near a fountain.

The enemy advanced, moving in bounding overwatch, one group covering the other. Leaning from around the clock tower, Deckard targeted the oldest looking shooter. He was a survivor, probably a retired Special Forces or Delta Force Sergeant Major. More than likely in charge of the element he traveled with.

The gray-haired man was barking orders, when Deckard triggered a shot, the steel core round tearing a baseball-sized chunk of flesh out the side of the man's face. The return fire from nearly forty enemy combatants was devastating. One of the Kazakhs crouched behind a metal trash receptacle, it being the only piece of cover nearby.

In seconds, hot metal had sliced through the metal slats and struck the Samruk trooper down. He fell to his side screaming when another shot caught him. With his head kicked back, the mercenary lay still, a bullet having stabbed through his eye socket.

"Right flank!" Deckard screamed over the gunfire.

Picking themselves up, the remaining gunmen ran to their side, heading into a pizzeria. The chain restaurant was their only chance to escape the onslaught. Continuing forward simply wasn't an option. Knocking over chairs and tables, Deckard ran to the far wall.

A C4 general purpose charge was retrieved from one of his pouches and slammed against the wall. The thin bulkheads wouldn't stand a chance against plastic explosives.

Initiating the time fuse, Deckard took refuge behind the pizza oven with the rest of his men.

"What's the plan?" JF wanted to know.

German troops had encountered a similar problem while fighting the Soviets in built-up areas. The streets were turned into kill zones by Russian machine guns and skilled sharpshooters. The German troops had no other option to advance other than to use explosives to blow through the walls connecting each building and house to move across city blocks.

"Stalingrad," Deckard answered.

The Composition Four roared, the blast tearing metal and plaster to shreds.

Nikita dumped the smoking hot M4 carbine. He had fired it until the barrel glowed.

The top deck of the ship was covered with swimming pools and hot tubs for guests, currently unoccupied. Maybe it was the approaching thunderstorm. Maybe it was the firefight. The deck was also littered with dead bodies.

His spotter, Askar, hadn't made it.

The rain was starting to come down in sheets of icy water, the super-liner rocking steadily from side to side in the choppy water. The Pacific Ocean seemed to be acting contrary to its namesake at the moment.

Resting his bolt action rifle on the railing, he dialed down the magnification on his scope for a two hundred and fifty meter shot. From the looks of things he had arrived right on time.

The sleek-looking executive helicopter was ready to go, rotor blades cutting through the downpour. A small procession walked towards the bow of the ship along a catwalk, heading for the helipad and their last chance to escape the carnage.

Talking a deep breath, Nikita pulled the stock into the pocket of his shoulder. Using the cross hairs in his scope, the sniper targeted the portion of the helicopter where the rotors met the fuselage of the aircraft. Letting half of his breath out, he squeezed the trigger, the rifle bucking hard and jarring his teeth.

The large caliber bullet flew on a nearly perfect straight

trajectory before striking the helicopter. The rotor blades continued spinning but now a tower of black smoke was rising off the aircraft.

Through his scope, Nikita could see the pilot freak as his dials went crazy and the aircraft began to shutter. His shot had wrecked something critical, and now the entire helicopter was beginning to oscillate back and forth in place before ever taking off.

Using the reticle inside the scope, he split the pilot's face into quadrants, the portion where the two cross hairs met resting comfortably on his cheekbone. The follow-up shot was drowned out by thunder crashing overhead.

The interior of the cockpit was sprayed with crimson, the helicopter now pilotless.

The small party that had been attempting to flee froze in place when the first shot was fired. After the second, they turned and ran back down the catwalk, desperate to get back inside the ship as they had been to leave it moments before.

The group had several bodyguards escorting them to the helipad who were attempting to get their clients back inside, pushing and screaming to drive them towards the door. Nikita focused on the armed men first, firing and rapidly sliding the bolt back and forth. Three dead mercenaries decorated the catwalk before he reloaded a fresh magazine.

One of the older members of the group was falling behind, old age having caught up with him. Samruk's intelligence section had printed off pictures of the three High Value Targets expected to be found on the Crown of the Pacific. Nikita winced. Unfortunately, he wasn't one of them. Taking up the slack in the trigger, the .300 WinMag boomed.

Shifting to his next target, he lined up his sights on another old man, this one stepping over the body of one of his late bodyguards. It was with grim satisfaction that the sniper watched the man's head disappear when he fired his next shot. The oligarch's lifeless body fell to the metal grating where blood dripped to the deck below.

Nikita's eyes went wide as he spotted the third and final target. He was one of the HVTs on the target deck handed out prior to the mission. He had studied the pictures during the flight from Astana, committing every detail to memory. He recognized the deep wrinkles around the corners of deep dark eyes.

His name was Jarogniew.

The sniper's finger tightened around the trigger.

Taking up the slack, he expected the stock to kick back into his shoulder in fractions of a second, when the entire ship suddenly rocked, pitching far on its keel to one side as a wave pounded into the super-liner.

The rifle cracked as Nikita slipped across the deck, the shot going wide.

Deckard was the first through the smoking gap he had created in the wall.

He emerged into a clothing shop full of overpriced jeans and t-shirts. Mannequins showed off the latest fashions in the display windows, and art deco pieces were hung on the walls.

The last of the Kazakhs were climbing through the breach as Deckard placed his second charge on the opposite wall where it held in place on its adhesive.

"Fire in the hole!"

The charge blew out the facade. The overpressure swept over tables full of the fancy patterned t-shirts, spilling them everywhere. Outside they could still hear gunfire in the mall. It wouldn't be much longer before the American contractors figured out what their game was.

Coughing through the smoke, Samruk mercenaries crossed into the next commercial venue, a medium-sized bookshop. At the sound of the blast, the enemy contractors turned towards the sound, trying to figure out what was going on just a moment too late.

From the bookstore Deckard and his men were parallel with the enemy's fighting positions behind a bar and a large fountain situated in the center of the mall's promenade. Taking cover behind the bookshelves, the Samruk team started firing on the contractors who still thought that their opposition was somewhere down range.

Deckard flicked his selector switch to auto. Firing a burst, he stitched the nearest gunman from crotch to chest. JF and the other mercs raked the enemy position with gunfire, cutting the gunmen down in short controlled bursts. The last of the group turned and cut loose with a burst of his own, catching one of the Kazakhs high, right across the collarbone and throat before Deckard emptied the rest of his magazine into him.

It was only superficially comforting to know that he probably never felt a thing.

Inching out into the mall, they came under fire from the second wave of gunners down by the atrium. They had managed to advance down through the mall by blowing through the walls but were still in the same predicament. Pinned down and unable to push forward.

Deckard ducked as a barrage of gunfire tore up a shelf full of recent best sellers. The individual books hopped as bullets slammed into them, turning pages into confetti and tossing them into the air like a New Year's celebration.

Turning to his men, Deckard gave them the hand and arm signal for grenades.

One of the dead men lying alongside the fountain had something he wanted.

When two of the FMK-2 grenades arched through the air, Deckard made his move. It took a moment for the enemy gunmen to gain target acquisition of him, the same length of time left on the grenade's fuses. They detonated simultaneously, shrapnel wreaking havoc as Deckard picked up the dead mercenary's weapon and rolled behind the water fountain.

The Mk 46 was a light machine gun that fired from a two hundred round drum mounted underneath the body of the weapon.

This particular model was fitted with a shortened barrel and reflex sight as favored by US Special Operations units.

He wasn't waiting for the opposition to recover from the grenade blasts, opting to hit them hard and fast.

Holding down the trigger, Deckard cut loose with a stream of autofire. Using the tracers as a guide he walked the rounds in a lazy figure eight pattern that pounded the enemy. They had taken refuge behind several overturned tables, a wooden bar situated in the middle of the mall, and some of the concrete planters with palm trees sticking out of them. The 5.56 bullets chased them like angry hornets, tearing through wood and sending splinters into the air.

With the enemy effectively suppressed, the Kazakhs rushed from the bookstore, adding their own gunfire to the chaos.

When the Mk 46's bolt locked to the rear on an empty chamber, one of the surviving contractors leaned from behind cover and took aim at Deckard. Dropping the light machine gun with a thud, Deckard snatched his side arm out of its holster, the front sight blade lining up on the enemy with muscle memory built by untold hours on the range.

The 1911 barked, the .45 hollow point coring the man's brain before exiting the back of his skull in a shower of gore.

Jean-Francoise kicked away a fallen opponent's rifle as he reached out for it and was preparing a final kill shot.

"Wait," Deckard said. With his ears ringing from the firefight, he was barely able to hear himself speak. "We need one alive."

One of the elevators pinged as it arrived at the mall.

The survivors spun on their heels, rifles and pistols trained at the elevator doors as they slid open.

"Holy shit," Deckard sighed.

"Warm welcome, thanks guys," Pat said, stepping out of the elevator.

"Weren't you supposed to be with Alpha Company clearing the starboard cabins?"

"Got separated from the team after getting hit by a second

group of reinforcements. They got this place packed with more security personnel then crew and guests."

"What was the status before getting separated?" Deckard asked. With their comms jammed he had no way of knowing.

Pat shook his head.

"You are not much better off down here with us," JF commented.

Suddenly everything in the mall that wasn't bolted to the floor started sliding. The mercenaries themselves were barely able to maintain their footing as the deck rocked to one side and then the other. The super-liner was getting broadsided with increasingly powerful waves as was demonstrated by the waterfall that suddenly came down through the atrium after sloshing down the elevator shafts.

Sheets of water cascaded down the open air shaft that led from the atrium up to the top deck. Somewhere above, windows and portholes had been smashed to pieces by the rogue wave, allowing huge volumes of water to wash into the ship.

"What the hell," Pat cursed as he grabbed a railing for support. "At least things can't get any worse," he said, smirking at Deckard.

Deckard eyed him angrily as the boat shook a second time.

THIRTY FOUR

Frank knew they were getting close to something or someone.

The opposition had hit them with wave after wave of gunmen. The Serbian and American contractors had worked in tandem to thwart Samruk's movement into the upper levels of the ship, deploying heavy machine guns and even antipersonnel mines in the hallways and stairwells.

The corridors of the ship were running red with blood, the viscous liquid clotting and sticking to their boots as it congealed in the carpeting.

The Serbs charged forward. Having deployed thick bullet-resistant riot shields, they pushed forward almost in a phalanx down the hall, shooting and trampling over the Kazakhs in their way. Frank was nearly black on ammunition when one of the Samruk troopers recovered a PKM from one of their dead and began to turn the tables.

The belt-fed weapon sputtered, slamming shot after shot into the riot shields and knocking the Serbs off-balance as they strode forward. With the shields flailing in their grip, several of the Eastern European mercenaries exposed their flanks, an opening that Frank and the other survivors were quick to exploit.

Draining the AK-103, Frank let the rifle hang by its sling and transitioned to his Glock 19. Firing shot after shot, he aimed for exposed feet beneath the protective wall of the shields. Screams filled the hall, filling the random hiccups between gunshots.

One of the Serbs tripped over his dead comrade and fell down on top of his shield. Looking up he found himself looking down the barrel of a Glock. Frank drilled him between the eyes. The dead were piling up like cordwood.

329

Reloading on the move, he took point, treading over the dead on his way down the hall. Stopping at a T-intersection, he knew they were nearly at the penthouse. The Alpha Company men would never have even known it was there if they hadn't suddenly encountered such stiff opposition as they got closer.

At the end of the hall, yet another layer of protection was present. They lined themselves in front of the penthouse's double doors, creating a wall with their riot shields. Having gotten a quick glance, he was about to duck back behind cover when a bullet struck him in the shoulder.

Mendez ran forward to pull him back behind the corner of the wall when the Serbs rattled off a long burst. The submachine gun fire threatened to reduce the former mortar man into pulp, the shots puncturing his side, instantly deflating both lungs.

Richie was the next on deck. He stepped forward and sidearmed a claymore mine down the hall towards the Serbs. Kurt Jager grabbed Frank by the leg and pulled him behind cover just as the British demolitions expert depressed the clacker.

The mine ravaged the hallway and everyone left in it. Even with the riot shields in place, the blast's overpressure alone was enough to kill the Serbs in an enclosed space. The steel ball bearings did the rest, severing flesh from bone.

The Samruk men struggled to their feet, many with blood coming out of their ears.

The explosion made a breach into the penthouse unnecessary. The wooden doors had been torn right off their hinges and deposited a few dozen feet somewhere inside.

Kurt racked the charging handle on a fallen enemy's MP-5k sub-machine gun, his own weapons exhausted of ammunition. Somehow, he knew that in the smoking wreckage of the penthouse was one of the HVTs, preparing for a desperate last stand.

Kammler held his head in his hands.

"Leave me," he bellowed. "Leave me!"

Half-naked children fled his bedroom. Their small feet padded away as quickly as legs would carry them.

Kammler had demanded a high price for a place in his new world.

Fellow members of the Council on Foreign Relations, The Trilateral Commission, and the Bilderberg Group, among others, had been brought in on parts of the conspiracy. They were key leaders in vital positions around the world, needed before, during, and in some cases, after the great cleansing. In exchange for inoculation to the trigger virus and safe passage on the super-liner during the crisis, Kammler had demanded their unflinching loyalty.

Not to mention their children whenever he felt the need to indulge himself.

He could not fathom how it could happen.

Guarantees had been made. Everything had been put in its proper place, and now it was falling apart. He was falling apart alongside what would have been his kingdom.

Gunfire grew near.

The outer circle of protection had been made up of Serbian mercenaries, veterans of the killing fields of Eastern Europe. He knew of their ruthlessness. He had seen it first hand as a child in Austria. His father had met his fate at the hands of such men in a war long since passed.

One of his bodyguards cracked open his door, looking in on him for a moment. The younger man's eyes were wide, pupils dilated. He closed the door on Kammler, seeing his resignation.

The inner circle was made up of the best men that his military-industrial complex could produce, or at least the ones who had been willing to compromise themselves in some manner. They were American and British. Ex-soldiers. They were the last line of defense.

The super-liner rocked, a wave pounding the decks.

Explosions sounded somewhere outside.

It was too real.

Enough was enough.

Check out.

Reaching inside his pocket he retrieved a small pill box. Flipping it open revealed a small white pill. It was fast acting, normally given to field operatives in case of capture.

Blinking absently, Kammler placed the pill in his mouth and swallowed.

In moments the room grew darker. Black walls were collapsing on both sides of his vision.

Gunshots and shouting seemed to close in from every direction. His vision growing hazy, he saw a large man kick open his bedroom door. Snow from the Bavarian mountains drifted in from between the soldier's feet.

Sliding with his back pressed against the foot of his bed, the old oligarch fell to his side.

Eyes fluttering closed one last time, he heard the familiar sound of his native tongue, almost as if the old gods were whispering in his ear, calling him away.

With drool dripping from the corner of his mouth, the voice came into focus.

"*Scheisse*," the German voice said. "That's him."

Deckard slammed home the breach on the M203 grenade launcher and let another HE round fly across the dining room. It exploded with a flash, creating a cloud of smoke. Screams of the dying sounded in between bursts of gunfire.

During a short tactical pause, he and his team had stripped dead enemy of weapons and equipment, including body armor and ammunition to replenish what they had expended. A hasty interrogation had netted them the information they needed before moving farther into the ship.

Once again, they were on the verge of being overrun.

Sliding the grenade launcher open, a smoking 40mm cartridge casing fell to the floor. Thumbing a fresh grenade into the chamber, he slammed the slide shut and took aim. The dining room would normally host formal dinners for the cruise's patrons. Now the dining room was converted into a war zone as Deckard's men were confronted by a few dozen triggermen, trying to prevent the mercenaries from reaching the Operations Center.

Hooking his finger through the trigger guard on his M4's under-barrel grenade launcher, Deckard was about to fire his next round at a trio of bad guys clustered behind a support beam on the other side of the dining room. Stumbling forward, the M203 discharged its round, as another wave rocked the ship. With his aim spoiled, the 40mm grenade went way low, skipping off the ground before slamming into the far wall and detonating.

The enemy gunmen were counting themselves as lucky, knowing the shot was meant for them as they took aim at Deckard. The next wave blasted everyone off their feet. Chairs and tables were sent tumbling across the floor. Anything that wasn't nailed down went skidding across the ground including the contents of the buffet.

Bracing himself against the wall, Deckard clung onto a decorative piece molded into the wall. It was with wide eyes that Deckard saw all three of the enemy contractors sliding across the deck amid a pile of furniture and loose silverware.

They were heading straight for him.

Chad slammed both fists down on the table. Wood splintered and the table hinged in the middle, sending a computer printer and a couple coffee mugs crashing to the floor.

Outsourced Indian technicians looked down at their toes as their security chief stomped across the room, throwing chairs and people out of his way. Muscles rippled under his shirt while his face had turned beet red.

They'd watched the entire assault on the wide screens, every detail captured by security cameras throughout the ship. It was now clear that his employers' plaything was coming back to haunt them. His ship was infested with the little Afghani-looking fuckers, not to mention their Western military advisers.

The group that was closing in on their Command and Control, or C2, node had interrogated one of his men in the shopping mall and apparently got an answer out of him. It was a good thing that they had finished him off afterwards, because he was definitely off Chad's Christmas card list. Currently they were holed up in the formal dining area, exchanging shots with his men.

There was no way shit was falling apart this quickly. He'd been throwing everything he had at his disposal at the problem. They were winning by attrition, but the question became whether they would exhaust Samruk before their command systems were overrun and destroyed.

They were closing in fast. Decks Seven and Four were both partially on fire. It was time to end this.

Picking up the phone, the ex-Delta man punched in one of the extensions.

"Get Maahir on the line right fucking now," he growled at the operator.

Crewmen Danuj Vyapari winced as voices crackled over his headset.

The high tech Zumwalt-class destroyers flanked the super-liner like twin bodyguards, watching the horizon for threats. Now it seemed a Trojan Horse had sneaked right past them.

The storm that beat all three ships was bad enough, giving even veteran Indian crewmen on board a case of seasickness. Now the hulking cruise liner was on fire, smoke billowing from its port side while gunfire and explosions flashed.

The Zumwalt was outfitted primarily with twenty-four long-range cruise missiles, Danuj fulfilling his role as the gunner on the ship's single rail gun. Working his control toggles, he swung the gun turret from facing outboard to take aim at the ship they were supposed to be protecting.

It was a concept that he had studied as an engineering student. The rail gun consisted of two parallel conductive rails that when connected to a power source would send electrons racing up the negative rail across a projectile seated inside the gun and then back down the positive rail, creating an electro-magnetic force. The EM energy produced utilized the Lorentz force to fire the metal projectile down the rails at unprecedented speeds of up to twenty kilometers a second. Useful as long-range artillery or a missile defense shield, to his surprise he was now being ordered to use it as a short-range sniper rifle.

The gun captain was screaming in his ears, no doubt due to someone else screaming in his.

While a five inch gun on a modern naval ship was traditionally crewed by fifteen or so men, the rail gun system made use of various automated systems, narrowing the crew down to three. The gun captain, gunner, and one crewman to run the fire-control system.

There were no trajectories to account for and no computerized calculation to adjust for the Coriolis Effect. Just a simple order. Really, a waste of talent for a graduate of the Indian Institute of Technology.

"Deck Five, mid-ship, third window from the left."

"Roger," Danuj acknowledged.

Someone was getting frustrated up there if they were firing on their own ship.

Originally, one of the Zumwalts had been crewed entirely by Indians and the other entirely by Pakistanis. Some white guy's logic was that it would prevent ethnic strife while on board. In a return to colonialism, both ships were captained by former British admirals, so no one was surprised at such a ridiculous idea. They

335

had to be convinced that having two cutting-edge warships manned completely by two groups of opposing national, religious, and political ideologies would not end well.

Like the others, he was well-educated and recruited while still in college. All he had to do was sit in a simulator and play video games all day, making thousands of dollars a month, supposedly testing out some new software. Then they had been contracted to fulfill their positions for real, this time on a destroyer that had just slipped off a dry dock in South Korea a month before.

The autoloader slammed the metal cube projectile into the breach and locked into position.

What had held back the development of the rail gun for so long was the massive friction created every time it was fired. The projectile moved so fast that it created more muzzle flash than a conventional cannon. The metal alloy cube created so much friction as it moved along the rails that it burned up the surrounding oxygen, creating a massive plume of plasma in its wake. Alloys and coatings had been developed to make the rails much more durable, but they were still expected to be replaced every month or so, depending on frequency of use.

"Confirm target," the FCS crewmen said, double-checking Danuj's targeting. "Fire when ready."

The gunner's hand was slippery with sweat as he palmed the joystick and pulled the trigger.

Deckard moved his hand back off the M203 and took up the M4's pistol grip.

He walked a line of 5.56 rounds up the first gunman's sternum until he popped the grape at the top. With his back against the wall, he targeted the second gunman rolling across the floor as the ship rolled with the crash of each wave. He was still sliding and fumbling with his rifle when Deckard double-tapped him.

The third managed to get to his feet and slide right into Deckard before he could sweep his barrel in his direction. The two crashed to the ground amid the tables and chairs that slammed into the wall next to them.

The mercenary was straddled on Deckard's chest, his rifle pinned under his attacker. Drawing the pistol from the drop holster on his thigh, Deckard saw the crazed look in his attacker's eyes leaving no doubt in Deckard's mind that he meant to finish the job.

Both men cringed unexpectedly as one of the supporting columns behind them disappeared. It sounded as if an invisible herd of elephants was crashing through the dining room.

Deckard saw the opening and lunged.

The mercenary had been foolhardy enough to mount his combat blade upside down on his body armor. Maybe he thought he could draw it quicker from that position, maybe he had just been watching too many movies. The blade was perfectly positioned for an opponent to make use of while grappling.

Reaching up, Deckard tore the fighting knife from its sheath and sunk it deep into the mercenary's neck.

The contract killer gurgled on his own blood as Deckard pushed him to the side and got to his feet.

The second shot was deafening.

The buffet lines were taken out in a flash, spraying whatever was left all over the ceiling. A fist-sized hole was left smoking in the wall. Strangely he noted that the hole was in the shape of a perfect cube, when a third shot pulped one of his Kazakh troops.

The American mercenaries looked just as shocked as the Samruk men who struggled amid the tangle of furniture and clutter they were trapped in. The fourth shot slammed into one of them, severing him in half. Another was showered with his comrade's blood before Deckard finished him with his M4.

The next shot disintegrated a flat screen mounted on the wall behind him.

The former soldier wasn't entirely sure who or what was shooting at them but had an eerie feeling that it was him they were

337

aiming for.

Deckard hit the floor as a super-heated blast passed just over his back and destroyed a grand piano in the corner of the room.

"Everyone out," he ordered to any of his men left alive. "We-"

His words were cut short as another wave crashed into the ship, sending him forward, face first. As they bounced off the hardwood floor, water surged down from the staircase in the center of the room in a quickly growing waterfall. The *pop, pop, pop* of a pistol continued to fire from somewhere. Another projectile flew through the room at blinding speed, taking out several chandeliers in its path.

Bits of glass dusted his hair as he shouldered the M4, sending a burst into an enemy desperately firing shot after shot from his pistol in a panic.

As the ship tilted from one side to the other, Deckard stopped fighting it and rolled away as autofire stitched across the floor off his flank.

Landing on one knee, he exhausted the rest of his magazine, punching down targets like bowling pins. Dropping an empty magazine, he thumbed his last round into the M203.

Thirty Five

A solid steel hatch slammed shut on the Kazakh assault team and locked shut with a *clack-clack* spin of a wheel.

Corporal Fedorchenko reached down and removed the night vision goggles from one of the dead American security contractors. Loosening the straps he slid the monocle over his left eye before tightening it in place.

Scanning the rest of his team, the Samruk mercenary smiled.

The AN/PSQ-20 Enhanced Night Vision goggles combined third-generation image-intensification technology with a scanner that read the infrared heat produced by the human body. You could see at night while also pinpointing targets by their thermal signature.

The corporal barked at Ospanov and the other four men in his team. Shifting through blood and spent brass, they recovered the PSQ-20s off the remaining bodies. Somewhere between decks Seven and Eight things had gotten ugly. For all he knew, they were the only survivors from Bravo Company. Whether they were all that were left or not, the Kazakhs intended to go down fighting.

Ospanov swung the thermal night vision goggles up on its swing mount while he worked the door. The others adjusted their equipment and reloaded their weapons for the final push. Fedorchenko readied a smoke grenade.

Nodding to his team leader, Ospanov was ready to initiate the countdown.

The team stacked up down the hall, giving Ospanov plenty of distance as he initiated the time fuse. Sparks flew across the corridor as he began the burn sequence. Running back, he jumped into the stack with the other assaulters.

When it blew, it was even worse than when they had run

over the land mine in Burma. The overpressure was nearly enough to do them in even though they had inserted hearing protection and covered their ears with their hands.

The heavy steel door had crumpled under the force of the plastic explosives and imploded into the helm of the ship. The crew members were ready, and gunfire blasted through the open hatch, anticipating the Kazakhs' entry as they approached.

Fedorchenko underhanded his smoke grenade through the hatch. Allowing the smoke to billow for a moment, the team pulled their newly liberated PSQ-20 goggles over their eyes as Ospanov lobbed a flash-bang through the door.

Pouring through the entrance, they alternated between moving to the left and right, leaving them staggered against the near wall. Underneath their equipment and inside a cloud of thick smoke their situation felt hot and claustrophobic.

Scanning from side to side, the thermal detection unit in their goggles cut right through the smoke, outlining human targets in blazes of red to indicate body heat signatures. The Kazakhs point shot each thermal signature, aiming their barrels through the haze as if pointing an accusing finger at the crewmen. Bursts of auto fire cut through the smoke for tense seconds before a creepy quiet left them alone in the room.

As the smoke cleared, Fedorchenko visually confirmed that his men were all still on their feet.

His assault team had captured the helm.

Deckard chambered the 40mm buckshot round into his grenade launcher and triggered the shot. The two enemy guns-for-hire were caught in the open absorbing twenty-seven buckshot pellets that spun them both around in a macabre dance of death.

The dining hall was rocked again, another superheated projectile slicing through the walls steadily turning the room into a slice of Swiss cheese.

Deckard heard a thump. Turning towards the source, he saw another of his men smeared against the wall, missing the upper portion of his shoulder, clavicle, and half of his face.

Running for the exit, the next hypersonic missile missed him by inches.

"What the hell do you think you are doing?"

Incredulous, Chad spun around, eager for confrontation.

"Cleaning up your mess."

Hieronymus' eyes went wild.

Chad grinned for the first time in days. The old man wasn't used to people telling him how it is.

"Stand them down," the oligarch ordered the Indian crewmen. "Stand them down immediately."

"Yes, sir," the senior captain on deck chirped.

"They'll be here in minutes," Chad said, crossing his arms in front of him.

"It's your job to make sure that doesn't happen," the old man reiterated. "And make it happen without destroying the ship. Johnston Atoll is gone, and all we have left is the enclave in Hawaii or one of our bunkers in Micronesia. With the ship on fire and you punching it full of holes we'll be lucky if the Zumwalts can tow us that far."

"What the fuck were you thinking hiring that guy?" Chad asked, pointing at the flat screen monitor bolted to one of the walls. The picture displayed live footage from one of the security cameras. A Caucasian mercenary in jungle fatigues fired a buckshot round from a captured grenade launcher, shredding two of Chad's men.

"O'Brien. Our calculations gave the odds of something like this happening as one in thirteen quadrillion chance of happening.

A statistical impossibility," the old man stated flatly.

"Your statistics count for exactly jack and shit when you don't even know who you are talking about. That guy on that monitor is named Deckard, not O'Brien."

"Impossible. Kammler Associates had their best people dig up the dirt on this guy."

"He must have had some deep cover. I'm telling you that guy's name is Deckard."

"Are you sure?"

"I never worked with him personally, but he has been on the CIA's targets of opportunity list for years now. He used to work for the Agency's Special Activities Division and had a little bit of a falling out with them, to say the least."

Hieronymus looked like he was about to have a heart attack.

"Sir," one of the Indians interrupted. "The helm has just been overrun."

At his age, Chad wouldn't put it past him.

"Fix this," the old man said through clenched teeth. "Fix this now."

Deckard slipped down the stairs amid a cascade of water flowing from somewhere above.

The situation had gotten a little hot in his opinion. Dropping to a lower deck, maybe they could avoid some security as they infiltrated through the ship, making their way for the enemy's operations center. Reaching the landing, Deckard was grateful that the cannon fire had ceased. Whatever the hell that thing was, it wasn't anything he had seen before.

The Kazakh behind him slid on unsure footing in the puddle of water as Deckard held up a fist.

They had moved down into a service area that guests

weren't supposed to see. The hold looked to be packed to the ceiling with luggage and supplies. The passengers were in it for the long haul, probably intending to stick it out for several months at sea before making landfall in their new world.

When the coast looked clear he took a knee, prepared to lay down support fire as he waved his men forward. Pat took point, rifle leading the way. There were only a few of them left. A couple of his C/co Corporals along with JF and Pat.

When the last Kazakh troop passed, Deckard glanced back checking their six, before picking up and moving with his team. As they began moving through aisle after aisle of stowed luggage, the ship trembled once again, the floor slanting at an angle as another wave tumbled over the Crown of the Pacific.

The mercenaries reached out and clutched anything in reach for support. Most of them grabbed onto the metal racks that the ship's supplies were strapped into. Pat found a metal attachment point on the floor that made a convenient handhold.

Jean-Francoise yelped as he somersaulted head over heels and crashed into one of the aisles at the end of the hold. He came to a stop on his rear end and was trying to regain some sense of orientation when Deckard heard a snapping like someone plucked a giant rubber band.

Metal clanked across metal as an industrial forklift broke free from its lashings and rolled down the aisle as the ship continued to list to one side.

JF looked up a moment too late, the forklift slamming into him head-on with a bone crunching crack.

A second later the boat righted itself, the forklift rolling back on its wheels. JF's body slumped to the floor, his face crushed, an exaggerated caricature of the man he had been a moment before. Deckard turned away. His comrade's face looked like a Halloween mask.

"Let's go," Pat said, grabbing Deckard by the sleeve.

Now wasn't the time to dwell on what could have been.

343

"Listen to me, Deckard."

Jogging through lifeless mechanical rooms and empty corridors, he tried not to.

"This is where you make the right decision and get with the winning team," the voice of the PA system blared. "I did what I had to do, to make sure my family is protected, that we have a place in what is coming. Hieronymus tells me he is disappointed in your decisions but impressed by your abilities. They are going to give you one last chance.

"Work with us. We have a place for someone like you. Call off your men and we can work something out."

Deckard had no interest in nihilistic explanations or apologies. They were making an offer because they were desperate. He pressed on, knowing they wouldn't be reaching out to him unless the rest of the battalion had been having their own successes. They were getting close.

"Join us."

Deckard looked into one of the security cameras as he passed and spoke.

"What the hell did he just mouth to the camera?" Chad asked no one in particular.

"Uh," one of the Indians struggled for the words.

"I think he said: *go fuck yourself.*"

Chuck Rochenoire came awake to the sound of gunfire.

"Sorry pal," someone was saying. "Nothing personal."

Chuck leaned up on his elbows, taking stock of the situation. Looking down the hall, he saw Adam down on his knees, his back pushed against the wall. One of the American mercenaries stood in front of him, a pistol pointed at Adam's face. A trio of trigger men stood around their leader, gawking at the captured man.

He hadn't been spotted, not yet.

"Business is business and Chad pays."

Blinking away the stinging sensation out of his eyes, he struggled to play catch-up. He lay among a pile of dead bodies. Two contractors came down the corridor, dragging a limp form under each arm.

"Fuck you," Adam said, glaring.

Chuck pushed a lifeless body away, reaching for a discarded AK-47 lying nearby.

"I'm sorry you think so."

The contractor had a smile on his face as he pulled the trigger, splattering Adam's brains against the wall. The Samruk intelligence agent's body hit the floor with a hollow thud. Chuck gritted his teeth against the pain in his side, his fingertips brushing against the Kalashnikov.

"Who's next?" the executioner laughed.

Sergeant Major Korgan was forced to his knees alongside Adam's corpse.

"Where the hell did all these Afghani fuckers come from?"

"Afghanistan?" one of the gunman's boys ventured.

"Very funny," he said, pressing his Glock into Korgan's forehead. "Guess it doesn't really matter what kind of Hodji this guy is."

The mercenary's finger tightened around the trigger as Korgan leaned forward, into the barrel of the pistol. With the slide pushed backward he had effectively knocked the weapon out of battery. The contractor snarled in frustration, the pistol seized up in his hands, refusing to discharge.

The staccato chatter of 7.62 rounds put a halt to the cold-blooded murder, Chuck holding down the trigger as the hallway turned into an ultra close-range firefight. Bullets crashed through bulkheads and shattered light fixtures as Chuck went cyclic, the contractors firing hastily aimed shots in return.

The AK barrel flexed as the former SEAL sprayed fire down the hall. One contractor wisely took a knee, avoiding the rounds that snapped over his head. Firing off a burst of his own, sparks showered off Chuck's AK. Still in a seated position, Chuck was thrown backwards and lay still.

Reaching for the downed executioner's pistol, Korgan stood and placed the muzzle against the shooter's temple. He squeezed the trigger just as someone fired, a muzzle flash catching his attention farther down the hall.

Catching a round in his side the Kazakh fell alongside the corpse he had just made, and struggled to breathe. He knew he was breathing at half capacity, the still rational part of his mind telling him that he had a punctured lung.

Clutching the pistol in his hand, he heard voices approaching.

THIRTY SIX

Jarogniew's heart threatened to thump right out of his chest.

He stopped, gasping for breath, his body having been exerted beyond his limit. Gunfire sounded all around him. Bodies were everywhere, death displayed on a grand scale. In other circumstances he would have basked in it as he had in countless wars engineered under his guidance. Terrified, he knew his last chance was to make it to a lifeboat. Once he activated the search and rescue beacon, his people would pick him up eventually.

Carefully, he stepped over the fresh corpses. Lifeless eyes stared at him questioningly. Flecks of blood were smeared across his expensive Italian loafers as he tried to tiptoe through the carnage. Some of the bodies belonged to the contractors employed by the moronic Chad Morrison. Kammler Associate's Human Resources Division fucked that one up at inconceivable levels of incompetence.

Others belonged to passengers. The chief executives of Fortune 100 companies, foundation members, even a former prime minister lay on his back full of bullet holes, unblinking eyes fixed on the over headlights. Still others looked Central Asian. They weren't under attack from some rogue military unit. This was their own creation, their own puppet, like Pinocchio finding a life of its own.

This situation can still be salvaged, he thought to himself, if he could just get away. There was always a back-up plan for the back-up plan.

"Hey, mate."

Jarogniew turned, hearing the wheezing words. An ashen faced man leaned wearily against one of the walls.

"Who are you?" he demanded.

"Name's Richie."

The British man was breathing hard, blood speckling the side of his face. A wound in his abdomen had dyed his field uniform shades of red.

He was one of them.

"Where are the rest of your people?" Jarogniew said, bending down to be eye level with the dying man. "You may still be of some use to me."

"Don't be such a fucking cunt," the Brit choked out.

"Just a damned minute--" Jarogniew grabbed the younger man by the collar.

"Piss off," Richie spat back.

Looking down at his hands, Jarogniew was too late to stop him from squeezing the Claymore clacker.

Deckard leaned out from behind the bulkhead and rattled off another burst from his M4 before the bolt locked on an empty chamber.

"Black!"

Shifting back behind cover, he loaded his last remaining magazine for the captured assault rifle. Pat took a knee and fired his own rifle, laying down fire for Deckard's movement as he bounded down the corridor. The enemy was sending their final wave forward, the last resistance to their forward progress. Attrition had nearly exhausted all of the Samruk men as they neared the operations center in the heart of the ship.

Shooting a controlled pair into two advancing Serbian mercenaries, Deckard indexed both targets center mass. Behind him, his two remaining Kazakhs bounded up to his position. Ibrashev and Garri moved into position with practiced precision.

Underhanding a frag grenade, Garri yelled something in Russian. The Americans needed no translation and braced themselves for the blast. Before the smoke cleared, they were moving forward, when the four survivors collided with the enemy.

The Serbs came pouring out of one of the side corridors, physically running into them. The Samruk mercenaries operated in synchronization almost like a gestalt. Each broke down their individual sectors of fire, overlapping with their comrades' sectors to the left and right as they swept the corridor.

In the narrow confines of the hall, the enemy was unable to mount a flanking maneuver; all they could do was attempt to force their way forward.

Serbian gunmen in the back pushed forward, stepping over the bodies as the battle quickly transitioned to ultra close quarters. Pat released his grip on his rifle as it cycled on empty and grabbed his Glock 19 pistol out of its holster in one fluid motion.

Garri grabbed the barrel of the closest enemy's M4. Pushing it away, the muzzle flash mushroomed with automatic fire that shredded the ceiling tiles. Finally he freed his own sidearm and managed to dump half a magazine into the Serb before he went down.

Pat engaged a second target with his pistol.

Ibrashev pushed the enemy closest to him away, attempting to create some space to spare him the fraction of a second he needed. Freeing his Glock, the Kazakh took up a two-handed grip and began shooting.

Deckard squeezed off another double-tap with the M4, and the dead mercenary in front of him was quickly replaced with a live one. Shooting again, the Serb soldier for hire disappeared in a cloud of blood. Locking on empty, Deckard brushed aside an enemy's rifle barrel as he attempted to bring his weapon into play. Getting inside the Serb's space, Deckard drew his 1911.

Pushing the muzzle up under his opponent's chin, he squeezed the trigger. The top of the man's head turned into a fountain of gray-white matter that sprayed the ceiling.

With his Glock in slide lock, Pat executed a combat reload in a blur of motion.

Ibrashev lost his pistol as he went hand to hand with two Serbs who were attempting to wrestle him to the ground.

Garri collapsed, lights off, a circular bullet hole appearing between his eyes.

Pivoting, Deckard snapped a shot into one of Ibrashev's attackers before having to turn his attention back to his front as he was charged. At least he had helped even the odds.

Two .45 caliber rounds ended the foolhardy attempt to rush him.

Ibrashev managed to draw his combat blade, sinking it deep into his second attacker's neck.

Pat snatched his final pistol magazine from his combat harness and racked the slide. Deckard stepped over a corpse, triggering two more shots into the next would-be shooter. The Kazakh pulled his knife free from the Serb, allowing him to bleed out on the floor.

Catching the man he shot before he fell to the ground, Deckard used the body as a human shield while burning off the rest of his magazine, firing one-handed down the crowded hallway. It was almost impossible to miss at such close range.

Pat dropped his empty pistol and bent to pick up one of the enemy's weapons. Acquiring an M4 from a fallen enemy, he sent half a magazine ripping into the Serbs' ranks. A shotgun blast ended the fusillade that threatened to drive the enemy back a final time. Pat collapsed against the bulkhead before crumpling to the floor.

Deckard released his hold on the corpse and went down to the floor with it. Kneeling he reloaded and thumbed the slide release.

Ibrashev's head snapped back, a stream of blood leaking from his forehead.

Firing wildly from side to side, Deckard ran forward with bloodshot eyes.

The Serbs back-stepped as a fresh salvo of .45 caliber hollow points slammed into their front line. The mercenaries saw that only one of them was left and were ready to overwhelm him. As they cut loose with a dozen automatic weapons, Deckard saw the open door and dived through it.

Bullets zinged through the operations center in three hundred and sixty degrees.

Rolling behind a rack filled with electronic equipment, Deckard stole a glance backwards. A half-dozen Serbs were mowed down by not-so-friendly fire from the OPCEN staff. Whoever they were, they were spooked, causing them to engage anything that appeared through the door.

Squinting, Deckard saw him from across the operations center.

Hieronymus was pressed up against the wall, his hands clenched around the edge of the table with white knuckles. His jaw hung slack, eyes glazed over as a torrent of gunfire slammed into the console that Deckard lay next to.

Straight-arming his 1911, Deckard saw the front sight post align perfectly with the rear sight, blocking out his target's nose. The old man stared into him with pure hatred. Deckard's finger tightened around the trigger.

The hard rubber sole of a combat boot stomped the side of Deckard's head, sending his pistol spinning across the floor. Before he could react, a second blow knocked the wind out of him, the booted foot coming down on his unprotected ribcage where the body armor didn't cover.

"Everyone out," a seemingly disembodied voice said. "Disappear!"

Coughing hard enough to gag himself, he heard a dozen or so footsteps as technicians in black uniforms fought each other to get through the door first. Hieronymus stood frozen in place for the briefest moment before rushing to follow them out.

Rolling to his other side, Deckard attempted to sit up, when hands grabbed his collar and pant leg in an iron grip. The next thing the former soldier knew he was airborne, sailing across the command center until a wall broke his fall.

Collapsing to the hard steel plated floor, Deckard broke out in another fit of hacking his guts up as pain racked his entire body. He was dizzy, too disoriented to gain his bearings.

"I'm going to take my time with you, asshole."

It was the voice that had spoken to him over the PA system.

His body stiffened, pain shooting through every nerve ending. Left unable to move, he could only hear a detached howl of agony that he was vaguely aware of escaping from his own throat. Just when he thought it would be over, the pain continued, stretching on for seconds that turned into forever.

Finally, the pain subsided and he was able to breathe.

"Heard about you from those pricks at Bragg," the voice snorted. "Said you were some kind of badass. Don't look so badass to me."

The pain exploded inside him a second time, every muscle in his body pulled taunt. Now it was only gurgling that sounded from his lips. Seconds later, it was over and he was able to take another deep breath. His nerve endings were frayed and still firing wildly.

With his vision clearing for just a moment, Deckard looked up at the hulking figure. A boxy pistol-like device was in his hand with two wires running out of the front of it.

"I can do this all fucking night," the man said with a sadistic laugh. "Holy shit, I am gonna fuck your world up."

Deckard rolled over, grinding his rib cage hard against the floor. The twin metal barbs broke off inside him, separating from the Taser prongs that had been embedded in his skin.

Chad squeezed the trigger on the Taser, a look of surprise washing over his face as Deckard pushed himself up on all fours, unaffected with the leads broken off under his skin and detached from the wires that led to the control unit.

"Piece of shit," the steroid-head snarled.

Chad detached the cartridge that had fired the prongs and discarded it. Moving forward, he squeezed the trigger again and the Taser clicked repeatedly as a charge ran across the leads sticking out from the front of the unit. Reaching down, he was prepared to drive stun Deckard back into submission.

Deckard's hand was a blur as he went on the offensive.

Chad recoiled, stumbling backwards into a console and dropping the Taser. The blade's edge was so sharp that at first he didn't feel any pain but saw his own blood leaking across the floor. Deckard clutched his side as he struggled to his feet, a bloody Ka-Bar fighting knife in his other hand.

The larger man flicked his hand back and forth before letting it hang limply on his wrist, dripping blood everywhere. Deckard was bigger and stronger than most, as well as being in peak physical condition before being tossed, stomped on, tased a few times, and completely exhausted from days without sleep. Chad was easily twice his size. Thick muscle was pulled across every inch of his body, veins in his neck and at his temples pulsing as his anger grew.

"Doesn't change shit," the ex-Delta operator laughed. "Dickhead."

Chad charged him, Deckard attempting to sidestep out of the way a moment too late. Built like a professional wrestler, he lifted Deckard clean off his feet, slamming him into the wall. Seeing stars, Deckard was sure he felt something explode inside his abdomen.

A hand the size of a catcher's mitt wrapped around his throat and began to squeeze. Black walls were closing in as Deckard stuck the fighting knife under Chad's elbow and sliced upwards towards his wrist with a single violent slash. Flesh parted under the blade's edge, sending the power lifter staggering backwards.

Enraged, Chad's eyes burnt like hot coals. Rushing forward he hit Deckard broadside as he struggled to breathe. Grasping his wrist, Chad twisted and curled his hand around until the knife fell from Deckard's grip.

Still holding onto his wrist, he flung Deckard back across the room and into someone's desk. Shaking his head, Deckard tried to clear his vision once again but to no avail. A clenched fist slammed into his guts, followed up by a brutal uppercut that dropped him to the floor.

"You're going to pay for that," Chad said, while examining the deep wound running down his forearm. "You should have gotten on the winning team when you had the chance."

Deckard groaned something in response.

"Still with us, huh? That's good."

Chad strode towards him on tree trunk legs. Reeling back, he raised one foot high into the air, bringing his knee up as high as his massive quadriceps would allow. About to bring his boot down on Deckard's skull, the former soldier squirmed to the side at the last moment. Chad's boot slammed down on the floor in a cloud of dust.

Vulnerable on his back, Deckard kicked out, striking Chad just below the kneecap with his heel. Chad's knees buckled, almost sending him forward into a face plant. Deckard got to his feet as quickly as he could, stumbling on shaky footing.

Chad was back on him in a flash, moving amazingly fast for a man of his size. Deckard barely avoided his punch and counterattacked with one of his own. The hammer blow thwacked into Chad's face with the sound of cold meat being tenderized.

With Chad temporarily stunned, Deckard followed up with a frontal kick to the mercenary's abdomen before delivering a right hook that pounded into his jaw.

Recovering from the initial blow, Chad growled and threw a punch of his own. Deckard easily avoided the haymaker that the muscle man had unintentionally telegraphed from a mile away. Still in pain and seriously disoriented, he struggled with his footwork, attempting to stay out of Chad's reach. Deep down he knew that if the larger man got hold of him again, the fight would be over fast. He couldn't sustain another attack.

The two circled each other for tense seconds, each avoiding the other's strikes. Finally Deckard saw an opening and reached out. His fingers formed a knife cutting edge, spearing into one of Chad's eyeballs, causing him to rear back with a scream.

Exploiting the opening, Deckard rained blows down on Chad's head. His fists acted like pistons driving the larger man back. Blinded, Chad stumbled and tripped, falling over a chair that some careless technician had left leaning on its side as he fled.

Deckard leaned in with everything he had left. Bringing his boot down on his opponent's groin, Chad's entire body heaved, his body trying to vomit up the contents of his stomach. As his knuckles split and bled, blood was flung in every direction. It came from his hands, from Chad's knife wounds, from the gash on Deckard's forehead that he didn't even notice.

Reaching up, Chad grabbed Deckard's collar and pulled him down.

Losing his footing, Deckard's center of gravity shifted as Chad yanked him down while he simultaneously thrust the top of his head towards him. Deckard's nose made contact with Chad's bald dome in an explosion of blood.

Pushing Deckard off him, Chad let Deckard brace himself against a desk while he grunted his way back onto his feet. Both men were beaten and bloody. One of them wasn't walking away. Both were equally determined to make sure it wasn't him.

Deckard tried to attempt another low kick as Chad vaulted forward like a train engine. The strike didn't even register in Chad's nerve deadened, steroid fueled body. The head of security seized around Deckard's neck and squashed him down onto the desk as he attempted to throttle him.

Trying to snake his fingers back into Chad's eyes, the larger man squinted and tucked his chin in as his hands clamped shut like a vise, depriving Deckard of oxygen. Thrashing, Deckard beat wildly at Chad's jaw, ears, neck, anything he could get a hold of. His body was well protected by sheets of muscle and Deckard was growing weaker for every nanosecond that passed.

Chad screamed, his fingers closing around Deckard's trachea.

Joining his hands behind Chad's head, Deckard grabbed onto something on his wrist and pulled. The rubber band securing the garrote wire in place snapped as he pulled the wooden handhold. The piano wire spiraled over his hand before snapping taunt around the leather bracelet he wore.

Tossing the wire over Chad's head, Deckard wound it under his chin even as everything was fading to black. On the verge of passing out, Deckard pulled on both sides of the garrote wire.

Chad convulsed, caught completely off guard as the metal

wire closed around his neck.

Sensing the opening, Deckard brought up a knee and placed it against Chad's chest. Able to take a quick breath he pushed Chad away with his knee while powering down on the garrote wire, attempting to bring both hands backwards and behind his own head with the wire wound around his opponent's neck.

The powerlifter's eyes went crazy, his face turning purple.

Large veins coursing through Chad's neck threatened to burst as he struggled uselessly as Deckard strained against both ends of the garrote wire. Every muscle and tendon in Deckard's brutalized body screamed as he flexed. Getting the toe of his boot up under Chad's chin, he pushed one final time with a gasp of exertion.

Chad's eyes went blank. His body fell to the floor with a thud.

With the garrote wire burrowed deep in Chad's neck, Deckard was pulled down after him and landed on the dead man's chest.

"I win," Deckard choked out in a whisper.

Closing his eyes, Deckard hyperventilated, trying to get air back into his lungs.

He was a wreck. Every joint felt blown out, every muscle burned with exhaustion. Warm blood dripped down the side of his face. Absently, he undid the buckles of the leather bracelet and left the garrote wire in place. There was no way he was getting it back. Having cut so deep into flesh and bone, it had become a permanent fixture of Chad's physique.

Holding onto the side of the desk, Deckard steadied himself as he stood up and looked around. Bodies, bullet holes, and shattered glass were everywhere along with splatters of slowly congealing blood. He still felt dizzy as his eyes swept across the operation center.

Deckard walked on feet that felt like jelly. Bending over to retrieve his pistol, he felt something pop in his back.

Too many of his men had died to come this far.

Looking at the exit he had seen the puppet master flee to,

Deckard checked the load in his 1911 before slamming the magazine home.

It was time to finish this.

THIRTY SEVEN

"He's right behind me!"

Looking at each other, the contractors stared dumbfounded until gunfire thudded somewhere below deck. Flicking off safeties, the security team descended down the steps. Hieronymus knew he was feeding them into the meat grinder. Hopefully a little cannon fodder would keep O'Brien, or whoever he was, busy long enough for him to affect an escape.

With the elevators out of commission, the old man thanked himself for taking HGH and stem cell therapy treatments, his legs carrying him up a final flight of stairs to the top deck of the super-liner. Emerging in one of the lounge areas next to one of the ship's many pools, he shook his head at what a wreck his ship had become.

Black smoke billowed up from the side of the Crown of the Pacific. Thankfully, the wind was carrying it away and not obscuring the deck, but there was also the issue of the boat taking on water. The entire deck tilted at an odd angle.

He wouldn't lose any sleep over Chad. The gun shots that seemed to be shadowing his every step left no doubt in his mind as to what had happened to his chief of security.

The old oligarch cursed as he made his way towards the bow. He could already hear the faint buzz of rotor blades in the distance.

Deckard flung himself to the ground as hot metal cut

through the air above him. Singling out the closest gunman, he walked a series of rounds up his body armor before they punched into his neck just under the jaw.

The last mercenary decided he had had enough. As he turned to run back in the opposite direction, Deckard cut him down.

Climbing the last flight of stairs, he moved out onto the top of the ship. Quickly scanning the deck, he spotted the white haired man fleeing as fast as he could towards the bow of the ship.

Feeling his blood boil, he ran.

"That's him right there!" Hieronymus yelled at his men while pointing back the way he had come.

A baker's dozen of contracted killers had just surged up from the lower levels. Black splotches of snot clung under their noses as they had just escaped the fire that raged below.

"Triple pay to whichever one of you manages to kill him."

One of them spat a black tar ball onto the deck before smiling.

They liked that idea.

Taking a knee, Deckard let his elbow rest against his knee to support the weight of the captured M4 rifle.

Cold rain whipped at his face as Deckard fired on the men forming a wall of bodies in front of Hieronymus' escape route.

The first contractor went down in convulsions, a single 5.56 round having cored through his brain after entering the eye socket.

His comrades jumped back in surprise as his body hit the ground, before training their weapons on Deckard.

Out on the deck there was precious little cover, leaving him with few options. Flicking the selector switch to automatic, Deckard did the last thing they expected.

Burning through the rest of his magazine, he held the rifle at his hip, spraying their front lines as he charged forward. The gunmen sought cover, a few finding it, others caught out in the open to absorb the auto fire. A few threw themselves down against the ground.

One of the American contractors looked wide-eyed, frozen in position, at the man running straight for him. The M4's barrel smoked, the bolt locked back on an empty chamber. His fatigues were ripped and torn, his face covered in a mask of brown colored dried blood.

Using his empty rifle as a blunt weapon, Deckard smashed the contractor in the face. He heard teeth and bone crack under his butt stock.

Releasing his M4 and letting it fall to the ground, he grabbed the rifle barrel of another opponent as he attempted to swing towards him and bring his rifle into play. The rifle spat a foot of flame as the contractor repeatedly pulled the trigger, Deckard redirecting the fire into another enemy as he grasped the barrel in his fist.

Clocking the rifleman in the jaw, Deckard tried to take control of the weapon only to find it strapped to its owner's body armor by a nylon strap that served as a sling.

Letting the unconscious body fall to the deck, Deckard transitioned to his 1911, double-tapping a gunner that appeared from behind the bar. The twin .45 caliber shots thumped into the contractor's shoulder and neck spilling him backwards.

Deckard shuddered as a rifle shot rang out like a thunderclap.

Behind him, a headless corpse fell to the deck with a thud, a wash of blood and gore sprayed out in a landing strip up to Deckard's feet. A readied sub-machine gun clattered next to the corpse.

The shot had been from a large caliber rifle.

A .300 WinMag if he wasn't mistaken.

Hieronymus ran.

Freeing a hand-held radio from his jacket pocket, the old man flipped it to the on position and turned the volume to high.

"I'm right here, dammit," he said, keying the radio and waving his other hand high above his head.

The gunfire was getting closer.

"Where the hell are you?"

Fear crept into his bones. It was then that it dawned on him that this was really happening. A piece of hot metal whizzed over his head, shaking him out of his epiphany.

The radio gave off a hiss of static.

"This is Juliet-23 to Package, do you copy?"

"Yes!" Hieronymus yelled into the radio with a rush of relief. "Yes, I'm exactly where you were instructed to rendezvous with me."

A black teardrop shape raced through the gray sky. It was well past dawn, but the overcast sky created by the passing storm left him standing cold in the rain. The teardrop raced forward, rotor blades bleating out a steady rhythm as the helicopter came in for the pick up.

"Roger, Package. We see you."

He'd called in the helicopter when it became clear that they were under attack. The pilots had rushed from the enclave off the coast of Hawaii, refueling once from a cache stored on an atoll so small it barely existed. Looking over his shoulder, he saw his soldiers-for-hire fighting it out with each other. Meat against meat, throwing themselves away for nothing.

Nice try, he thought as the helicopter closed in on final

approach.

Once he reached minimum safe distance, he'd radio in a massive air strike on the super-liner, nuking it into oblivion right along with the rest of civilization after his pandemic got a minor jump start. Really, Samruk had done him a favor getting rid of Kammler and Jarogniew, saving him the trouble.

Hieronymus was just getting started.

Every muscle in his body felt like it was on fire.

Sprinting forward he vaulted over another dead body, as the sniper rifle snapped another round down range.

The bullet smacked into the nearest enemy, picking him up off his feet and throwing him on his back as if struck by some invisible force. Deckard didn't know which of his snipers was still alive, he was glad to have someone providing cover fire.

Landing on one foot, Deckard held his pistol steady, triggering a shot into another one of Hieronymus' patsies.

Running straight up the middle, he leaped over another piece of pool furniture, heading directly to his target.

Another gunman appeared to his side, brandishing a sub machine gun, pointing it in his direction. The WinMag cracked, dropping the man in his tracks.

The matte black Little Bird Helicopter swept in, its skids hovering just above the deck.

Hieronymus hurried forward, his tie flapping wildly in the rotor wash. A square-jawed mercenary with blonde hair sticking from under his Kevlar helmet reached out to grab his hand and help strap him in. They would both ride on one of the exterior platforms that were bolted to each side of the helicopter to accommodate passengers, usually Special Operations troops inserting onto the rooftops of terrorist strongholds.

Without warning, the crewman was thrown backwards against the fuselage of the helicopter, his hand ripped violently from Hieronymus'.

Suddenly the interior Plexiglas bubble that encased the front of the cockpit was sprayed with crimson, multiple gunshots sounding from behind him. The old man was hurled backwards as the helicopter veered out of control.

Brushing up against one of the ship's metal railings, the entire tail boom of the Little Bird sheared off. The rear rotor blades turned into deadly shrapnel as they spun through the air. Now the helicopter pinwheeled wildly. The torque created by the main rotors was no longer countered by the opposite force provided by the rear rotor blades.

With the skids bouncing off the deck, the entire body of the helicopter spun like a top, destroying everything in its path.

When the helicopter finally came to a halt, the pilot began recovering from a temporary blackout. The surviving pilot reached for the Beretta holstered in his survival vest but didn't quite make it.

Deckard executed the pilot with a single shot before putting a similar insurance bullet into the co-pilot who hung limply in his five-point restraining belt.

What was left of the Little Bird steamed as exposed metal parts were subjected to the cold rain.

Hieronymus blinked several times while attempting to concentrate on something in front of him.

Tongues of flame flickered amid dark smoke from the side of the ship while wind howled across the deck. A soldier walked towards him, a pistol held in one hand that laid flat against his side.

Looking back and forth he saw the helicopter in pieces. The two pilots were slumped over in their seats. The man who had reached out to help him on board was nowhere to be seen. His mind catching up after the fact, he realized that the mercenary had probably been thrown overboard.

The blurry figure stopped a few feet in front of him, boots squared up with his own supine form.

Finally the man in front of him came into focus. He looked nothing like that mercenary he had met months ago. He looked like a demon, like hell itself had come for him.

The demon's ambassador came ambling up to stand alongside him. The Kazakh cradled a large scoped rifle in his arms. A bloody cloth was wrapped around his hand as a hasty bandage.

Pushing himself up on his elbows he looked down at where his legs should have been. Streams of blood gushed from his ragged stumps. The out of control helicopter had amputated both his legs.

Going white in the face, he looked back up at the demon. "Why?" the old man asked.

Deckard leveled his .45, pointing it at Hieronymus' face. "Because perception isn't reality." His voice sounded like sandpaper. "Because truth can't be created."

Nikita craned his head, looking at Deckard expectantly.

"The truth?" the old oligarch croaked. "Which one? O'Brien? Deckard?" Looking up at the dark sky, the old man laughed. "Do you even know who you are?"

Deckard stared into his eyes, seeing how far down the rabbit hole they led. How far gone they really were.

"Justice."

Deckard pulled the trigger.

EPILOGUE

T O P S E C R E T SECTION 01 OF 05 BEIJING 003765

TS-SCI/NOFORN

FM: AMBASSADOR BROOKS
TO: SECSTATE/WASHDC PRIORITY 00949

SUBJECT: QUICK LOOK RE: US-CHINA INTELLIGENCE EXCHANGE WITH NON-OFFICIAL REPRESENTATIVES

CLASSIFIED ISIS-FOUR AND GHOST-SIX

- - - - - - - - -

SUMMARY

- - - - - - - - -

1.   (TS) Meeting took place the morning of 17AUG with OGA officer Jeremy White and Chinese economics professor

Lin Zhang at Beijing University. Since the Myanmar event Chinese intelligence has been especially hostile to Western overtures of accommodation, however, Professor Zhang has been fairly amicable. Our analysts state that Zhang is a long time asset of the Ministry of State Security. Zhang is believed to be cooperating with official sanction as the MSS hedges their bets, wanting to keep an open line of communication while expressing official displeasure. This is atypical of operations in this region.

2.   (TS) Intelligence liaison proceeded with mutual compromise of several fronts. Issues raised by Professor Zhang included recent cyber-attacks, US-South Korea war games, and QE2. Zhang remained noncommittal regarding North Korea, signaling a possible shift in Beijing's rhetoric while also expressing grave displeasure of currency devaluation. Officer White brought up issues regarding the recent activities of Samruk International and related events.

Myanmar Incident:

1.   (TS) Professor Zhang surprisingly admitted to official embarrassment over the shooting down of the two J-10 Fighter Jets during the cross border incident. We were given assurances that it was merely a case of two pilots who had recently graduated from the flight academy having a navigation error due to a technical malfunction. The Defense Ministry is conducting an investigation into the matter according to Zhang's sources.

2.   (TS) Zhang was quick to bring up the persistent rumor that Americans were present on the ground during the incident on the Myanmar side of the border. Shockingly well informed, he told us that [REDACTED] was the ground force commander. Unwilling to announce that our analysis concurs with MSS on this issue, Officer White gave promises that no Americans were present in that region in any official or unofficial capacity.

3.   (TS) At this juncture the meeting suddenly changed tone. One of the unidentified men sitting in on the meeting, more than likely Zhang's minder, insisted that before being shot down the PRC pilots had fired on and destroyed an American made UAV. To support his argument he produced pictures of what he claimed was the latest generation Global Hawk UAV. Officer White countered with evidence that both J-10's were shot down with Chinese clones of SA-7 surface-to-air missiles. The unidentified man took his seat in the back of the room without another word.

Afghanistan Event:

1.   (TS) Zhang opened by saying that he wasn't going to give us an opportunity to lie and queued up a radio intercept on his computer. Officer White states that the recording began with an American voice, "-soldier but it turns out the old guy is MIK's number two, his brother actually. What do you want me to do with these clowns?" After a slight pause another American accent replied, "Do 'em." This transmission was almost certainly intercepted by the Chinese telemetry station, designated SV-11 in the Xinjiang region along the Afghanistan border.

2.   (TS) Zhang insisted that they had intercepted other transmissions at the time of the Myanmar incident and had performed voice spectrum analysis on them for comparison. Chinese experts concluded that many of the voices were identical matches.

3.   (TS) Officer White denied any and all knowledge of Operation Dark Star.

Samruk International:

1.   (TS) Zhang demanded that we share any and all intelligence we had on the Private Military Corporation known as

Samruk International. Zhang was assured that at no time was Samruk Int. in the employ of this Agency or any other US based entity.

2. (TS) Officer White saw no harm in offering Zhang and his handlers a few facts from recent observation in order to gain future bargaining capital with the MSS. Zhang was told of recent investigations carried out by unnamed US Agencies into Samruk International. It appears to continue as a small firm specializing in executive protection for Kazakh oligarchs and governmental officials.

3. (TS) Professor Zhang told us that his people had uncovered evidence of a massive training camp and headquarters out in the steppes outside Kazakhstan's capital, Astana. Zhang was shown photographs taken by our regional assets showing the abandoned compound. Newly built barracks were stripped clean, including plumbing and electrical wiring. Several ranges were identified and a variety of shell casings were present. At this time we confirmed to him that our Agency is still looking into the matter. As of now we believe it to be a training area for Kazakh Special Forces teams.

4. (TS) It appears that neither Agency knows the current whereabouts of any surviving Samruk International employees from the previously mentioned incidents, rumors notwithstanding.

Israel:

1. (TS) Professor Zhang asked if we knew anything about the imprisonment of IDF Corporal Liora Shoshan at Confinement Base 396 near Atlit. Officer White said that he would look into it. A Request for Information has been submitted with the Mid-East Department.

"Crown of the Pacific" Incident:

1.   (TS) Inevitably, the sinking of the Crown of the Pacific was brought up by Zhang. He came right out and asked to hear the whole truth. As suspected, MSS is too savvy to believe media reports and probably has sources close to the incident. Officer White maintained the official story given to the press and restated that a steering committee originating from NATO nations was meeting to discuss foreign relations issues in a roundtable type format while underway. Why the cruise liner caught fire and sank so abruptly is still under investigation.

2.   (TS) Zhang fidgeted with his shirt sleeve at this point. He told us that Beijing questions nearly every aspect of the official story and that they know that we know more than we are prepared to reveal. He told us that they are aware of the USNS Safeguard and the USNS Grapple conducting salvage operations on site. Zhang wanted to know what we had discovered about the cruise ship but did not seem to know the true purpose of the salvage operation.

3.   (TS) One of the two unidentified men in the room spoke up and asked us what happened on Johnston Atoll. Officer White insisted that Johnston Atoll had been decommissioned in 2003 and converted into a nature preserve. Reports of the island on fire must have been due to confusion, the only recorded fire in the area was on the adjacent cruise liner.

Chinese Intelligence conspiracy theories:

1.   (TS) The two unidentified men became frustrated with Officer White's explanations and were increasingly upset with us. They told us that they have information about the so-called assassinations of Admiral Thomas Banks, Colonel (ret.) Lynn Chapman, and Former Chairmen of the Joint Chiefs General (ret.)

Walter Huffman. Officer White tried to convince them that the initial media reports had been correct. Banks and Huffman had been involved in a boating accident while on a fishing trip. Chapman was killed in a similar accidental drowning the same day by coincidence only.

2.   (TS) The Chinese representatives were aware that on the same day of the accidental deaths and the sinking of The Crown of the Pacific that Continuity of Government had been stood up for several hours before being quietly stood back down. Zhang told us that Chinese nuclear submarines were positioned off the coast of California and near the Panama Canal during that time frame and were waiting for orders. He told us this was not a threat but a warning. Beijing felt that the US Government was on the verge of initiating World War III. Such paranoid delusions give some idea of the increasing irrationality of the Chinese ruling elite.

- - - - - - - - - - - - - - - - - - - -

MEETING PARTICIPANTS

- - - - - - - - - - - - - - - - - - - -

Accompanying Case Officer Jeremy White in this meeting were:
>-James Kellogg (Kammler Associates executive)

Accompanying Professor Lin Zhang in this meeting were:

>-Two unidentified men

Now a preview of PROMIS: Vietnam, an exciting new series that chronicles the life of Deckard's father, professional mercenary Sean Deckard as he drifts across the dirty little wars that took place in the twilight of the Cold War.

05MAR70

Border region

Laos

Staff Sergeant Sean Deckard spun on his heel, taking a knee in the dense foliage and shouldered his CAR-15 rifle as enemy gunfire cut through the jungle to his side. Letting the rifle's front sight post nose up into the center mass of a charging North Vietnamese soldier, he stroked the trigger, dropping his target with a single shot in a spray of crimson.

Behind him, Pao threw a fragmentation grenade, its flight path riding a lazy arc in the enemy's direction before disappearing into the jungle.

Expending the rest of his magazine, Sean put suppressive fire down range, the carbine heating up in his hands as he fired on automatic. Screams sounded as Pao's grenade detonated, shrapnel cutting through NVA flesh. With the enemy advance temporarily stalled, Sean grabbed the American crouched beside him by the sleeve of his flight suit and dragged him to his feet.

Now it was Pao's turn to fire. Sean bounded back with the downed fighter pilot, their actions choreographed as they executed the well rehearsed battle drill.

Tom quickly extended a Claymore mine's metal legs before sticking it into place in the jungle underbrush. With the command detonation wire back stacked onto a wooden spool he was the next to bound back just as Sean set down near a thick tree with his package in tow.

Vang jumped over a fallen tree trunk covered in slick green moss, his AK-47 in hand, taking cover behind it just in time.

"Fire in the hole!"

Tom squeezed the claymore clacker, detonating the mine. Hundreds of explosively propelled steel ball bearings ripped through the NVA skirmish line that had threatened to over run them for the third time in less than an hour.

Even as the front line was cleared out by the anti-personnel mine, Sean knew they weren't going to make it. Loading his rifle with a fresh magazine, he shook his head. The dice had been loaded against his team from the beginning.

There were just too many of them.

Hot brass glinted as spent cartridges were ejected from his CAR-15. The sickly sweet smell of gun power wafted with the sour sulfur stench left by explosive residue, all combining with the ever present rot that existed in the jungle. Tracking from one target to the next, Sean squeezed his trigger in rapid succession, knocking the enemy down like bowling pins. As he burnt through magazine after magazine, the NVA kept coming. They were like rows of shark teeth, automatically replacing themselves by rotating into position.

Pivoting at the hips, a Chinese made bayonet ripped through the commando's OD fatigues and sliced across the surface of his skin before burying itself in the bark of the tree he had taken cover behind. The North Vietnamese soldier yanked at his AK-47 attempting to free it. The khaki uniformed soldier had come out of nowhere, emerging out of the foliage from their flank.

RPD machine guns opened up, more lead tracing figure eights across Sean's Recon Team.

The pilot jumped to his feet and tackled the NVA troop to the ground. As they wrestled each other, Sean was left pinned to the tree until he tore himself free with a grunt, his bloodied uniform hanging open where the bayonet had nearly killed him.

Finally, Vang stepped forward and pressed the muzzle of his rifle against the NVA soldier's head. Sean turned to the disheveled pilot as Vang's AK barked.

This time they ran together, with Vang close behind as Pao and Tom provided cover fire. The other two Montagnard mercenaries assigned to Recon Team Key West had been killed a kilometer back where the team had dumped their rucksacks. Weighted down with heavy loads, they would have been unable to maneuver as they attempted to break contact. Dropping their rucksacks, they had each initiated a short time fuse just as the NVA hit them a second time.

The time fuse detonated soap dish charges in the bottom of each team members ruck, destroying the excess military equipment, leaving nothing for the North Vietnamese to scavenge and exploit for intelligence value. They hadn't had time to even consider recovering their dead comrades before the enemy was pouring over them.

Running light on supplies, Sean spoke into the hand mic trailing from the single radio they still carried, the long whip antenna wobbling behind him. For some damn reason command wouldn't authorize close air support, Cobra gunships or Phantoms, but didn't seem to have a problem with B-52's carpet bombing well into Laotian territory, the territory they currently occupied. After calling in a *prairie fire*, all he could do was hope for an extraction.

Sweat poured down his face, stinging his eyes, as the garbled voice came through the receiver. It was barely audible above the gunfire.

"*-andby, five mike-*"

Sean choked down his frustration, sweeping gunfire into the jungle as Pao and Tom bounded towards him. In between shots he could hear angry shouts in Vietnamese, they were still damn close. The pilots told him five more minutes but they would be lucky to last five more seconds.

With the Recon Team back on line with each other, Vang and Sean hurled smoke grenades between themselves and the enemy. With a hiss, the grenades began billowing clouds of high concentration white smoke. Now that the NVA's line of sight was obscured, the team collectively picked up and ran further into the jungle, once again attempting to elude their pursuers.

Gunfire continued to crack behind them as the Vietnamese forces popped off random shots. Once they had moved a sufficient distance, the team moved into a file, cutting through the jungle as fast as they could. Sean muscled the pilot into the center of the formation to make sure he could keep tabs on him.

Good men had already died on the rescue mission, and Sean would be damned if he was going to lose the pilot now.

The Recon Team scrambled downhill, sometimes sliding down the slick undergrowth on their backsides, before combat boots broke their fall in the stream at the bottom of the gully. After the briefest of glances at his map, Sean motioned for the team to continue downstream.

He was known as being *good in the woods* among the operators who made up their covert paramilitary unit. Staff Sergeant Sean Deckard came alive out on patrol, instincts flaring and keeping him alert. Tactical decisions were weighed and acted upon in fractions of a second. He was the One-Zero, the team leader of RT Key West.

Reaching for his hand mic, Deckard raised the Huey pilots who were inbound to their position. Quickly, he made them aware of their situation and gave them new grid coordinates he wanted them meet them at. They didn't have time to find a landing zone, but it would be a hot extraction, of that there was no doubt in any of their minds.

"Roger, One-Zero. Gator Three-Five, out," the pilot's voice crackled over the handset.

Sean gritted his teeth as the team continued to splash through the stream. He could hear more shouts and the occasional gun shots nipping at their heels. The enemy hadn't reestablished contact with the team, but would shortly if they didn't extract soon.

"That way," Sean ordered, pointing up hill.

There were no clearings for the choppers to land. All they could do was find some high ground and hope for the best.

As they slogged their way up hill, pushing branches out of their way, the radio came back to life. Their extraction was one minute out. Down below they could hear the NVA sloshing through the stream, looking for spoor they almost certainly left behind in their haste.

"I'm popping smoke," Sean informed the pilots in between pants as he struggled to catch his breath. The bayonet had only opened a glancing wound against his side, but it still burned like hell.

Twisting and pulling the pin on another smoke canister, Sean tossed it to the top of the hill. When the grenade began to billow yellow colored smoke, he spoke back into his hand mic.

"Confirm my smoke."

"I've got yellow smoke, One-Zero."

"That's us. Coming in hot."

In the distance RT Key West's One-Zero could hear the buzz of rotor blades.

At the summit of the hill the Recon Team dug in as best they could, taking positions behind dead fall and the fan rooted jungle trees. The Khaki clad NVA troops were now scurrying up the side of the hill, pith helmets bobbing up and down as they negotiated a path, following in the footsteps of their quarry.

Sean motioned for his men to stay behind cover and concealment. Wait for the enemy to come within hand grenade range.

Freeing his final hand grenade from his web gear, he yanked the pin with a index finger while holding the spoon down. Breathing shallow breaths, his uniform was now soaked through with sweat. His arm pits had gone soppy, grit gathered in the corners of his eyes.

Dropping his free hand, the surviving members of the team lobbed M33 frag grenades downhill. They detonated in quick succession, their efforts rewarded with screams of agony. Now that contact had been reestablished the NVA opened up, dozens of muzzle flashes lit up with staccato bursts of gunfire.

Suddenly a shadow appeared overhead, rotor blades beat at the jungle foliage, whipping broad leaves back and forth.

Tom moved underneath the Huey with their package, the Navy pilot. A rope ladder was kicked and dropped from the helicopter, uncoiling it's way down to the ground. With the rest of the team burning through what little ammunition they had left, Tom got the pilot into a climbing harness and snap linked him into the ladder.

Next, he called the two Montagnards over from the defensive perimeter. Each team member wore a STABO extraction harnesses as their standard equipment, which magazine pouches and canteens were attached to. The short, indigenous tribesmen quickly snapped into the ladder. A nervous look passed between them before all eyes turned to their team leader.

Sean hammered another long burst downhill before turning and making a mad dash, darting under the helicopter. NVA were just cresting the hill as he got his snap link around the last strut on the ladder. Before he could even signal that he was hooked up he found himself yanked into the air, no longer moving under his own power.

With his CAR-15 hanging over his shoulder by it's sling, he was lifted straight up and through the jungle canopy, Kalashnikov fire chasing them away as they made their extraction.

Undulating waves of green moved beneath them as the pilot banked hard, taking them on a heading back towards South Vietnam.

Sean strained in his harness. The STABO rig was uncomfortable as hell, but it was better than being dead. Feeling something wet dripping on the back of his neck he swiped a hand across the back of his head. It came back coated in bright red blood. In a moment of panic he ran his hand all over his scalp, fingers probing for a wound that wasn't there.

Looking up, he saw Pao's body slumped lifelessly in his harness. The corpse rocked back and forth in the wind as they were towed under the helicopter, bouncing off a terrified looking Vang every few seconds. Pao must have eaten a round on the way out. Half the team cut down to rescue one pilot.

It was a long flight, made longer by the straps digging into his thighs and the thought his dead comrade dangling above him.

* * *

Command and Control North or CCN headquarters was little more than a collection of oblong military buildings along the shore of the South China Sea and surrounded by concertina wire. The extraction Huey had thankfully landed at a Special Forces Camp after crossing the border, allowing the Recon Team to detach from the ladder and climb into the helicopter. Pao's body was wrapped in a poncho and sat between the surviving SOG members.

The Huey, or slick, as the men called them, circled around the CCN camp, establishing radio contact before coming in for a landing. Peering down below at the landing area, Sean could see a half dozen slicks with rotors spinning.

They would have gotten word about RT Key West's successful extraction. The only explanation was that another RT was in contract somewhere else. At any given time multiple teams were running operations in Laos, Cambodia, and North Vietnam. In the past, they had inserted teams who never even established contact with HQ at their first comms window. Entire Recon Teams swallowed up by the jungle.

When the helicopter finally set down, a team of doctors and medics was waiting with stretchers. They led the fighter pilot away, his eyes reflecting the fact that his mind was still somewhere back in Laos. His psyche would be playing catch up for a long time to come.

Pao was carried away and Tom laid on one of the stretchers. He had suffered a grazing wound across his shoulder. The flesh wound would require some stitches but he'd be back on patrol in no time. Deckard knew from experience.

One of CCN's medics, named Jim, came running up to Sean and pressed a bandage against his side where he had almost been skewered by the bayonet.

Looking over at the Montagnard mercenaries boarding the slicks on standby with their American advisers, Deckard leaned in and yelled in the medic's ear.

"Where is Hatchet Force going?"

Hatchet Force was the quick reaction team composed of American SOG commandos leading the Montagnard tribesmen and South Chinese Nung mercenaries that responded whenever the smaller six man recon teams got in over their heads.

"We got two teams inserted over the fence a few hours after yours," the medic yelled back. "Both are in contact and we're just waiting for the green light from higher. Now, let's go, we need to get that cut cleaned out."

The team leader nodded his head, holding the gauze in place over his wound. Grabbing Jim by the collar he screamed over the sound of the helicopters.

"Hey, my boy Vang took a round through his shoulder," Sean lied. "You better catch up with him and make sure the docs know about it. You know how some of these 'Yards are about shit like that. Sometimes he thinks you can just suck it up or some shit."

"Fuck yeah," Jim grunted. "I'll go take care of it. See you up at the aid station, okay?"

"Sure thing," Sean replied patting the medic on the back as he chased after Vang.

Looking around to see if anyone was watching, Sean quickly tied the combat bandage around his abdomen to hold it in place before buttoning up his spray paint covered OD fatigues. Running over to a water basin next to the airstrip he refilled both of his one quart canteens and secured them on his web harness.

Dashing over to the helicopters, still on standby, he found Rogers, one of the supply sergeants, handing out bandoleers or ammunition. Grabbing two for himself, Sean flung them over his shoulder and jumped on the nearest Huey as the rotors cranked at a higher pitch.

Seconds later, Jim was left wandering the camp looking for the Recon Team leader as the olive drab colored helicopters shot over the camp, heading for Laos at full speed.

Read the conclusion to PROMIS: Vietnam now and look for the forthcoming sequel, PROMIS: Rhodesia in the near future.

Acknowledgments:

First and foremost I want to thank the very first Deckard fans, Rob, Karl, and Doug. This book would never have existed if it wasn't for you three spurring me on with encouragement and enthusiasm for a full blown Deckard novel. I would also like to acknowledge Glenn and Terry at MackBolan.com for hosting the very first Deckard shorts about ten years ago while I was still just a kid.

I want to thank my awesome proof reader, Gloria for her professionalism and tolerating my misuse of the English language.

It goes without saying that Marc Lee did a slamming job with the cover image helping to fully realize what this book is about. I highly recommend his services, just contact him at "the_saint_iz@hotmail.com".

I also want to thank Hank Brown and Jack Badelaire for their feedback and support for this project to include impromptu tech support!

Last but not least, I want to thank Caterina for putting up with me hiding in my corner of the apartment while I hammered away at this book day and night. Thanks for understanding honey.

<u>Glossary</u>

.300 WinMag: Sniper rifle chambered for the .300 Winchester Magnum cartridge

1911: .45 Caliber pistol

2REP: Elite airborne unit within the French Foreign Legion

40mm grenade: A grenade fired from a grenade launcher rather than thrown by hand. Also see: HE and

HEDP for different types of grenades

727: Civilian passenger aircraft

AAR: After Action Review, conducted post-mission to establish what happened and critique mission performance

AC Milan: Italian soccer team

AG: Assistant Gunner, carried ammunition, spare barrels, and tripod for a machine gunner

AH-60L: Black Hawk helicopter outfitted with a machine gun and rocket pods

AK-103: An updated form of the AK-47 rifle that can be fitted with a variety of different optics

AK-47: Avtomat Kalashnikova-1947, following the standard Soviet weapons naming convention. Avtomat meaning the type of rifle: automatic. Kalashnikov comes from the last name of the inventor, Mikhail Kalashnikov and the year 1947 is when the rifle went into production. The AK-47 is the world's most ubiquitous battle rifle, having been used in virtually every conflict since the

Cold War.

AN/PSQ-20: Advanced form of night vision goggles that also incorporates thermal heat vision to help detect targets.

Antonov 125: Large Russian-made cargo airplane

AO: Area of Operations

APOBS: Anti-Personnel Obstacle Breaching System

Arystan: Kazakh Anti-Terror unit

Aurora: Allegedly the code name for a classified spy plane

Bilderberg Group: Secretive, yearly roundtable type meeting of the world's most influential leaders in business, politics, and the mass media.

Bohemian Grove: Occult ritual taking place in California once a year and attended my much of the US political and business establishment

BOLD: Blood-Oxygen Level Dependence, used to measure which parts of the brain are active

C130: US Air force military cargo airplane

C17: The C130's big brother, can carry more equipment and personnel

C4: Composition Four, plastic explosives

Camelbak: Plastic bladder used to carry water in, commonly carried on a soldiers back and drank through a long tube that acts as a straw

CDC: Center for Disease Control

CFR: *see Council on Foreign Relations*

CO: Commanding Officer

COG: Continuity of Government

College Park: *See Special Collections Service*

Council on Foreign Relations: Has been described as a parallel government. A think tank that discusses various foreign policy issues.

CZ75: Czech-made 9mm pistol

Delta Force: US Army counter-terrorist unit

Det Chord: Detonation Chord, used to sympathetically detonate larger explosive charges

DevGroup: US Navy SEAL counter-terrorist unit

Dragonov: Russian-made sniper rifle

DShK: Soviet era 12.7 machine gun

EM: Electromagnetic

ETA: Estimated Time of Arrival

EUC: End User Agreement, a legal device that attempts to prevent arms transactions from happening among blacklisted countries or groups.

Exfil: Exfiltration

FDC: Fire Direction Center, used to coordinate mortar fire

FM: Frequency Modulation, a form of radio communication

FMK2: Argentinian made fragmentation grenade

fMRI: functional Magnetic Resonance Imaging

FN P90: 5.7 50 round sub-machine gun manufactured by Fabrique National of Belgium

FNG: Fucking New Guy

Glock: Austrian made brand of pistols

GPS: Global Positioning System

GROM: Polish counter terrorist unit active in the War on Terror

GSG-9: German counter-terrorist unit

GUARD: Global Unconventional Aid, Rescue, and Defense, a US-based Private Military Company

Gulfstream 500: Luxury private jet used by corporations and the wealthy

H&K G3: German-made 7.62 battle rifle

HALO: High Altitude Low Opening, also known as Military Free Fall or MFF

HE: High Explosive

HEDP: High Explosive Dual Purpose

HGH: Human Growth Hormone

HK: Heckler and Koch, German arms manufacturer

HN-5: Chinese copy of Soviet era anti-aircraft missile launcher

HTT: *see Human Terrain Team*

Human Terrain Teams: A military project that provides socio-cultural experts to help commanders on the ground understand local cultures.

HVT: High Value Target

IED: Improvised Explosive Device

IFF: Identification Friend or Foe

IMF: International Monetary Fund

Infil: Infiltration

IR: Infrared

IZLID: Infrared Zoom Laser Illuminator Designator

J-10: Chinese fighter jet

Jet Ranger: Civilian helicopter manufactured by Bell

JP-8: Military grade jet fuel

Ka-Bar: Military fighting knife

KIA: Killed In Action

Little Bird: Special Operations helicopter used to insert small teams of operators onto objectives

M203: Under barrel, breach loaded, 40mm grenade launcher

M4: Shortened M16 carbine, commonly carried by US forces

M81: Fuse ignitor

Main Core: Classified US Government computer system

MC-130: Special Operations variety of the C130 cargo transport aircraft

MC-5: Free fall parachute used by Special Forces personnel

MH-47: Special Operations variety of the double rotor CH-47 transport helicopter

Milkor Mk14: Six-shot 40mm grenade launcher

Mosin-Nagant: World War Two era Russian bolt action rifle

Mossad: Israeli Intelligence service

MP5: Heckler and Koch 9mm sub-machine gun

MRUD: A Yugoslavian copy of the US-made Claymore anti-personnel mine

NCO: Non-Commissioned Officer, Sergeants

NSA: National Security Agency, handles signal intercepts

NVG: Night Vision Goggles

O2: Oxygen

OPCEN: Operations Center

Operations Order: Written mission format distributed to combat leaders

PETN: Pentaerythritol tetranitrate, used instead of blasting caps to detonate larger explosive charges

PG-7: Anti-Tank rocket for an RPG-7

PKM: Belt-fed Russian machine gun

PMC: Private Military Company

PRC: People's Republic of China

PsyOps: Psychological Operations

RAF: Royal Air Force

Rangers: US Airborne Light Infantry unit

RDX: Research Developed Explosives, also known as hexogen

Remington 270: Short barrel 12 gauge shotgun used for ballistic breaches

RFID: Radio Frequency Identification

RPD: Russian belt-fed machine gun

RPG: Rocket Propelled Grenade

RPK: Heavy barrel AK-47 with an extended magazine

RV: Rendezvous

S2: Intelligence section of a military unit

SA-7: Russian anti-aircraft missile launcher

SADF: South African Defense Force

Samruk: Kazakhstan based Private Military Company

SATCOM: Satellite Communications

SEAL: SEa Air and Land, naval commandos

SEC: Securities and Exchange Commission

Sergeant Major: Senior ranking Sergeant in a military unit

Short 360: Mid-size passenger aircraft

SIG Blaser Tactical Two: State of the art sniper rifle with interchangeable barrels to allow more than one caliber of bullet to be used by the same platform

SIGINT: Signals Intelligence

SITREP: Situation Report

SOP: Standard Operating Procedure

Special Collections Service: A joint venture between the CIA and NSA that conducts "black bag" operations such as surreptitious entry to plant surveillance and monitoring devices

Special Forces: Also known as Green Berets, specialize in training indigenous forces. A separate unit from SEALs, Rangers, and Delta Force

Spetsnaz: Russian Special Forces

SPG-9: Russian-made recoiless rifle

SQL injection attack: A type of computer code injection that allows hackers to exploit security flaws in computer systems

Sunkar: Elite Kazakh police force

TNT: Trinitrotoluene explosives

Trilateral Commission: An international off-shoot of the Council on Foreign Relations that fosters cooperation between the US, Europe, and Japan

TRP: Target Reference Point

Type 63 APC: Tracked Chinese Armored Personnel Carrier

UAV: Unmanned Aerial Vehicle, typically used for surveillance

UH-60: US Army general purpose helicopter

Unit 8200: Israeli signals interception unit

UWSA: United Wa State Army, a Burmese narco-militia

VSS rifle: Russian-made rifle with integrated sound suppressor for use by Spetsnaz units during covert operations

WIA: Wounded In Action

World Bank: A private international lending institution

XO: Executive Officer, second in command after Commanding Officer

Yaa baa: Methamphetamine pills

ZSU-23: Twin barreled 23mm anti-aircraft machine gun

Jack Murphy is an eight year Army Special Operations veteran who served as a Sniper and Team Leader in 3rd Ranger Battalion and as a Senior Weapons Sergeant on a Military Free Fall team in 5th Special Forces Group.

Learn more at: http://reflexivefire.com/

Contact the author at: reflexivefire@yahoo.com

Hell and Gone

By Henry Brown

"Highly recommended." - Midwest Book Review

HALA'IB TRIANGLE, SUDAN

Allah has given two generous gifts to Khaled Ali: a surplus tactical Russian nuclear warhead, and the perfect martyr to deliver it into the Jewish enemy's heartland—15 year old Bassam Amin.

VIRGINIA, USA

CIA planner Bobbie Yousko knows what Ali's likely target is, and must somehow push her plan through cobwebs of red tape and her politicized chain-of-command in time to preempt the bomb plot before the Israelis take matters into their own hands.

IDF HIGH COMMAND, ISRAEL

Mossad handler YacovDreizil is dispatched to Sudan to join his field agent there and infiltrate the American commando team blasting a bloody swathe through the war-torn dictatorship toward the camp where the warhead awaits final delivery.

BOR, SUDAN

Retired Cold Warrior Dwight "Rocco" Cavarra must organize a dirty baker's dozen of alpha-dog mercs into a crack raiding party to steal the nuke away from Ali's cult of murderers. Trouble is, the raid has little chance for success and even less chance of their survival; he's got kill crazy loose cannons and possible moles in his rag-tag outfit; and the mission has been compromised before it even gets started.

"A top-notch military thriller."- Bookvisions

"An action novel that hits you like a brick through a plate glass window." - Post Modern Pulps

www.hell-and-gone.com

Buy the exciting first issue now!

http://postmodernpulps.blogspot.com/

Made in the USA
Lexington, KY
15 March 2012